THE BEST AUSTRALIAN

STORIES

12

THE BEST AUSTRALIAN
STORIES

12

EDITED BY SONYA HARTNETT

Black Inc.

Published by Black Inc.,
an imprint of Schwartz Media Pty Ltd

37–39 Langridge Street
Collingwood Vic 3066 Australia
email: enquiries@blackincbooks.com
http://www.blackincbooks.com

ISBN 9781863955805

Contents

Introduction

Sonya Hartnett

On summer days when my brothers and sisters and I were young we sometimes used to visit our cousins, who had a swimming pool. Our cousins' house was plush and tidy, very unlike our own home. The swimming pool was not the only attraction: my aunt was a librarian, and her house – also unlike our own – was filled with books. I would often pass our visits there reading on one of my cousins' beds, or exploring the urban pine forest which reared, dusky and spooky, beyond the back fence. But this particular day was a hot day, and we were in the pool, my brother and younger sister and two of our cousins. We all must have been around ten or twelve years old. The swimming pool wasn't large, but it was lovely. Our uncle had built a deck around it, and you could hang on the pool's edge and rest your arms on the warm timber and let your feet drift unmoored. Glancing up, you would see the pine forest, a shadowy field of towering trees which shifted watchfully with the wind. Beyond their piked tips would arc the hot blue sky, and in the lulls of our laughter and splashing there was silence: I don't remember any noise in the places of my childhood.

My sister Lucy, also a reader and usually a swimmer, wasn't in the pool that day. She came out of the house carrying one of our aunt's paperbacks, knelt by the edge of the pool and called us over. She was going to read us a story, she said, a short one. Occasionally at home she would do this – she'd read the entirety of *The Chrysalids* to me, so I knew her taste was trustworthy – but I doubted my cousins and brother, being boys, would have the patience for such an interlude. Lucy, however, was the eldest of us, and thus could sometimes force submission, and did so now. We trod water, the beach ball bobbed away, silence fell, we glided nearer; Lucy opened the book. I could see its cover was a strange one, ugly and stylised. 'It's written by a man called Roald Dahl,' she told us; the name meant nothing to me. 'The story is called "The Man from the South."'

Thirty years later, yet I remember the day so well – not the whole day, perhaps, but the hour. Maybe my whole life found its shape as I hung listening on the edge of a swimming pool, the cool water choppy around me, the sky whitely arid above. While my sister read the story of a dapper little man who makes a startling bet with a young sailor, the stake being the little man's car against the smallest finger on the young man's left hand, I felt the heat of the deck rising through my palms, smelt the forest and heard it move. The bet involves the young man's cigarette lighter: if he can make its flame catch ten times in a row, the dapper man will give him his green Cadillac; but if the lighter fails, the dapper man will chop off the sailor's finger with a meat cleaver. The young man's hand is tied to a tabletop to prevent him reneging on the deal, in an expert fashion that makes the narrator wonder if the gambler hasn't done this before. The dapper man speaks with an accent – the writer, whose own name was peculiar, had written his words in a peculiar way – but my sister was good with voices. 'Now pleess,' she read, 'clench de fist, all except for de little finger. You must leave de little finger sticking out, lying on de table.'

The forest, the sun, the water, the words: we hung suspended, we all did, our chins on the scorching metal of the pool's rim, the beach ball bumping lightly, ignored, the boisterous boys quietened, listening to the sound of the cigarette lighter flicking and catching once – twice – three times, four times. It reached seven, and our fingers were digging into the deck, the forest itself was bending closer to hear. It was such a hot day, an airless afternoon, and the butcher's cleaver which hovered above the sailor's finger hovered over us too; we could draw breath no deeper than could the narrator, the sailor, the blonde girl in the bathing costume who'd been invited along as a witness to the folly – she wore bathers because it was a hot day in the story too, there was a swimming pool in the story, and a forgotten beach ball.

The sailor flicked his lighter, and my sister and the narrator cried, 'Eight!'

*

I thought often about that long-gone afternoon in my cousins' swimming pool as I read through almost 800 submissions for the 2012 edition of *The Best Australian Stories.* Eight hundred stories is a lot to read, and it took a long time, and often the sheer size of the project might have swamped me with indecision had it not been for the memory of that day, and the anchoring lesson which Dahl, that dazzling devil, that dark trickster of a short-story writer, taught: short stories are *stories.* Intrinsically and essentially they should be about *plot.* Among the submissions there were so many beautiful and skilful pieces of *writing* that they alone could have filled several anthologies: but in the face of so much choice – so much work of such quality that the whole experience has been an exercise in humility, for I've spent my life trying to become a decent writer and now I know for sure there are hundreds as good, and far better – it became vital to refine the conditions of acceptance. There are a couple of exceptions, pieces of writing which pleased me so much they just had to be included, but in assembling the collection I have generally adhered to Dahl's great law: that the purpose of a short story is *to tell a story.* Nothing – not the author's standing or lack of one, not the subject matter or style – has been more important than the degree to which the story keeps and holds the reader's interest. Yet even under the guiding light of the master storyteller's rule, finalising the selection has been one of the most anguishing things I've ever done. The anthology could have been three times longer than it is, and still I would have been forced to omit pieces I'd have liked to include. I will never look at the anthology without thinking of those left behind.

Nonetheless I'm proud of this year's selection: one can never please everyone with such a collection, but I quite vainly hope Roald Dahl would like it too. I hope he would enjoy the black humour which runs through many of them, and the calm cool voice of others, and the craftsmanship which characterises them all. The stories come from all over Australia, as well as from Australian writers in far-away places around the world, but they share a delicate complexity and a vibrant cleverness. Decades ago, I held my breath as my sister cried 'Eight!': these stories, too, are breath-takers, the ones which render no thing more important than discovering what happens next. They are thirty-two fine examples of what well-placed words should do in tight confines.

Sonya Hartnett

Someone Called Rob

Martin Lindsay

It was an unknown number. I usually let them through to voicemail.

'Is that Rob?' A male voice, holding a temper ready to explode.

My 'who wants to know?' came across a little more abrupt than intended.

'The boyfriend of Kate.'

The call now involved three strangers. I asked who Kate was to narrow things down.

'Kate is the girl whose birthday card you signed at the pub the other night.'

Oh. Vague recollection. But wasn't that my mate's card? I asked the angry voice if he was sure.

'You left this phone number.'

Oh.

More recollections. Later in the night. In the swing of beers. When many ideas suddenly seem unbackable winners. There was a chance Kate had been gorgeous, though equal chance beers were talking. At the time, she'd been gorgeous enough for me to cheekily gate-crash her birthday gathering next to ours. Then sign her card with a flirtatious witticism and … oh God … my mobile number.

The witticism. Less a sonnet, more a mildly pornographic pick-up line.

'What are you playing at, making a pass at my girlfriend?'

Ah. That would explain the anger thing. I babbled an apology. Me drunk, hour late, beers many, and most definitely unaware he was on the scene in a romantic sense or otherwise.

'Well,' he said, fury barely subsiding, 'just see it doesn't happen again.'

I hardly remembered it had in the first place.

He hung up with a parting cuss, and I vowed hereto never to be talked into shooters when birthday cards were around.

It was twenty minutes later when the second call arrived. Another unknown number. 'Is that someone called Rob?' a female voice asked. I confirmed with less courage this time. 'This is Kate. You wrote in my card.'

I explained that her boyfriend had just pointed out the error of my 'harmless' prank.

'What did he say?' she interrupted. 'He didn't threaten you, did he?'

'Threaten' had an insidious tone. I asked in what way.

'Violently. Physically. Christ, you didn't tell him your address, did you?'

I answered no, my mind on speed replay of the conversation. Had I given anything identifying? I hadn't even confirmed my name. Safe. Reasonably. I assured her no threats were made besides some perfectly understandable anger in the circumstances.

'You don't know Adam,' she warned.

This was true. I didn't. Or her for that matter.

She thanked me for being so understanding, and I apologised again for the birthday card and trouble caused. Though I couldn't help flirtatiously adding that if she didn't have a boyfriend, the call might've turned out much better. She laughed politely, with the distant patronising tone that the contentedly coupled give lame approaches.

The phone rang again minutes later.

'I cannot believe you,' snarled the angry voice.

'Adam?'

'Barely half an hour after I tell you off for cracking onto Kate, you're giving her secret calls behind my back.'

'It wasn't a secret call.'

'It was secret from me.'

'That's as may be, but I wasn't calling secretly. In fact, I didn't call at all.'

'What are you saying about Kate, then?'

'Nothing. She didn't say the call was secret.'

'What did you think, her calling you?'

'Not much. I don't normally deduce the secrecy potential of calls from strange numbers.'

'Mr Fancy clever talker, eh?'

'A clever guy would've hung up by now.'

'You do and I'll crush you, mate.'

Fortunately, diplomacy genes run in my family. I invoked the universal signal of utmost seriousness between guys. 'Dude,' I said carefully, 'I don't have designs on your girlfriend. You're a lucky man and I wish you all the best with her. Nothing is going on.'

A wavering silence. The 'Dude' had done its work. Then, 'There better not be. Because if I find out you're calling each other again ...'

'I don't even know her number,' I fibbed. I would be clearing my phone history as soon as the call was over. 'It's as good as forgotten.'

His silence suggested uneasy contentment. I bade him goodwill on his way. There was a conversation about to be had between them, and I was glad to be no longer involved in it.

*

According to call history, she rang three more times.

I put the relevant numbers on block, deactivated my voicemail, then steadfastly refused to answer unknown callers for the rest of the week.

A completely different number called on Sunday afternoon. An ill-thought-out sense of security led me to answer.

'Who the frick do you think you are?' a venomous female voice asked.

'I don't know. Who do you think I am?'

'Some thoughtless bastard stirring up trouble in someone's relationship for a laugh. Surely you know how rocky things are between Adam and Kate?'

I groaned at the names, then asked hers.

'I'm Kate's best friend. I look out for her when pricks like you come along to screw things up for her.' My protest was ignored. 'Adam's furious. He's talking about ending it all.'

'What, suicide?'

'With her. He doesn't trust her anymore. What with you leaving messages and suggesting things.'

'I don't even know her. If anything, she's been ringing me.'

'Don't try blaming this on her, you bastard.'

'I'm not.'

'Just as well, arsehole. Things are still tense between them about the whole Scott thing.'

'Who's Scott?'

'Don't try acting stupid.'

'I'm not acting.'

'Scott was the guy Adam thought Kate was seeing behind his back. And we all know what happened between Adam and Scott.'

'No, we don't.'

'Well, you wouldn't want it to happen to you.'

This is exactly what you don't want to hear in the information age. In fact, the information was ageing me at a fast rate. I had visions of this Adam guy googling me down. A mobile number and first name were probably enough to clean out my bank account, let alone trace my address. He might sneak round while I was in the shower and strangle me with the last of the toilet paper.

For all I knew, there was a picture online of my house, with me looking out the window wondering who was driving the strange van going by with a camera.

'Why does Adam keep jumping to these sorts of conclusions?' I asked. There was a scoffing sound at the other end. She was either disgusted by the question or clearing her throat. 'Why did he think Scott and Kate were seeing each other?'

'Because they were. God, everyone knew that.'

'Except Adam, presumably. To begin with, anyway.'

'This isn't a laughing matter. Adam's severely pissed.'

I glanced at my door to ensure it was locked. 'My intentions in all this were entirely honourable.' I gave my inebriated self the benefit of the doubt. 'I didn't even have any intentions. It was just a drunken joke.'

'Oh, charming.'

'I thought Kate was single,' I said, slowly and deliberately. 'I discovered she isn't, so I've backed well away. Over the hill and miles away. I explained that to Adam. I thought, anyway. So hopefully this is the last he, she, you and especially me hear any more of this.'

'Dick,' was her final summation before hanging up.

It took me a moment to work out who Dick was. Hassle be damned, I was getting my number changed first thing in the morning.

Through sheer self-discipline, I looked at my phone only once in the next twenty minutes. 'A drunken joke am I?!?!' was the only message received.

I turned the phone off for the rest of the evening. And took the SIM card out, just in case.

*

I changed my number online to a random new one. It would take a few hours to take effect. A Google search on myself revealed little. Fortunately I'd never taken to social networking, and my unremarkable day-to-day life didn't warrant a blog by or about me. Later, I restored the SIM, then deleted every trace of them from my phone. Short of relatives who were ASIO operatives, I was hopefully rid of Adam, Kate, Scott and whomever else they knew.

I slept well.

Till a message at 7 a.m. The phone company, asking if I was happy with their online services. I gave them my thoughts about being startled by unexpected morning messages.

Taking advantage of the early start, I padded downstairs and threw the front curtains open, welcoming a fresh day's sunlight.

A strange car sat in my drive.

I pulled the curtains straight back, praying I'd not been seen, then scampered to the kitchen to hide. An immediate scan for potential weapons. Nothing.

No knock on the door. Had they seen me? Or were they toying?

I let minutes pass, then snuck along the side wall to peer out a gap. I saw now that semi-translucent curtains were a mistake in the event of psychopathic attentions. I edged my eye round as far as I dared. A carport column blocked my view of the driver. But the car was definitely lurking. The driver could only be sitting, watching the house.

Adam.

I stood, not sure how to act. What did he intend to do? How might I escape? To where, now that I wasn't safe in my own home? To walk out and confront, armed and dressed, or sit it out until sense was seen and he left without issue?

Inertia. Twenty minutes? More?

My neighbour popped out of his house in tennis gear, climbed into the stranger's passenger seat, and they drove away.

I would *never* visit that pub ever again.

*

Late afternoon, another strange car pulled into my drive and hovered, engine running.

The curtains open, I was in full view on the couch.

The car sat, idling. I couldn't make out the driver, but I waited, confident after my earlier paranoia. And waited.

This was different. The car lurked with intent. Purpose.

The driver leant over for something. A weapon?

A street directory.

*

I'm rational enough to recognise imagination running away with unrelated events. But they kept happening.

I awoke next morning to my phone ringing. Work enquiring if I intended to grace them with my presence that day. My alarm clock was dead to the world, sitting in a near-noon sunbeam. On inspection, a circuit breaker had tripped during the night. The power box was prominent on the front wall. Child's play to waltz in and tamper with. I looked for footprints in the garden bed. The mulch layer revealed nothing. I attached a small padlock to the power-box cover. The power company told me to remove it after one of their inspectors tried to read my meter a few days later. The box became a sitting duck again.

Mail kept accidentally arriving in the wrong mailbox. Too many times for my neighbours to comfortably joke about our dopey postman.

The home phone would ring, stopping before I reached it.

Sometimes one ring. Sometimes three. Sometimes ten if I was out in the backyard.

Then a flat tyre on my car. The spare was under-inflated too, though that was more my own neglect. I checked for sabotage. Adam hadn't struck me as a psychological terrorist, but who knew with the insanely jealous. And what had happened with that other guy?

A screw, embedded in the grooves. It was entirely possible a screw might lie on the road. And I might happen to drive over it. Exactly in the weak spot of my tread. Who was to say it wasn't just misfortune?

Until the day I came home to find the mouse head. Just a head, in the middle of my doormat. Waiting for me. Its cold dead eyes staring untold menace. Neighbourhood cat? Exactly dead centre?

Then my phone rang.

Fumbling the lock, I raced to the receiver and demanded caller identification. An Indian voice asked if I had considered an automatic roller door for my garage. 'Only to lock out psychotic boyfriends,' was my reply.

'You are having boyfriend troubles?' The telemarketer asked.

'Am I ever.'

'My advice: take him for a nice night out then give him a foot rub when you get home.'

*

A mobile and first name, to an address and home phone. From there, a letterbox could give bank and credit card details. What could be told from my statements, besides that I spend my money on an awful lot of crap? Pin numbers? Had I received anything recently that might have my signature?

Had the neighbours blabbed? The old lady next door was notorious for knowing too much about our street, and all too keen to broadcast tidbits. The things she tells me about that couple at number fourteen. You should hear what they get up to. All it would take is someone to say they were a friend and the old girl could blab anything, from my whereabouts, work hours, recent visitors, to what day I put out my washing.

Good lord, hadn't I lost a T-shirt in the last wash?

What had I started?

You hear of nutters in the news. Road rage stirring short-fused people to insane acts of violence. Just for pushing in a queue of traffic. What could a misconstrued pass at a girlfriend bring about?

I bought locks and stoppers for my windows and sliding doors, and requested a deadbolt from my landlord.

*

I couldn't live like this.

The only sensible course of action was to ring this Adam and explain it once and for all. And if need be, threaten to call the police.

I picked up the mobile. The numbers no longer existed in the phone. I had been too thorough with cutting them off. I contacted my phone company for a log of incoming calls on the previous number. It was no longer associated with my account. I explained it was vital to ring back an ailing relative whose contact details I'd lost. For additional weight I said I'd just learnt they had barely days to live.

'How'd you find that out?' the phone company guy asked.

'Another auntie told me.'

'Why not just get the number off her, then?'

'She told me by Twitter,' I replied in a flash of inspiration. He sounded even more dubious when I said I'd lost her email too.

'And your entire family doesn't know the number either?'

'I'm adopted and they all hate me. They're my phone records, let me have them.'

'We don't keep that sort of information, anyway.'

Surely they were archived?

'Have you any idea how much storage that would require?'

'What if the federal police wanted to check a person's call history?'

'They probably already do.'

This seemed a fair point. 'So you can't help me.'

'Not besides suggesting you keep in touch with your family more. They're your kin, man. Blood is thicker than water.'

'Is this conversation being recorded for quality purposes?' It was. 'Plenty of storage space for that, then.'

He called me something that might be considered an issue on later review.

Online, I changed my number back – luckily it was available. Then I waited.

Nothing.

*

I started visiting the pub where I made the fateful birthday card blunder. After-work drinks at first, then Friday nights, Saturdays and Sunday sessions. No sign of them. They were obviously not regulars.

A barmaid became quite friendly as my visits grew frequent. She smiled as I handed over my phone number, but was less interested when I said to call me if she saw a girl of Kate's description from what I could only vaguely remember. When I said to especially call if a big strong guy answering to Adam came in, the barmaid found another part of the bar that needed polishing.

I tried other bars in the area. Did they even live in this suburb? Would I have to spread my search?

My friends noted I was looking ill and stressed, and seemed to be going to the pub an awful lot. I couldn't explain, it sounded irrational, but I had to find them. Before Adam found me. Before Adam did whatever happened with Simon to me.

I would leap at any sound in the night, ready to attack, my cricket bat by the bed in case someone got in. I had nightmares about dark shadowy figures chasing me, my legs like lead, stuck in quicksand, snowdrifts or Kafka novels. People at work were noting bags under my eyes.

Then one night I fell asleep on my couch, a finished DVD menu looping incessantly, but not enough to rouse me. I had no urge to watch horror movies anymore.

A thundering knock on the door woke me. Half-asleep, I automatically stumbled to the door and turned the handle, before realising the news was full of stories like these. My breath gasped in preparation for an attack I had witlessly invited.

Some drunk bloke was looking for number twenty-three, evidently too inebriated to notice the shiny brass six on my door. I gave directions. He eyed my bare torso and expressed admiration for my patterned boxers, then apologised if he had interrupted anything. As if anything could go on in my life while a nemesis lurked over every thought.

I began the slow trudge upstairs to bed when my mobile rang. It was a completely unreasonable hour for anyone to be ringing.

The number seemed familiar. Was it him? Her? I dithered to answer, then pressed the green button.

The line was filled with a static of background music and crowd hubbub, then a female voice sing-songed 'Pen-ny' with well-lubricated good humour. The good humour instantly deflated when I said hello. The drunk girl asked if I was Penny, somewhat unnecessarily.

Kate's friend. Bingo! 'But I am someone who needs to talk to you,' I said.

'This isn't that creepy bloke from the pub a month ago? I told you to piss off.'

'No, this is Rob.'

'Who?'

'The guy who left his number in Kate's birthday card.'

'Kate's birthday was ages ago.'

'I know.'

'Why are you ringing me about it?'

'I'm not.'

'Well, what the fuck, dude? What's with you?'

'You rang me.'

'I was ringing Penny.' She sighed woozily. 'Frigging calls list. I need to organise my thing. I need a new phone.' She groaned. 'I need a lift.'

'Well, I'm not giving you one.'

'Dirty bastard.'

'I'm not giving you *a lift.*'

'Shit no, you weirdo. Ringing me up like this, trying to crack on to me.'

'You rang me. It doesn't matter. I need to talk to Kate.'

'Kate isn't here,' the girl said, annoyed by the obviousness of the matter.

'Not now. I need her number.'

'You can't ring me, then ask for some other girl's number.'

'Cheek of it,' said another female voice nearby.

'It's some perve. Trying to score an easy root while I'm pissed.'

'Tell him to fuck off.'

'Hey,' Kate's friend almost yelled into the phone. 'My mate says I should tell you to fuck off.'

'I will,' I said. 'As soon as you give me Kate's number. I'm not trying to pick you, her or anyone up. I just need to talk to her.'

'She's seeing someone anyway.'

'That's why I need to talk to her. There's a big misunderstanding that needs sorting out once and for all.'

'Kate's birthday was weeks ago.'

I breathed a calming five seconds. 'Yes, I know. Can I have her number?'

'Hang on.' There was a major shuffling, followed by a loud clunk and a 'Shit, fucking dropped it.' I held the phone from my ear. 'Can you call us a taxi?' Kate's friend asked with utmost weariness.

'Sure, when you give me Kate's number.'

'I want to go clubbing,' demanded another drunken female voice. 'Where are my shoes?'

'Kate's number. Do you have it?'

'What? Yeah, sure. It's …' There seemed to be an awkward juggling of phone and address book. I would've asked her to SMS, but couldn't trust the request to be remembered, the right number sent, to me or anyone. Short of calling her in the morning, when I would have her hangover to contend with, I persevered.

'Who is this again?'

'This is Rob.'

'Is he sexy?' asked the other female voice.

'Where are my shoes?' said the third with growing frustration.

One more insistent request later, finally, blearily, I received the digits. Feeling brave, I asked her to repeat it. Besides some additional expletives, the numbers matched. I asked their current location.

'What the fuck do you want to know that for?'

'You wanted me to call you a taxi.'

'I'm perfectly fine,' she retorted. 'We're going to the club.'

'Have a great time,' I said, hoping this would be the last I'd talk to her.

'Tell Penny to come down and join us.'

'Will do,' I said.

'Where the fuck are my shoes?'

I hung up. Mission accomplished. I had a number. One call remained to sort this whole mess out at last.

For the first time in a fortnight, I slept well and contentedly.

Until a bottle was broken somewhere in the street. I remained awake till near dawn, the number memorised.

*

Kate didn't recognise my voice. 'Who is this?'

'This is Rob.'

'Who?'

'The guy who wrote on your birthday card.'

'My birthday was weeks ago.'

'I know.'

'What did you write?'

Precious life moments seemed to be passing. 'My phone number.'

'How did you get mine?'

'From your friend. Look, I need to speak to your boyfriend, Adam.'

'That wanker. He's not my boyfriend.'

'Yes he is. Isn't he?'

'We broke up. Well, I dumped him, anyway. He was a cheating prick.'

'He was cheating?'

'Yeah, the cocksucker. Why do you want to talk to him?'

'Because he thought I was cheating with you.'

'What would I be cheating with you for?' I was almost affronted enough to list a few of my good points. 'I don't even know you.'

'I know. That's what I wanted to tell Adam.'

'That I cheat with guys I don't even know?' she asked, maintaining a rage.

'No! That it's stupid for him to think you're cheating with me.'

'I don't cheat with anyone.'

'Except for Simon,' I said without thinking. Or was it Scott?

There was an iceberg of silence. 'What do you know about Simon?'

'Nothing. I don't even know Simon either.'

'How did you find out about him, then?'

A good journalist never reveals his sources, but I no longer gave a bollocks. 'One of your friends told me. The point is, I need to speak to Adam.'

'It was Fiona, wasn't it?' Kate railed. 'I knew she wouldn't keep a secret. Just because she got with Simon before I did.'

'Simon must be quite a guy.'

'I'm not speaking to him either. He got with Stacey.'

'Does that stop you giving me his number?'

'Simon's?'

'No, Adam's!'

'I erased it. I don't want anything to do with that cheating prick again.'

'You have no contact details for him at all?'

'Just so you can go tell him about Simon? No way.'

'I don't give a toss what you did with Simon. Or Scott. I just want to tell Adam to stop hounding me like some jealous psycho.'

'How did you know about Scott?' Her anger was overtaken by surprise. 'Adam's jealous?'

'Either that or sociopathic.'

'What's he done?' I drew a blank on actual proven cases of anything really, but gave a vague list of recent 'incidents,' with only minimal embellishment to get the direness of my point across. 'You're sure it's him doing this? Out of jealous rage, you reckon?'

'I haven't anything concrete yet, but I'm pretty sure he's out to get me.'

'You really think he cares that much about me?'

'He seemed pretty angry back when he called. Furious, even. Half demented.'

'So he does still care for me!'

'What?'

'He didn't seem to care that I dumped him. But if he's actually angry and jealous ...'

'It was a while ago.'

'I'm going to call him.'

'You said you didn't have his number.'

'I'll get it off his mate, Kev.' She stopped. 'Shame. I thought something might've been starting to happen with Kev.'

'But I need to talk to Adam.'

'So do I. We might have made the most horrible mistake.'

She hung up. I could only hope they worked out whatever there was to work out.

I kept the cricket bat ready by the door just in case.

*

Days went by without incident. I approached something near regular sleeping habits. I began to calm, joking with friends and workmates, and not jumping with each sweep of headlights through my front window.

It was a Wednesday evening when a vaguely familiar number rang.

'Is this someone called Rod?' Adam's voice.

'Rob,' I corrected, then instantly regretted it. Perhaps the only reason he hadn't hunted me down properly was the difference of just a single letter.

'Mate,' he said. 'You are a champion.'

I remained silent, the words *It's a trap* in my head.

'I dunno what you said to Kate, but mate, it worked a treat.'

I gave a noncommittal 'Oh.'

'We're back together again. Better than ever. And yesterday, I popped the question. And, mate – she said yes.'

I offered what I hoped sounded like hearty congratulations. The way Adam was gushing I suspected he had rung the wrong person. But he continued, and it became clear I had somehow corrected all the ills of their relationship. They'd 'come to their senses' and were now completely in love. Proper love.

'Not just rooting,' Adam explained. 'All that other shit like buying a house and having kids, too.'

Growing in confidence, I gave further congratulations. 'I guess this means you'll stop stalking me,' I blurted, carried away with the new-found rapport.

The line fell silent. Then he said, 'I've been doing what?'

I stammered a tentative list of terrors. Adam paused, then laughed. 'Not me, mate. I barely knew you from a bar of soap before today.'

Fortunately I restrained myself from recapping the whole ordeal. *Keep quiet, you fool!*

'Gotta say, that's sounding a bit bloody paranoid to me.'

I had to agree, in retrospect.

'You're a single fella, aren't you?' Adam deduced.

I admitted this was so, but remained adamant that it was not a factor.

'Been single a while, too?'

Who has time for romance when a psychopath – real or imagined – is out to get you?

'What you need is a good root, I'd say,' Adam concluded. 'Soon set you right.' I struggled for a reply. 'Tell you what,' he said. 'I'll send your number off to a nice girly. Mate's ex. She's been having a dry stretch herself.'

I assured him this wasn't necessary. He didn't take no for an answer, much less even notice it.

So he did.

And she rang.

We met.

Now we're seeing each other. And we both agreed wholeheartedly never to go near Adam, Kate or any of their friends again.

Apparently they sent us a wedding invite. Christ only knows who received that.

[untitled]

And Senseless Acts

Eva Lomski

This big man in a furry coat, he gets on at Flinders Street and walks down the carriage, people all avoiding looking at him. He's wearing a black beanie pulled down low, and he has a wide, white face – reminds me of those husky dogs you see pulling sleds on TV. Malamutes, they're called. One eye's funny, and he's got these three bags stuffed full of stuff. He shuffles past and says, *Sit down mate, sit down,* and I know he's not talking to me, not talking to anyone, and wouldn't you know it, of all the places he sits right behind me.

My leg with the veins starts twitching, but at least he's quiet, and he stays that way while the train pulls out. It's busy for an afternoon train, which means one in four seats is taken, people making sure not to sit next to anyone else. Weather like this, clothes are all stinky from rain. I check to make sure I don't recognise the faces. I finally got myself in a tidy place after Lev was killed walking the dog. Anxiety levels are way down, but I still try never to take the same train twice, doesn't pay to let anyone know your routine. Who'd believe it's been a year already?

Meantime, I feel the man's fingers on the back of my seat and I shift, because who likes to be touched? Poor thing, reckon he's homeless, but at least he's not next to me. I can sit calm and read this book for class. Doctor made me enrol, said I needed to *connect*; I said, people like me, *disconnect*'s a blessing. It's the book of a movie I saw for the first time maybe twenty-five years ago, back when Lev and I celebrated wedding anniversaries with movies and such. The character, McMurphy, turns up at a nuthouse and rattles the cage of a nurse called Ratched. Funny, sad. Tragic, actually.

*

The man behind me whimpers and I think, hell, maybe he's seen what I'm reading and thinks I'm making fun of him, sitting here reading about nuthouses and crazy guys. I peer at his reflection in the window across the aisle, but he's not looking at me. In fact his back is turned, and he's staring at some poor girl in a tartan parka in another seat, small and chewing gum. Reminds me of my Lucy. Wonder where she is now?

I start to worry he's going to say or do something to the girl. What if she starts crying and screaming? What would I do if she did? Would I stand and say, leave her alone, and if I did, would he yell and smash me about the head with his bags, maybe taking out a knife?

But in the reflection, Malamute-man just sits there before turning back my way. I pretend I don't see. That's the beauty of sunglasses.

He starts whispering. *Sit down, mate, sit down.*

The train's emptying and I notice something. The more people get off, the louder the man gets. *Sit down, MATE. Sit down.* And then he starts having a conversation, like there's someone in the seat next to him. *Horses, mate. The gee-gees. Didja get that money on? You what?*

So I'm thinking, should I move? Would he think I was moving because of him? Would he turn on me and start smashing me about the head? Should I get off at the next stop and run to a carriage in front and get on again? One thing's for sure – *he's* not thinking about getting off. He's happy as a puppy in a sausage factory. Far as I can tell, he's having a conversation and calling the race too. *Get your money on Balcony-In-Blue. Horsham races, mate, gotta get there. And they're racing. Come on, Blue, come on. Coming to the first turn.*

This woman in the seat in front of me, I see her start to stiffen like a slug when you first touch it. She's got her ears on, listening to Malamute-man, same way I am. The backs on her earrings are so straight and perfect I know she's never had to cope with a crazy before.

Keep the spirit, Horsham. Let us pray. Coming into the last turn. Go! Pulling ahead is Balcony-In-Blue. WE DID IT! Fifteen-thousand dollars! We're RICH.

He's slapping his knees, whooping. I think the woman in front might very well vomit. She's scooping up her things, and she shoots out of her seat and down the aisle to the door. Old crazy is muttering away, and the next thing he's walking past me, still chuckling, shuffling up behind the woman. I see her eyeing the emergency button. *Fifteen-thousand dollars, can you believe it? Come on, Blue, sit down.*

At the next stop he gets off and I watch him through the window. He walks like he's walking into the wind, the funny eye pointing in my direction and the other one glaring straight ahead. I reckon he has all his clothes in those bags of his. Peeking out the top of one is a stuffed blue bunny.

I forget about him when I get to my stop, because some dopehead has stolen my old bike, and I have to go to the police station. *Whacha mean did I lock it up? Do I look like an idiot?* I'm angry because that bike has been better to me than most people I know, and what that dopehead's caused me is trouble I don't want or need. What I want and need after a day surrounded by noise and people is to get home as quick as possible, feed the cat, pray for forgiveness and sit very, very still.

*

But later that week, I see some stuffed toys in an op shop window and remember the man, and for the hell of it, I google it in the library. 'Horsham. Horses. $15,000.'

And I see this: *$15,000 to the winner of Horsham Garden Mint.* And I realise the article is dated the same day as the day on the train. But here's the thing. The race didn't happen until long after I'd gotten off the train, probably around the same time I was filling out my name at the police station.

*

I don't see Malamute-man again until the following Thursday. I'm in the front carriage this time, thinking there's less chance of crazies here, but wouldn't you know it, he finds me. Wearing the same coat, he's walking up and down, trying first one seat and then another. People are doing the shifty knee thing, bunching their legs together whenever he passes, like he was intending to stick his bags up their wazoos.

He's talking more than last time. I'm thinking, if he talks about the gee-gees, I'm off this train and into the nearest betting shop to put my money on. I've been googling it. There are these scientists doing experiments, and they found these people, they respond to things that are about to happen five seconds before they happen. And here's the thing – their *heart* responds faster than their brain. So some other scientist hooked up machines all over the world measuring people's responses, and get this; before the planes crashed into the twin towers in New York, four *hours* before, the machines went crazy.

This time the man's real restless. Foot's jiggling, funny eye swivelling in all directions. He's talking, same thing over and over, but he speaks in a whimper, and it takes me a while to figure out the words.

One dead and thirty-seven injured in train crash.

My heart does a little skip, and I check to see if anyone else has heard. There's a woman in green and purple – the type to chain herself to trees; a jerk in a suit talking into his phone about fridges – if he were American the accent would be Brooklyn; and two teenage girls in school uniforms. No one is paying Malamute-man any attention. They're ignoring him the same way I used to be able to. He sits one seat up, opposite me, with his feet in the aisle.

One dead, thirty-seven injured, he keeps saying. *Thirty-SEVEN.* He glares at me.

Now I'm really worrying. Exactly what train is he talking about? Because if it's this one, I'm getting off at the next stop.

The train halts, and before I get my wits about me, these three boys come on, all swagger and something else nasty. They spot Malamute-man and zoom in on him like those cruise missiles you read about, so good they can zoom in on a boil on a baby. The man shifts in his seat across to the window.

Hey stupid, says one of the boys. He's wearing a hoodie and his pants are hanging so far down his crotch, I'm thinking, boy, how big is the thing you think you got down there?

His friends laugh. They know their roles.

Stupid, I'm talking to you, says Crotch-boy.

It seems to me the man is getting smaller. His head is shrinking below the back of the seat. I'm worrying for him, and I'm worrying for me. What if these stupid boys start smashing him about the head? Should I say something? No way these other people are going to do anything. What if Crotch-boy turns on me and sticks his pimples in my face, yelling stuff about nosy old women? What if he sprays me with spray paint before slicing me up with the knife he's got hidden down his stinking pants?

Crotch-boy spits. The spit lands on the man's cheek. His friends spit too. They laugh and head down the carriage and out the door and into the next carriage, and I know they're off to make sure their crotches get their fill of fun for the day.

Malamute has found a hankie somewhere and he's wiping his face, scrutinising us – Suit-jerk, Greenie, the schoolgirls and me. When he inspects me, I'm glad I'm wearing the sunglasses, because I'm sure I've got the same shamed look in my eyes as the sick crank who stopped beating his dog only after realising the pee hadn't moved and the dog was a trembling, desperate-to-please mess. What did I do wrong, Master?

The man pulls things out of his bags. Greenie is watching, and I see her thinking about switching carriages. Onto the floor tumble the blue bunny, the black beanie, a plastic mug, a pair of jeans, a newspaper and a pencil case.

You ask me, says Suit-jerk into his phone, you ask me I'd do it *smarter*. I'm telling you, ring the fridge mechanic in Sydney.

Your boobs were hanging out, says one schoolgirl to the other.

More bra than there was top, says the second.

More underwear than there was wear, says the first.

One DEAD, let us pray, says Malamute-man and unzips the pencil case. He pulls out rosary beads.

How could I have forgotten about the train crash?

Mate, says Suit-jerk, you're not listening to me. Frank is redundant to this argument. My advice to you is this, get onto the fridge mechanic in Sydney.

All these people going home to their husbands and wives, says one schoolgirl.

Losers, says the other.

Slow is how I have to manage it, says Suit-jerk. You're not doing this smart. You're losing focus … FOCUS, do you hear?

Malamute-man jumps from his seat, waving his rosary beads like he was warding off vampires. *Sit down,* he barks at Suit-jerk.

Suit-jerk pauses, the phone in midair. He half smiles, half frowns, a salesman dealing with an irate customer. Okay, big guy, he says finally, I'm sitting down.

Gotta go, he says into the phone.

Malamute's watching back and forth while the guy shuts his phone, and then he shuffles back to his bags and starts piling everything back in again.

One dead and thirty-seven injured in train crash, he says to the carriage. *One DEAD.*

So now I'm spooked and remembering what else I googled. 'Presentiment' is what they called it. Get this. All four of the hijacked planes on 9/11 only had half the regular number of passengers, like the other half knew something terrible was about to happen and decided to stay home for an extra serve of pancakes.

Can't do that, says one of the schoolgirls, same as if it were your man.

I love you too, says the other, you're such a whore.

Don't need that shit, seriously, says the first.

One dead and thirty-seven injured.

The train starts to slow.

What now? says Suit-jerk, and glimpses around to see if anyone's heard him talking to himself. I heard you, I'm thinking.

An announcement comes over the speakers, but it's feeding back, or maybe the driver's got some accent you need to be Santa Claus to understand. Anyway, the train stops on a bridge over the highway before the overpass tunnel, nice view of the carbon dioxide and electrical retailers down below.

What's happening? says a schoolgirl.

Delay at the next station, says Suit-jerk, puffing up like she was the heat and he was the popcorn. She giggles at his weasel-male puffiness.

Thirty-seven injured, Malamute-man says. *Thirty-seven injured and one dead.*

That's it, I have to talk to him.

Excuse me, I say across the aisle.

Everyone stops what they're doing. Their ears are quivering like mice in the dark.

Excuse me, I say louder.

Malamute-man gives me a 'What, me?' expression, and I realise it's probably been a long time since someone was polite to him. He's examining my old coat and my sneakers and cut-off gloves. The rosary beads hang around his neck.

I can't help but hear you talking, I say to him. What's that you said about a train crash?

For god's sake, says the Greenie. We eyeball her. Leave him alone, she says, can't you see he's not *right?*

Sit down, he says, quiet.

This is too creepy, says a schoolgirl.

There's another announcement I don't understand. Malamute-man shoots over to the window, scrunching his body. He starts crying.

Now look what you've done, says Suit-jerk to the air.

Malamute-man's hands are clenched near his face. *Balcony-In-Blue,* he cries softly. *Let us pray.*

Greenie stands and hightails it to the door even though the train is stock still, and so does one of the schoolgirls.

You be right, she says to the other schoolgirl.

Fine, the other one says. Ta. Love ya.

I didn't mean to offend you, I say to Malamute-man.

He glances around, tears like icicles on his white face.

Suit-jerk is back on the phone. Train delay, he says. Have you talked to the fridge mechanic?

Malamute-man kicks over his bags. Stuff flies everywhere, across the aisle, under the seats. He's stopped crying, but he has the beaten-dog look about him.

My chest feels heavy as asthma. I hate that look. Since Lev was killed because of me, and I don't care what the doctor says about *bereavement* and *blame,* I see it in the mirror way too often, even after all the counselling, even after I've made the effort to go out to the supermarket or to class. Before I can think, I'm out of my seat, gathering things I wouldn't normally touch for worrying about insects and germs and things. This man's a big kid, I'm thinking, and kids I know how to deal with. I've even had some of my own, though I've lost them somewhere on the other side of the world.

Here, I say, here, and hand him the blue bunny and the newspaper and a roll of toilet paper and something furry that may or may not be a muff. We're both on our knees and up close his eye's not that bad, and he doesn't smell like I thought he would. More like mothballs really, and who doesn't smell like mothballs in the winter?

I catch his eye, the good one, and it darts down to where he's stuffing something into his bags. It's one of those plastic ziplock things and it's full of cash, must be thousands of dollars in there.

God almighty, I splutter. Then, Be careful with that, don't let anyone see.

He nods.

The voice comes over the speaker, and again Suit-jerk plays translator, telling us there's an electrical fault with the signals ahead and the train's staying put. Greenie and the schoolgirl sit down.

We finish the rest of the bags and I turn to my seat, but Malamute-man tugs at my sleeve. *Sit down?* he says.

Oh no. One thing to pick up the man's ratty old muff and another to sit down next to him and have a conversation. Lord knows he doesn't need more conversations going on in that head of his. What if he likes me and decides to follow me off the train or something, or follow me home even?

That dress just so sucked, says one schoolgirl.

We're totally cooler, says the other.

Please, the man says to me.

I'm no good at saying no to people, never have been, and that's exactly the reason, *exactly* the reason why it makes so much more sense to avoid them altogether. No mess, no fuss. I'm thinking, boy, will I be glad to get home to the cat tonight.

I sit down next to Malamute-man, worrying about what we're supposed to talk about and the cash at his feet. Worrying that Crotch-boy and the Crotchettes will come back to steal it.

One dead and thirty-seven injured in train crash, he says.

He's not saying it like he said it before, as if it was some crazy talk, but like he's heard the word of God, and it's his mission in life to pass it on. I get hot all over and my eyeballs flicker.

Presentiment is what they called it.

What train? I whisper. This one?

Crotch-boy bursts through the carriage door, his friends laughing behind him, and Malamute-man shrinks in his seat like a worm who's found himself at a bird convention. Crotch-boy's swaying, something's wrong with him, and I'm thinking maybe it's drugs. He staggers to the seat in front of the schoolgirls and kneels on it, facing them. They lean back as far as the seat lets them.

Ya wanna feel? he says to them, grabbing at the space between his pants and his jeans.

Hey, says Suit-jerk. That's enough.

Crotch-boy isn't impressed. You wanna feel too? he says. Ya fuckin' faggot.

Greenie's off her seat, heading for the emergency button. The Crotchettes head her off. Crotch-boy laughs.

How d'ya reckon the pigs will get out here, he says, and he points to the bridge and the overpass and the cars way down below.

Suit-jerk's on the phone. Crotch-boy notices Malamute-man and me.

Hey stupid, he says, happy birthday. Get his bags, he says to his boys.

They come towards us. Suit-jerk's yapping, those girls aren't helping, and Greenie's got the Crotchettes in the way.

All these years I've been avoiding this. All this time I've been keeping it tidy.

*

Wait a minute, we'll walk the dog together, I had said to Lev.

You don't want to come, Lev replied, either with the dog or with me.

And the truth of it, after so many years of living in the house like strangers from the time Lucy left, was like a slap, because I'd never admitted it to myself, and I had never guessed that he'd known.

So I let him leave, and some young offender on drugs smashed him across the head, kicked the barking dog, and stole the five dollars Lev had taken to buy a coffee at the shop.

*

Even as I stand I know I don't want to do this.

Leave him alone, I say.

Crotch-boy doesn't pause. He pushes me aside.

Don't touch me, I say, and even as I say it, I hear the tears coming, and of course Crotch-boy doesn't take any notice, some stupid weak woman who wouldn't know how to deal with an emergency if it came and spat in her face. He pushes me harder.

SIT DOWN!

Malamute-man has swollen up, and he's climbing past me, shoving Crotch-boy back, and his arms are swinging left, right, left, right, and Suit-jerk is yelling that the cops are on their way, and the girls are screaming, and Malamute-man's going chest to chest with Crotch-boy, pushing, shoving, and because Malamute's bigger and heavier and madder, Crotch-boy is falling back and calling on the Crotchettes who are guarding the door, but now Suit-jerk is in there too, swinging, and Greenie has pulled a can of something out of her bag and is yelling, GET BACK, GET BACK!

Crotch-boy and his friends see the can and make a run for it through the carriage. The train jolts, and then starts moving.

Thank god, says a schoolgirl. The pair of them are upset mewling kittens and Greenie fusses over them, saying, There, there, and stuff like that, while Suit-jerk storms into the next carriage and I hear him asking, Which way did the dickheads go, who'll come with me?

Malamute-man's handing me a hankie, and I realise I've been crying all this time, and my throat is sore, because I've been yelling too, but I don't remember yelling, and I don't remember crying. He pats me on the shoulder, can't remember how long since anybody patted me on the shoulder, makes me cry harder.

Sit down, he says, and I sit.

I believe you about the crash, I say. When's it happening? How do you know?

He points to his funny eye. *I see.*

The train's coming to the tunnel, and Malamute-man grabs hold of the rosary beads around his neck with one hand, and then he grips my hand with the other.

I didn't love Lev enough, I tell him. Was it my fault?

Coming to the last turn, he says. *Let us pray,* and as the train enters the tunnel, and he shields my body with his own, it gets me thinking as to how the heart responds faster than the brain.

The Sleepers Almanac

So Far North

Sarah Holland-Batt

It has been a week since the Aboriginal boy came to squat in the shed down the road. He has been watching. The shed is on the boundary of the old McCullough place, a shoddy A-frame of sheet iron and scrap cladding. The McCulloughs cleared off once talk of the blight started spreading north, and when the place didn't sell, left the land to grow over. The boy must have a billy rigged over there, because the electricity has been off for months.

He does not like the look of the boy. The boy is rangy tall and has been wearing the same clothes all week: a too-loose shirt and jeans. He also carries a rifle. In the evenings he disappears with it slung over his shoulder into the state forest. He is killing things in there. All week the old kelpie, Bully, has been bringing in animal skins with bullet holes in them. Possums, sugar gliders. Soft things that come out at night. There is something strange about the boy, something not quite right. So he has been watching. And the boy has been watching him too, he can feel it. Out in the thicket of leaves, on his trailbike, he can feel eyes on him.

There are too many places around here a body can hide. Whiskygrass as high as the windows around the house, then the plantation's fringe that gives unbroken cover all the way to the road's edge. The crop is towering this year, plants twice his height, thick and dark. When he stands in the middle of them, huge ragged leaves cross over each other in a humid weave that blocks out the sky. Some of the fruit is ready to cut, heavy hands of green bananas with skins so bruisable they will need wrapping in foam before they are packed in crates.

The harvest will wait until the new pickers come. Illegals probably, but they will get the job done. The last lot were drifters, but they were the best he could get. Town people warned all the good ones off, so he was lumped with two kids who spent their time off talking hippie stuff, night swimming in the creek, smoking and stringing hammocks in the gully. The girl had huge drooping tits and a cone shell through her ear. Her boyfriend had tattoos on his forearms and stank like tobacco. Turned out in the end they were junkies. He found a blackened spoon down near the creek and sent them both packing. Hard to get anyone to come up here at all. Hard to get help so far north.

*

At midday the house is a hotbox. He leaves the back door open and opens the kitchen shutters. No breeze. He has been bagging all morning, tying blue and silver striped sacks over the stems. Backbreaking work and too hot for it, worse without help.

He lights the gas stove and puts an enamel pan on the ring of blue flame. He empties in a can of corned beef. The pink brick of meat hisses and sticks to the side of the pan. Bully is at his feet, jowls wet. When it is warmed through he scrapes it onto a slice of bread. He drops a few spoonfuls into Bully's bowl and the dog noses into it.

Bully is missing part of her lower jaw and makes a terrible wet noise as she eats. He tries to ignore it. The sound is enough to put him off his lunch.

He is waiting for the water to run cold in the sink when he sees the boy. Just a glimpse through the fringe of banana leaves: his face, the whites of his eyes. He fumbles in the drawer for his butchering knife, but by the time he gets his hand on it the boy is gone. He thinks irrationally that the boy has crossed the distance between the plantation's edge and the house and is standing beneath the kitchen window like a shadow.

He resists the urge to stick his head out of the window and check. He reminds himself that he has been alone for a long time, maybe too long. The boy is stealing bananas, nothing more.

*

That afternoon he is inside boiling tea when the phone rings. There is no chance it will be Jean, none at all, but he picks it up.

Yep, he says.

I know what you fucken done. It is a man's voice this time.

You got the wrong number, he says.

No I fucken don't, the man says. You hear me? I fucken know.

*

Down in the long hot idleness of the night he wakes to hear the plantation whispering around the house. A lush shifting of leaves, the hush of prickling silence. Bad dreams. He can hear Bully breathe on the floor beside him. There are brown snakes out there in the leaf litter, poisonous things muscling through corridors of dead matter, curling in layers of husks and fronds. At night this place is oppressive, seething with roots and suckers, too dangerous to walk in. He sits up. Out in the absolute darkness, a sound like trickling rainsticks. When he is tired like this he imagines the plantation creeping towards the house, all those ripening things crowding him, leaning in.

He reaches for the lamp switch. His room is small and plain: a bed with a blanket kicked to one side, a closet, today's shirt over the arm of a wicker chair. It looks foreign to him. He goes to the window and pulls the shutter closed.

The boy will be out there somewhere in the dark of the night now, hunting. His mind strays to the forest's edge. Past the wire fencing are the cool ferns, staghorns that ray out like green suns from the colossal trunks. Strangler figs that braid around the bark and sap the trees, plaiting their way up. And above are the night animals moving from branch to branch whose huge blind eyes shine in the blackness and whose soft bodies unnerve him, chase him in dreams.

When he was a child and afraid of the night his mother would sit with him. He thinks sometimes of her cool quavering voice, calls it up. He imagines her face, the seam that ran from lip to nostril where the darkness of her hare lip was stitched shut.

*

The next day he packs the trailer and drives it to the boundary of the McCullough place. The trees down here are not even close to ready for bagging, but he pretends to check them anyway. He works the rows methodically. Bully walks with him, the skin of her belly wobbling low and stretched.

When he sent her out for a piss earlier that morning she came back with a possum's pelt, perfectly skinned from the neck down, paws intact. The paws were skinny grey with slate-coloured claws. There was a small ragged hole above the hindlegs. When he picked it up the fur was thick and coarse. He could feel the weight of the bones in its limbs like sinkers.

Down by the shed there is no sign of the boy. He walks to the stump at the edge of the property. The shed is empty. The walls are panels of fibro siding and the roof is a patchwork of rusted-out scrap iron. The door is a knock-up job, a piece of green PVC usually used for greenhouse roofing. Hanging over a pile of sleepers there is a filthy pink blanket. Just to the left of the shed there is a billy rigged over a pit. The boy could be inside now, sleeping.

Bully has strayed over near the shed and is sniffing in the grass.

Bully, he says warningly.

He follows her and that is how he spots them in the grass. Empty cans: corned beef and syrup peaches. His. The boy has snuck into his pantry and taken them. The boy has been inside his house.

He yanks the door open. Nothing. The shed is hot and closed up and has a sharp reek of rust and oil. On the floor there is a sleeping roll on top of flattened cardboard boxes. Beside it are a yellow rucksack, a flask and a torch. On the old sorting bench, he finds a box of matches and a pouch of Drum tobacco, a pocket knife and a comb. There are old things of the McCulloughs', too: an old tine ripper, a few pallets stacked up against the wall, lengths of hose and rope. The shed has been in disuse for years, well before the McCulloughs left; the plantation goes for hectares and the huge cooling sheds and house are a twenty-minute drive down the mountain.

He looks at the rucksack. If he opens it he is no better than the boy. He leaves the musty shed and wonders why the boy has come here, where he came across the rifle, how many times the boy has broken into his house.

*

Later he takes Bully for a long walk to the gorge. He thinks often of the time it has taken the creek to insist its way through the rock. Today it is a quiet place full of the sound of water, but when the creek swells after storms the noise is deafening. It is a monstrous sound, violent, like the roar of longhaul trucks. He looks up. Above the large faces of rock wet with moss and lichens, ferns are growing. They nod down secretively.

Bully is wading in the creek.

The creek is low today, though there are several waterholes close by where it is possible to swim. Even in huge rains their surfaces are silent and unmoving.

He and Jean used to come here to swim. She would breaststroke out, ripples rolling out in front of her, then call him in. He was never much of a swimmer. He would ease his way in cautiously, shot with a plummeting panic at the blackness below. That is his idea of fear: dead things brushing his feet, the slime of cold smooth stones.

This is also the place he brought the daughter of the woman who came picking that year. Only a few times, it is true, but that was enough. She was fourteen, Vietnamese. He still does not know what made him do it. When he tries to reinhabit those thoughts, that desire, he finds he cannot. It was not lust, exactly, but something else, the precise nature of which is lost.

He stands at the water's edge. Huge dragonflies are mating just above the surface. The sheer mechanics of how they hover there without drowning is a mystery. They move as a single thing: two heads and sets of wings.

When he brought the girl down here, in the joy of the act, the force of it, he felt himself becoming heavy as stone. It was as though he was moving below the water's surface and the water was thick as molasses. When he tries to sieve out details of that time, they arrive in flashes, swift-moving, like gold flecks in a pan, too small to be of any use to him or anyone. Nothing is left of that time, nothing at all. He used to think you had to put time between yourself and a thing like that to understand it, but he was wrong. Time only breaks things down.

*

He is going to put a padlock on the pantry to keep the boy out. He will do it after breakfast. The boy must be a runaway from a boy's home or borstal. The problem of how and why the boy has found his way up here niggles at him, strikes at his skull like a blowfly.

He opens a can of beans and pours it into the frying pan with some strips of bacon from the freezer. Supplies are getting low. Soon he will need to drive down the mountain to town, where he will face the same grudging silence at the supermarket, the petrol station, the pharmacy.

Petty gossips, all of them. Full of talk and hate.

Although he is not yet what he considers old, lately he has come to wonder about what will happen to him when he dies. If it happens when the pickers are here his body will be discovered quickly. Any other time of the year it could be months before someone finds him. And what if no one comes? What happens then? He scarcely knows. Since Jean left, the scope of his life has become so minuscule that its particulars are known only to him.

He opens the kitchen window and whistles for Bully. That is when he sees the boy. The boy is standing out in the open grass between the plantation and the house, looking up at the window. It takes him a second to really see what the boy is holding. It is Bully. The boy has Bully in his arms. He can see a scrap of the pink blanket dangling from her hindleg.

He is running down the back stairs and towards the boy before he realises what he is doing.

You bastard, he yells. You mongrel bastard. I'll kill you.

The boy holds the dog out in his arms awkwardly. The rifle is dangling loosely over his shoulder.

Get away, he yells at the boy. Put her down.

The boy just stands there.

Are you slow or something, he snaps. Fucken put her down.

The boy lets the dog down in the grass. Bully takes a few steps. There is something wrong with her leg.

He looks at the boy. What the fuck have you done, he says.

Up this close the boy does not look well. He is too thin and there is a swelling the size of a cricket ball on his right ankle where the skin is taut and shining.

What the fuck have you done, he says again.

The boy gives him a sideways look and runs pell-mell into a row of banana trees.

He takes one look at Bully and goes haring after the boy through the whipping leaves. He does not know why he is running or what he will do when he gets hold of the boy. His heart is walloping in his chest and there is a huge rushing in his ears. He is running as fast as he can, the most he has run in years. The boy dodges into another row and disappears. He veers right and stops to listen. He does not know what he will do if he catches the boy. The boy is much swifter and younger, and although he does not think the boy will use it, there is still the question of the rifle.

Everywhere he is surrounded by the rustling of banana leaves. The boy has lost him. Then from the corner of his eye he catches a glimpse of white. It is the boy's sleeve. The boy is hiding, crouched down beside a tree with the rifle in his hands. He feels a bolt of excitement slide through his gut. His steps are silent and deliberate. The ground holds beneath his feet. He makes it to within arm's length of the boy before the boy turns, and by the time the boy stands up, he is there, with his hand bunched in the boy's shirt, his fist moving like a sledgehammer into the boy's face. Even he is surprised by the violence of it. He feels the boy's nose mash under his knuckles.

The boy holds one hand up to his nose. Blood is rivering down his face.

Hey, the boy says thickly. Hey. What I done.

What the fuck are you doing here, he says.

The boy stares at him defiantly. You fucken crazy. He spits and it is bloody. I done nothing.

When he lifts his arm to hit the boy again, the boy is ready and smashes the butt of the rifle down on his head. The pain is huge, as though his skull has split. He drops to his knees.

Crazy old fucker, you, the boy says, softly this time. Crazy old fuck.

*

When he opens his eyes again, leaves are swinging sickeningly overhead. It is still light. He gets his arm around a tree trunk and hauls himself up. White starbursts scatter like buckshot across his temples. His head is throbbing, great stabbing pains that come in a dizzying rhythm.

He lurches through the corridors of leaves. Everything is keeling and pitching around him.

Bully, he yells. His voice comes out muffled, like a piano on soft pedal. Bully.

When he staggers back to the house he finds her lying by the back stairs in the grass. She is breathing.

He collapses beside her and concentrates on his own breathing. He lifts one hand up and feels a wet patch on the crown of his head. The blood is sticky and dark as motor oil. Bully makes a faint whimpering noise when he touches her flank, and he sees his blood drying as brown ridges in her coat.

A few years ago he would have driven Bully to the vet in town and had her leg looked at, but that is no longer possible. He cannot imagine what would happen if he walked into the vet's now with his head split open and Bully in pain. He has come to accept that he is a pariah, that no one will help him or his dog.

He uses the railing to pull himself to his feet and carries Bully into the house. She is heavy, much heavier than he expected. Her body is unbearably soft. He lays her down into the bathtub, then goes to the kitchen. He takes three aspirin for his own head, which is thundering, and brings back scissors, an old rag, and the bottle of whisky.

Once he has undone the boy's shabby tourniquet and shaved her leg, the two entry points are there, clear as day. Snake bite. He washes the bite and dried blood off with soap and rewraps her leg tightly with the rag, just above the joint. Her breathing is shallow but quiet enough.

At times like these he feels as if he is impossibly far from the place he grew up, so far away that he is clinging to the edge of things. That is why people come this far north. To disappear, to be swallowed up. And he is being wiped out, he is being swallowed up. He is vanishing day by day in this place.

He carries her to the sofa and sits beside her. Bully is old, he does not know how old exactly, but even if the bite is not badly venomous it may still finish her off. He strokes her head. He cannot do anything to bring Jean back or undo what he did to the girl by the creek. He cannot even take care of Bully. His life has come to this.

*

In the middle of the night he wakes in sweat and kicks off the blanket. There is a disorienting sound all around him, a patter like a car engine ticking over. Rain. He reaches over. Bully is breathing.

He lies in the dark and watches the shadows on the walls. Follows the shape of the chair, the lamp, the open wardrobe door, the whole negative world. It is a trick his mother taught him as a child. On his back, he would first hold his hand in front of his face until he could make out its edges, then his arm, then the rest of the room would materialise from the itching velvet.

The rain is bucketing down now on the iron roof. He imagines the boy down in the shed, holed up in the darkness like a rabbit. He shouldn't have hit the boy, but he cannot change that now. Whatever the boy has done, whatever brought him here, the boy still did the right thing for Bully. He has managed to make the boy hate him in spite of that.

He sinks down further into the dark and closes his eyes. All he can remember of the girl is the faint smell of cold cream on her neck, the way pain changed her face, pulled it sideways. There is no point in going over it. He took what he took and would take it again. This is the one true thing he knows. If he could go back it would all still end here, this room, this bed with its wool blanket, the small house leafed in by plantation, this seedless fringe of green that could be left wild for a thousand years and still would not multiply.

Perhaps he will wake up in the morning to find the boy gone. But if the boy is not gone, tomorrow he will get up early and take some canned fruit and potted meat down to the shed.

There can be no fixing what he has done to the girl, to Jean. But he will keep an eye out for the boy. It strikes him that he is the only one who knows where the boy is, who knows that the boy is alive at all. And in return, the boy is evidence that he himself exists. They will watch each other. It is the right thing.

Ringroad

Alex Miller

Now that the time for such a visit is already in the past, it seems that I really am going to visit Vienna at last and will be able to walk around the Ringroad as my hero, Sigmund Freud, once did every morning for his constitutional. Richard talked me into the trip. He was so pressing and insistent that despite my reluctance to commit myself to such a journey I had no alternative in the end but to tell him I would go. I was afraid he would be ill if I resisted him any longer. 'Be sure you do go,' he said as he turned to leave my office. 'I want to see the ticket.' I have been putting off a visit to Vienna for thirteen years and I had no substantial reasons left to offer him for not going. In three years I shall retire. I shall go alone of course. I have lived alone since Annabelle left me nearly seven years ago. After my wife left me I made several unsuccessful attempts to form new relationships with women. But there were too many difficulties. So to settle the problem of sex once and for all, last year I decided I would remain celibate. It has not been as difficult as I had thought it was going to be. Indeed it has been easier than giving up smoking, which is something I managed to do more than twenty years ago. In getting rid of my beloved Dunhill pipe and throwing out my last packet of fragrant Erinmore I suffered greatly and still consider giving up smoking to have been the one truly heroic renunciation of my life. And I'm not a young man. I'm in my fifty-seventh year and have had time and opportunity for heroism. It was Annabelle, my wife, who made me give it up. She disliked the smell of it so much that she began to find me repulsive. It was either my wife or my pipe. I struggled for quite a while to resolve this dilemma, but in the end I had to decide for Annabelle and against the Dunhill. No more sitting alone in my study reading and puffing away on my pipe. The brief affair I indulged in with one of my honours students following this act of self-deprivation, the event indeed that triggered my wife's abrupt departure from our home, ended by causing me a great deal of grief and unpleasantness in addition to the long-term suffering associated with the loss of my wife, Annabelle, whom I loved and whom I still love and believe I shall always love.

After Annabelle disappeared into the hinterland of North Queensland with an Aboriginal stockman – an unlikely story but true nevertheless – I decided my life would be easier if I dispensed entirely with the problem of women and sex. Beginning new relationships is complicated and difficult for a man of my age. I know that Simone de Beauvoir has assured us that men's bodies don't matter and that women don't make love to men for their physique. But I'm not sure that I'm convinced by Beauvoir. I am, to be perfectly frank, rather overweight and am sensitive about my appearance. I know I do not repel women and from time to time one of them will even demonstrate an eagerness to get to know me. I have never made the first move in any relationship, whether with a man or a woman. In fact I find it difficult to respond even when a friendly overture is made towards me. The desire to have friends and lovers is not lacking. It is just that the reality is always so much more complicated and difficult than one had ever imagined it might be as one lay in one's bed alone in the middle of the night dreaming of a companionable companion. The truth is, I would never have married Annabelle or had the affair that ended my marriage if both women had not been as insistent as they were.

It is difficult for me to imagine anyone finding me attractive. I'm six foot three in the old measure. I don't know what that is in centimetres. I have narrow and rather rounded shoulders. Some might say that this is from all the years of poring over books, but the truth is I've always had narrow rounded shoulders. I had them in primary school. I think I was born with them.

From the outside looking on, that was me. I also have very thin legs and a rather distinctive manner of walking. My distinctive manner of walking began when I was thirteen and was in my first year at a new secondary school. During that year I grew almost twelve inches and became a stranger to myself. I ceased, during that year, to be the person I had always been. In order to compensate for my immense height and in an attempt to return to my old familiar self, I began to effect a crouch and to develop an extra long stride. I'm sure that ergonomic engineers have tabulated the optimum stride length for a given height or length of leg and that this optimum is usually arrived at unconsciously by the normal walker. I set out to override the unconscious optimum and to exceed it in order to bring myself down a little. The unforeseen result of the combined crouch and longer stride was that as I walked I bobbed up and down, as if I were running on the spot in neck-deep water, or was imitating an English comedian whose name I can't at this moment recall. I also developed a fixed stare, which was no doubt due to the concentration required from me to override the natural and unconscious rhythm of my body. My parents were already sensitive to the fact that I had suddenly become six inches taller than they, and were so alarmed by my new way of walking, the purpose of which I had not thought to explain to them, that I abandoned the slight crouch almost at once. I have, however, retained the lengthened stride to this day and it would probably require many probing sessions of psychoanalytic therapy for me to recover my repressed optimum stride length. But would it be worth it at my age? I do wonder, however, if this determined repression of my own normal walking style may not have had other effects on my personality of which I have remained unaware. But the intention in writing this autobiographical account is to tell the strange story of my visit to Vienna, and is not to assemble ideas about my attractiveness or lack of it for the opposite sex, or indeed for my own sex, or how it is that I walk in a way that draws upon me the curious stares of complete strangers and the ridicule of young students, who imitate me, some with such virtuosity that I have once or twice over the years imagined I saw my companion-self bobbing along ahead of me through the cloisters.

I didn't play sports when I was a boy and have always felt this to have been the cause of a certain weakness in my character. I have a considerable stomach. I struggle to control it. It varies in size as the struggle varies in intensity, larger as my morale sinks and I abandon the attack and smaller as I gather my resolve and assert the firm discipline of a new campaign. I believe my stomach is with me, however, for good now and will be buried with me when I go. Although I would never admit as much even to my closest acquaintance, since Annabelle's departure, my stomach has become a substitute for the friend and companion of my bed. I caress it when I am lying alone at night under the sheets and I often find myself confiding little confidences to it as one would to an intimate. My standing silhouette resembles rather the silhouette of that great Frenchman, General de Gaulle. I don't believe I need be ashamed of this.

When I decided on celibacy, as a precaution I told my students it was a principle of mine never to make friends with students. So as to preserve my objectivity in the matter of marks, I said, for how could one bring oneself to give a poor mark, no matter how deserved, to a dear friend? Or, and I did not add this, a lover. But of course when you are faced with a group of ten or twelve fresh new honours students at the beginning of the year, some of whom are young women with golden skin and who gaze at you as if they are already in love with you, to renounce the possibility, the dream and illusion even, of friendship is by no means an easy thing to do with conviction. I will say however that I managed it for seven years. As I said, giving up sex has not been as difficult as giving up smoking. As the reasons for this are not obvious I shall go into them in some detail later. For now I must cut to the chase, as Richard always says.

Richard is the dean of our faculty. He is a decent, honourable man and not at all like deans usually are. He likes to read and even to write and was much happier as a professor, but he allowed himself to be talked into the promotion. So now he has become an administrator and no longer has time for reading or writing and this has made him sad. He is one of the new managers and it does not suit him. He is deeply alone and unhappy among the accountants and marketing people and pro-vice-chancellors and the other deans. Richard has become spiritually isolated at the prime of his life. I feel sorry for him. But there is nothing I can do to help him. Our situations are so very different that we have lost our old intimacy and we can no longer share a joke without a certain sadness coming over us, a nostalgia for the old days when he was at liberty to laugh at himself.

It was Richard who convinced me to make the trip to Vienna. Which is, after all, what this story is about; the extraordinary events that unfolded once I reached that distant city. I applied for outside study leave, which with Richard's support I was certain to be granted, and decided to go. The vehemence of Richard's argument in persuading me sprang in part at least from his sense that since his promotion he has become a man under sentence of death. He sees nothing good now between himself and the abyss of nothingness that awaits us all and he does not want his old friend to share such a sad fate. Richard is a man without illusions. And without illusions to comfort him in his lonely hours he is naked and alone. Our illusions, after all, are our most precious possessions and make the sense of happiness a possibility for us. Illusions, indeed, are surely half the meaning of human existence. I'm not sure what the other half is. But whenever I hear a fundamentalist anti-religious person speaking with contempt of those who hold to the illusion of faith it is the fundamentalist for whom I feel some compassion. To have reached maturity in life and to have not understood that our illusions are the treasure house of the imagination is a sad fate. For many years when I was a student of English literature and a devout reader of the volumes of *The Cambridge History of English Literature* I thought Caroline Divines was a woman author and I looked for her work in vain.

I should explain that I've been writing a biography for a number of years. Far too long. I hardly dare commit the number of years to paper, but it is in fact almost thirteen years since I began to research the life of John Robinson of Norwich and there is still no sign of a book. The old contract I had with the university press is years out of date, the publisher at the press has changed due to the death of the dear fellow who signed me up, and the research grants I once had are used up and accounted for long ago. Ten years ago at our university my discipline was subsumed into something called Cultural Studies.

Now Cultural Studies is itself about to be subsumed into something else that does not even have a name yet. It's rather like the old American folk song in which an old woman swallows a spider to catch a fly which she has already swallowed, and so on, until at last she swallows a horse, and ends with the line, She's dead – of course!

From an unfinished fragment of memoir found among the effects of the writer after his death.

Sidney

Emma Schwarcz

He stares at the fruit compote. A small mound of apples and pears and sultanas, or at least that's what he assumes – the fruit is so far gone it could be anything now, boiled down to nothing specific. A little note sits beside it on the kitchen bench: 'Sidney, this is for *after* your lunch.'

He flips the note over, but there is nothing further. And lunch itself? He looks around the cupboards, peering past mugs and bowls and special silverware. A puddle of Ant-Rid has crystallised beside the food processor; the wine glasses have been moved to higher ground. He considers the refrigerator. Inside, a raw chicken breast sits next to a head of broccoli. Sidney presses a finger to the cling film: perhaps he's meant to cook the chicken himself? Paula usually leaves him a sandwich, when she leaves him at all – for the hairdresser or to pick up groceries, never for longer than an hour. It's always something vegetative on rye: lettuce or cucumber, or tomato, which she keeps separate so the bread doesn't soak, or that green muck he swears he's told her he doesn't appreciate, what's it called again? Japanese-sounding. Starts with 'o.' He strains for a moment and then returns to the fridge. He'll have to cook the chicken then, if he can just find the frypan.

The pan is on the heat when it comes to him – avocado! – a sudden flare in the dark. Fetid stuff, though his daughters all goad him to try it; health-obsessed, their generation. It's a 'superfood,' they say, full of antioxidants and good fat (whatever that is): just like a vitamin, but tasty. Personally, he'd rather take vitamins, which he does, each morning, along with some other medication the doctors have prescribed. He stops short. Has he taken them today? He walks back to the bedroom and finds the blister pack from the pharmacist – so clever these days, the way they allocate the pills to the right date, like an advent calendar for the aged. Except instead of small chocolates there are about eight pills of varying shapes and sizes, one of which lodges in his throat each morning and seems to leave an imprint that scratches for the rest of the day. Tablets shouldn't come so large and unwieldy, he thinks, not when there are electric windows in cars.

He looks at the last day's dose and wavers. Wednesday. Is that today or tomorrow? Could just as well be either, the days having long since lost their markers. Retirement has had that effect on them; they jiggled around in your pockets, rubbing against one another until the edges and markings were worn down and what was left were only seven shining nubs, roundly polished to obscurity.

The paper! He clicks his fingers and grabs the pills. The paper will tell him whether it is Tuesday or Wednesday. He feels a rush of pride at this sudden onset of lateral thinking. It isn't all beyond him.

On his way back to the kitchen, he notices another sign, this one posted to the study door. 'DO NOT ENTER.' He frowns. Is this note for him? Surely not. He considers the room's contents – mostly books and old photo albums, nothing top secret, certainly nothing to warrant a note of this authority. It is still his house, still his years of mechanical engineering and nimble stock shifts that allow them its shelter. The study is technically Paula's, given over once the girls were married and Paula discovered a need for hobbies. Reading didn't seem like much of a hobby to Sidney back then – golf or checkers were hobbies – but other women of Paula's age seemed to disagree, and she left him bi-weekly to discuss the latest fictions. She had a lot more time back then and the books started to gather in small stacks along the shelves until there was nowhere for them to go but the floor. The towers of books unsettle Sidney now, with his higher centre of gravity and propensity to topple things. He doesn't generally have cause to enter the room, which is a relief, though he's noticed of late that Paula also avoids it. Perhaps he should encourage her to return to the book club? He can handle a night alone.

An acrid smell reaches him and he is pulled back towards the kitchen, where someone has left a chicken breast to burn.

He fans the smoke away from his face as he reaches for the gas knob. The place smells like one of those corner shops that have popped up in recent years, manned by Mediterraneans. He looks for a way to activate the exhaust fan but the damn thing is new and its switches are hidden. He opens the windows and doors instead and catches the eye of their neighbour, Mrs … He stops, panicked. *Mrs* … The name won't come. She smiles through the window and waves, but he is fumbling along the sink, knocking over detergent bottles and clean cutlery. He *knows* her, has lived next door for years. The details of their lives laid bare by the construction of their houses – ill-conceived – which aligns their windows like primary school kids on excursion: side by side, hand in hand, buddies for the duration. He tries to relax. If he places it in a full sentence, sometimes that's enough to unstick the cogs. 'Her name is Mrs …' He bangs the counter. Starts again. 'You know, I went next door the other day and bumped into Mr and Mrs …'

He really focuses, sends the messengers off down the eroded pathways, again and again and again, but they fall short of their goals and instead idle on the side somewhere or hit unexpected culs-de-sac. He spends so long trying to retrieve it that when he looks up at the window across the way – now empty – he realises that he's lost sight of what he was seeking and it's time for lunch anyway.

After a brief search of the kitchen, Sidney decides the only option is the chicken. It's burnt through on one side but at least it's cooked, which he's heard is imperative when it comes to poultry. He scrapes some of the charcoal into the sink and sits down to his meal. It sticks in his mouth it's so dry, any moisture just a concept at this stage, not at all like Paula usually makes. He rummages through the cupboard for some tomato sauce but finds only a pot of tomato paste, which he assumes can't be too dissimilar. He is wrong.

'What on earth?' He reaches for some water, wishes the whole lot gone from his mouth, the whole charred, desiccated, acidic lot. Paula was wrong to leave him. Where the hell is she, anyway? He walks into the hallway to see if her car is in the drive. It's not, so he turns to the bathroom to see if he can't rinse this atrocity from his tastebuds. He sees a sign on the study door and, confused, decides to inspect further. Paula generally looks out for him, but nothing should be off-limits in this house – everything shared, everything known – isn't that what a marriage is?

He opens the door and switches the light on, but instead of the literary turrets he's come to expect, there's a large zippered bag – gigantic, really – hanging from a coat-hook against the wall. He squints. It looks like a Christmas tree it's so big, so A-line, but you don't usually zip Christmas trees up in body bags, he thinks, so chances are it's something else. Could it *be* a body? he thinks, for an exhilarating moment. It certainly looks like the bags he sees on those police dramas Paula watches. He checks himself. He lives with his wife of fifty-six years in a quiet suburb mostly populated by retirees. Logic dictates it's neither a Christmas tree nor a murder victim and, as he's exhausted his sole possibilities, the only option left for him is to unzip the thing and stand back.

'Good God!' The cream silk seems to rush at him once the zip's undone, the ruffles and layers barely contained by the bag. He looks closer, peels back the nylon. There's lace and a small beaded section and a neckline so reinforced it almost stands upright unaided. A wedding dress? But for whom? He hasn't been told of a wedding, and if the dress is in his house it must be for someone close. His three daughters are already married – happily, for the most part, but either way they're not the type to jump ship – and his grandchildren are all too young to consider it, the oldest just out of high school now, about to study medicine. And *he's* not about to wear this frippery in any case. Sidney sits down on the floor.

He has a strange taste in his mouth, which he worries might be the onset of a stroke, but the mystery of the dress keeps him from calling anyone. What if he's not supposed to know about the wedding? What if he's being kept at bay because he's likely to object to it? He presses his toes into the carpet and watches the grain shift and resettle.

He recalls, for a moment, his daughters' wedding dresses. The first had gargantuan, bulbous sleeves that kept Sidney at an awkward distance as he walked her up the aisle. The second was sleeveless and elegant; the third dipped so low in front that Sidney was forced to deck a cousin for his comments. This was all aeons ago now, but he could still feel the clutch of their hands on his wrist, their small wobbles as he steadied their pace.

And to think they're now staging a wedding behind his back! Who will pay for it, for a start? He played the role of negotiator at the last three functions – chipping fortunes off car hire and catering and flowers that weren't half as pretty when you knew what they cost you. He'd saved thousands. The girls were lost without him – a wedding without his input would send them all to the poorhouse.

He paws his way to the back of the dress, feeling blindly past oceans of material for a receipt or tag of some description. Silk, silk, silk – paper! He grabs a hold and pulls it out to the light. As he squints to read it, he notices a patch of red on his thumb – blood? He sniffs, then licks it and is relieved to taste tomato. The relief dissipates. 'Oh *no*.'

He heaves the dress out and there it is – right at the back. Maybe he can replace it? He checks the receipt: $6700. For a dress? A name is scrawled above the figure: 'Natalie Banks.' He blinks hard. Little Natalie? But she's still in school and hasn't even mentioned a boyfriend, let alone a fiancé. How can her parents allow it? And, more importantly, why has he not been invited? He's her grandfather – it makes no sense that she should slight him like this. Unless … Perhaps she's in trouble? He returns to the dress and checks its girth. Tight as a drum; she'd have to be in her first trimester, if at all, to fit in this waistline. He smiles but then notices another spot of red, now on the front.

He thinks of his granddaughter, of her small white teeth and elegant hands – hands made for music, for piano or violin. He slumps to the floor. Invited or not, he has ruined it. There is no coming back from that.

Why didn't they just tell him? Why all the secrecy? If he'd known, he would have ignored the room with the dress, sat down to watch CNN and tracked fingerprints over his trousers instead. Paula would have come home, tut-tutted and given him a change of clothes, plain and simple, whereas now he'll be strung up and quartered while they all gather round the soiled dress and cry for its potential.

He turns away when they cry, which they seem to do more and more. You'd think that as the knee grazes and schoolyard taunts faded into history, so too would the saline, but if anything the tears have increased and from such a well that the promise of ice-cream no longer suffices. In that sense, boys might have been easier; looking at his sons-in-law, however, he thinks that maybe daughters are not half-bad. Yes, it would have been his son-in-law, Peter, who excised Sidney from the celebrations. Always so concerned about what others were thinking, whispering behind a hand that Sidney had odd socks or a piece of omelette in his stubble or shoes that, if you don't mind me saying, Dad, could use a bit more polish. Well, he *does* mind and – Sidney freezes. Shoe polish!

He rushes down the hall and flings open the wardrobe. Paula's Special Occasion Wear, now lying fallow, takes up most of the space, but somewhere in the underbrush lie his good leather shoes. He's half inside the cupboard, shoving aside shoeboxes and handbags, when he finds them. He hauls them out into the light for inspection. The old scuff marks are covered; the toe-tips, which have thinned and softened with the years so that there is no rebound to their give, have been polished for the army.

He sits back on his heels. He tries to remember when he last wore them. Nothing surfaces. He closes his eyes and tries to coax back the occasion – was it a wedding? An anniversary? His birthday? He tries to situate himself in time so he can then work back to the most likely scenario, but nothing is coming to him and it takes so long – too long – that he realises nothing will be coming to him from here on out. His breaths are shallow. The veins in his calves are starting to pulse noticeably from this kneeling position. He runs a thumb over his shoe. Still, they're polished – that has to be a good sign. He'd need them shined if he's to go to a wedding, so perhaps it's a surprise – an uncommon tradition, to be sure, but not outside the realm of possibility.

He leaves the shoes to attend to the dress, which has not shifted from its ruined slump on the study floor. He stares at it for a moment. He can still save it, if he acts quickly. It's not too late for him.

'Right.' He unsheathes the dress from its bag and hoists it over one shoulder, unbalanced momentarily. It's heavier than he'd expected and with all the layers there's only one viable option for him. He stumbles down to the ensuite and, blinded by the swathes of silk flying this way and that, almost catapults the thing into the bath.

The stain looks to be settling in now, with a moat of grease surrounding the original tomato, so he grabs a round of soap – Lavender Fresh – wets it and applies it to the dress, at first tentatively but then briskly, as he's seen Paula do with the tablecloth and his undergarments. The tomato starts to shift – a step back into the fold! – but then he notices a mauve shadow in its place.

'No. Please no.' He takes off his shoes and steps into the tub, unhooking the shower nozzle and letting loose the water. His socks are soaked and he slips a little, and he thinks he hears some beading skitter across the enamel. The water gathers in a small pond at the waist, sending little rivulets down the seams, which darken as they're absorbed. He scrubs at the material, losing control over the nozzle briefly so that it flashes in his face and drips water down his shirtfront. Still he wipes his cheeks dry and goes back to work; he can save this, he can be of use. This new stain can be washed away with the old and he can resume his place on the head table, with his wife, his daughters, his child bride of a granddaughter, and his polished shoes.

*

When he is done, he steps out of the tub. He walks away from the bathroom, down the hall to the kitchen, where the compote is waiting. On his way, he hears a key in the front door and Paula's voice, high and bright.

He sits down and tries to remember what he was meant to have done with his day, if there was something else he might have achieved. He can hear Paula humming as she puts her things down on the sideboard. He lifts the spoon to his mouth, pushing the puree around his palate with his tongue, the fruit so tame now it meets with no resistance.

The Big Issue

Oxtales

David Astle

Howqua to Jamieson

My name is Nelson after the Pommy sailor who lost an eye to grapeshot. Or in my case a whip. My left eye is gristle. I can't see Yella the newblood walking beside me. I can't see the Goulburn River. I can't see the fucking mountains. You might say I'm blind to anything sinister, giving rise to my namby-pamby folklore (Orion's words) that helps us pass the time tramping through the backblocks.

Orion walks in the rearmost span closest to Cusack's whip, gaining my stories piecemeal from bullock to bullock, yoke to yoke, Chinese whispers down the line.

Yella is a virgin to the open road, this trip his first beyond the outskirts of Mansfield. A willing beast, the kid is riddled with questions – Why do birds sing? How far is Jamieson? What's a barouche? – as Nigger is with heartworm. I envy the breath Yella finds to verbalise uphill. I long for the novelty he feels on fording creeks. The nonsense code of insects. No doubt Yella is braced for a long haul, most of it without me. This road to Aberfeldy shapes as my last.

Cusack our driver has an ironclad rule when it comes to choosing yokemates. Old must accompany new, he believes, the likes of Yella by the likes of me, world-weary by world-hungry. Cusack hopes the coupling will see the new ox 'break' but I prefer the opposite idea. Yoking I see as the vital step on the road to completion. Twice the beast for the stories I feed him, Yella is shedding his innocence by dint of miles and campsites. As two, we merge into one. The ox, he's learning, owns more than a walk-on role when it comes to the landscape we brave, the snaky road, the watchful bush, the kilns and mines and scratch-out farms we encounter on the road. Only this morning he mistook our species as Johnnies-come-lately to this island's saga until my oxtale told him otherwise.

Presnell's Comet

Engine of an empire, the ox has blazed this colony's way from the outset. The original migrant herd crept from the lobes of Botany Bay, beyond the leases, the outer parishes, sneaking north of the Tweed, sheltering in the lap of the Darling Downs. There, in pioneer times, a drover named Presnell goaded a medley flock – cattle, sheep and assorted bullocks – across the loam. Early evening, a long summer twilight, when suddenly the sky turned magnesium.

A fireball creased the air! Chased by sparks! All bar the oxen bolted for shelter. Even Presnell bunched his reins, horror-struck by what he saw. Coconut, his mare, reared – and Presnell toppled off. The scene was chaos save for the oxen, content as ever to ignore the heavens, dining on native grasses and turning our rumps to the alleged omen.

Ancient Romans understood the sky, unlike Australians who view the blackness as a threat in itself, a derisive anagram of the English sky they'd known, a mystery more ancient than Old Rome itself. In light of Presnell's Comet, as the fireball would come to be known, only *Bos taurus* was prepared to graze in the face of disaster, our broad rumps an endorsement of the colony's longevity.

Presnell at length passed the tidings onto outlying graziers, allowing the news and kudos to filter slowly south. The image of the steadfast steer afforded heart to a million cowed Australians. Here was a five-star investor in the new land's future! Faced by comets in the sky a nag will baulk, the swine run, all udder milk curdle overnight, but the stable ox is a beast heaven-made for this skittish folly of a continent.

Jamieson to Gaffneys Creek

The clay is slippery. Stepping is a case of hoof by deliberate hoof, our task to keep the trace chain taut, the going fluid, the cargo poised, the headstall square. Steam floats from Sergeant's hide. Cusack curses the rain and team in turns. For every pinch and quag our load adopts a subtle ton.

We march in a train of six, twelve steers hauling the stage that Australian life is played upon: the open dray. Yella thrives amid our company. He whiffs something epic in the going, while I confess to feeling less ennobled, servant as I am to the umpteenth leg in the colony's odyssey, dragging Progress one inch further inland. This week Progress comprises planks and flour, oats by the hundredweight, fuses and picks, fencing wire, a barouche.

What's a barouche? asks Yella, not for the first time. As an answer I speak on matters pedestrian.

Oxley's Moccasins

I kid you not, the explorer's name was Oxley. (Little by little Australians are paying their bovine cohorts their overdue tithe.) A surveyor, Oxley was responsible for measuring Illawarra, the unkempt sprawl extending to Port Jackson's south. His bullocks hauled chains, stakes, astrolabes across the brutal seaboard. We blazed Bulli Pass, waded Kembla Rip. In short, the oxen gave Oxley's inroad the necessary legs.

If road is the right word: the path was nonexistent, the sun malicious. Lesions bloomed on the animals' spines. Gashes festered. Hooves fell into disrepair with nary a farrier in cooee.

Too kind a soul to qualify as bullocky, Oxley granted ample spells for the team along the way, but the foot sores worsened. The odour of pus overpowered our sweat. Creeping across the escarpment, a chorus line on tiptoes, the broken hooves steeped the outcrops in blood. Ten days into the trek, holed up at Wollondilly River, the surveyor struck an idea.

It should be said, to make matters clear, that during such an epoch the ox was Australia's chief source of leather. (Cows were few in number and daily wrung for curd, while kangaroos were too chimerical for colonists to contemplate.) Yet so highly were oxen deemed, the lure to exploit our leather was often scorned.

Most settlers were content to ply their trade unshod, or tricked up in London hobnails such as Oxley wore himself.

Hence the enigma when Oxley that night opted to hunt opossum and native bear, indeed any marsupial asleep to his designs. Five long nights in Wollondilly, the sixth a bee of makeshift needlework, Oxley hunted and skinned, he smoked and oiled, cured and stitched, all the while his bullocks watching and left to second-guess their driver's intent. When the slippers were done, a full two dozen lace-up shoes, four for each beast, the master bowed before his team and kitted out each ox. Aye, the first fancy-shod steers in history! Explorations resumed on slippered hooves. Thus did John Joseph William Molesworth Oxley, trailblazer and makeshift cobbler, pay one part of this colony's extravagant debt.

Two Bob Night

Rain has eased. Darkness enters the valley. We gain the eastern bank on Two Bob Creek and Cusack calls a halt. Aberfeldy is nine miles distant going by memory's map.

Egg-and-bacon flowers, boronia, morning glory – the feed is good around these parts. Yokes off, we are hobbled as a group and eat in silence. Come dark we congregate close to Cusack's fire, his fresh mutton spitting in the pan, the flames licking shapes against our pelts.

Rudolf, an ox of few words, disturbs our lull with an outburst. 'Catastrophe waits on tomorrow. I can see it.'

'The seer bloody steer,' brays Sergeant. 'Shut your fucking gob and go to sleep.'

Rudolf persists. 'Believe me, brothers, this trip is short-lived. Trip is the pivotal word.'

Nigger shushes the clairvoyant. Mortgage, another tyro, sneers in tandem with his yokemate Orion. Yella is camped beside me.

I sense his fear and thus speak softly of Elijah Puplick.

St Treacle

Convicts are the breeding stock of Australian life, men whose flesh has tasted the lash, the cat-o'-nine-tails and every other number in between. Elijah Puplick was one such wretch, a devil in pyjamas with rape and sedition his calling. But the devil escaped, breaking shackles in a Pitt Town quarry and killing a string of lieutenants en route to freedom. The 46th Regiment combed gully and byre but the wilderness offered outlaws ideal camouflage.

The monster prospered, strangling the Madden clan of Wallerawang station and adopting their airs and chattels until a bullock team passed. The load of gunpowder kegs murmured destiny to Puplick who planted a mattock in the bullocky's brain and so inherited the dray. He set his sights for parliament, not so much as candidate but as self-anointed destroyer. He whipped the team hard towards Port Jackson. Treacle, the senior ox in the span and a conservative by nature, was first to register the nihilism that coursed in Puplick's veins.

Twelve miles from Sydney – in scrub on Parramatta's margins – the oxen were obliged to pass the night in their shafts, feigning sleep as Puplick, weary with raillery, slept like a child on the flatbed. A dying fire shone like an impulse in Treacle's eyes. Softly, using the age-old curses, the bullock roused his brothers into action, urging them to ease the juggernaut above the firebed.

As one the oxen were doomed. So too anything in a hundred-yard radius. Parramatta locals still recall the night Quaker's Hill shook like never before, a modest Armageddon, with modest repercussion, in light of what might have been. The load's true intention vanished with Elijah Puplick and a dozen hidebound martyrs.

Two Bob to Woods Point

Orion walks before us this morning, his hind legs deliberately ajar. 'Take a good look, Yella old mate. See that ball sack? Looted! Picked clean! That's what fucking humans do, beefing us up to excess then fleecing the best of us.'

The team is rounding Mount Irwin on a corkscrew path known as Jacob's Ladder. The rain is gauzy. All around us the slick bush shines like something newborn.

Orion feels the urge to go on. 'Take no heed of Nelson's namby-pamby folklore. I too was once a bull! Look at us now. Fucking slaves is who we are, eunuch serfs for the mealy-mouthed bullocky. Look at mine, look hard. A ransacked sack is nothing to crow about, son. Ask Nelson how a eunuch bull can be anyone's ancestor. His talk is tripe. His stories are worse than the knife what done this.'

As decoy from the tirade I whisper to Yella another.

The Golden Ox

Gold is the human panacea, the reason for Australia's being. Why do you think Aberfeldy *is*? Or half the forlorn fleabites an ox team will pass in a calendar year? What sane farmer would sow and reap in these cruel hills? How else to explain the picks and fuses piled high on our dray?

Years ago Samson was likewise employed. A Lancashire longhorn, the ox was a regular on the goldfield run, Ballarat to Melbourne, a perilous trip as Mad Dog Morgan owned the turf.

Morgan was a cutthroat with no god for compass. He loomed from the she-oaks edging Emu Ford and ordered the men to throw down arms. Stand aside! Billy Sing, a part-Chinese dogsbody with stupendous cunning, distracted the bushranger with a fan of treasury notes while the drivers slipped the gold into several nosebags. Morgan was conned. He took the notes and other trinkets, killing Sing and co. nonetheless, leaving the bullocks to munch on a mix of rapeseed and bullion. By the time a wayfarer encountered the bloodbath the nuggets were a sound part of the animals' constitution.

Until weeks later at Port Gellibrand, the colony's southern gateway. There stood Samson, awaiting his cue to haul a swarm of flywheels from the dock, when the urge to defecate arose. Samson released. He shat a drayload, an undammed bonanza through his colon's own southern gateway, dumping the compost in eyeshot of Giles O'Cullough, an *Argus* reporter saddled with the duty of annotating new arrivals.

O'Cullough himself was fresh from Eire, as hinted by the credence he paid to Samson's stool, telling his readers and the world by default of a land so munificent that even its livestock dumped treasure.

Rumours rebounded over the ocean. Hip pockets itched across meridians. Gold fever had a relapse as all peoples of the atlas made sail for Australian shores. Just think, the colony harvested new blood owing to a single ox's extraordinary evacuation.

Jacob's Ladder

Mortgage, the newcomer with too much time to spare for Orion, slips. The bank is steep. Cusack snarls, tugs the brake, but the end is over before the tragedy begins. Chains groan. Braces tug. Orion follows. Downward. Headlong. Yella and I are next in train, Nigger and Lofty, Ollie and Rudolf, Sergeant and Hercules. In one mad moment Jacob's Ladder becomes Jacob's Snake as the team plunges helter-skelter into the abyss, Cusack and the load, lock, stock, box and dice.

Despite the rain there's dust. When it settles the reckoning begins. Sergeant is dead. Ollie is dead. Rudolf the prophet is dead. Blood as thick as axle grease drips from Yella's open jaw. 'I'm going,' he says – but not before I pant the final story.

Snowgum Angels

Feathertop, a mountain not far from here, is a heron plume of snow, so cold one day a driver named Garner Pegg froze blue and fell like a plank from the dray seat. The sky thickened – flurry turned to blizzard. The world went white as the bullocks, plus Pegg's two useless dogs, lay stranded high on Feathertop.

And then the killing began. Ten steer, two dogs, horns and fangs and claws all scoring flesh and fur, an orgy of red on white. Come the thaw, by the time a search party reached the castaways the aftermath was chilling: bones in the main, but no commonplace bones.

Pegg's remains were gone, taken by the winds, the dingoes, the dogs. The dogs were gone, lost to civilisation, perhaps alive in this very scrub around us. Only the angels remained, the searchers' words, the snowgum angels.

At first they took the flashes in the trees for laggard snow. The next speculation was birds, a murder of albino crows nesting in the lower branches, but closer inspection found the creatures to be skeletons, an airborne boneyard dangling in the wind.

You see, the gums had offered oxen shelter, fodder, a place to breathe their last like here, for you, dear Yella. Down to their withers, melting into scaffold, the team slowly turned to bone, a carcass queue embedded in the snow. Ravens came. Wild dogs. Scavengers wolfing the last of the gristle. Next the spring, and the summit thawing, the empty ribs and fetlocks looping like bangles over boughs once the snowline receded, leaving the eeriness of so much aerial anatomy that hung in wait for the searchers, its music elegiac.

'Just as good bullocks attended the birth of Jesus,' spoke one searcher on the mountaintop, 'so do the beasts remain in the Lord's favour.' The quote is Yella's last morsel.

What's a Barouche?

Yella is oblivious and so too the good souls of Aberfeldy. Cusack is banking on the fact. He borrows the muscle of Orion and me to haul the remnant freight back to the road.

I can only imagine Aberfeldy's mayor as a self-important man, one who demands a token of aristocracy, a viceregal touch to flourish his might in the bush. Bring me a barouche, he probably demanded. A what? asked his people. Whatever Cusack can fudge from the catastrophe is what will ultimately be delivered. Our driver is desperate to claim his haulage fee.

Yella lies among us, his cooling beef a larder to add to the Aberfeldy load, a corpse of excellent meat and leather. Orion and I watch Cusack at work. Building. Tinkering. His improvisation knows no bounds. The purpose of our trip was to deliver a symbol of order to the wilds, but the symbol (and ten oxen) have been obliterated, and a new symbol needs inventing.

Cusack is industrious. Kegs become wheels, planks the chassis, chaff bags the upholstery. Fusing wire is plied into pinions, a pair of shovel hafts the make-do axles. A bolt of canvas mimics the hood. On the third day the only detail missing from Cusack's crackpot vehicle is Australia's coat of arms. The driver doodles in the clay, unsure. He combs the gully's smithereens to find no such emblem as a stencil. His pockets are empty of money or any clue to the government's authority.

A unicorn? The English lion? He chews a stick, dabs its gnawed end in a pool of sheep raddle, painting a couchant emu on the upright panel. He deletes the heresy with banksia and wonders what next to sketch. He looks around him. And thus he sees Yella's inert repose, the noble *Bos taurus* that he was, his power and wasted generosity lying prone, an image for the ages, the soul of the road itself and all who travel on it. Strong, silent, callow: Australia embodied, the land's true emblem, and who would be Aberfeldy to controvert this truth?

Orion and I drag the barouche into town. Cusack has lost his whip; he lapses to banter, the journey a peaceful cortege for the dead we leave on Mount Irwin. The dray is no longer a dray but a vehicle of Cusack's ingenuity. The driver rides high with haywire for reins, steers for steeds, the man as punch-proud as we, the journey a steady procession into oxlore.

Starved of spectacle, the people of Aberfeldy cram the single dirt track to cheer their barouche, an indigenous chariot, a bullocky's work of art and craftiness coasting into town. Still wet, the emblem on the facing panel is the outline of the noble ox, who is St Yella, who is every Ox.

Aberfeldy

As sources of power Orion and I linger in town for a season or more, too spent to be hounded back to Mansfield, too canny to travel of our own volition. Besides, Aberfeldy suits our stage in life, a brittle outpost with laziness in bucketloads. We haul pay dirt from the penny-ante mines, we shoulder whims to draw summer water, we drag carts. Cusack himself has retired to the neighbouring hills, kept in tobacco by the language he possesses, the blue rapport that can coax a bullock from mud.

With yoke life waning our retirement soon follows. We pass our days by the schoolhouse grubbing lucerne, silk grass, getting fat on native dogwood, arguing less, finding time for philosophy. Orion is a fair companion. We exchange yarns – the great freight stories. The strongest beast, the vilest driver.

In quieter times I like to focus my good eye on Miss Stanhope's lessons, picking up the basics in lettering and whatnot. Did you know OX, for example, is a furtive hug beside a kiss? And going by the crisscross games the children gouge in the playground, an O seems timeless foe to the X. Proof the ox comprises affections and contradictions.

Around us Aberfeldians have learnt to rely on horses, plus a flash green contraption dubbed a *locomotor* with no visible means of propulsion. But the barouche remains a cherished icon of village life. If only St Yella could see the love the people afford his gay mausoleum, brighter for a coat of paint, rollicking on the roadways. Just now the mayor clopped past the butter factory with topper and quirt, winning a blush from Miss Stanhope at her gate. I know the young martyr would be proud.

As is a man named Owen Molloy. A month down the track he leads us by the nose to a shack reminiscent of the accident, its complex aroma of blood. Orion goes first. With a silver flash the cleaver unlatches the ox's neck. His pelt is shucked like a glove. I stand to one side in naked admiration, ogling the might of Orion's flanks, the chrism of his hooves, his tallow fat, the gristle glue, and last the sacrament that launched this telling, that flexes now and commemorates those before us and those magnificent oxen to come. Of course I speak of the coveted tongue.

Griffith Review

Crumbs

Bram Presser

In the region of T., not too far from the city of U., there once stood a small village that for a while was in Poland, then Hungary, then Subcarpathian Ruthenia, then Czechoslovakia, then Slovakia, then Hungary again, then the Union of Socialist Soviet Republics, then the Ukraine and now cannot be found on any map.

This village, satellite to a satellite, was passed around like a decaying heirloom, each time losing a small part of its being, until one day it simply ceased to exist. Even its name is forgotten, for there is nobody left to lament it. In its place now might be a field, or a forest, though no animal would dare play there. Or perhaps God, in His infinite wisdom, removed that small tract of land altogether, so that the world might be a little smaller and less full of sorrow.

In the beginning, God had etched a natural border along the outskirts of what would become this village, a wide river that flowed gently for most of the year, until Elul and Tishrei as its people would know those months, when it raged with what most took to be righteous anger. For centuries the river served to hide those on either bank from one another but, as Man is wont to do, this natural order was destroyed as soon as the King's stonemasons, drunk on hubris, told their Lord that they could stop the water so that his empire might expand.

Many men died in the process but a bridge was eventually

built and so began the millennia-long period of conquest and succession, none of which really concerned the village folk, except inasmuch as it affected their trade and taxes. The two villages on either side, one predominantly Jewish, the other predominantly Jew-fearing, shared a market, a common heart crucial to both of their survival. Depending on where the greater power lay – royal families, landed gentry or municipal councils – this market often shifted from one side of the bridge to the other, so that the lowest tithes would have to be paid each fortnight when the collectors rode into the area with a great sense of entitlement to take what by right was not theirs.

And so it was that sometimes the village folk would hesitantly welcome the traders from the other side of the bridge, and at other times those traders would begrudgingly welcome them and they would put their differences aside, if only for the morning.

'It is because God sighed on our shtetl,' said Mottel D., who would later choke on poisonous gas, feeling the jagged fingernails of those trying to climb above him digging pathetically into his back, but for now is a teacher of young children. He was pointing at the sagging thatched roof of the little shtiebl where older men went to pray when called by the shammas.

The children giggled, savouring the thought that God might take time out of his busy schedule to check on their insignificant village. How could He not be moved by the devotion of these people in their simple clothes who spent as much time praising Him as they did trying to feed their families?

Mottel liked to tell stories and the children liked to listen. 'Beware the bridge,' he would say when the border shifted to the further shore. 'Under it lies a dybbuk, who would just as soon eat you as one of Reb Shlomo's sweet buns.' This wasn't altogether false. Many in the village believed in the dybbuk under the bridge and blamed it for most of the misfortunes that befell them. Crop failures. Stillbirths. Disappearances. Those who doubted quickly came to believe when Lazar V., who was only trying to take his wares to the market on the other side, was swept over the railing in a freak storm, never to be seen again.

It was this dybbuk, not God, upon whom the blame was placed. Which is why each year for Tashlich, as the village folk went to cast their sins into the flowing water, they would make sure to do so downstream lest the dybbuk find in their time of heavy heartedness and repentance a reason to rejoice.

Across the bridge, it was the same, but in relief. 'They hide there and will take you and use your blood to cook their special bread,' said Karel T., who would later stand guard at a perimeter fence, but for now was also a teacher of young children. It was true. He had read a case in which there was incontrovertible proof that a young Christian child had been killed and her blood used for their dirty ritual. And what a great shame it was that his esteemed president, Thomas Masaryk, had besmirched his reputation defending these heathen murderers. Sure, thought Karel, it was fine to trade with them, and for the most part they kept to themselves, but it was still best to warn the children not to go near the bridge alone because no matter how nice they might seem at the market, you never really could trust a Jew.

Back in the village, the women gathered around the well to listen to the wet-nurse, Hanicka O., who would later die standing over a ditch, staring down at her shrivelled, empty breasts, embarrassed, counting the bodies of the children she remembered suckling, but for now was the source of all gossip. She was welcome in most homes and knew their secrets. 'They say dybbuk, I know better.'

Hanicka had her own opinion on such matters. She had not forgotten a certain child brought into this world, a boy, who was not right and who, according to his parents, failed to come home one day. The travails of everyday life soon superseded the pity bestowed upon them by the village folk, but Hanicka did not forget. Nor did she fail to notice that at Tashlich, these parents would stand at the very end of the line, upstream from the bridge, and empty their pockets which, unlike the crumbs that fell from most other people, contained large chunks of bread and, if Hanicka was not mistaken, meat and sweets.

'Let's see what horror our people have caused this week,' smirked Jakub R., the Rabbi's son, who will die in a most peculiar way, in a far away land, but is now making mischief. He unravelled the paper and showed the article to his little brother Shmuel, of unknown fate, pointing at the smudged ink. It was unusual for boys on this side of the bridge to read the papers brought in on the back of Hermann F.'s cart. They were expected to devote their time to studying Torah in cheder or learning a trade, not wasting it with the frivolities of an irrelevant wider world. As Reb Shimon D., the blacksmith who would die covered in blood and shit in the back of a cattle train, often said, 'A horse doesn't shoe itself.'

However, young Jakub was different. Each fortnight, when Hermann's cart would pass through the market, he would secretly buy a copy of the city newspaper with the few coins his mother had given him to buy bread and cheese for lunch because, he reasoned, an empty stomach might grumble but an empty head will most certainly scream. Then he would gather his brother and three friends and read it to them on the lower riverbank, by the bridge. 'Knowledge is their dybbuk,' he would often say.

Of the outsiders that regularly passed through the village, Hermann F. was both the best known, and the least liked.

Destined one day to swing from the gallows for treason, though it is not altogether clear against whom, he would arrive in the village each time from the northwest, walking alongside his poor donkey as it dragged an over-packed cart with one or the other wheel broken.

He would demand a drink from the first villager he encountered, as if he had walked all the way from B., or whichever city he was said to have come from that time. Amongst the villagers it was rumoured that he was rich, that his weary façade was simple chicanery, and that he offloaded surplus papers and trinkets from the trays of trucks that had driven to the forest to dump them and thereby amassed the seeds of his fortune. His books, often missing pages, or not matching the title printed on the cover, were always sold for a premium, as were his other assorted wares. He had grown accustomed to the wants of his customers, bringing for each what he knew he could sell and nothing more. Pity the donkey, who would be carrying a greater weight on departure, for coins weigh more than paper and tin, particularly when you demand so many for each worthless item.

Hermann F. appeared to hate these Jews, and would rush across the bridge as soon as he had offloaded his lesser wares. But he liked Jakub R. He particularly liked that the boy would always meet him on the other side of the bridge, away from the prying eyes of the village folk. Hermann would bring the latest newspaper for Jakub, always the one that cast the Jews in the worst light, perhaps trying to entice him to see the error of his people's ways. And Jakub would invariably be thankful, in Hermann's opinion too thankful, and never question the vast discrepancy between the price printed on the paper's masthead and the one he was being charged.

In fact Jakub did notice all of these things, but was too afraid of losing his one connection to the outside world and was therefore willing to play Hermann's nasty little games. He also knew that the paper he would buy each time could only have been popular amongst the rabble in town. But from it he discerned the odd bit of truth, and gained perspective on his place in the world. He also learnt that he had friends out there, friends in high places, like this man Masaryk, who had risked his career to help Jakub's people.

'That Jakub is trouble,' whispered Old Chava, who would not live to see what was to come but instead die in the drowning-like discomfort of consumption.

'Well of course he is,' said Marta B. 'He is friends with the dybbuk.' She smiled crookedly, much as she would again when, but a few years later, she was packed into the back of a truck only to feel the air slip away to a symphony of crunching gravel and laboured sobs.

'And to think, our poor Rabbi ...' Old Chava trailed off into a wet cough and then nodded thoughtfully. 'With a son like that, studying in cheder to take his father's position, what will become of our children?' Old Chava was right.

She foresaw the disaster though it did not come to be in the way that she anticipated. When the children died in hails of bullets, or in gas chambers, or thrown directly into furnaces to burn alive, Jakub R. was nowhere to be found. For years before, on the night the Beth Din was to arrive so that he could sit his final Rabbinical examinations, Jakub packed his bags and fled the little shtetl along the road to the northwest, in the direction from which he would often see Hermann F.'s cart approaching.

And so it was that he left behind those ever-changing borders, the river, the bridge, the dybbuk, his family and the hundred or so condemned souls whose paths to their final fates were many but the destination a cold, dark one. All that remained of him was a note, scrawled in haste.

'Dearest Maminku,' it read. 'I pray that one day I too shall be redeemed. If only in your eyes.'

Like the town itself, the note would also burn; a pyre to the lost and forgotten. Burnt crumbs cast from empty pockets. It was as if none of it had existed at all.

The Age

Scissors

Rebecca Harrison

We met the town's first policeman in church. He had come to the Sunday morning service in the first week of his posting in Wren to ensure that we all knew he had arrived. Of course we did; the town was rife with gossip over it. We hadn't had our own police officer or station before now and this was the source of all manner of speculation. Some were pleased – if a shearer took off with a fleece or a bit of equipment that didn't belong to him, a station master wouldn't have to go all the way into Yanco to report the matter – but others seemed to take it personally, as though the town being appointed an officer meant we weren't trusted and needed watching over.

My father fell into the latter category. He was cagey and distrustful as he eyed off the young officer who had come to the service dressed in his dapper uniform, dark navy and buttoned to the chin. The officer was tall and fair with straight shoulders and a trim moustache. The ladies were clearly taken with him, smiling away, shaking his hand and twittering that since he was a bachelor and all alone, new in town, they would invite him over for tea so he wouldn't be too lonely. Some of the older wives appeared to be appraising him for his suitability for their daughters and more than one nudged a skinny eldest into his path. The men were more reserved and I noticed that many of them glanced at my father before they made up their minds on how to proceed.

My father, the great Jack Turner, had been a Wren man since before the war when there was not much more here than a few shacks and the church was a few boards cobbled together. The church was still a weatherboard cottage, but it was whitewashed and surrounded by a neat garden and had a bell in the steeple.

My father strode up to the young policeman, who tall as he was still did not quite match my father's towering frame, with his hat in his hand. The church doorway was enough inside the church to keep him from putting it back on and so he held it lightly in his left. If some men might look humbled or respectful holding their hats this way, my father wasn't one of them; he was more intimidating without the hat on and he knew it. He bore down on the younger man with his wiry golden hair brushed dramatically back off his high forehead, his chin jutting forward so the red bristles of his beard appeared to point directly at the officer's chest. He looked like a kind of lion as he thrust out his big calloused hand.

'Jack Turner,' he said gruffly and gave the officer's smaller hand a firm pumping.

'Ah, yes, Turner, I have heard the name. You're a cattle man, yes?'

'That's right.'

'Well, Jack, I expect we'll be getting along fine.' The officer laughed lightly in an attempt to break the ice, but my father's chin just jutted further and his hand retracted to sit stiffly in his pocket.

There was an unease about the exchange, an unease that was calculated. My father didn't welcome the officer to town or invite him by the homestead as he might have done. His short replies gave nothing away. It was construed by those who looked on that he had reserved judgment on the officer and so the other men who followed in greeting the new fellow were similarly reserved, saying firm, polite hellos and offering little more.

I marvelled at the way my father seemed to lead the town even if he had no formal right to it. They respected him, my mother said, as if being shit scared of somebody was the same thing. I kept my mouth shut because that's what I do. I like to watch, I make up my own mind, but I keep it mostly to myself. What I saw when people met my father was their reaction to the force of his waiting violence. They may have been afraid of him, or respected him, but I wondered that they didn't see that shifty look in his eye, his terror that they might see how scared he was. At least that's what I had always thought. When you've built yourself up as the toughest bloke in town, what was left but to fear? Fear being beaten, fear being proved mortal, fear falling from that position; it seemed, to me, a shaky place to stand.

*

I am more than eighty years old now; I live here in the old house on the land that used to be the station my father ran. The outbuildings, the old barn and stables, the hay lofts and sheds are rust and ruin now; the fields are swathes of broken grass that lie untended, wild and lonely. The house creaks and sighs in the wind and in the winter it's a ghastly business going out the back to the dunny, so I have gone old-fashioned and taken to using a chamber pot, at least at night. Everyone is dead now: my mother, my big brother Frankie, and wee Bess who was never very resilient and died quietly in her fifties of some defect of the heart.

Also dead is that shiny new police officer who locked Frankie up for public drunkenness one day when Frankie was fifteen. My father, who went to collect him from the town lock-up, who stormed in and demanded Frankie be handed over, is long dead now too. When the officer refused to hand Frankie over, Father challenged him to a fistfight and intimidated the younger man until he yielded. Father brought Frankie home laughing and skiting that the cop was nobody in this town; that a man was only as good as his own two fists, no matter how many badges some official from Sydney might pin on him. Then Father wiped the smile right off Frankie's face by beating him, there in the yard, with all of us watching on. He beat him because Frankie had caused trouble and it just had to be that way, the way my father saw it, even if the copper was a fool and a bullshitter.

Frankie sat in the dirt in the yard, wiping at his bloody nose and holding back his tears with that kicked-dog look he always had when he realised that our father was never going to be his friend, that his love had no softness in it, that the dark clouds would always roll over to obscure it. Frankie went off to the war in '39; he rushed to it, eager as can be to make his father proud, to be a soldier just like he had been. Father sent him off with a hard look and the words, 'Don't try to be a fucking hero, Frankie, and come home to your mother.' Only Frankie didn't come home and I once heard my father say, sprawled across the kitchen table in a deep drunk, that this was probably for the best.

I always thought that if it were women who'd gone to war, they'd have come home, tied their aprons back on and got on with things. Men, they drank and cried and writhed around in terrible dreams; they were too soft for the business of life and death; they were always shocked that the world could be cruel. It was women who knew this all along.

The night we learnt that Frankie had died, my sister and I slept together in his bed. Mother came in and curled around us like a mother cat protecting her litter, or what was left of it anyway. I was fourteen by then, long and bony, but we curled up together in Frankie's narrow bed that first night in a pile, drawing comfort from the weight of each other, sometimes crying softly and holding our mother's hand in the warm dark. The next morning Mother was up as early as ever, and Bess and I awoke to the usual sounds of the chooks loose in the yard and the scratchy stroke of the broom on the kitchen floor. Mother hung laundry and rolled dough that first day as though it were any other day; our father did not come home for days and when he finally did the stench of whisky on him was so strong it made us gag.

*

I have been crowded with memories since the photographs the other day. I was reaching for the dustpan that was perched on top of the mouldy meatsafe in the back room when I knocked over an old biscuit tin, the metal kind with Victorian ladies printed on it. There was a sharp clatter as the metal struck the floor, the tin opened and a small spill of photographs fanned out. As if they'd been conjured from the grave, there was Frankie in his soldier's kit, stern faced and painfully young; there was Bess, a slender hand on her curved hip in her new tartan dress, off to the ladies college in Griffith. She had begged mother to send her there. She was breaking her neck to get out of Wren, smart girl that she was. Bess looks sassy in that picture, a rounded, sensual thing with her fair hair in pin curls and a red swipe of lipstick that is black in the black and white photograph.

And there were older photos, too; Father in sepia with Mother beside him, their mouths pressed into grim frowns because that's how all photos had to be posed at the time. It must have been their wedding photograph judging from Mother's pale lace dress and Father's suit. He was so young in that picture; the beardless line of his jaw looked soft, but even with his face frozen you could see the mischief there, the desire to smile. They had loved one another at least for that short while before the war. Mother often told me about the man she had married; she spoke about him as though she was speaking of an old friend, a lost love, not like it was the same man who might have been, at the time of her telling, kicking the mud off his boots at our front door.

I think she just drew a line through her life, clean as that. My father, her husband, was a different man on each side of the line she drew. The only husband of hers that I ever knew smelt of horses and whisky and the outdoors; he'd stamp in trailing the heat or the cold depending on the season. You'd just best be sure your chores were done and you were out of his way. The dinner table was where we saw him the most and that was a pretty solemn affair; you weren't allowed to talk unless he asked you a question; you weren't allowed to laugh or scoot the food around your plate with your fork or put an elbow on the table. You had to ask to be excused and there was no point doing that if your plate and everyone else's wasn't clean. If he asked you a question you answered it politely and you looked up at him, but not too boldly, and you made sure your legs weren't kicking about under the table, even if you were nervous, especially if you were nervous.

*

I watch TV shows, those American shows about families with that annoying canned laughter rattling out after every second or third line that's spoken. Those families are all eating and chatting and laughing with the teenagers and kids cracking jokes and rolling their eyes at their parents and I think, the world is, surely, a whole new place. I admire young people. I like the way they move, all free and easy. I like the young girls in their boyish shorts and long legs all over the place with their lipstick and black eyeliner and clunky shoes; they laugh with their mouths wide open; they smile broadly and say what they like. When I was young we were always being told to be more polite, more demure, to sit this way and walk that way, until it felt that the idea was to somehow disappear completely in order to be the perfect girl child. It looks to me, from the TV mostly since I don't get out much, that this is a good time to be a girl and I look at myself and think, it's not my time, though. No, this is not my time.

I stay up here in the old house and wait; I wait it out. Sometimes the grocery boy comes up and I'll have forgotten he was coming and I'll head toward the door, unaware until after he's gone, legging it quick-smart back to his battered ute, how awful I must look. In some ghastly housedress, probably stained, I must look a fright; Old Maggie the smelly witch with a fright of white hair like fairy floss whipped around my bony skull.

Once my hair was rich and full and dark and long. I had my mother's hair and when we stood together at Father's funeral, people said we looked like sisters in our black dresses that we'd made for the occasion. That was in '51, Mother was nearing fifty, but she had aged well with only a few lines in her fine skin. Her bony, veined hands were where her body told the true story of its age; her hands and the dramatic streak of silver that ran from above her left eye in a wide trail down the length of her hair. I was young then and still in the prime of my life, my hair full and my flesh plump at the lips and cheeks, though I stayed skinny and tall all my years.

Mother and I held hands as they lowered Father's coffin and the crowd murmured and fidgeted in their dark clothes, solemnly watching one of their own go to his rest. He was like a king in this place, a hero, and they were sad to see he was mortal; I think they had expected him to rise up and laugh or shout out to God or whoever or whatever governed the business of living and dying, to fuck off and fight like a man. But he didn't. The coffin stayed closed over the wasted remains of the man. He lay still, shut up with his war medals pinned to the breast of his best suit, and when the dirt tumbled over the box it stayed there.

*

I get confused about things. I confuse memories, thinking they are just stories in my head or films I have seen. This morning I woke up with the pain of my arthritis coursing through my body so bad I would have cried, but it's hard to cry or even moisten my mouth these days. It's like I'm all dried up, desiccating, the way the old husk of a cockroach or a spider will curl up on itself and dry until it's nothing but the clean shell of itself. I feel like I am doing that already; I'm drying up alive. I think that maybe I'm dead, or close to it, or cursed so that I'll never die and I'll just wander around this old house forever, slowly drying, curling at my edges, forgotten. But the pain won't leave me and it makes me wish I *would* just die.

I lie still in the hard bed, the whole left side of the bed straight and smooth as tile because I lie still and barely disturb the covers and I'm dreaming and awake all at once, but not dying, not even close. If Mother were here she'd help me along. I remember Mother coming through the door with her sewing scissors in hand, the silver scissors with the gold-plated handles that had been her mother's before hers, and I think she might be here with me, come to cut this final loose thread after all.

*

When I wake, it is to a memory of Father holding Mother against the kitchen wall by the throat, saying something so low I could not make it out. The memory of Father's violence is nothing new or strange, but there is something that *catches* about this memory. It's my mother who is remarkable. In this dream, or whatever it is, she is sagging to the floor meekly, not fighting, as my father towers above her, having just released his grip on her throat, but something is happening in her eyes. I think that what I'm watching is the last light of any love she had for him dying.

Imagine a darkened house, and inside that house there is a tiny candle burning, burning so low that it gives off no light at all. It would seem that it couldn't matter if that flame blew out because it is so small, but then, when it is snuffed out completely and the absolute dark falls, you can see that that little almost-flame was actually so bright, so bright, in contrast to this final darkness. That is what I see happening in my mother. Darkness falling. The tiny almost-flame being snuffed. I see her later, stoking the fire, making tea or something else mundane, and the way her knuckles go white around the iron poker is pure menace and I am eager, I am hungry for her to do something with that poker; my mind is a red field of blood.

*

I remember a children's book with a brown fabric cover and worn gold script on the front. I was too young to read it, but the book had illustrations and I was fanning through the pages looking for them. On one page I found a beast. It was something like a dog or a bull, but like nothing I had ever seen as well. It was half submerged in a lagoon, a lagoon that looked remarkably, to my eyes anyway, like Horse Head Lagoon that sat at the farthest end of our property. In the illustration the beast stared dead ahead with rage in its eyes and its mouth was a fright of teeth, all sharp and uneven. Its tongue lolled out obscenely; its eyes were wild rolling orbs.

From the day I saw it, and took the book over to Mother to have her read to me the inscription underneath the picture, 'The Bunyip,' I was rapt. I dreamt of that bunyip, drew endless pictures of it and invented my own versions of it from my imagination.

In the dreams it would come for me and tear through the house trailing gushes of fetid water, pulling the stuffing out of the armchair, snapping the kitchen chairs in its jaws like they were twigs, its teeth white and long and foaming with bloody ropes of saliva; it had killed and it would kill again. It stalked through the house and sometimes it reached me and stood puffing steaming breath at my bedroom door with its yellow eyes glowing. I was never afraid of it in this dream; I knew that it waited for me, for my command. It was my beast. But there were other dreams too. In some dreams, it reached Mother first and I would wake with a scream caught in my throat. In every dream the bunyip was the same, the dark slick hide gleaming over the flexing muscle, the red around the rolling yellow eyes, and the teeth, the awful teeth.

*

There is a noise; it is piercing my sleep and keeping me awake. Something out in the dark night is calling, or crying. The sound is a terrible moaning, a groaning of despair so absolute I am not sure if it makes me afraid or sad. It makes me dream of the bunyip, when I can get to sleep at all.

The noise has kept me awake nearly all night for two nights in a row now. I don't get much sleep in any case, but it is growing difficult to keep my head together throughout the day. I lie in bed with the dreams and memories fogging my mind and that ghastly bellowing that comes keening across the paddocks in the dark of night. I don't hear it in the day, but I know it is there, waiting, or just drowned out by the sounds of the daytime, by the burbling of magpie song and the cawing of the crows and the endless susurrus of the wind in the grass and the trees.

I'm losing my grip on things; I tipped the kettle too sharply this morning and sloshed so much water over the mug that it tipped and the boiling water lashed across the table. I skidded back in time to avoid getting splashed and scalding myself, but the shock gave my heart a jolt and I had to sit in the armchair for several minutes afterwards.

The more tired I am the harder it is to keep the past at bay; people keep coming through doors. There is Mother, after Father died, airing out the house. I can see her as though she really is here and it is sixty years ago and she has taken to humming and singing as she scrubs and dusts. She fills the house with sunlight and the scent of yellow soap. I think my mother drew another of her lines after we put Father in the ground. And she had started her new life by cleaning the house and opening windows and dusting and polishing until the house felt clean and golden and new again.

*

In the last days of his illness Father lay in the darkened front room, in his and Mother's bed. Mother took the sleepout bed as her own; she draped it in her favourite pink and red crocheted blanket and cut a handful of roses, which she placed in a crystal milk jug on the windowsill. The roses were falling open and so fragrant that it nearly knocked you over when you entered. She seemed happy in that room.

Father sweated and groaned in the throes of his sickness in the front room with the curtain drawn. He had tried to tough it out, but it wasn't long before the sickness took him and he could no longer get up and get himself dressed and into the paddocks. His boots stood in the doorway where Mother had put them after giving them their last clean, but he never put them on again.

He began to rant and rave; his head tossing on the pillow looked like a hollowed pumpkin. His skin was yellow and waxy and his beard, gone mostly to a dull grey, was tangled over his dry lips. The things he began to say, lost in his fevered dreams, oh, they were dark things, secret, violent things; things he had seen in the war, things he had done. If Mother or I entered the room he would snarl at us and talk to us as though we were the ghosts of people he'd known. Once, he muttered, 'Stewart asked me to shoot his hand, fucking coward wants to go home. To his fucking *mother*.' Then he laughed, a dry-throated cackle, 'I shot the bloody hand right off his arm.' Another time, it was something crass about 'French pussy' that sent me tiptoeing out, embarrassed, my heart hammering, and disappointed that this was the only time I had ever heard my father talk of his time in France.

The doctor said there wasn't much we could do. Mother hurried him back to his car, pressing biscuits wrapped in a tea towel into his hands. She was embarrassed for the doctor to hear the things coming out of Father's mouth and maybe she was worried because she didn't know what he might say next, about whom.

Weeks passed like this, Father hollowed out by the cancer that was consuming his organs and Mother and I tending him; we washed him, ducking his limp attempts to swat us away, and all the while the poisonous nonsense he could not contain filled our heads until we were both irritable and pale with exhaustion.

*

It was night, just after dinner, and Mother was changing the pillowslips under Father's head. He was so thin now it was as though some different man, some stranger, had taken his place. It was very dark inside the room. The small electric lamp buzzed faintly to the far side of the bed; Father was muttering something I could not hear. Mother slid the pillow into a crisp white slip in one efficient flip of her wrists. Her mouth was set in a line, her brow was dark; she looked so tired, so grim. I stood in the doorway. Neither of them had seen me arrive and I didn't enter; I just watched.

Mother's skin was a creamy white in the dimness; Father was yellowed with his sickness. Shadows crowded them. Father muttered and Mother shushed him, plumping the pillow between her hands. The pillow slipped from Mother's hands and fell lightly onto my father's face. I jolted forward, but stopped myself and recoiled behind the door. I waited. Mother reached out for the pillow, but when her hands met the white cotton, rather than grasp it to lift it, her fingers remained splayed and she *leaned.* From under the pillow Father produced a few muffled bleats, and his thin legs twitched, trapped beneath the heavy blankets. His arms rose, spidery hands opening and closing, reaching for Mother, but she simply leaned further, silently but resolutely pressing his arms down with the weight of her own body. He stopped moving finally and all was still.

Mother lifted the pillow and plumped it a little. She lifted his head gently and placed the pillow under. She stood over him then and looked at his face for what seemed like a very long time. Then she looked up at me, directly. She'd known I was there all along. Her face was not severe as I thought it would be; rather it was suffused with gentleness, more gentleness than I had seen in her face for many years, maybe since before Frankie died, maybe even longer ago than that. She didn't smile; she just looked at me enigmatically, her face glowing with its new gentleness. I think she let herself love him again, now that she had killed him.

She walked up to where I stood, unable to move, in the doorway. She squeezed my hand. 'It was mercy, Maggie darling, mercy.' I nodded. I looked at my father, or what was left of him, on the big bed, and I turned and looked after my mother, who had walked slowly into the kitchen to prepare tea, and I felt a great and terrible relief, so much so that I cried in great choking sobs. When I sat at the kitchen table later, my face still red, hiccupping from the crying, Mother put tea into my cup and spooned extra sugar in and smiled lightly at me. She said, 'I know, it's such a relief, isn't it?'

*

Later that night my mother and I sewed at the table together with Father's body in the bed down the hall; we would call the doctor in the morning and he would be told that we had gone to sleep and woken to find Father had passed, unnoticed, in the night. I watched Mother sew and, as always, admired her small clever stitches. She could make the cleanest hemlines I had ever seen. For a moment the yellow kitchen light caught on her silver scissors as she pulled a thread to cut it and I remembered the Greek mythologies I had read.

Mother, in her housecoat and apron, her black and silver head bent over her work as she cut the thread, was Atropos, the eldest of the fates, the one called 'the inevitable' who was the cutter of the thread of life. Her silver scissors made a clean zipping sound as she snipped the thread that she held taut in her creased hands; she pulled the remaining thread away and let it fall into the wastebasket at her feet.

*

There's a thunder of footsteps on the front porch, a burst of giggles and loud stage whispers. Kids. I don't have the heart today to go to the window and pull the curtain aside and scowl theatrically at them, as I normally would. They come up here to see Maggie the Witch and usually I give her to them. I glower from the window, and sometimes I run a hand through my hair to get it to stand up madly before I go – they're after a madwoman and I don't want to disappoint them.

After all, it's me and Jacob Ghost who provide half the entertainment in this town, only he is a ghost and has no say in the matter. I, on the other hand, could dispel the mystery of myself, should I start going into town and talking to people, and letting the kids see me walk down high street with a Zimmer frame and a plastic bag full of canned tuna and toilet paper. Then I would just be a regular old bird. But it has been a long while since I was anyone's kind of regular, so I just can't be bothered trying. After Mother died in '85, I just didn't really have the heart to keep up appearances. I was in my late fifties by then anyway and had long given up the notion of a family of my own, a husband or children.

I got close to all of that just once, with Billy Bird, the baker's son. I'd see him nearly every week when I went into town for the shopping. I was twenty-five or twenty-six, Father was dead and Mother and I were enjoying our freedom up at the house; we were listening to records, baking sticky sweet jam-drops and gossiping viciously; I wasn't thinking of courting anyone. Bess had always been the boy-crazy one, the romantic; I think that was half the reason she wanted to get out of Wren since she had, in her teens, stepped out with every eligible boy in town and found none of them to her standards. But Billy was cheeky and handsome. He wore his shirtsleeves rolled up high so you could see the long, wiry muscle along his forearm and when he smiled at me I'd feel the heat creep up my chest and over my face. Billy came up to the house a couple of times to chat and have tea – I think he would have liked something stronger but Mother would have no alcohol in the house after Father.

In the warm dark of a summer night, sitting with our knees touching on the porch seat and the cicadas drowning out our feeble attempts at conversation, Billy slid his hand up my skirt and along my inner thigh, far enough that his fingertips brushed the gusset of my underwear. I gasped and he whispered in my ear, his breath hot, 'Car'n Maggie, ya don't want ta be a virgin your whole life do ya?' I pulled away and escaped inside, but the next time I saw him I let him go all the way.

We walked out along the southern fence line where there was a copse of trees under which I knew the grass was green and soft. I took off the light coat I had slung over my shoulders for the walk, even though in the warm afternoon it would have been unnecessary. I took it off and lay it on the grass beneath the milky gum trees and sat down. Billy lay beside me and for a while we lay there, on our backs, watching the sky turn a vivid pink through the branches and listening to the birds caw and call, telling each other the day was over, it was time to roost. I could hardly breathe and then Billy rolled over on top of me and stopped my breath altogether. He covered my mouth with his and his kisses were fierce and wet and I could feel the plunging of his tongue and the scratch of his stubble grazing my chin and I wrapped my arms around him and surrendered to it, thinking, I don't want to be a virgin all my life, I don't. But I didn't love Billy.

Once it was over we tidied ourselves and walked back to the house. Billy kissed me goodbye and in his eyes was a puppy-dog look that made him seem just plain stupid to me, full of gratitude and eager affection. I went inside and made tea for Mother and myself and settled into my chair with Billy's stuff trickling out of me.

The next time Billy came to call I had Mother tell him I was ill and the same again the second and third times he came. Two weeks later, I went to the bakery and ordered the bread and flour, and when I met his eyes and saw the hurt there I did feel a little bad, but I couldn't imagine marrying Billy Bird, spending all day with him, talking to him night and day about the stupid things a man might want to talk about. I was happy with Mother and that was that. So, now I am the old spinster Maggie the Witch, Old Maggie, Mad Maggie, The Turner Witch. I know all the names they have for me around the town. I don't make any effort to change their minds.

*

Truth be told, I like my special status; it's a laugh. Today, though, I'm bone tired and can't be bothered going over to the window. I wait until the noises fade off and I think they're gone and I shuffle to the door to make sure the kids haven't lit something on fire or lain anything dead at the door; something dead might draw a feral cat over or at the very least a damned stink to high heaven. Kids from town usually don't do such awful things, but there's a bad egg or two among them, just like anywhere.

I crack the front door and peek through: nothing dead, no fire or damage, just a bunch of flowers. Picked flowers, stringy dry weeds and such, from the roadsides and fields, among them the yellow dandelions we always called wet-the-beds. I open the door a little further and bend down to grab them. I hear a gasp further down the front path and see my visitors haven't left, but are trying to hide by the front gate. I can see them clearly through the gate's crooked arch, the arch over which my mother tried tirelessly to grow something, anything, and was thwarted by the summer heat that burned the leaves and killed her best efforts. I gave up on gardening years ago and have let the front fence sag and the paint peel.

The kids are about ten or twelve years old, two fair-headed boys and a dark girl. They look at me with wide eyes; the girl has her hands over her mouth, hardly able to contain her excitement. I grasp the flowers in my right hand and look at the kids; I leer and reach out with my left and waggle my fingers at them in a 'casting a spell' fashion; they squeal and bolt away. I hear, a little farther off, the clatter of bikes being picked up and kicked into motion. I take my flowers inside and put them in the crystal milk jug, which has been a makeshift vase now for sixty years even though I still call it a milk jug. I wonder if Jacob Ghost gets flowers.

Jacob Ghost is supposed to haunt the trees by the edge of the Horse Head Lagoon. Horse Head Lagoon, a crooked little watering hole that starts at the farthest edge of this property, sits near the cattle bridge that crosses the Murrumbidgee and leads over to the Sturt Highway. I don't know when the story started up; it must have been sometime during my twenties. I remember a sign just appeared one day. It was handwritten with black paint on a piece of white fence post and had been nailed to a tree down by the lagoon; 'Jacob Ghost walks here,' it declared. The handwriting was heavy and childlike with dried runnels of black paint streaked from each letter. I never knew who put it there. Mother was tight-lipped about the whole thing; even when I was excited and bursting to talk about the great mystery of it all, she dismissed my eager wittering.

'You're too old for such nonsense, Maggie,' she'd snapped.

When Mother snapped, that was that; we didn't speak of it again. I think of it now only because, since I have become the local witch and a famous spook myself, I feel a kind of kinship for old Jacob. I hope he's getting flowers too.

*

The howling starts again, a few hours after the darkness falls. It's getting dark faster now, with the heart of winter coming, and don't my bones know it. My knuckles, knees and hips scream with pain and I swallow some of the pain pills the doctor brought up for me last time he came. They are supposed to make it easier to sleep, but they just fill my head with a cottony fog that further blurs the edges between my sleeping and waking.

I wish whatever it was groaning out there would just die, or come for me, or do whatever it damn well has to do so it would shut up. Sometimes, when I can think clearly, I tell myself, It's just a cow or a calf, you've heard the sound of a bovine in distress before. You grew up on a cattle station for God's sake, stop being so imaginative. I say this to myself in Mother's matter of fact voice; the voice she would use to admonish the actors on TV if she thought they were being silly.

Some years after Father passed, Mother went down to town and ordered us a TV. It was the late 50s by then and a few young men brought it here on a truck. It was an extravagance. We were among the first in Wren to have one of our own and we pretty much settled in to watch it as our main pastime. Oh, there was plenty of gossiping and sewing, knitting and the brewing of tea, but all of it took place under the pale glare of that TV light. We developed a taste for it, sure enough, and it has kept me company in my solitude, though the set itself is new and the third since that hulking first box. I can't count the times I have fallen asleep in its company.

*

I'm awake again; it's late as hell. The howling is worse; it is deep, urgent and afraid, and I just can't stand it anymore. It's the bunyip; I will have to go to it. It's stuck down there somehow. It is waiting for me. It is Jacob Ghost and Father's angry ghost. I know it is not any of these things. If I could make it quiet I could get some sleep and I could, I don't know, I'm forgetting what I need.

Mother is sitting in the kitchen, she is sewing, her lap is overflowing with black silk, she looks up and her hair as all white now, her face a series of folds and hollows. She is hunched over so far that her back is a full half circle and her face is bent close to her work. She pulls the thread taut, out come the silver scissors and with one clean snip it is done.

'Mother!' I cry, but no sound comes out because Mother is not here and I am not quite awake. I want to cry and I get angry with myself for the thought. 'Mother, please. I am done with it,' I blubber and I know I'm talking rubbish. If I could just get the awful noise to stop I could collect my thoughts, I could sort myself out. Even the TV can't soothe me now, and it can't drown out the keening.

I will have to go out and stop it myself. But first, of course, I'll need a coat. I'll need something warm and thick, to keep off not only the night chill, but the bugs and whatnot that might be out there. There's an old parka on the hall hook; I give it a few firm shakes to get the dust out and it still fits okay, even if it is a bit baggy. I button it down over my housedress. I wish I had some trousers, but I can't think where any might be. I look down at my battered slippers, their sheepskin innards pilling and brown with dirt. I'll need some sturdier shoes for walking out in the grass. I rummage through the wardrobe floors, the shoe rack and the laundry room. I have a ratty pair of slippers and a pair of Homey Ped sandals that I mail ordered about fifteen years ago. The sandals have a weak strap and are entirely inadequate to my purpose. I haven't got any good sturdy shoes at all. But what would I need them for? I don't go anywhere. Now I'm frustrated because I'm determined to sort this out, once and for all. I need to find out what is making that awful bellowing and I need to get it to stop.

I stumble around looking through boxes and cupboards I haven't peeked into for many years, since Mother died, since before Mother died. There is so much clutter, so much rubbish and, oh, everything is loaded with the past. I pull out the coat that I lay on for that one tryst with Billy Bird and a lump presses upwards from my chest to my throat. How can this old thing still be here? But nothing has been thrown away so everything is here, of course. The ridiculous hat that Bess sent me in her first years away from home; a funny little cap made of a deep blue felt she must have thought I would like, but I stashed it away and forgot it, embarrassed by its stylishness and what it revealed about the distance that had grown between Bess and me. A bag of marbles that must have once belonged to Frankie clunks heavily along the bottom of another drawer.

There are boots that were Father's in the piles of junk that have been stacked along the sleepout wall. I try them on but they are too large. I can't walk in them. I haul open an old chest and scatter motheaten blankets and greasy stubs of candles and there! Boots. They are brown leather riding boots of the kind Father always wore, but these are a little smaller; maybe they were Frankie's, but I don't remember them. I pull one on and it is stiff with age and disuse. The dry air has hardened the leather and the inner soles feel like they have curled up a bit on the inside, but altogether the fit is not bad. I pull both on and stamp a little in the dark room, getting the feel of them. The hard wood heel makes three loud raps like the casting of a spell.

The air outside is still and cold. The moon makes an intermittent appearance between fast-moving clouds and bathes the landscape in flashes of silver. Each time the clouds roll back over I have to rely on the weak yellow beam of my torch. It jitters and jolts as I bump along. The long grass whacks wetly into my bare shins. The boots hold together, though, and for this I am grateful. I half expected they'd have sat so long untouched that they had perished and would fall apart and leave me barefooted in the dark grass and weeds.

I walk in a straight line and I am tuned in to the beast that bellows and groans in the night. I walk for ages. The cold air is getting into my bones and my hand is a vice around the old plastic torch. I think I couldn't let go of it now if I wanted to. Maybe hours pass, maybe minutes; the holler of the beast comes and goes but it is getting louder, so I know I am getting closer. I see in silhouette the sparse line of trees on the horizon ahead and I know I am reaching the lagoon. The sound is coming from the lagoon and I become momentarily sure it is the bunyip after all and it is not hurt, but waiting, with its teeth gleaming in the moonlight and waiting, waiting and hungry, and even though fear spikes in my belly, I quicken my steps because an end is an end I am so tired now, so tired.

Something catches my foot in the grass, a rock or a tangle of weed, and I trip in the too-large boots. I fall flat, smacking my chin against the hard ground, the torch bouncing away. The dark falls over me and the pain is everywhere. I lie a while with the damp grass scratching at my legs. The pain in my chin and my scraped palms burns and I hear myself whimpering as though I am far, far away. Something flickers ahead, a whitish flash beneath the trees. It looks like a man shape and then I see the spindly legs, a pale elongated head. Jacob Ghost walks out from under the trees. I am stomach-down in the grass, propping myself on my palms and trying to summon the strength to get up as the willowy ghost walks forward. He has no face, but I know it's *him*. 'Jacob,' I try to call.

Then the moon clears through the cloud cover and the world is illuminated again and there is no ghost, but the white flicker is something: a beast, a creature with a white hide, thrashing under the trees. Not the bunyip, then, since my bunyip is an oily black, always black, unless of course the bunyip has aged too and is as white-haired as I am now.

I scramble up, my energy renewed by the light and the creature that is surely there beneath the trees. Its eyes are glowing in the dark; it thrashes and makes its terrible bawling. I brush the wet grass from my creased knees; they are grazed and bloody now and the stinging does not abate. My heart is hammering in the cage of my ribs and I feel so faint for a moment that I might fall again, but I collect myself and make it to the red plastic torch before the moon is obscured again and I am left with nothing but its weak beam. I stumble toward the lagoon's edge.

The creature must know I am near; it has picked up its bawling and it is calling and mewling urgently now. I know what it is even before I shine the torch on it. It's a calf, a big pale calf caught in some fence wire which is cutting into its leg so deeply that in at least one spot it is grinding against bone. The creature is mad with pain and distress and its eyes roll wildly. I try to calm it, but it is jerking its head in a mad panic. I count three or four days since the crying began, so I know it's been down here at least that long.

I can't think of what to do for it. I don't know whose calf it might be. We haven't grazed our own cattle since Father's illness and Mother sold off two thirds of the land to sheep farmers. For the first time in my life I wish for one of those portable phones everyone uses nowadays. I can't leave the beast here and I'm too bone tired to think of walking back just yet in any case. My body feels like a pile of sharp bones inexpertly packed into an old sack; they jangle about and sharp spears of pain slice through me. I am holding a palm out to the beast, whose nostrils are foaming with snot, and I try to make calming noises. I know I am grimacing in my own pain and tiredness and I think, If the cow has a thought in its bovine head, it is probably that I am naught but a scarecrow, a woman made of old branches. We sit together, this dying calf and I, and neither of us can do a thing for the other.

I am panting and the dark is deep and cold and the calf bellows and bawls away. I need to make it stop. I grasp at branches and anything I can to get to my feet. I sweep the torch over the area, looking for anything that will help. A darkness drops over my eyes, deeper than the dark of the night around me, and at first I don't even realise that I have collapsed. The darkness is sleep, or something close to it, sleep trying to steal over me. But I still hear the crying of the calf until my hand, flung out now with the torch gone from my grasp, feels a slap of damp heat. The calf has stopped crying and is investigating my hand, licking the dew I have brushed from the leaves and grass in my scrambling. The calf is blessedly quiet as it snuffles and licks. I can barely open my eyes, but I do; I am lying on my back and the clouds are parting over my head.

The moon is gone and the black sky is deep and pinned with stars. The night is entering its deepest chapter. Watching the sky through the reaching branches I am reminded again of that night with Billy Bird, lying in the grass with the night over us and the soft grass underneath. As the stars wheel and the branches sway overhead I feel a pang of regret for the first time in my long life. Oh, is this what it comes to?

The calf has gone quiet, not nuzzling my hand anymore, not thrashing or bawling. It has gone still as a stone. I let my head fall to the side and I see, back the way I have come, across the wild weedy paddock in which nothing of use has grown for years, coming toward me from the place where the house sits like a hulking shadow darkening the horizon, a human shape is nearing, nearing. It is Mother. Her hair is flying, her face is young and old at once and her expression is gentleness, such infinite gentleness and in her hands are her silver scissors. I smile. I close my eyes and I wait.

A Lovely and Terrible Thing

Chris Womersley

What a burden it is to have seen wondrous things, for afterwards the world feels empty of possibility. There used to be a peculiar human majesty in my line of work: the woman with hair so long she could wind it ten times around her waist; old Frankie Block, who could wrestle a horse to the ground; the boy with a fox tail. There was a good reason we referred to ourselves as the Weird Police. Now it's more likely to be a conga-line of Elvis impersonators sponsored by McDonald's. Somewhere along the way the job lost its magic, but perhaps that was just me.

*

It was dusk when I pulled over to phone my wife. I would be gone for only two nights, but caring for our daughter Therese was gruelling, melancholy work, like tending to a fire perpetually on the verge of going out. More than once I had come home to discover Elaine sitting in the near-dark, weeping with the endlessness of it all, and there was nothing I could do but hold her until she felt better. It took hours, sometimes. At others, all night.

My phone didn't have reception out on the back roads. I trudged into a cold and muddy field with it held foolishly over my head, but it was no use; I would have to call from the motel in Kyneton.

When I returned to the car, the damn thing refused to start. I fished out a torch, popped the bonnet and peered at the engine, but the mass of wires and pipes might as well have been Sanskrit hieroglyphs for all the sense I could make of them. No cars passed. There was not a house in sight. I cursed my decision to take the scenic route. At least on the highway someone might stop and help. On the highway my phone would have reception.

I jiggled a few wires and checked the radiator, but it was no use. By now the horizon was darkening and the wind had turned sharp and bitter. Again I stared at the mute, incomprehensible engine and it occurred to me that a mechanic might have fared better with Therese than any of her medical specialists had over the years. I held my freezing hands over the engine, but the heat it gave off was minimal and diminished noticeably as I stood there.

I was beginning to resign myself to the prospect of spending the night in the car when a voice startled me. I swung around to see a large man approaching through the gloom. 'G'day,' he said again.

Embarrassed to have been discovered warming myself over a dead engine, I took my hands back and greeted him.

'Everything all right?' he asked.

I gestured to the engine. 'Car's broken down on me. I pulled over to make a phone call and now it won't start.'

The fellow was about my age, dressed in overalls, with a shock of grey hair that flapped about like a bird's broken wing. He stood nodding at the roadside verge and considered me for a moment. 'Want me to take a look?'

'Yes, that would be great. Thanks.' I held out my hand. 'I'm Daniel Shaw, by the way.'

The man grunted and shook my hand, reluctantly, it seemed. 'Dave. They call me Angola round here.'

'An*gola*. Like the place?'

He started. 'You've heard of it?'

'Of course.'

He paused. 'Well, I spent a few years there.'

He took my torch, positioned it on the rim of the bonnet where it would provide the best light, and set about poking around inside. After a few minutes he urged me to try the ignition again, which I did, but without any luck.

'Dunno, mate,' Angola said, wiping his hands on a rag he produced from a back pocket. 'Reckon she's stuffed for now, though. Where you going?'

'Kyneton. How far is that?'

Again he looked at me as if puzzled to find me there at all. By now it was almost dark. The only light was that of the torch which, at that moment, splashed its light across the right half of his face. I imagined us from a distance – two men, strangers to each other, on a lonely road – and felt a jolt of fear.

'Too far to walk,' he said at last above a roar of sudden wind. He undid the bracket supporting the upraised bonnet, grabbed the torch and let the bonnet fall. 'But you can stay the night at my place, if you like.'

'I need to be there by 2 p.m. tomorrow afternoon. There's something I have to verify. I work for Ripley's Believe It or Not, and there's supposed to be a parrot that can count to 150. I have to check it's true. We might use it in the next annual.'

That piqued his interest. It usually did. Angola sauntered closer and looked me over. 'You work for Ripley's? Like the TV show? Ha. You musta seen some pretty weird things.'

I laughed. The world's most-tattooed man, the girl with eighteen fingers, the ultra-marathon runners. He didn't know the half of it.

With his thumb he indicated the field beside the road, beyond which, presumably, he lived. 'My daughter has a pretty special trick, actually. Maybe you should come and see her? Put her in your big old book.'

He said this in a mildly lascivious manner I didn't care for but, as usual, that word pricked my heart, deflating it ever further. *Daughter.* I thought again of poor Elaine, poor Therese; my silent, waiting family. I hoped my wife had at least turned on the lights before pouring her first Scotch.

'You got kids?' Angola asked me, handing back the torch.

'Yes, I have a daughter too, as a matter of fact.'

He grinned. 'Then you know what a lovely and terrible thing it is.'

It was an incongruous and curiously poetic description, particularly coming from his gap-toothed mouth. I nodded. For a moment I could not speak. I looked off into the bleak distance, then at this man, and there was something about the sad shake of his head and the way his hair flapped about on his scalp that filled me with unreasonable warmth. A decent man out here in the country, with mud on his boots and the grease of a stranger's car on his hands.

For reasons best known only to the darker parts of myself, I felt immense shame about Therese, and rarely told anyone of my troubles; I had colleagues, for instance, who were completely unaware of her existence. But, for some reason, out on this road, I felt compelled to tell this man what had happened to her.

I coughed into my fist. 'But my daughter is – she was in an accident. Eight years ago. She cycled onto the road when she was eleven and got hit by a car. She lost the use of her legs and became brain damaged. We don't even know if she knows who we are – my wife and I, I mean. They say – the *experts*, that is – to hope for a miracle, that she might recover some of her movement and coordination. It has happened before, you know. Small breakthroughs, they say. Keep an eye out for small breakthroughs, whatever they might be.' I could have bored the poor fellow with talk of trauma and lobes and the ripple effect, but instead I tapped my head with my index finger. 'We don't really know what goes on in there.'

It was at this point that people usually said something consoling, along the lines of *I'm sure she'll come good one of these days*, but the man called Angola merely stared at me, listening, until I said all I had to say. And it was perhaps for this kindness that I enquired after the 'trick' of his daughter's. Normally I would not follow up on every stranger's claim – for we all believe our children to be possessed of special talents, even those of us whose faith has been worn so thin – but I felt I owed him this small courtesy.

Angola waved my polite query away. 'Oh,' he said. 'You'd never believe me.'

'I've heard some pretty wild stories, you know.'

He looked at me for a long time, as if attempting to peer into my soul. It was unsettling. I saw now – by what light I couldn't say, for the sun had well and truly set – that his face was pitted with acne scars and that his left earlobe was malformed. But there, by the road, he told me something so bizarre, and in such a strange manner – looking from side to side, shrugging, mumbling – that I had no choice but to believe him.

*

I carried the torch as we squelched across a field and ducked between the barbed wire of several fences. I asked him about Africa, but he was reluctant to disclose his reasons for being there and became curiously sullen, saying merely that it was a terrible place and that he hadn't deserved to be there at all.

It was only when we saw the lights of his small house in the distance that I realised, and stopped. 'Your name,' I said, trying to keep the panic from my voice. 'It's not for the country, is it?'

My companion paused and wiped his meaty paw beneath his nose.

It was freezing. My shoes were sticky with mud. 'It's for the prison, isn't it? In America.' I recalled an entry from the 1972 Ripley's annual; an inmate who – although he had never left the state of Louisiana – built a precise scale model of central Paris from toothpicks, complete with street signs and roadside markets, tiny apples and pears.

'Course it is,' he growled, and continued walking.

I stared after him until I could barely make him out in the darkness. I pondered my options, which were few. After a minute, I staggered after him.

It was a decision I have come to regret.

*

Angola's house was large, but cluttered with thick-legged furniture, piles of toys and the detritus of domestic activity: mounds of knitting, fishing bags, a cricket set. Angola's wife, Carol, elbow-deep in dishwater, seemed perplexed to see me in her house but shook my hand with her own sudsy one and offered me a beer. A teenage boy appeared and grunted at his father before sulking off. I peered around for the daughter about whom I had heard such amazing things, but there was no sign of her. Another son materialised, dutifully shook my hand and vanished. The television blared and I recognised the dopey voice-overs of *Australia's Funniest Home Videos*. The sons laughed themselves stupid at something. *I think I'll just take a walk up here on the icy roof …* Angola and his wife bickered good-naturedly about an unpaid bill. *Boinggg.*

With their permission, I phoned Elaine from the dim, unheated study at the rear of the house. The window sills were lined with children's sporting trophies. Football, cricket, tennis. *Best and fairest. Under-12 Champion.* The small desk was covered with bank statements, shopping catalogues, letters from a local school.

Elaine sounded harried – but not drunk, at least. Her French-accented voice was damp with unshed tears. Not for the first time I felt I might have been starring unwittingly in some mournful, European film. She had had a bad day of it: a tradesman had tracked mud into the house and then been unable to fix a pipe we had been waiting on for two weeks; Therese had to be changed three times.

'But she did a funny thing, Dan. You won't believe this but I went in this afternoon, she was in the sunroom – you know how she loves to stare at the birds at the feeder – and I swear she reached out to stroke my hair as I leaned over her.'

I paused to take this in. I heard our fridge humming in the background. 'Are you sure?'

'Yes.'

'She stroked your *hair*?'

'Yes.'

This could be a breakthrough. I leaned forward, elbows on the desk. 'For how long?'

'Well. A few seconds.'

'It could be something, though, couldn't it?'

'Sure. Yeah.'

'It wasn't just a—'

'Dan. I'm sure.'

Pinned to the wall above the desk where I sat was a child's drawing of a dog. Bulbous shapes conjoined by stick-like limbs, a scribble of blue cloud. I imagined Therese in her low bed staring at the ceiling where I had stuck luminous stars; her implacable face, her shining eyes. She might have contained entire oceans, shipwrecked galleons, dragons, concertos. I loved my daughter more when I was away from her; her actual presence only highlighted my inability to help her. My beery breath bounced back at me from the plastic receiver, and for the thousandth time since her accident I was flooded with sudden, acute disappointment at how I had so quickly reached the limits of my love.

I told Elaine I would be back the day after tomorrow at the latest, depending how long it took to get the car repaired.

'Dan?'

'Yes.'

'Do you promise?'

She often asked me that. 'Yes,' I said.

*

Returning to the lounge room, I passed a carpeted hallway I hadn't noticed earlier. Pop music drifted through a part-open door at the other end and a long matchstick of light fell on the swirling carpet. This must be the daughter's bedroom. I paused to listen, as if the music might offer a clue. 'I Should Be So Lucky,' by Kylie Minogue. Hysterical laughter from the lounge room, Angola asking his sons something. I shuffled down the hall towards the daughter's room. She was singing along to the music in a low voice. Despite myself, I sensed the thrill of discovering something truly incredible. What if her father had been telling the truth? I crept closer, almost holding my breath.

'You right, mate?'

I swivelled around to see Angola standing at the other end of the corridor. Although he was in silhouette, I could tell he was glaring at me. 'Yes, I was just—'

'That's Chloe's room.'

'Oh. I was, ah, looking for the bathroom.'

It was clear he didn't believe me. He wiped the back of his hand under his nose, then pointed the way I had come. 'That way. And dinner's ready.'

*

In any case, I didn't have long to wait before seeing the daughter. When I returned from the bathroom, the family was gathered at the dinner table and looked up expectantly at my entrance. The daughter, Chloe, was seated opposite me. She looked ordinary enough, but I couldn't help inspecting her whenever the opportunity arose.

Dinner was roast lamb with mint sauce and vegetables. Everyone talked at once. The boys bickered and thumped each other. Carol lit up a cigarette at the table as soon as she had eaten. Angola talked on his mobile phone for several minutes. The television raved away in the background. It was disconcerting to be at such a rowdy family dinner, but gradually, with the help of a few beers, I began to enjoy myself. *So,* I thought, *this is family life.*

Angola had cooled towards me, but I regaled the gathering with tales from my years as a verifier for Ripley's. Soon they were all laughing and wide-eyed, gasping in astonishment at South Pacific cargo cults, at the man who dived into buckets of water from great heights, the parachutist who shaved and smoked a cigarette in the time it took to float back to earth.

Angola picked something from his teeth. 'And do people make, you know, *money* out of these things?'

'Sure,' I said. 'Sometimes.'

At this, Angola's wife uttered a curious sound. I could restrain myself no longer and turned to the girl, Chloe, who had been quiet the entire meal. 'So. Your father tells me that you have quite an unusual talent yourself. Would you like to show me what you can do?'

The family fell silent. Then Carol put her head in her hands. 'Jesus, Dave. I *knew it.* You told him, didn't you? I knew it ...'

Angola started to protest, but his justifications were trumped by the only words I heard Chloe speak. 'No,' she piped, 'that's my sister Emily. She's in the shed.'

*

The shed was really a stable about one hundred metres from the house. A wind buffeted us as we made our way across the yard with a torch. I was anxious. Many years ago I met a woman who claimed to have a portion of Hitler's jawbone – complete with some piece of paperwork or other that verified it – but from the moment I stepped into her stinking, ramshackle entrance hall I knew she was just a lonely madwoman with a house full of junk. That I fell for it has long been a source of embarrassment for me, but in my business one needed to check all reasonable leads. Would this perhaps be the same? Or even worse?

Angola unbolted the massive door and swung it open. The stable was dimly lit. Pausing on the threshold, I could smell wet hay and the sweat of animals. I knew the rest of the family was standing at the kitchen window, watching to see what I, a stranger, would make of their daughter. After Chloe had spoken up at the dinner table, there had been a heated discussion of money, of fame and reality TV that I did my best to dampen while still allowing them enough enthusiasm to show me their curious prize.

I stepped inside. Angola followed and closed the door behind me. Something stirred in a far corner; I heard a clank of chain. Angola brushed past me and went to another door on the other side of the stable. He paused with his hand on the wooden knob. 'You ready?'

I nodded. By this time my heart was hammering. The miraculous has a smell, and this godforsaken place was ripe with it. Angola opened the door and went in. Another rustle of chain, the swish of straw. Murmured words, kindly words. He beckoned me over. 'Don't be afraid,' he said, then to his daughter, 'This is Mr Shaw, love.'

I said hello and sidled into the room, which was spacious, decorated like any fourteen-year-old girl's room: posters of pop stars, family photographs, drawings of horses. The girl, Emily, was sitting on a low bed placed along one wall. She was slight, pretty, with long brown hair and large eyes. She looked momentarily startled but quickly recovered, said good evening and smiled. It was clear we had interrupted her reading a book; it was placed face-down on the bed next to her. Then I saw the iron hoop around her ankle and the short chain attached at the other end to the bedframe. Emily noticed me staring at it and shrugged. Angola seemed nervous and asked her if she might show me her trick.

'It's not a trick, Pa,' she admonished.

Angola unlocked the iron hoop. 'Well. You know what I mean, love.'

Emily rolled her eyes.

Angola dropped the key to her bolt into his coat pocket and stepped back. He offered me an apologetic smile. 'Teenagers, eh?'

Emily swung around until both legs hung over the edge of her bed. Angola and I waited by the door. Horses moved around nervously in their stalls nearby.

'Are you sure, Pa?'

Angola nodded.

'But you said that—'

'Emily. This man might be able to help us.'

'Okay.'

And after a few minutes, it happened, as Angola had said it would. Almost imperceptibly, Emily began to levitate from the bed with no apparent exertion. The space between the hem of her dress and the rumpled bed expanded. Her face wore the beatific expression of one rapt in an interior activity like, say, listening to a favourite piece of music or contemplating a scene of sublime beauty. The entire thing happened in silence. When at last I could speak, I asked Angola how long she had been doing this.

'Oh, only two months or so. Not long.' It was clear that, behind his anxiety over what was happening to his daughter, he was very proud.

Meanwhile, Emily rose higher and higher. After several minutes, she put out a hand to prevent her head bumping against the high ceiling. Gently she shoved herself off, whereupon she drifted down and across the room before again floating to the ceiling. Finally, Angola took a length of rope, flung it up to his daughter and hauled her down to the floor, as one might a boat to a pier.

He secured Emily to her bed with the iron bolt. They exchanged tender words. He thanked her, kissed her on the forehead. We left the barn. Then he turned to me with an avaricious gleam in his eye, and I knew instantly what I had to do.

*

In the middle of the night, when I was certain the family was asleep, I eased the ring of keys from the hook by the kitchen door and crept out of the house.

Emily didn't seem surprised to see me standing in her room. I sensed her looking at me as soon as I unlocked her door, but she said nothing, uttered not a sound. It was so quiet out there in the country I could hear her breathing in the gloom. I crouched by her bed and told her not to be afraid and she nodded as if she had known all along – known even before I did – what I intended to do. Some girls were like that. I unlocked the iron clasp from her bony ankle, gave her a moment to put a robe over her pyjamas, then lifted her from the bed and carried her outside.

My shoes crunched on the gravel driveway. I registered the familiar pleasing sensation of a girl's warm and trusting breath on my neck, a cheek bumping against my shoulder. I had intended to carry her far beyond the edge of the property, but she was heavier than I anticipated – or I older and wearier – and I was compelled to put her down in the driveway seventy or so metres from the house. The girl uttered a startled laugh, wobbled, then grabbed my sleeve as if momentarily unbalanced on a beam.

I held her by her wrist and we stood there for several seconds staring at each other in silence.

'I'm scared,' she whispered.

'I know. But there is no need to be.'

The moon was high and full. By its light I saw the silvery outline of her jaw, tendrils of her hair waving in the breeze. Experimentally, I loosened my grip on her wrist and we stood there in the driveway, the girl and I, for a few seconds longer until she, too, let go of my sleeve.

I sensed animals moving around us in the darkness, the soft and furry blink of their eyes. Emily smoothed her knotty hair and looked around. For a second I feared she would run or cry out for help but, instead, she looked at me and smiled. 'Goodbye,' she said.

Gradually, she rose into the air as she had done several hours earlier and the sight of it thrilled me anew. Her knobbly knees floated past my face and I realised I was weeping. She stifled a giggle with a hand across her mouth, then relaxed and held out her arms, and it seemed to me that she was not rising so much as the earth on which I stood was falling away beneath her feet. She waved. By the time lights came on in the house and I heard angry voices, the girl was already out of reach, floating above a nearby stand of gum trees.

Angola and his family ran up behind me with mouths full of oaths, but instead of escaping, as I should have done, I closed my eyes to better imagine the world from the girl's new height. I wondered if she saw trees in the distance, the yellow gravel of a driveway. Did she hear her father crying out and sense the stars close at hand, the vast and ancient universe into which she was being drawn? Far below, did she make out a man beating another man over and over with his fists, and hear a dog yapping at the commotion? People clawing at each other, throwing up their hands, shrieking?

Finally, when her family below fell silent and looked skyward, their faces glowed strangely and were so small they might have been coins on a road as, free at last, she disappeared from sight.

Granta

Benny Wins Powerball

Erin Gough

Benny wins Powerball, the entire jackpot.

It's a Saturday night. In Gran Donna's lounge room the heater's on and they're watching the draw on Channel Seven. All three of them crowded in front of the screen, eyeing the coloured balls as they whizz down the plastic tubes and plop into place.

There's Big Dave, shouting out the numbers as they land – twenty-three! thirty-seven! fifty-five! There's Jube, marking them off on each of their tickets with a texta. And there's Benny, gazing from his sister to his brother and back again; at the way the colours on the television – the blues, yellows and pinks – dance across their hopeful eyes like New Year's fireworks.

Out on the street, everything is closed and dark: the chicken shop, the surf shop, the bank. Even the pub, which overflows in January, is shut tonight for lack of customers. It's a dead little town, especially at this time of year, when the sea is cold and the colour of a five cent piece. But the sky is clear and the stars are out, thousands of them.

Not that Benny, or Big Dave, or even Jube who goes nuts for stars, who lives by her daily horoscope, would know it. It was hours ago that they drew Gran Donna's curtains across the window. Hauling the rings along the rod as her sherry glasses – round-middled and short-stemmed, just like Gran Donna – chattered on the sideboard before settling down onto Gran Donna's couch, three in a row.

The stars are up there all the same, though, even if no one's looking: stars like diamonds, like winking eyes. Stars like the stars on the cover of Gran Donna's *Star Wars Trilogy* boxset.

Gran Donna herself is not in the room. She hasn't joined them for the weekly draw since Big Dave decreed the front half of the house a no-smoking zone. No matter that it's her house – if he catches her in the lounge room he goes wild.

'Either quit your filthy habit or stay out,' he'd bellowed the last time she'd stuck her head through the door, waving his fists at her.

So while the rest of them watch for their numbers, she sits in the kitchen sucking at her tobacco pipe and blowing smoke into the fireplace.

The Powerball music tings; it's the sound of coins falling onto other coins. 'Sixty-five!' shouts Big Dave as the last ball tumbles into place. Jube lines up the tickets and runs her finger across them, her french-polished nail with its painted white moon whispering over the little squares of paper.

'Well?' Big Dave asks, leaning over her.

Jube furrows her brow, and double-checks the numbers on the television. Her eyes widen. 'I don't believe it,' she says, and it comes out more like breath than words.

'What is it?' Big Dave bellows.

'It's Benny's.'

All three of them stare at the ticket.

'Benny's?' says Big Dave, grabbing the slip of paper.

On the screen, the studio lights glare off the row of coloured balls. Big Dave stares hard at them and then down at the ticket, mouthing the numbers to himself. When he looks up, his eyes are as wide as his sister's.

Benny looks at Jube. He looks at Big Dave. Could the numbers really be his? He waits for the room, and the coloured ball growing large inside him, to burst.

But nothing bursts. For a drawn-out moment, nothing happens at all. Nobody screams out, or cheers; nobody says a word. The heater hisses. The sherry glasses, with their cut-crystal sides like Gran Donna's argyle jumper, gaze emptily. Only the television sings, and now that the draw is over, its song is about flat-bottomed tacos.

Then Big Dave clears his throat.

'Benny has never won a thing in his life,' he says. 'Not a raffle. Not a spelling bee. Not even a game of Connect Four.'

'It's true. He's a born loser,' says Jube, and the way she says it it's as if he's out of the room – in the bathroom, maybe, or getting a glass of water – not sitting next to her with a warm bit of his thigh against hers.

'He's actually *un*lucky,' says Big Dave. 'Remember the holiday we had at the snow? When Benny was caught in an avalanche, and broke both his legs?'

Jube and Big Dave laugh.

When they have stopped laughing, the room falls quiet again. Quieter than it did last week after nobody won.

Jube grabs Benny's hand and slaps the winning ticket into it like she's never been so disappointed with him in all her life. Like he's back in high school and she's his teacher, not his younger sister, and the ticket is a detention slip for failing his exams. Like the windfall, which was descending so quickly a moment ago, so heavily that the air's seams strained to hold it, hasn't landed in his hands at all but whistled through his parted fingers.

Benny takes the ticket off his palm. His skin stings from where Jube slapped it. He turns the ticket over, stares at the blank white square of paper. He turns it back and brings it up close, an inch from his nose, to read the single sentence written in tiny font beneath the numbers. He has never noticed it before, so faint and small are the letters.

You could be a winner, it says.

*

It's the biggest jackpot they've ever had! It's the biggest ever because no one has won it in years! It's the largest amount ever won in Australia! That no one else in the whole country has chosen the same numbers as Benny is amazing in itself; but for it to happen this week, when the amount is enormous, is the most improbable thing to occur in the history of Powerball!

The media are quoting startling figures now that Benny's won. They're referencing the cost of vast infrastructure projects, and the GDP of smaller nations. As if the digits lined up like that

– stretched out across the front page of the *Telegraph* – don't speak for themselves.

On *The Morning Show* they devote an entire segment to what Benny could buy with the money. They make up lists of expensive things in interesting combinations –

a Mercedes Roadster and a Boeing 747,

a Vanuatu island retreat and a Collette Dinnigan wardrobe,

a Hilton Hotel and a lifetime's subscription to the *Women's Weekly*

– things that also happen to be products of the companies that sponsor *The Morning Show.*

On *The Evening Show* they ask callers to ring in with lists of inexpensive things that Benny could buy a whole lot of. The phone lines are engaged for three hours. Twenty-five million Paddle Pops, is one suggestion. One million, two hundred thousand squeegie mops. Seven million, five-hundred thousand caramel-flavoured cappuccinos.

*

In an empty phone room, Big Dave is spraying disinfectant onto a cloth. He squirts the cloth and the liquid foams and bubbles. He slaps the cloth onto a table and the bubbles burst.

It's Monday. Big Dave always works in the phone room on a Monday. Every Monday, before the other staff arrive to take calls from dissatisfied customers of the insurance company that employs them, he wipes down the headsets. When he has finished with the headsets, he wipes down the touch pads on the phones. He's always happy to do it – more than happy, in fact, to contribute to the hygiene of the office, even though he is Floor Manager and arguably above menial tasks like cleaning.

But this Monday he feels differently.

The phone on the desk rings. Big Dave wrenches it from its cradle. 'It's not even nine o'clock,' he shouts into the receiver.

And hangs up.

It's unusual for Big Dave to act this way at work. Rarely is he rude to a customer. At the phone room he makes a special effort to be pleasant and congenial. It's his pleasantness and congeniality and all-round commitment to company values, in fact, that got him promoted to Floor Manager.

Today, however, he's sick of being a good employee. For the first time since he started managing the phone room he feels he should not be disinfecting headsets and touch pads. He should not be working at all. He should be rolling up the highway in a new Ferrari: a red one, with alloy wheels and leather seats the colour of milk.

Big Dave pours some more disinfectant onto the cloth. Its fumes, which don't usually bother him, sting the back of his throat. The taste is metallic and sharp, like a coin: like the money he should have won, which is right now sitting in his brother's bank account.

Big Dave grits his teeth. He thinks about the millions of dollars, piled up in a safe somewhere under Benny's name. Towers of it, sitting in bundles in the moisture-free dark.

He pounds a fist against the table, and the row of headsets rattles like dice.

It's been two weeks since the draw and still Big Dave can't believe it – that his lousy brother, Benny, is now on the nation's rich list. Benny, who's never had a dollar to his name! Whose most prized possession is a stupid toy car, a model DeLorean like the one in *Back to the Future*! When it comes to money, Benny is the most thick-headed person he knows. It's no surprise that in two weeks of being a millionaire he hasn't made a single withdrawal.

Big Dave has a few ideas about how *he'd* spend the jackpot. And a decent share of his brother's winnings is not, he doesn't think, too much to ask for. Not from someone whose backside he covered for four long years in high school.

How many balls did he break in the schoolyard for Benny? How much flack did he cop on behalf of his brother? Benny the loser, who sat on the schoolyard wall reading dumb science fiction books while everyone else played cricket or football – it's no wonder the other kids picked on him. Benny the layabout, who's never had a steady job in his life.

It's simple, really. Big Dave has not worked this hard to progress in the world, to have his useless brother trump him like this.

Which is why last night he and Benny had a little talk.

Big Dave sighs moodily and scrubs a glob of unidentifiable facial excrement off the plastic. He doesn't like what he had to say or do last night, not at all. But Benny can only blame himself.

Of course if they'd bought their tickets as a syndicate none of this would have been necessary. He had wanted to do a syndicate but Jube, the selfish cow, had said:

'If I win a thousand bucks there's no way in hell I'm splitting it with you.'

He bets that she regrets it now.

If only Benny would hurry up and do as he's told.

Big Dave wipes down the final phone and screws the lid back on the bottle of disinfectant, not caring that he's spilt some of it on a chair and that the whole room now smells like a hospital corridor. He could be trout fishing in New Zealand. He could be high-rolling in Vegas. He could be drinking champagne on a yacht bound for the Maldives, his hair blowing giddily in the breeze.

*

A chilly wind has blown in from the water. The Hills hoist creaks as Benny takes the last piece of clothing off the line: a pair of tracksuit pants with a hole in the left buttock. He folds the pants in half and places them with the rest of the clothes in the clothes basket. Cradling it against his chest, he peers out over the shrubs at the back of the garden to the sea.

The beach is deserted except for two people at the southern end near the rocks. One of them is lying on a deck chair while the other one crouches nearby. They must be crazy, thinks Benny, to be out there today, with the promise of rain in the air and the sand hissing up in clouds. The sky is a misty blur, although he can just make out the moon's skeleton, so pale that it's almost transparent, like a mint that's been well and truly sucked on. Everything else is covered in haze. There's no clear way of telling where the sea finishes and the sky begins.

No horizon: it makes Benny think about the man from Powerball who gave him his cheque. He wore a suit and a tie covered in colourful, numbered spheres. 'The world is your oyster,' he'd said, slapping him between the shoulder blades as if he'd known him forever. 'Nothing is beyond you now.'

Benny lowers the washing basket. He remembers Big Dave in the hallway last night – the heavy press of his arm as he held him to the wall. It was enough to make him lose his breath. Only when he'd started wheezing had his brother let him go.

Benny blinks, and looks up at the sky again, but the sliver of moon has disappeared.

Gran Donna is in the lounge room, watching *The Empire Strikes Back.*

'Washing's in,' says Benny.

He sits down beside her. She reaches across and squeezes his hand. Her skin is dry and soft like flour. When did her skin get like that, Benny wonders – dry and soft and sort of loose on her bones, so that it shifts against his skin like jelly? One day, he thinks – perhaps one day soon – she'll be gone, and he'll be left alone with Jube and Big Dave.

The thought is terrifying.

She releases his hand slowly and picks up her pipe, which she lights with a match.

Benny likes the smell of her pipe. He likes the cinnamon and aniseed waft of the smoke, the way it drifts in whirls and loses itself in the folds of the curtains. He likes, too, the quiet of the house when, like today, Jube and Big Dave are out. He likes the whole town in fact: its seasonal rhythms, the way the sea changes colour with the weather. He couldn't imagine living anywhere else.

He wonders where Jube is. Big Dave is probably at work. Jube should be at home studying for her exams, but Benny hasn't seen her since breakfast.

On the screen a shuttle explodes, shattering into a million pieces and rocking the Millennium Falcon. The soundtrack dips and soars.

'You know, er, this money I've won?' Benny asks Gran Donna when the scene is over. 'Well, I've been thinking. What would you say to a world cruise?'

Gran Donna looks at him blankly, and turns back to the television.

'You don't like boats? What about a regular holiday, then? In a five-star hotel like the one we saw on *Getaway*?'

She reaches for the remote and presses a button with a floury finger. The soundtrack music grows louder.

Benny covers his ears. The empty sherry glasses rattle on the sideboard. The television hums with volume.

*

'Is this the right angle?'

'A bit to the left.'

'Here?'

'Kind of push your hips up like … mmm, yes, more that way.'

'How about now?' asks Jube.

'Perfect,' says the photographer from *Gentleman's Eye Magazine*, giving her a slow-lidded wink.

Jube balances carefully on both elbows. A metal bit from the deck chair is sticking into her leg. She ignores it. There are goose bumps on her arms and legs from the cold, and her thighs are beginning to shiver, but she tries not to think about how she'd prefer to be wearing her sloppy joe zipped up to her neck instead of the zebra-skin bikini she's actually wearing. A professional model, thinks Jube, would not be put off by close-to-zero temperatures.

The photo shoot at the beach was the photographer's idea. His name is George.

'We'll have the water as the backdrop,' he said when he arrived. 'And you in the foreground on this chair. You said your star sign's Aquarius, right, sweetheart?'

'That's right.'

'Then a water backdrop is perfect.'

'I'm pretty sure Aquarius is an air sign,' Jube said.

But George ignored her. Instead he began to sing a song about the moon and seven houses. He is still humming the tune now, as he shoots her with an extended lens from every angle.

Jube sucks in her cheeks like she's seen the models do on *Project Runway*. George is clearly an ignorant, over-the-hill hippy as well as being not very attractive, she notes, holding in her stomach and clenching her thighs and bottom; but this is probably a good sign. It probably means he is good at taking photos, since why else would he have gotten the job? As long as the photo is good and she looks thinner than in real life and they photoshop out the birthmark on her shoulder, she'll be satisfied.

They have already told her what the article will look like. They even gave her a mock-up of the page before getting her to sign a wad of papers at the *Gentleman's Eye Magazine* office. After she'd seen the mock-up, Jube had signed the papers immediately.

Millionaire's Sister: This Lady Luck plans to spoil you rotten, the heading read.

Underneath the heading was a blank space for her photograph, and underneath that there was a fake interview, which went like this:

Q. What do you plan to do with your share of the winnings?

A. Pamper the man of my dreams in my new hot tub overlooking the Pacific.

The way Jube figures it, the article is a kind of insurance policy. She can use it to guilt Benny into handing over her piece of the pie if Big Dave's little talk doesn't work. She doubts it will be necessary, though. He's probably learnt his lesson from the last 'little talk' he and Big Dave had, when he borrowed Big Dave's car without permission. She remembers the funny way his face had looked afterwards: his nose all lopsided, like a squashed pear.

'Can you straighten out your legs for me, darling?' says George.

Jube straightens out her legs. She doesn't care that the interview is fake. She wouldn't mind having a man of her dreams, or a hot tub to pamper him in. When she gets the money she just might buy a place with a hot tub. Then she could move out of Gran Donna's house, which she hates. The television doesn't even have a flat screen! And Gran Donna is old, and she has strange habits that are not acceptable in the modern day, have probably never been acceptable at any point in history.

'Is your grandma still alive?' Jube asked her friend Kylie the other week.

'Dunno. I guess,' Kylie said.

'Does she smoke?'

'Could do.'

'Cigarettes?'

'What else would she smoke?'

'Like maybe, a pipe?' Jube ventured.

'Who ever heard of an old lady smoking a pipe?' Kylie said, and she laughed so hard that she choked on her gum and Jube had to do the Heimlich manoeuvre on her twice.

Jube looks in the direction of George's camera and presses her lips into a pout.

'That's right, sweetheart,' says George. 'More of that right there.'

Once she gets the money she will definitely move out. She will live in a penthouse in the city. She'll get room service every day, and have her hair done twice a week. And she will not feel guilty, not for a second, because she deserves it. If she were to, for example, sell herself on eBay – not for sex of course, she would never do that, but for friendship, say – then the amount of money Benny has won is how much she would get. She is definitely good company. She is a cack – that's what all her friends tell her.

Jube adjusts her bikini top so that more of her breasts are showing. People would pay what Benny has won just to be around her. Not just the share that's owed to her, but all of it.

*

When *The Empire Strikes Back* is over, Gran Donna puts on *Return of the Jedi*. The theme song begins to gallop; Benny and Gran Donna lean forward in their seats.

Return of the Jedi is their favourite of the trilogy. It's the one in which Luke Skywalker fights Darth Vader; the one in which the Empire is finally destroyed forever. Their favourite scene is at the start of the movie, when Han Solo, who has been frozen in carbonite by Jabba the Hut, is rescued by an anonymous bounty hunter.

Gran Donna's favourite part is when the bounty hunter takes off the helmet and it's Princess Leia, shaking out her hair like someone in a shampoo commercial. Benny's favourite part is just before that, when she presses the button that releases Han Solo. The hard shell covering his face disintegrates. His arms, raised in protest, slacken. His frozen rage melts. He is free.

Outside it is now dark and has begun to rain heavily. Benny hears the front door open. Someone squelches up the hallway.

It's Jube. She sticks her head through the lounge-room door.

'I'm soaked right through,' she wails, and begins to sneeze. 'Better not let Big Dave catch you in here with that pipe,' she adds with a sniffle, looking sternly at Gran Donna.

An hour later the Rebels are being captured by Imperial Forces and Big Dave returns from work. At the sound of his footsteps, Benny's heart gets racy in his chest. He snatches the pipe from Gran Donna's mouth.

But it's too late.

'I can smell tobacco smoke,' Big Dave roars from the hallway.

His footsteps draw nearer. Benny squeezes his grandmother's arm. 'You've got to tell me,' he urges in a whisper.

Gran Donna looks at him silently, carefully, with her watery eyes.

'Whatever you want, that's what I'll spend the money on. I don't care what the others say.'

She plucks her pipe from Benny's fingers and tucks it carefully into her dressing gown pocket.

'Anything, Gran. It doesn't matter. It's your decision.'

But she will not answer him.

*

That night Benny has a dream. He dreams that his body is light, weightless. He dreams of distance and endless quiet, of days as empty as balloons. He dreams of a place where not even the sound of his own voice can break the silence.

And it's just him there, in that soundless paradise; just him and Gran Donna. He wakes up with the sun on his face and an ache in his chest. And knows what to do.

*

He is dismantling the Hills hoist when Big Dave comes outside. 'What's going on out here?'

'I'm making room,' says Benny.

'What for?'

'A delivery.'

Big Dave shoves his big hands into his pockets and looks around the garden. The garden furniture has been stacked neatly underneath the kitchen window. The garden gnomes have been lined up along the back wall. The few shrubs that had been growing in the middle of the lawn have been pared back to ground level with a hacksaw.

'It's something big, I take it,' says Big Dave. 'This delivery of yours.'

'You could say that,' says Benny.

Big Dave kicks at the lawn and a clump of grass flies up in the air and smacks into the laundry wall. He narrows his eyes at his brother. 'You remember what we agreed, don't you? A third to me and a third to Jube?'

Benny nods without meeting his eye.

'Because if you've spent all the money ...'

Benny hauls the clothes line from its pole and lays it down next to the stacked-up furniture. He digs around the pole with a spade and lifts it out of the ground.

'What are you two doing out here?' It's Jube. She and Gran Donna are standing on the back step – Jube sniffling in her sloppy joe, Gran Donna in her dressing gown, dipping her floury fingers into a pouch of tobacco.

'Benny's having something delivered, apparently,' growls Big Dave.

Jube screws up her face, which is a blotchy red. 'What is it? And how much did it cost?'

Benny taps the pole of the Hills hoist with the edge of the spade so that the dirt comes loose, and stacks it with the rest of the furniture. Dave and Jube are watching him like hawks. Now the garden is an empty, grassy square.

Jube has an idea. 'Is he getting a house, do you think?' she asks Big Dave.

'A house!' Big Dave's eyes glimmer dimly. 'That could be it. How much are houses?'

Jube shrugs. 'Depends on the house, I s'pose,' she says sniffling. 'What's that noise?'

They cock their heads to listen. It is a funny sort of noise, like the grumble of the winter sea, or the roar of a Wookiee. As they listen it gets louder, so loud that Jube plugs her ears with her fingers, and that's when they see the road train back into the driveway.

A man with a clipboard jumps down from the cabin and walks towards them.

'Delivery for Benjamin?' he asks, glancing at his clipboard.

'That's me,' says Benny.

The man turns his head in the direction of the truck and nods.

Two men get out. They unlock the doors at the back and open them wide. They unlock the rivets that hold the side panels in place and fold the panels back. Sitting on the tray of the truck is a rocket ship. It is a pale grey, the colour of Gran Donna's pipe smoke. Each of its wings is painted with a single red racing stripe. One of the men shifts a gear stick in the cabin and the tray begins to jolt upwards. It slides out over the lawn and descends.

'Sign here, please,' says the man with the clipboard when the rocket ship is settled in the middle of the lawn.

Benny takes a pen from the man and signs the clipboard. The man hands over a package, which is small and rectangular and wrapped in brown paper. He walks back to the road train and climbs into the cabin and pulls out of the driveway.

Big Dave stares at the rocket ship open-mouthed. 'What in the devil?' he says, his face growing as red as his sister's.

'This is a joke,' scoffs Jube, and blows her nose derisively on a handkerchief. 'It's a fake. It's got to be. You can't just *buy* a rocket ship.'

Benny puts down the brown paper package and walks towards the rocket ship. The door beneath the left wing is open. He climbs inside, into a room that is comfortable and warm. He looks around, and a smile begins to play at the corners of his mouth.

The floor is carpeted a deep, plush red. Soothing music wafts from a set of speakers in the roof. A row of mahogany cabinets makes a crescent-shape beneath the window. It is nothing like the Millennium Falcon, he thinks; it is ten times better.

He hears a scrabbling at the door: Big Dave and Jube are climbing inside. They stand up, Jube coughing and wheezing, and take in the view. Big Dave begins to open the cabinets and drawers, one at a time. Each one he opens is stacked with something different: crisp white linen, bottles of water, gleaming saucepans, tins of food. 'You've been planning quite a trip I see, Benny,' he says through a clenched jaw.

As Jube gazes around, her brow darkens. 'You've done it, haven't you? You've spent every single goddam –' She stops suddenly, and her eyes light up. 'Ha!' she says triumphantly.

'What?' says Big Dave.

She smiles, at Big Dave first, then menacingly at Benny. 'I was right. It *is* a fake. This thing's going nowhere. There are no controls!'

Big Dave scans the interior again. He opens and closes every cupboard and drawer that he hasn't already explored. He begins to grin. 'Dimwit Benny,' he gloats. 'Thinks he bought a real rocket ship.'

Jube and Big Dave begin to laugh. Clutching their stomachs, they laugh until tears streak their cheeks.

'A rocket ship!' wheezes Jube.

'Of all the things!' roars Big Dave.

That's when Benny remembers the package the delivery man handed him. He hops down onto the lawn and walks over to the step where he left it. Gran Donna is still standing there, stuffing tobacco into her pipe. Standing beside her, Benny picks the package up and peels the tape off. Carefully he unfolds the paper.

Inside it is a box. He opens the lid and pulls out its contents: a black plastic panel covered in buttons. He turns it around so he can read the labels on the buttons. With the tip of his index finger, he presses one.

He watches as the door of the rocket ship slides closed.

'Hey!' shouts Jube, but it's hard to hear her from behind the reinforced metal door. A clanging noise accompanies her shouts: Big Dave must be bashing his fists against the inner walls.

Benny presses another button, and the motor begins to roar. The rocket ship shudders. Flames flicker from the hole at its base. Slowly, it lifts off the ground.

Benny watches as it ascends into the hazy sky, quickly gaining speed. Up it goes past the roof, past the tallest trees, past the misty clouds. Up past the last migrating birds, past the jumbo jet flight path, past the moon that looks as small, from here, as the painted white moons on the tips of Jube's fingernails.

In the middle of the lawn, smoke drifts from the charred circle of grass.

When at last the rocket ship is a tiny speck, a morsel, an eyelash in the sky, Benny crouches and swings back his arm. He tosses the remote control out beyond the garden and towards the sea. He turns to face his grandmother with his knees still bent, his whole body shaped like an inverted question mark: the crescent of his legs and torso, the oval of his head.

'Well?' he asks her.

It has started to rain again. Fat droplets sizzle on the burning grass. Gran Donna looks at Benny. She strikes a match on the matchbox cupped in her floury palm. She lights her pipe. She sucks at it deeply, and says not a single word.

Going Down Swinging

Underwater

Romy Ash

'What do you reckon it's about?' she says.

'Yeah,' he says, looking up from his mobile for a moment, then back to the screen.

'My dream,' she says, but he doesn't reply.

She looks out the train window. Futons are hung out over sunny balcony railings. It seems strange that futons are flung out for all to see when on the train everyone's books have privacy covers on them. She thinks about asking her brother about it, but he sits up suddenly.

'Change here,' he says. He's begun to speak like this, in simplified English, even to her. She follows him out the doors, which on this old train open as slowly as a yawn. The air is hot and stinky, like bad breath.

She is the eldest, but here she follows him a step behind. When they were kids she always made him hold her hand whenever they crossed the road to the beach. Her brother let her, but when they reached the curb he would throw her hand away from him, disgusted.

She follows at his heel along the platform, down into the underpass and then back up again into the light. They stand behind the line. They have a strange collection of bags, a little esky, beach towels.

The next train arrives and they step on. They sit down across from one another, him facing the way they are going, the esky an awkward square between their legs.

'*Ohio goziamas,*' she says, to practise but also because she knows the mispronunciation will annoy him. Annoying him is a habit she finds impossible to break.

'It's *mus,*' he says, and she smiles to herself.

'*Mus, mus, mus, mus, mus. Ohio goziamas.*'

'*Mus.*'

'*Mus.*' She tastes the sound in her mouth. Their esses sounded like snakes hissing.

'*Mus,*' he says.

'I'm saying *mus,*' she says, and rolls her eyes. He takes out his mobile. 'How much longer to the beach?' she asks.

'A while.'

*

A giant blue blow-up slide makes a triangular silhouette against the horizon. Through it is the flat expanse of water, little waves lapping at the shoreline. They have settled on grass in the shade of the concrete underpass. There is a wide lick of sand between the grass and the water. Her brother has a hibachi out and lit. He lays four silver fish on the heat. Their skin sizzles and spits.

'I'm hot,' she says. He looks pointedly at her. She's still wearing all her clothes. He's stripped down to board shorts and is applying sunscreen. She looks down at her arms, at the marks on them – bruises in the shape of fingerprints, her boyfriend's hands. She licks her finger and tries to rub one off, but it stays there, persistent.

'What does it matter? They stare anyway,' her brother says.

She peels her shirt and pants off, and quickly lies down on her towel. She can feel each bruise, even with her eyes closed. On the top of her thigh, the corner of the kitchen table. Each place where his hands had grabbed and squeezed and pushed her away. A bright blue bruise blooms out from under the top of her swimsuit. That one from pulling her back in. Some are an older, dirty crayon yellow.

*

She had mewled kitten-like over the phone to her brother, curled up on the floor around her bruises. Her brother had said,

'You sound like sorrow,' in that strange way he'd begun to talk. 'Get on a plane. I've booked you tickets. You've just got to get on.' Then he'd hung up. She had felt quite clearly that this was the last time anyone would try to help her, and that if she didn't go she would stay on the floor forever.

*

She feels someone looking and opens her eyes. A man with his goggles still on. He's dripping water.

'Where are you from?' he says in heavily accented English.

Her brother wipes sweat from his face and looks up at him. He answers in a long string of Japanese, the syllables sounding to her like gunfire: bang, bang, bang, bang.

The man looks across to the blow-up slide and says, 'It's a nice day, isn't it?' Her brother answers in Japanese. The man in the goggles leans down to the barbeque and picks a sizzling fish off the grill with his fingertips, grabbing its burnt tail, silver-black in the sun. He crunches it in his mouth. With his goggles he looks reptilian. He walks away without saying goodbye.

'Was that rude?' she says.

'I said he could have a little fish.'

'I don't understand anything.' She sighs.

'There are so many men like him here,' her brother says, putting his hat over his face. From within the hat he says, muffled, 'Lonely.'

She closes her eyes. She can only hear the sound of the cars on the overpass above. It's the same sound a waterfall makes, a booming hush. She can't hear the sound of the little waves on the beach at all.

'Let's go for a swim,' her brother says.

*

The water is a cloudy brown, though it had looked blue from the beach. It feels thick around her legs. Japanese float like flotsam, on rings and blow-up mattresses, inert, fingers trailing in the water. There's no current, just a dirty stretch of water right out to the tankers lining up to go into the port: on the horizon they look small as toys in bathwater.

'I don't know if I can do it,' she says, hovering, arms out, trying not to touch the water. A plastic bag floats towards her.

'Maybe it will be better a bit further out.' He has his hands in the water. His arms look brown and sinewy as beef jerky. She feels glowing white, straight from winter to this humidity, this air so wet that everyone carries a little white towel around with them to mop the sweat.

He walks out further until he loses his footing and is forced to swim. She follows, and because she's short she has to start swimming almost straight away. The water feels like a hug from someone large and strange. She thinks she might cry.

'It's not better out here,' he says. 'Don't put your head under.'

She looks back at the shore. A girl bobs in front of her, a bubblegum-pink floaty ring around her waist. She is wearing perfect make-up.

'I've got to get out,' she says.

They swim back in. She unwinds a plastic bag from her foot at the shore: she holds it as it disgorges brown water but can't decide what to do with it. She looks at the beach, at the water. She gulps air and drops the bag to the ground. The water claims it back, and it looks like it belongs there.

'Why did we come here?' she says.

'I didn't know it would be like this.'

'It's awful.'

'It's not Australia,' he says, and starts to walk back up the beach, leaving her there alone.

She picks a strand of noodle-like weed off her arm and begins to cry. Swimming has always cured her of hangover, melancholy, tiredness. She's grown up making her decisions underwater, in the quiet there, or out the back past the breakers, with the water surging around her and the about-to-break waves lifting her way up high and back down again. This is the first time that swimming has made things worse.

*

A girl is smiling and walking towards her. She must be about fifteen but she wears a childish one-piece swimsuit. She stands out among the other teenage girls who walk across the sand, crippled in their heels, fingernails painted into bejewelled claws, triangles of cloth over their bits.

'I can't believe to find you here,' the girl says in an American accent.

'Pardon?'

'This is my grandmother,' the girl says, offering a wrinkled version of herself, a twin with the juice sucked out of her.

'Hello,' the grandmother says. They are both wet, dripping pools onto the sand.

'Do I know you?' she says and laughs, her tears gone.

'I can help you,' the girl replies and takes her hand, gently pulling her back towards the sea.

She looks behind her, but she can't see her brother or pick out their towels among the bright patchwork beneath the overpass. She follows the girl and the grandmother closes in behind.

They are nearing the slippery slide. She can hear people screaming as they careen down it. Plastic blue against the plastic blue sky. A very tall Japanese man turns to her: he's wearing Okanui shorts and a Hawaiian shirt, and a large golden cross hangs on his hairless chest. He smiles.

'My father,' the girl says. As she speaks she squeezes her hand reassuringly.

'Come,' he says.

The girl releases her hand and the father puts his arms around her shoulders.

'We're baptising people,' the girl says, her face hiding nothing in the bright sunlight.

'Really?' She nearly says it in Japanese: *honto ni.*

'Yeah!' the girl says. 'It's so exciting.' She does a little jump in the sand.

The father's hands on her shoulders are hot and heavy. She tries to shrug them off. He squeezes her. She looks up at him and he's blocking out the sun.

'I'm sorry. My English very bad. God speak all languages,' he says, and switches to Japanese.

*

He is walking her to the water; she looks back, trying to catch sight of her brother. A semicircle of people holding hands surrounds her. The girl and the grandmother grip one another. They all have faces too bright with smiles. The water licks her toes. He walks her deeper until the bottom of his shorts are wet, and she is holding hands with the water. The people push in closer around them.

His hands on her shoulders, he leans down and deftly knocks her legs out from under her. He has her like a baby now. The water is cradled around her. She smells his aftershave and rotten weed.

'Come now,' he says, and pushes her under. She tries to protest, gets a mouthful of warm water. She holds her breath, blowing out her nose. His arms are unmoving as pylons, impervious to her struggles. It's dark. She waits for him to lift her back up out of there.

The water is warm, and she makes little circles with her hands. She feels something: a tendril of weed, she imagines, but then it feels like scales, slippery scales.

Breath starts to burn in her chest. Still he holds her down, cradling her body. She kicks up, tries to grab at him, to scream. She relaxes – and begins to breathe the water. Her brain buzzes with the hot hum of cicadas.

*

Suddenly she feels her brother's hand wrenching her out of the water. Everything is bright. Her feet find the ocean floor and she vomits brown liquid.

She looks around. Her brother is clutching her hand. The semicircle is broken, and the priest's Hawaiian shirt is dark with water. No one is smiling. The priest is firing Japanese phrases at her brother, angry.

'Hey,' she says, 'you're hurting me.'

Her brother loosens his grip but doesn't let go, and she sees he is crying.

'It's okay,' she says.

She touches him gently on the back and they walk through the group, sand gripping their feet. He follows her.

They find themselves back at their towels, and she gathers up their belongings. They leave, the water drying crisp and salty new skins.

Griffith Review

A Willowy Woman

Marion Halligan

She is a woman who flirts with priests. I have been around churches long enough to recognise one of them when I see her. A genre, rather than a stereotype, and within that her own particular characteristics, her own individuality.

A woman who flirts with priests is not to be confused with a priest's housekeeper, pronounced with a certain intonation. The one flirts, the other sleeps with him. Thus helping him keep his vow of celibacy. A lot of people don't know that being celibate is nothing to do with not having sex but with not being married. Had there been more housekeepers available perhaps there would have been less material for the husband Eric's book on tender young men who tried but failed to become priests. That whole lost generation which is responsible for the emptiness of the priesthood these days. Housekeepers housekeep, they clean and iron and cook, they share the clean-sheeted master bed, and sometimes they produce children but then the system's gone wrong, celibacy is designed for the non-production of children, so the priest can keep his mind and his energies on his flock. The housekeeper might be young and even pretty, or else cosy and middle-aged, possibly one and then the other. I am speaking of course of the ideal. She will often love him and he her. But priests can be boozy horse-racing creatures who smell of smoke. Not nice to be near. Of course so are some husbands. Certain priests are known to molest small boys and sometimes small girls. How much safer to have a comfortable housekeeper. Why not. Everyone deserves the comfort of skin touching skin in the soft spaces of the double bed.

Flirting with priests is a very ancient art (well, so is the housekeeping, you'd have to say) and one which has provided many women with an artless hobby, so it has seemed. A given is purity on both sides. Physical purity, purity of deed, is one thing, and can normally be ascertained unless the protagonists are exceptionally clever and secretive. But mental or spiritual purity is another. I've observed these things carefully. It is possible to be pure in word, but what about intention? A cup of tea is a hostessly act, but what about the heart in the hand that passes it? What gets mixed into the cakes, what seasons the casseroles? The spoon turns, the fork stirs ... passions and longings and yearnings translate from hearts to hands to the mixtures shaped with desire. The tender thoughtful priest is the vessel of God's love. The husband is not sensitive; not a brute, perhaps, though he may be, but he is not a vessel of love to be held in delicate cradling hands; he is mundane, he is not precious. Or there is no husband, simply a space, an emptiness waiting to be filled with the overflowings of the vessel of love.

Of course there is already an odour of antiquity about this. Lavender scented like linen in a glory box. Maybe in small towns and villages, you will say, but surely not in city parishes, priests aren't what they were and women work, they do not arrange cucumber sandwiches on oblong plates with oblong doyleys to fit. There is something anthropological about this. The next time a young woman finds in her mother's drawers or her grandmother's these odd small oblongs crocheted in cream thread or embroidered on white linen that she won't have seen even her grandmother use, she will not know they are for lining plates of cucumber sandwiches. There are still old women who know this. And there are still priests and parishes and women who yearn to make gifts of love.

And the priest is after all a bachelor and of some long standing; he needs womanly care. Like the widower who, looked after for so long by a wife, cannot be left alone. A wife dies, look out for the women bearing casseroles. You could write a thesis about widowers' casseroles. Like food in fairy stories and old tales, they are not what they seem. Proserpine's pomegranate, Snow White's apple, Hansel and Gretel's gingerbread house, the casseroles brought to widowers by helpful women, they are a trap, they will drop you right in it, be warned before you take a mouthful.

We talk about these things, over the flowers, voices soft but messages clear, as we primp the vases, quite a lot of them there are, in a church this size, and the glorious blooms from rich old gardens. The ancient rituals are by no means dead.

Of course Vanessa was not a woman for making cakes or stewing up casseroles. Nor for arranging flowers in churches. Tea was not her thing. A cup of strong coffee in a small cup, a tidy whisky in a crystal tumbler, even a glass of good red; she was a sophisticated woman.

Here is what she looked like. She was tall and appeared slender; she arranged her body so you noticed this fact. In her mind (oh, I have observed her) her body is willowy. It is pliable, it bends, it twines. Willows are anthropomorphic, they shake out their green hair like mermaid's tresses, they dance in the breeze. Willowy: we all want to be willowy. Any woman in the world, you ask her, I bet she'd say willowy.

There are things you could say about willows. You don't want to let them near your drains, otherwise you'll find yourself spending a fortune on plumbers. Those delicate weaving tendrilly roots will find their way into the toughest of sewer pipes and block them solider than concrete, your lavatory will brim over, your dishwasher flood the kitchen, the washing machine waste well back. Admire willows from a distance, so beautiful, so useful, for aspirin and cricket bats and in the past for tying parcels, but keep them out of your gardens unless you live in a Capability Brown-sized park.

Her face is long and bony; you can suppose she was handsome once in a horsy way. She never shows any skin to speak of. The willowy body is long and bony too but nobody ever sees that, it's always enfolded in layers of fabric that cling and smooth and float, in scarves that wind and slip, in skirts cut on the bias that swirl about her black-stockinged legs in shoes with heels high enough to give her that slightly difficult vulnerable walk that is the point of high heels.

Ethereal. I reckon that's a word she's embraced for herself. The slippery diaphanous fabrics. The hair. Fair hair. Not blonde or bright: pale.

Once it had been reddish gold; now she has it done just pale. We all grow out of the reddish gold. It's fuzzy. She pins it in a knot on the top of her head and tendrils escape, curling on her neck, floating round her face. She bends her long thin neck and the little kiss curls touch the heart. A cloud of hair, you could say. Every now and then it will slip out of its knot and then with languid impatient fingers she twists it up again and skewers it with an antique tortoiseshell comb. In her youth she went to mass in a mantilla, but nobody does that anymore.

Willowy. Ethereal. A cloud of hair. None of these things is true of people. But some people make you believe them.

Oh, Vanessa, the flower ladies say. They purse their lips, or narrow them. Oh, Vanessa. You can see them not speaking ill. If you haven't something nice to say, don't say anything.

Her air is helpless, but this is a deception. She is cunning and clever and always gets her own way. You see I am not a good woman like the flower ladies. The flower ladies ... they sound like a chorus out of a Gilbert and Sullivan operetta.

Vanessa. Once when I was still in her good books we drank tiny cups of coffee and she told me – probably more than she wishes she had. That she didn't care for the name Vanessa. Something of a cross to bear, she said. It was invented. Not like a saint's name. Invented by a clergyman, indeed, but it was so he could write to his mistress Esther Vanhomrigh in a secret way, and he wasn't a particularly religious clergyman, not a Catholic, a very secular Anglican. Dean Swift belonged to a time when preferment was political.

Esther Vanhomrigh: you sort of invert it and you get Vanessa.

Wasn't he into eating babies? I asked, and Vanessa said, Oh no. But I was sure he was, he wrote an essay about it.

It was satire, said Vanessa.

Vanessa said she thought that at least Esther was a good Jewish name, but it turned out to be Persian, meaning a little star. Father Bede told her that. He said it's another form of Ishtar, the Babylonian goddess of love. Ishtar the goddess of love, said Father Bede. That cannot be of interest to me, she said. (See how she flirts with priests?) It's idolatrous, she said. I sometimes think I could be an idolator, said Father Bede.

It turned out Father Bede had this idea in his head for some time before he mentioned it to Vanessa. Then he called her Ishtar, and she gave little moues of distress, I saw her. And maybe it was clever of him to make this connection, for Ishtar is a fierce and terrible creature, whereas Vanessa appears all gentleness and meek eyes. Ishtar is the goddess of war as well as of love. You'll notice this if you cross her. Vanessa, I mean. Priests never do. She never lets them.

She has children but they are grown-up and live in another city. So does her husband. But they are not separated. They are devoted spouses. So she will tell you. His name is Eric and his surname is different from hers. He's the headmaster of a distinguished school for boys. Not a Catholic school since he isn't a religious. He had been for a while in his youth, had spent several years with the Jesuits, and when he retires he's going to write that book about why so many gentle clever ardent young men of his generation had tried to become priests and failed. As I've remarked, a sentence would explain that, a word even. You don't need a book.

Being devoted to your husband but not wanting to live with him strikes me as curious. But I am no longer on good enough terms with Vanessa to ask. She purports to love the city he lives in, to find the one she lives in tedious, but still, here she is.

She occupies a small city flat in an old warehouse. Small in floor space but considerable in volume since it is lofty. Her bed is on a mezzanine, climbed up to by a ladder. She is limber enough for this. Where the money comes from no one seems to know; she doesn't seem to earn any. Perhaps Eric pays. Perhaps she has a private income. Nobody in this country ever supposes that a person might have a private income, but in fact they do, on occasion.

I happen to know that at least two of the flower ladies have private wealth. They come from families who made a lot of money in ways that could well be doubtful, and have left this to be paid in pleasant regular sums to their children. This is one reason why they have the leisure to be flower ladies. Highly prosperous husbands is another.

On the other hand, Vanessa purports to be doing something, and that is writing a history of the Irish and Catholicism. This is a highly intellectual activity; it needs a lot of talking about, a lot of planning. Especially with priests. Are any words written? Who knows? I may suspect, but I do not know. Any work of the intellect needs a lot of thinking about, beforehand. She never has written anything, but that's not to say she won't.

Perhaps you will be thinking I have not given much evidence of this flirting with priests I keep mentioning. It is very delicate. She has a particular way of touching them; she stands close and puts out her hand – against their chests, on their sleeves – but doesn't actually connect. She almost does, and a nervous person might flinch, but the contact is not made. It is a kind of hovering. Like royalty, their persons are sacrosanct. And it is quite thrilling, this possibility, this suggestion, this mirroring of touch. It is more powerful than the actual meeting of hand and body would be, because it insists that it be in the mind. It makes its own warm place, as though a kind of radiance of connection has been made. I think when I observe it that it has a kind of violence in it, and yet anyone would insist on the chastity of her gesture.

She seems helpless, and is not, but people do not know that. She is devout and respectful, as in that not-touching. She is a handmaiden. So it is safe for them to enjoy her company. So they believe. But she is an opportunity, occasion, vessel, of temptation. She leads them astray. They believe it is her piety and her intellectual approach to it that they are responding to but it is her woman's body in its modest but deceiving draperies and her meek eyes whose guilelessness is only a veil.

Watch her, across the room. The occasion: the launch of Anthony Tindale's book. The lean elderly Jesuit has finally produced the promised fat tome. He smiles his abbot-by-the-fish-pond smile. Vanessa stands beside him as though refusing to take any credit for the great oeuvre. He is a very holy man and this is the distillation of his years. He reads a poem; he is famous as a poet as well. It is elegant and difficult and nobody is quite sure about it. He wears half-moon spectacles on the end of his finely chiselled nose, holds the book up and gestures with his long-fingered white hand. His voice is deep and beautiful, so you can listen to this and not worry about what the poem means.

Father Bede is the master of ceremonies. He is a stocky young man, with dark curls and fine white skin with a round red spot on each cheek that burns more brightly when he is excited. You want to put out your hand and feel if it is hot. Maybe Vanessa's not-touching would feel the radiance.

Vanessa sits on a low chair. As is her wont she puts out an arm and snaffles a passing child and cuddles it on her lap. She sits with her back to the light so it shines through her fuzzy hair, haloing her shadowed face, and bends her long neck at that willowy angle and murmurs in its ear. Charming woman, says the bishop who is seated nearby. Charming woman.

Vanessa's lids veil her eyes. She glances sidelong from under them. People seem to think this is a pious look. I reckon it's sly. Her lips form a faint tender smile. *If you see a crocodile don't forget to scream,* the little children sing. I feel like screaming.

Anthony Tindale murmurs to Father Bede: A good woman is a pattern of the Virgin Mary, regard, how she is here amongst us for a moment as fallen women reflect her glory. Something like that. How true, murmurs Father Bede back.

The chid is less keen, and wriggles off as soon as it can. Vanessa looks around for another one. The escaped child picks up one of the books being launched and carries it back to her mother. Book, she says loudly, with terrifyingly pure vowel and consonants. As toddlers do she trips over her own feet and drops the book on the bishop's foot and then falls on top of it. The bishop shouts and then says in a soft but penetrating voice, Fuck. The child's mother snatches her away and Vanessa's lids fly open, her eyes rounding. She recovers, and hovers her hand over the bishop's knee.

I know what's wrong with him. A friend of mine looks after him. He has a tendency to gout but doesn't like people to know. That's why he wears those baggy wide shoes that look a bit like Goofy's in Walt Disney. Mostly he's all right but occasionally he suffers. I know about the pain of gout; it's excruciating. The faintest touch is unbearable, but a heavy book, a heavy child – seems to me a quiet fuck is really rather restrained. Of course the bishop is used to making his soft voice heard. Father Bede brings him a glass of red wine and he drinks it down as though it would cure him.

Vanessa stands up to talk to Father Bede. She stands close to him, so that he has to arch his body to avoid touching her, so he seems to be bending over her, as though he is the one trying to get close. She lowers her lids again, tips her head back so she can see him. Her hand sketches the surface of his cassock. She is speaking hesitantly, as though too shy to say what she means. At such moments she is inclined to lisp.

I'm sure she is a nice woman, says Enid, my friend who looks after the bishop. Very kind, really, and truly devout.

No she isn't. She isn't. She is the dirtiest fighter in the game, totally selfish, only interested in her own advancement. I don't say this to Enid. I know I will only make myself look mean and petty. Quite possibly, is all I allow myself to say. I think: she is a crocodile.

Advancement? you wonder. She edits the *Catholic Times*, which is a surprisingly serious journal. I used to do this but she took it over. That said, she doesn't do a very good job; the old team including me still do the work but she takes the credit.

I have to confess my husband found her rather cute. She is quite a wonderful woman, in her way, he said. If you like that kind of thing, I said. He smiled. He was always quite sweet to me. That conversation was not long before he left me for a man. Or men, rather. As politely as ever. So I don't know that I know what it means.

The mother is still holding the book. The child says *book* again, in her firm clear voice. Father Bede nods at it: Are you going to buy it? he asks her.

The woman shakes her head in horror and puts it back on the stand. Anthony Tindale on *The numinous in a daily world* at sixty dollars a copy is not her thing. Looking interested at a book launch is one thing, buying let alone reading quite another.

Vanessa buys it and gets him to sign it, pointing her long crocodile (all right, my imagination, but I can see it) face at him, keeping her teeth hidden, masking her fishy breath. I'm not making that up; her breath does have an odd fishy odour. She slaps on a lot of Dior's Diorissimo but it doesn't help. I know that's what it is because I asked her.

Lovely scent, I said, what is it? Diorissimo, she said. I suppose she was telling the truth.

She's back to Father Bede. Seductively saying something. He frowns slightly, looks around. Looks back at her, his brow smooths, he smiles and walks off with her, she leaning into him, her hand hovering, still not touching. She has a room in this complex of buildings, an old convent, most of which is no longer needed for its original intent. The book launch is here in the old refectory, a large room with beams, with windows made of panes of coloured glass; very new world I always think it is, imitation somehow, not very convincing. But a good space. The journal has an office here, and she has a sort of study in which to write the great work. I assume that's where they are going.

I suppose you think I might sidle off, slip up to the door, knock and throw it open in one swift gesture. No, of course not. What do you think I am? What she gets up to in there is her own business. I say I don't think it's anything. She doesn't want to sleep with priests, she wants to flirt with them, pull them to her, hold them by her.

Later, when I am leaving, I walk past her room. The door is open and she is sitting at the desk, he in an armchair on the other side, a brightly coloured Turkish rug under his feet, a cut glass tumbler of I suppose whisky in his hand. She is leaning forward, speaking softly. She gives a little laugh in her throat. The kind, if you heard through a wall, you would think, I know what's going on, in there.

*

Time passes. The book progresses, she says. She has been busy judging a prize for religious writing, open to any faith. There's a committee, my friend William who is on it complains that she takes no notice of any of them. They are not at all happy with the choices she is making, he says, but they don't know what they can do about it. None of them likes to make a fuss so she will doubtless have her way. That is how it goes.

And then she is gone. Her husband had been offered a visiting chair at one of the New York Catholic colleges and suddenly she is off with him. Not living with him in the city of his boys' school is one thing, New York clearly another. She sends us all mass emails, blog-like spiels, nothing personal, describing the delights of life there. She is a parishioner at the cathedral of New York, St Patrick's, in Fifth Avenue. Vast new fields of priests to flirt with, I expect. Pastures new.

Other People

Matt Gabriel

The rental market is tight, an article in this morning's paper tells me. It is not the first time I have read this. Newspapers publish articles like my uncle tells stories. There is an accompanying photo of a real estate agent with only half his eyebrows. It makes me a little nauseous over breakfast. To his side is an inset textbox. A series of dot points reads: booming population, high demand in inner-city stock, continuing investor confidence.

I only finish reading it because we put up an ad in a bookshop window yesterday afternoon. It described us as friendly and considerate. As soon as it went up, my phone didn't stop ringing. I only answered the first three times. Each person had plagarised our adjectives. They repeated them twice in their initial description of themselves without synonyms and then once more as they said goodbye to reinforce the message. I got suspicious that people were using a guide to answering rental ads in a tight market and didn't pick up the phone again.

Beth is in the kitchen. She's pouring cold coffee into a pan. She tries to convince me that, if we want to fill the room, I am going to have to return the missed calls. This is in place of my preferred method, continuing to ignore them. In the past, when I was on the other side and looking for a new room, I always felt relief hearing the call I'd made ring out. I could apply this generally for my telephone conversations, or the lack of them. For me, the trying fulfills my end of the obligation. I never expect people to call back. I'd go so far as saying I feel good when they don't. I often assume other people are like me.

It's been said I have confidence issues. Beth reminds me that on the phone I am the one in control and that I shouldn't let people turn my shit around. My therapist is also helping me with this. She gets me to visualise my imagined masculine ideal. I can't help but think of Steve McQueen. She sometimes doubts whether it's confidence where my issues lie.

That said, I am bare-chested and standing poolside in my compound. I am somewhere in Beverly Hills. Feeling better, I call the first number. I try to organise a time for them to come over on Tuesday, but there is a foreboding sense that they have already turned my shit around. I watch Beth pour half the reheated coffee back into my cup. My Californian sunshine fades. The guy on the line is looking at houses today and insists on coming over this afternoon. I say the kind of 'yeah' that means 'not really.' He replies with a 'great' that says 'I will be outside your gate soon.'

I say my housemate will be out this afternoon. Steve leaves me and is somewhere shaking his head and grabbing the keys to his shit-hot Mustang. Beth rolls her eyes at me. She mouths, 'Hold onto it, Steve.' I appreciate the support, but Beth obviously can't hear the roar of the Mustang's engine.

'Two o'clock is perfect,' he says. He just wants to check out the space. I try to suggest that there is no point if Beth and I aren't both in. He asks me some more questions about the 'space' on the phone. I wish he would call it a room or maybe a home.

He is a remedial masseur. He has a list of requirements. These are not for him, but necessary for making his clients feel comfortable. I am not listening because I am thinking about the naked people in towels walking through my house. I think about our lounge room full of the pained, injured and lonely, waiting for their professional touch-up. The nakedness changes its hue. The thought of all that expectation starts my nausea churning again. I tell him the room is really small and not suitable for his clients. He says he will loft his living space and multi-utilise its functionality. I have lived in the room. I tell him that you can't fit a queen-size bed in there, but it fits a double. He doesn't understand that I am euphemistically telling him that the room is the size of a double bed and barely facilitates the function of a nightly sleep. He interrupts and asks me to describe the layout of the house. His clients require a bathroom outside the general living area. Since we didn't put 'must have a small business to set up in our home' in the ad, I assume it's part of a remedial masseur's habitat to set up practice in their nesting grounds.

I am imagining naked strangers in my house again, but this time I am back poolside and I am Steve McQueen and I am not interested in the other, less attractive naked people anymore. I tell him it won't work. He has a studio he can work from in the city is his reply. I am unnerved. He almost sounded vulnerable, a touch desperate. At this point, I wish I had hung up, but I don't because as quickly as Steve returns, he's leaving the building again. The vulnerability I heard was indigestion. The masseur punctuates his response with a short series of smothered burps. He then informs me that our location is central enough for him to compromise on certain requirements. I'm not sure if I owe him one for this, but I feel like I do. I find myself booking him in, so that he can check out the space. He insists on two o'clock this afternoon.

I realise I don't know his name, so I ask. It sounds like a variation on Josh, although I am not certain. I ask him to spell it. I look at the letters I have written on the pad. S, C, H, T and S. I repeat them for him. He corrects me by repeating his name. It sounds like a variation on Josh. I ask him if his name is Josh. He says if it's easier for me to pronounce, then he is fine with Josh. I like to get a person's name right, so I insist on calling him Schts when I say goodbye.

When I hang up, Beth asks me where the hell Steve went. I answer by asking her if she will be home this afternoon. I explain the situation. She says he sounds like a creep. I question the objectivity of the way I have portrayed Schts to her. I feel sorry for other people sometimes, but I know him moving in isn't going to work. I message him this. He calls straight back. I let the phone ring out. The phone beeps a forewarning of his voicemail message. My coffee has gone cold again. Beth listens to the message. She tells me he has one more question and that he wants me to call him back. I know the question. I don't need to call him.

*

By Tuesday, Schts is back. He booked in with Beth to check out the space. He used the name Seth. Also, he is no longer a remedial masseur. He is a myotherapist who works in the city. Beth said she didn't like him at first, but that she changed her mind. A myotherapist she assumed worked with the vision impaired, but didn't ask. I understand, career people are strangely offended when you haven't heard of their professional specialisations. I also defer to pretending I know.

I knew it was Schts by the way he pronounced Seth. I return his introduction with 'Hi Josh. Nice to meet you.' He flinches, but only slightly. I say it more for Beth's benefit. She doesn't seem to pick up the significance. I try to stay on the front foot, as they say in the sports, and declare that we have already decided on someone. Beth gives me a surprised look. She laughs and asks who. I find her tone unsupportive. I say Calvin. She laughs harder this time.

She says, 'What, that French guy? The one who could only describe everything as either fucking boring or fucking stupid?' She does a pretty good impression of Calvin and punctuates this comment with another laugh. I even find myself giggling. Josh takes the opportunity to turn to me and smile. It's giggly too, but strangely he hasn't met Calvin. He walks past us both and into the house.

I pull Beth aside and tell her that this Seth guy is really Schts, who also goes by the name Josh. She gives me a look. It says to me, Why did you give that creep our address? I tell her to call her friend Victor. He can come over and pretend he is another person looking for a room. I also think that Victor can be especially mean and will protect us from this guy pretending to be Seth. Beth says that I just want to invite Victor around because I think he is a bigger arsehole than this Josh guy. She's right, but I say it isn't true. She doesn't believe me but still calls Victor. I go inside.

Josh is smiling at me again. His smile is saying, I forgive you, or perhaps it's just that he has no idea we have talked before. Either way I wish he would stop because I can't help but smile back. I have no idea what my smile is saying. I might be at this moment inviting him to carve his initials into my forehead. Thankfully, he just asks about the furniture. He wants to know whose it is. I say Beth's. He says he loves it, but his is much nicer. It's newer. This confuses me a little. He informs me it's in storage, but this is perfect because Beth can share the storage space. It will halve the cost. I tell him that we haven't decided who will move in yet. I am smiling at him. Without trying I think my smile is telling him I might carve my initials into his forehead. He says he has a technique. His technique is projecting. Projecting helps him to get where he needs to be. He is writing a book about it. If I had his technique I assume that I could think of better places to project, but maybe it doesn't work like that. I'm not really interested in buying the book to find out.

I am out of questions before I have a chance to ask him one. I think he is too, so we stand and look at each other. He breaks first. He is distracted and runs his finger over the top of the stereo. I say something banal about being close to trams creating a lot of dust. I fill the next awkward silence by asking if he would like a drink. I'm reminded of first dates. A first date at which the participants realise there is no attraction between them. In general, politeness dictates that both of you must wait at least thirty minutes before making excuses. We abide by this masochism of manners. I think of my parents.

Josh asks if he can see the other room. I suggest we wait for Beth. He says the kitchen needs a complete clean out. He will organise the schedule. He likes that kind of thing. He was once a personal assistant. His use of the past tense shocks me, but also gives me hope. He must have had a better offer somewhere else. I ask him if he has seen any other good houses. He answers by telling me he is a fantastic cook. He informs me that he cooks three times a week. I don't ask which days. He always shares his food, but Beth and I will need to give him money for ingredients. He explains that this will mean we needn't feel like we have to reciprocate.

I break. I tell Josh that the interview is over. It just won't work. We are seriously different people and Beth and I are really looking for someone a bit more relaxed and accommodating. He looks shocked. He asks if he can ask one more question. My silence tells him he can try. He does. In a genuinely concerned voice, he says, 'Do you let anything touch you? I mean really reach you, or are you so used to it by now that nothing really touches you?'

It doesn't quite make sense considering the context, so I answer, 'You believe what you want. You work your side of the street and I'll work mine.'

Actually, I lied. I didn't break. I just let Josh wander upstairs and found myself daydreaming about Steve McQueen again.

I notice Beth still hasn't come in from the back. I go looking for her. I want to tell her I have things to do. I am trying to think of what those things are. I look out the back of the house. She has left. I decide I need proper coffee and leave too.

At the café, Beth is sitting with Victor. She isn't happy to see me. I tell her that the Josh guy is just checking out the rooms upstairs, but he won't be too long. I try to make my intonation say, 'Me and Josh have made a deal that he will lock up after he leaves.' She accuses me of locking a snowdropper in our house. I'm not sure what that is, so I ask. It makes her angrier. I assure her he is not interested in our underwear, unless compelled to reorder and launder them and charge us for the favour.

By the time we have finished our coffees we order some beers and we are talking about where we think Josh comes from. Victor, having ignored me for the most part, is kind of interested now. Beth puts forward the theory that he waits around in IKEA for the store to close and each night chooses a themed area to act out his sickest of domestic fantasies. I say that he is a terrible mythical tale told to children and he hides in unmade beds waiting till dinner time and then appears uninvited and expecting a place set for him and murders the whole family with stories of his time organising others as a PA. Victor says that he is giardia incarnate and lives up people's arses and fills rooms full of stench in the most unexpected social situations. I feel Victor has gone too far, but I am afraid to say this and laugh anyway. I think of Josh as a bad habit that we all have but wish we didn't. We then go to great lengths to hide it from others or sometimes from ourselves. I think the beer is making me feel a little nostalgic for his company.

It's been a while, so I convince everyone it's time to go back to the house by offering to buy some more beer on the way. We all agree that he must have left by now, although when we get back no one is willing to move beyond the kitchen. We keep drinking and try not to mention Josh. It's not long before we hear a noise from upstairs. It's loud enough to stop our conversation. We all look worried, then laugh, then look worried again. He is waiting and he isn't happy. Victor directs this towards me. I say it's nothing, but my voice comes out high-pitched and vibrato. Victor looks in the drawer and tells me the kitchen knife is missing. The nervy high-pitched squeaky vibrato he uses is very similar to mine. This time the smile standoff is between Victor and me. I notice Victor's eyes slowly appraising the rising colour in my face. His look is locked on the dial of my body temperature. I can't stop him turning it up. I think of asking to look in the drawer, but I am sure Victor has pocketed the knife himself. I think it would be safer in Josh's hands.

There is another noise from upstairs. It's more of a pitter-patter. Victor asks whether we have seen *The Brood* and suggests that our guest has laid a nest of mutant children. Beth tells Victor to shut up. I try to remember whether the mutant kids were psychological manifestations or egg-laid. She declares she has to go to the toilet and will go up. I tell her that she can't go alone. I ask Victor to go up with us. I still think he has the knife. Not my problem, is his reply, but he also reminds me that I was the one who left the egg-laying freak alone in the house. He is right, except for the egg-laying bit. I tell them I will go, hoping that we can come to a compromise and go together. Instead Victor and Beth turn and start talking as though I have already left.

I pause at the bottom of the steps. There is a pair of gumboots by the stairs. I look back and make sure neither Beth nor Victor can see me. I put the gumboots on my hands. I can never tell when Victor is serious or not. I clasp my best karate-chop knuckles under the protective sheaths of rubber.

Upstairs there is no sign of Josh. Instead a cat is spraying what isn't Josh's room, just about where his bed won't be. I can tell this because he has roughly chalked out lines for his furniture. It looks like he moved in this afternoon and his life died under suspicious circumstances. I flick a gumboot at the cat. It misses, but makes a loud thud. The cat hisses at me. It doesn't move. I am sure in the rehearsal it runs away. I respect its tendency towards improvisation, but still toss the other gumboot. The cat then scampers out the window.

The room is now empty apart from chalk lines, a puddle of piss and a note. Josh won't be moving in, the note informs me. I'm a little taken aback. For a moment I think about the great location. The note says he did show someone else around while we were away: a woman called Irene. He has organised to sublet the room to her. The note ends with 'Give me a call to sort out the details. Seth.' There is a series of handwritten smileys running across the bottom of the page. Their bracket lips are smiling ninety degrees askew. They are in lateral position. I hear the toilet flush. I look for their vital signs. I assume I have more in common with Irene.

Meanjin

The Crow

Ashley Hay

Warm in the sun, his eyes closed, Clem thought: *What you see behind your eyelids, it's never black – black as coal, black as pitch.* He concentrated, and saw a gash of purple and a soft, round brownness, like middle distance. He tried to focus on that distance and winced; must be something that eyes weren't supposed to do. Or he was getting old. At forty-three, with his kids grown and his daughter pregnant now herself, he didn't want to think about that.

He heard the bird's claws then as they collided with the deck's railing, and opened his eyes fast to see a flash of its black feathers as it rocked a little, and steadied itself. Eyes closed again, Clem saw that flash of black across the brown darkness, and shuddered.

Crows: they made him nervous.

Back when he and Elsie were looking to buy a place, they'd walked down from Clem's mum's, up the hill on Gladstone Road, to this one – a little box at the end of a row of similar boxes, and the backyard a mess of mud and clay and paspalum. But it was new, and it might be theirs, and Elsie liked the view out through the kitchen window towards the swamp and the sky.

Skitting about among the green as they stood on the back step, a baby crow had been following its mother, mouth open, squawking.

'Look at that, Clem,' Elsie said, softly. 'I've never seen a baby crow before – their feathers glisten, don't they? Such a beautiful thing.'

Then she wanted to live in the house more than ever, and talked about it in terms of the crows – that it had been a special thing to see the baby, that it boded well, surely, for two people raising their own family. The twins were seven now, she said, and perhaps there might be another one, one day, *soon*. She blushed when she said this, the way he liked, a tiny frill of pink rising up from her chest towards her throat. She did say some silly things about adoring him for all time – he suspected she got them out of the women's magazines she read. But she was always willing for whatever he wanted in bed, and that was something, he said to himself, he'd been very happy to get used to.

The day the mortgage papers were signed, he could hardly speak for the shock of the amount they owed. They shifted down from the rooms they'd had at his mum's since they were married, seven years before, and put the twins' beds in the bigger bedroom, taking the smaller one at the back for themselves. He and a mate added the deck as the first summer came round.

'Our tropical paradise,' Elsie said, installing a palm in a pot. 'Never so fancy as to have lived somewhere with a deck before.' As if she was the practised inhabitant of any number of grand residences, rather than the young mother who'd lived in her parents' house, her mother-in-law's house, and now this weatherboard cube.

She washed the floors daily and the windows once a week, and he was careful to comment on this. Another thing to make her smile; another thing to make her blush.

'My little homemaker,' he'd say, hugging her around her waist, and then the kids would run up and burrow in as well, and he'd say something expansive about their mum. That was love, he'd thought in the middle of those moments, not whatever those silly magazines of hers said.

But she never stopped wondering about the crow – 'never saw it again, did we, love? I was so excited to have it to show Lainey and Don, but we never saw it again.'

'Must've moved away – maybe crows do that. I don't know.'

He never said, never told her about the day he and a mate had brought the bathtub – a day or so before they moved themselves in and settled the twins. Straining across the grass, the white enamel blinding him as it caught the sun, Clem had turned at a strange noise and seen a rough brown dog busy with something by the back fence.

'Take a spell, mate,' he said, lowering his end of the burden and walking towards the noise. Knew what it was before he got there, and there was the little crow, crumpled and bleating among the sticky paspalum stalks. 'Go on with you!' he shouted at the dog, his hand flinging out across its head and his voice harsh. He watched it slink back into the shadows that filled the swamp beyond.

What now? he thought. *What the devil do I do with you now?* But as he crouched down he saw the gash in the bird's body, the way its wing was creased out awkwardly from itself.

His mate was beside him then, and Clem shook his head. 'Young crow – that dog was at it. Poor blighter.' He raised his boot and stamped before he could think about it twice. It was only then that he noticed a strange silence as if every nearby bird had stopped calling.

And then the cries began, a litany of long, wide laments – *every bloody crow in the neighbourhood.* He plucked some paspalum, lining his hands before he had to touch the bird. His hands, he saw, were shaking; and that was when he remembered what he knew about crows and their mourning.

'Don't tell Elsie, ay.' He heard his voice catch as he carried the mess to the lowest corner of the yard where the dirt was moist. Scrabbling a hole, tucking the baby bird inside, he hunched his shoulders against the swoop and peck he half-expected from its mother at any moment.

Overhead, the crows' noise built and built, and then dropped away. And Clem, leaning over his brand-new diamond-wire fence, let his head drop and his stomach empty, as if every piece of food he'd ever eaten was raking itself out of his guts.

'Geez you're a soft touch,' his mate said then. 'Put it in the bin, I would've. All that fuss for a blinking crow.'

All that fuss for Elsie, thought Clem now, *and for all the crows,* watching as this new black bird balanced on the railing and eyed off his last piece of toast. He'd never told her about the little bird. He'd never told her that crows made him nervous.

Behind him, in the kitchen, she was murdering Elvis Presley's latest swooning song, her light voice losing its foothold as it dipped towards the lower notes. She'd be after Lainey to call her little one Elvis, he thought, if it was a boy. Let Elaine have the good sense to shut that idea down.

'Time for another cuppa, Clem?' she called, coming out onto the deck and pulled up short by the sight of the crow. From the corner of his eye, Clem saw her stop, and in front of him the crow tilted its own head to take her in its sights. 'You did give me a fright,' she said to the bird, and Clem knew what was coming next. 'Do you remember that morning we walked down to see the house? Remember the baby crow after its breakfast in the backyard – I've always wondered where it went. I'd've fed it the scraps, you know, watched it grow up.'

'You had the twins,' said Clem, short. 'What more watching did you want?' It ate at him, the memory of how frail the bird had felt under the heel of his boot. It ate at him that he hadn't told her all those years ago, and couldn't now, no way. 'And I never thought them crows were such a good omen anyway.' *If we'd come down half an hour earlier or later; if we'd come down the day before, we'd never have seen the bloody thing – would she have wanted the house then? Or if I'd come with the tub in the afternoon instead; that dog would've finished it off and probably eaten it as well.* She was a practical woman, his Elsie, but she did invest a lot in these small, strange things.

He knew perfectly well why crows made him nervous, and it was nothing to do with that tiny death in the sticky grass back in 1948, no. It was what he'd remembered with that wide, awful lament. He watched Elsie watch the crow as he finished his tea and held out his cup towards her offer.

'Fill this up, love, and I'll tell you a story about crows. Back when I was a kid.' The bird shuffled along the rail, first one way, then the other, as Clem heard the noise of the kettle and the tea canister coming from inside.

'When I was a boy,' Clem began, as she set the tea on the table and leaned towards his words. He could smell her hair, and it still took his breath away sometimes, to be close to her, to know her. *We're still young,* he thought, *even with all those bootees she's knitting for our first grand-kiddy.*

When Clem was a boy, his dad was one for pig-shooting, down near Lightning Ridge. First time he'd said he'd take Clem, the boy would have been only six or seven years old, and he'd spent his days fossicking around in the dust and the gravel, pulling out tiny flecks of opalled stone, their colours firing like rainbows. Clem wanted nothing to do with the shooting, the killing. The sound of the rifle and the way it jumped back against your body when it fired; the way an animal's eyes dulled down to horrible, blank milkiness when its breath stopped: these things terrified him. The chance of a bucket of treasure, that seemed to Clem a better plan for a holiday.

But out there, past Lightning Ridge, where the sky was as brilliantly blue as the incandescent lines in an opal; out there, his dad and his dad's mate had a bet on who could shoot the most creatures – pigs, primarily, they agreed, but there'd be points for anything that moved, and extra for birds.

His dad dropped a wallaby; the mate dropped two more; and Clem inched further and further away from them, busying himself with getting water, or sticks for a fire, or folding swags – anything to avoid the gun's weight, its sudden jerk, its report.

On the last morning, with the mate leading the tally by a nose and just starting to boast, Clem's dad looked up from the tea he was stirring and smiled.

'There was no warmth in that smile,' Clem said to Elsie, 'just something nasty, and hard.'

Clem's dad had set the billy on a rock, set the spoon he'd been using very carefully alongside, and reached for his gun. Propping it, adjusting it, he pursed his lips into something like a kiss. Then he pulled the trigger and fired, shooting a single crow – 'a big one, huge, its feathers so black' – from the top branch of a silvery dead gum.

'So fast,' said Clem, 'I didn't have time to cover my ears or shut my eyes.'

The crow had dropped to the ground – Clem could still hear the thud, feel the way the ground shook, and his very body seemed to shake now so that Elsie, across the table, felt some echo of the fall.

And there it lay, a tiny pile of darkness against the rich red soil.

'I was seven years old, and I couldn't hear a thing. Thought the bloody gun had deafened me. Then it started, this angry, angry sound, and all these crows were flying in, diving and wheeling. They damn near covered the whole tree, and they yelled and they wailed and they howled. Must've been a hundred of them in the end – I remember when I learnt the word cacophony in some poem at school. I knew what it meant; it was heartbreaking.'

Crouched down by the fire, Clem had watched the black shapes swoop and settle, more and more coming from as far as he could see.

'Then a dingo came too – wanting the body, you know – Dad hadn't scooped it up the way he did with pigs and roos, the stuff he called "real game." And blow me if these crows didn't go down after the dingo, swooping it and pecking until it slunk off and left them to their funeral. Most mournful sound I've ever heard, Els, like the wailing those foreign women set up when someone dies.'

In front of Clem, now, the crow startled and took flight as a truck clattered along the street, its tray laden with ironwork and scrap metal.

'The pigs, they were one thing, even the roos – and he'd never shoot one with a joey. But a crow, a crow; they're magnificent. I dunno why he would've thought to do it. Just trying to win the bet, I suppose, but it seemed so mean, so unnecessary.' Clem sat a while saying nothing, staring into the middle distance of the yard – seeing the crow, the dingo, the dead tree, the sky.

'My dad drove home without a break – petrol here and there, I suppose, I can't even remember whose truck we were in now, but I was glad of its noise. Didn't want to have to say anything. Didn't know what to tell my mum, either. But I was terrified of being taken on another shoot after that. I even wished he was dead, so I wouldn't have to go again.

'And then I was eight years old, and he *was* – pneumonia in the middle of winter, and that was it. Me and Mum, and then it was boarders, and peoples' mending coming in, and the typing she did for one of the university blokes, me going to sleep to the clicking of that ruddy machine. Still, still,' he patted Elsie's hand, 'she made me a good life, and she gave us a good home till we got sorted here. Never told her about the crow, neither. But I always wondered if it'd marked Dad somehow—'

Clem cut himself off; it was a crazy thing to think, a crazy thing to say. He drank the fresh tea and watched a couple of kookaburras fluff their feathers in the poinciana. He'd always wondered if it was his wishing his dad gone that had done that too, the pneumonia. But that was even less sayable.

They sat in silence.

'Does he still work over there, that professor your mum used to type for?' Elsie was leaning back and stretching, her hair lit by the morning sun so it shone.

Clem shrugged. 'Dunno – I never thought to look. He'd be old by now; he was older than Mum, and she'd've been heading for seventy if she was alive. I used to wonder if he was sweet on her – he'd bring her chocolate sometimes, and a card once for her birthday, which made her blush.' A different life, he thought, if your dad was a smart man, and a living one. Maybe Clem could have gone to the university instead of just polishing its floors and fixing its window sashes. He shook his head and stood up, passing the empty cup back to his wife.

'I'm off then, up to the punt. Shouldn't be late tonight, if you want to wander up and meet me.' He liked it, looking out from the barge as it crossed the river from St Lucia to Dutton Park, and seeing her there, her hair light against the shadows of the foreshore and its tall, dark trees. They'd cut through the cemetery and head home, the river turning and lapping alongside them.

'I'll do that, then,' Elsie smiled. 'And something nice for tea – a bit of lamb, or some steak, if you like.' She paused in the doorway, watching as he stretched himself. 'Maybe he was showing off, your dad. Maybe he thought it'd impress you, taking a great bird like that when it could just as easily have risen up and flown away.'

'It was never me he wanted to impress,' said Clem, shrugging his arms into his coat and feeling in its pocket for his cap. 'Just his mates, always his mates. Might've been different if I'd been older and he'd thought I could shoot something myself. But I don't think he really minded what I thought about him – don't think it occurred to him I thought anything. Nicest thing my mum ever said to me, when Don and Lainey were born, that some men were made to be fathers, and I was one of them. "Not like your Pa," she said to me, Els. "You'll not make the mess of it your Pa made." I never saw her cry once when he died, you know,' he said, checking for his wallet and starting down the stairs. And it occurred to him then, for the first time, that maybe his mum had wished his dad dead too.

As the punt reached the end of its crossing, Clem wedged himself against its railing to take the force of the bounce. He did love the river, its twists and curves, and the quietness of it. If he could have anything, he thought, he'd have a little boat, go rowing on the weekends, maybe throw in a line. *Wonder what Els'd think of that?* Probably pack up a picnic and want to come too.

She was plucky; he'd always liked that – and he wondered, out of nowhere, what she'd have done if she'd been the one to come across the mangled little bird and the dog. Because she'd fed that dog for weeks after they'd moved in, a bone here, an end of meat there, wondering aloud what sort of person could let a dog be so skinny and unloved, and making a sack-bed for it in the laundry, out of the chilly night wind. Another reason he'd never told her what he'd found, what he'd done; he didn't want that generosity compromised.

Him and Elsie: twenty-three years now, he figured. He could remember the first time he saw her, the day war was declared and he was stomping through Brisbane trying to feel like a grown-up and wondering if he should enlist. A tram slowed on Adelaide Street and she'd swung out before it fully stopped, bright and young in her pale green dress. The sun caught her hair, the wind caught her skirt, and she looked so impossibly pretty that Clem paused and put his hand up to help her down without thinking. That was that – he wasn't going to war; wasn't going anywhere. When they were married, the next year, she wore the green dress, its skirt overlaid with something sheer and its top prettied up with lace. His mum had loved her – thrifty enough to make do with a frock she had, and alive enough to make Clem stay away from getting himself killed. They had good times, the three of them – and then the five of them, with the twins – in the old house on Highgate Hill. He still missed it, and his mum, though she'd been dead now a decade.

The boy threw a rope out towards the jetty, and Clem braced again as it tightened and held – he liked to feel the decking shift as everyone rushed off before him. First job was something in the physics building today, he knew, a dodgy door into one of the lavatories – shouldn't take more than half an hour, and if he got to it while there was a lecture on, he shouldn't inconvenience anyone about the convenience. He smiled at his pun as he climbed the hill, took his tools, and cut into the Great Court, dazzled by the colour of the morning sun against its sandstone.

Scoping the halls of the physics building, he saw students hurrying towards a class and stood a moment in the foyer, his eyes adjusting to the low light while he waited for the crush to pass.

'Mr Gormley, is that you?' Clem recognised the quiet voice of one of the tutors, and nodded. 'You're here about the lavatory? Because when you've dealt with that, I'd appreciate you having a look at my office door as well – I'm teaching now, but you'll see it's left open, down the hall. If you could pop by, if you've got a moment. I really do need to be able to make it secure.'

Clem turned in the direction the man indicated, and turned back to see him disappearing into the lecture hall. As Clem carried his tools towards the bathroom, he heard the man bark, 'All right, all right' – such a different tone from the one he'd just used.

They were cold, these buildings, no matter the season. Clem shivered as the men's room door swung behind him – the smooth cold floor, the tiled walls, the doors that clattered against the two stalls. He saw the problem, rescrewed the hinge, and was done in ten minutes, washing his hands at one of the basins and smiling as the hot water came through at last.

The tutor's door, and then he'd get out into the sun and take a breather.

He found the man's office and pushed at the door, feeling the way it sagged out of kilter with the weakness of its upper hinge. Clem pressed at the rectangle of metal, reaching for the screwdriver in his back pocket – *A man could've done this himself, if it was so important,* he thought, but perhaps physicists didn't work with anything quite so blunt.

Still, he thought, glancing at the desk behind him, *this one's not as messy as most* – taking in the neat papers, squared with each other and the desk's edge, the pot of pencils, the half-empty cup of tea set on a coaster. There was a typewriter too, pushed to one side – no women tapping away for this man – and behind it, slightly obscured, a dome of glass on a varnished wooden stand.

Inside was a funnel full of black stuff – tar, thought Clem, or maybe pitch. He'd had an uncle who built a boat when he was a boy, and Clem had spent weekends by the river, smoothing over the joins in the little craft's hull, proud to be involved with something as grand as *caulking*.

He leaned back against the now-closed door. Uncle Perc: he hadn't thought of him for years – and then what? The boat finished, the man had kissed his sister – Clem's mum – goodbye, and prepared to set off, across Moreton Bay, and on towards New Zealand.

'But how do you know how to sail her, Uncle Perc?' Clem, tiny and pleading, desperate to be taken for a turn. 'Oughtn't you to take her out for a run, before you try for the whole horizon?'

'It's in my bones, Clem, the wind and the water – ask your mum about growing up on the shoreline with such a bad influence for a brother. Once I go, I don't turn back.' He'd named the boat for Clem's mum too: *The Pearl*.

'She sounds like a pirate ship,' breathed the boy.

There might have been a Christmas card that first year, from New Zealand, Clem thought now, but nothing after that, and he'd never asked his mum where Uncle Perc had gone, or why. It was funny, the way family was so disposable: *If Donny upped and moved to another country,* he thought, and then smiled. Elsie would never let her children get away. She'd know where they were, and what they were doing, until the last living breath left her body. 'My babies,' she still called them sometimes, though she swore it was accidental.

Breathing deep, Clem rubbed the heels of his hands against his eyes: he'd get on then. And maybe he would see about a little boat – call it the *Pearl II*. He bent down to gather his tools and imagined leaning forward to pull at some oars. Stroke. Stroke. He could feel the muscles that would open up across his shoulder blades, muscles he hadn't used for years – it was as if he'd suddenly remembered how to fly. *Reckon I could row Elsie all the way to Indooroopilly Island, if the tides were right.*

Straightening up, his leg knocked the desk and something moved. Clem turned towards the glass jar: the pitch that had been dangling down the neck of the funnel, thick and heavy, was creaking and stretching until it broke free and folded into the small beaker below.

No, no: Clem stared at it – had he done this? Had he broken this thing? All the possibility he'd felt – the lovely idea of a boat, a day on the river – shattered and closed down. *Just get out*: he grabbed his bag and reached for the door, fumbling in his haste. The tutor was standing outside, his hand in his pocket for the key.

'All done? Grand, thank you. I've just come for my book—' he stepped around Clem, stopping as he saw the jar. 'No,' he said quietly. 'Oh no.'

'I don't know how it happened,' Clem stammered. 'I was rescrewing the hinge and when I turned, it was like ...'

'So you didn't see it?' The man was holding his arm now, and leaning in close. 'You were in the very room, and you didn't see it?'

Clem blinked, swallowed, and took a guess at the right answer – this was worse than being hauled up and asked about algebra in school.

'No, sir, no, I didn't.' Fourteen years old again and desperate to be away.

The physicist laughed and inched the bell jar a little towards the window. 'Eight years since the last drop – that one was only the fourth since Parnell began the experiment, you know. And you know the mad thing? No one's ever seen it happen. Ever. I've had it in here for a year now, waiting. And the blessed thing waits till I'm talking to first-years – and waits, may I say, till your back's turned and you're busy with the ruddy door. Then off it goes. An historic moment. Unseen by the scientist or the janitor – pah!'

He grabbed at the book, so fast that Clem jumped aside.

'Shut the door on your way out, would you?' he called, rushing and almost halfway back to his class.

'But should I wait? If it's going to happen again, I could wait and watch for that? If it matters that I missed it this time?' From deep in the hallway, Clem heard the man laugh.

'Come back in seven or eight years,' he said. 'That's when the next one will be ready to taunt me.' And he disappeared into the gloom.

Alone in the room, Clem crouched beside the jar, staring at the glass, the pitch, the empty space below the funnel. *Eight years of waiting, and here I was.* He cupped his hand around the jar's curved top, trying to think of another thing in his life to which only he was witness. There was Elsie, he thought, although she spoke sometimes of a young fella she'd known before she met him, and Clem wondered in the middle of some nights how much there might have been to that. But all right then, Elsie sleeping, maybe – but then there were the twins, and always one or other of them ending up in the bed before morning. The pitch was so shiny, so sleek – he could have stood and watched it forever. In the end, it was his hand, sweaty, against the glass that made him step back, wipe it down, and walk away.

Outside, in the elegant loggia of the Great Court, he took the long way towards the workshop, visualising the pitch's drop again and again. Maybe he'd tell Elsie, as they walked home together. Maybe he'd tell her as they had their tea. Or maybe it'd take him as long to tell her about the silly pitch as it had to say something about his dad and the crow. There was something nice about a story you kept inside yourself; there was something nice about a secret, or a fear.

The sun inched across the sky and the day passed, Clem's stomach rolling now and then as if he was on the brink of falling in love. *A bit of pitch,* he told himself more than once. *All this for a bit of pitch.* At the end of the day, waiting for the punt to cast off, he watched the late afternoon light pick up the currents on the river's surface and saw himself caulking the perfectly smooth keel of a dinghy or a skiff. From the trees above, a chorus of corellas broke out, and Clem smiled at their song.

Then, behind him, came the physicist's voice – the polite, hallway tone, not the rousing bark for students. 'And blow me if it didn't go today – I was giving a lecture. Parnell's pitch gave way, and there wasn't a blessed soul there to see it.'

At the punt's rail, Clem saw his knuckles grip to whiteness. *Hang on,* he wanted to call across the deck. *There was a blessed soul – and the blessed soul did see it.* But the man's voice had dropped into the next part of his conversation, and Clem knew he would never have made himself heard.

He stared at the water and saw nothing but its usual murky brown. Overhead, the corellas rose as a block, bright whiteness against the dusk.

What a man might expect; what a man might get – *If I'd had a learning man for my dad, that pitch would be mine to claim.* But his dad had shot birds and died young, and that was all. Clem wouldn't tell Elsie about the slow black drop folding itself into the jar; he wouldn't tell her he was dreaming of a boat. He wouldn't even dream.

He let go of the punt's rail and stumbled, seeing himself as the physicist might – a plain man with ginger hair and stubble, pushing through his forties; worked a bit too hard and disappointed a bit too often.

All these moments, he thought as the punt eased away from St Lucia to take him home. They added up to something, but he could never quite see what.

She Knows How to Look After Herself

Michel Dignand

Jennifer Essambot sits alone in the carriage. She has worked late, as sometimes happens in her business, so is alert to the possibility of danger. When she started her journey there had been a scattering of other travellers occupying the carriage, but at each station along the way passengers have alighted, until now she is alone.

Realising this, she leaves her seat on the upper level and moves down the stairs to the open area near the doors. There is a pimply youth with his head in a book sitting in a seat in the corner, but it takes Jennifer no more than a brief look to decide she will face no threat from him. There is a bench seat on either side of the carriage, each capable of seating only five passengers. She takes the seat diagonally opposite the pimply youth. His name is Arthur Bartholomew, but of course she is unaware of that.

The train continues through two stations with no passengers joining or alighting. Jennifer is relaxed, but still alert. She opens the book she has been reading and finds her place on the page.

The door leading to the next carriage is suddenly opened loudly as if thrown to the side. Jennifer looks up and watches as a young man enters, followed by another. They leave the door open, and the noise from the wheels on the rails is very loud. The two men stand in the open area before the main doors, holding on to the central column of handrails for support as the train sways from side to side. The pimply youth sitting beside the open door cautiously slides it shut without looking at the two men and the noise in the carriage returns to its previous level.

The two men in the open area are bending to peer along the lower deck of the carriage. They can see it is empty. One of them steps up to the upper deck and notes that it, too, is empty.

Jennifer is feeling slightly uneasy, a feeling she often gets when travelling late; so far, though, she has never been subjected to any sort of harassment. Jennifer is twenty-four, and believes she can look after herself.

Arthur Bartholomew, on the other hand, is a little frightened. He is eighteen, and has been bullied all his life. He is an only child. His mother is a single parent. They lead quiet, frequently frightened lives.

From the corner of his eye he can see the two men looking towards Jennifer, nudging each other and laughing. Arthur can sense danger here and wishes he was in another carriage.

Jennifer decides that if the two men show no sign of leaving the train at the next station, she will leave herself and take a taxi the rest of the way home. She pretends not to have noticed the men, and continues reading. In fact she hasn't read a word, her attention being entirely on her safety. She turns a page to give the impression she is reading. She will find her place again later, when she gets home.

The man furthest from her moves around his partner and takes a seat beside Jennifer, his partner breaking into a guffaw. The partner's name is Peter Onslow, and he would have liked to have the self-confidence to do what Jimmy Parker, his friend, has just done. But he is a follower, not a leader, and he has never successfully approached a girl before. The woman Jimmy is seated next to is a stunner: blonde, a pony-tail, well-dressed. Peter can't actually see her face, but he knows she will be a stunner. He wishes she would stand up so that he could see the whole of her.

Jimmy has had many women. He is twenty-two years old and knows how to force a girl into a corner for a snog. He knows how to feel them up, often in public where they don't want to make a fuss in front of their friends. He stares at Jennifer now, lowering and tilting his head so that she cannot help seeing him, his head nearly in her lap. She notices that his hair is a little greasy, and that he has a crop of blackheads around the flare of his nostrils. The standing man sniggers and she knows she is in trouble now.

Arthur knows it, too. He watches frozen as she sits up and snaps the book closed. Peter has moved closer, crowding her on that side, and Jimmy is still bent, close to her face.

Jennifer has had no training in any form of unarmed combat, but is nevertheless confident that she can handle the situation. She watches a great deal of TV, and has rehearsed the moves she has witnessed so often; the ones that might prove helpful to her, anyway. She knows that ruthless action is the key to success.

With adrenalin pumping, she quickly reassesses the situation. Is she sure she is under threat? Yes.

Could they be just messing around? Yes, but they have gone much too far.

If she does nothing, if she allows them to have their fun, will she remain safe? No.

At that moment Jimmy, the confident one sitting beside her, raises his head and puts his hand on her knee, sliding it under her skirt and along her thigh.

Jennifer lifts her bag from beside her and puts it in her lap, opening it and dropping her book into it. Without pausing she feels for the hard drive, an almost-new two terrabyte device in a steel case, and folds it in her fist, her thumb wrapped around one end of it, the other end protruding rather like a heavy dagger. Smoothly she lifts the hard drive from the bag and with all her strength smashes it sideways into Jimmy's face, aiming for the bridge of his nose. She feels great satisfaction at the crumpling sensation in her fist, knowing that it will not be the sturdy case of the hard drive that is crumpling.

Without a pause Jennifer rises and performs a lightning-fast *fouetté*, the ballet movement adopted by street fighters and kick-boxers to bring the foot crashing into the faces of opponents. Jennifer, as we know, knows nothing about fighting; but she took five years of ballet lessons during her teens, only to discover that she has grown too tall to become a successful ballet dancer.

Peter, who has registered almost nothing of all this, just a flashing of arms and legs, takes the toe of Jennifer's boot in his throat. Jennifer has lifted her leg as high as her short Lycra skirt allows, and while she aims at his head, hoping to hit beside the ear with the solid side of the boot, it is the flattened point of the boot that catches Peter behind his Adam's apple. With a roar of pain Peter falls to the ground clutching his throat, rolling under the seats.

Arthur is standing, horrified, at the end of the carriage, his eyes wide with fear, his body slightly bent as though preparing to flee, his book still in his hand, his satchel hanging behind him. He wants to scream but something is preventing him from doing so, maybe an element of empathy with Peter, who is having great difficulty breathing, his trachea swelling dangerously.

Jimmy is bleeding copiously, his shirt front soaked by the blood running over his chin despite his efforts to stem the flow by pressing both hands to his shattered face. He will never again be able to view himself as the laughing, handsome boy his mother has always told him he is.

He will have breathing problems for the rest of his life, and in fact a great deal of surgery will be necessary before he can breathe through his nose at all. He lies on his side on the seat Jennifer has so recently vacated, making a terrible mess of the upholstery.

Jennifer takes a brief look around her. Her foot has been badly twisted by the angle at which the boot struck, and her ankle is already developing a swelling that will make removal of the boot a bit of a problem later that night. She hopes the hard drive is not too badly damaged, but consoles herself with the knowledge that it is quite new and contains only ten days of back-ups, which she has duplicated on her work computer anyway. On the whole, she is pleased with herself. She retrieves her bag from under Jimmy's head, a little cross that he has bled on the lower corner of it, then moves towards Arthur and the door to the next carriage. He steps back as she passes close to him, and she slides the door wide to leave the carriage. She turns to slide the door closed behind her, but Arthur isn't staying there alone with those two thugs. He hurries after her, and only then is the sliding door closed behind them. Arthur looks for some sort of lock, but there is none.

Jennifer walks calmly through the next two carriages, both empty. The train is slowing, she realises, and will soon arrive at the next station. She stops at the end of the next carriage, holding the column of handrails for support. Arthur stops beside her, feeling a sort of team spirit with this fearless girl. She looks at him, looks at him properly for the first time. 'You okay?' she asks. He is the colour of snow on a mountainside.

'Yes. Yes,' he stammers. He looks down. 'I wanted to help, but you had finished it before I was even on my feet.'

Jennifer isn't sure what to say. 'It sort of all happened in a flash,' she tells him. 'I didn't have time to think.'

They stand silently as the train enters the lighted station, slowing as the brakes are applied noisily, their bodies brushing each other as the deceleration drags their hips sideways. The big doors open with a hiss of compressed air and they step off together, turning right along the platform. They are the only ones leaving the train. What will they do if the two thugs get off too? Arthur doesn't know, but he is glad she is with him. He decides he will join a kickboxing class.

As the train starts to move they stop, turning to watch the carriages moving away. They can see Jimmy still lying on the seat, but there is no sign of Peter. They each assume that he is still on the ground. Jennifer turns to Arthur. He is taller than she is by fifteen centimetres or so, and he looks down on her face. As Peter thought, she really is stunning. 'Do you think we should call someone? D'you think they're badly hurt?'

Arthur is surprised that she is asking his opinion. 'They must be,' he says. 'You didn't half wallop them.'

Her air of self-confidence is dropping away from her. Tears start in her eyes, glinting in the uncertain light of the station. 'I was just defending myself,' she says, and she leans towards Arthur, resting the side of her face against his jacket. He can feel her shaking and, hardly believing that this is happening, puts his left arm around her. She sobs for a while, her shoulders moving, leaning more and more heavily against him. He brings his other hand up to touch her hair, to hold her head against him. 'I'd better call someone,' he says eventually.

He feels her nod, but the sobbing increases. He doesn't want her to stop. This is like a wonderful dream. They stand together on the platform for several minutes until her sobs decrease and he feels it is no longer the decent thing to do. He leads her to a bench, and takes out his mobile. 'What's your name?' he asks.

Without thinking, she tells him. 'Jennifer,' she says. He starts dialling, but at the second zero she puts her hand over his mobile. 'Don't tell them my name,' she says. 'Tell them you just saw it at a distance, then saw them hurt when the train pulled away.' He nods, and presses the final zero.

'Police,' he says to the operator, and when he is put through explains that he has witnessed a fight on the train, and that there might be two badly injured men who need help. No, he says, he didn't see who did it, just the injured people as the train passed him. They might have been fighting each other, he suggests.

Jennifer squeezes him in silent thanks as he rings off, but she starts to cry again as he stands. He has more confidence now, and he leans down and helps her to her feet. He is hoping for another long hug. 'Come on,' he tells her, 'this is no time for tears. You'd better get a move on if you don't want the police to talk to you.'

Jennifer nods. 'I'm not sure how to get home now.'

'Can you call someone to come and pick you up?'

She nods, and pulls out her mobile.

'Will I see you again?' he asks her quickly.

'What?' Jennifer thinks she has misheard him, this spotty boy.

'Will I see you again?' he repeats. He knows she won't let him, but he has to try.

Jennifer pauses, obviously giving it serious consideration. 'Why don't you give me your number, and I'll call you in a while?'

He nods, and fishes out a scrap of paper from his satchel, hastily scribbling his name and number before handing it to her self-consciously. 'Only, you know, I'd like to see you again, when it's not like, you know, like this.'

Jennifer flashes him a smile. 'Of course,' she says, and tries the name on the paper. 'I'll give you a call, Arthur.'

'You'd better go,' he says as they hear a police siren drawing closer. She nods, reaches up to kiss his cheek and turns away. He is shocked, his hand rising without conscious effort to the cheek she has kissed, watching her as she walks out of the station.

She sees she is in a well-lit street with shops and a bus stop only a few metres away. She waits there as a police car, lights flashing, pulls in to the kerb in a no-stopping zone outside the station. A bus arrives, and it is going in the right direction. As she climbs aboard she drops the scrap of paper to the floor. 'Silly sod,' she mutters to herself. The bus is half full. She finds a seat and sits looking at her reflection in the window and smiles.

She knows how to look after herself.

fourW

The Other Room

Liam Davison

The day the girl came to visit, we were going to feed stones to Neary's horse. It had taken clayballs and clods of dirt from us before, but Lonan wanted it to choke. I remember it, because we'd planned to walk the long way past the new cutting where Brendan had said you could walk right into the storm drain and be gone, underground, before anyone knew where you were. But when the day came, it was Lonan who was gone. I waited for him at the gate and when he didn't come, I pushed it and stepped into the Crielys' backyard.

The gate was Lonan's gate really. Brendan could remember Mr Criely cutting the railings and our father worrying at the damage to a good fence. Lonan was the only one who ever used it. Sometimes, he'd be on the back step before anyone had woken.

Mr Criely kept birds. There was an aviary pushed to the fence and when I stepped through the gate, there was a flurry of wings and a pardalote stuck hard against the wire as though it saw only open space.

'He's not here,' Mrs Criely said. 'He's gone for the day.'

'Where?' I asked.

Lonan never went anywhere but with us. There was nowhere for him to go.

'If he'd wanted you to know, he would have said,' she said. 'And mind you shut the gate on your way through.'

She wore slippers like my father wore and yellow rubber gloves.

Later that day, I noticed my father had placed the wooden plinth back across the bottom of the gate and looped the top with wire so the fence was a straight, unbroken line again.

'We'll be having a visitor,' my mother said. 'A girl from the country.'

We didn't have visitors unless they were people we already knew. The bottle men came once a month and Mrs Marriott from the other side borrowed tea or sugar and sat too long at the kitchen table. Mrs Pereira tried unsuccessfully to sell perfume and cosmetics to my mother but rarely gained entry to the house. She left her order book stuck behind the flywire door where it stayed till she collected it the following week.

And there were the nuns. Apart from Mrs Pereira, they were the only ones to come to the front door.

'You can sweep the front porch,' my mother said, 'and bang the mat before you disappear.'

'Is she a nun?' I asked.

'What?'

'The girl who's coming. Is she a nun?'

'Of course she's not a nun. What would make you say that? Don't even think for a minute ... Don't even.'

*

Brendan said Neary would cut your balls if he caught you tormenting his horse. You don't mess with men like Neary, he said.

Brendan spoke of Neary with the authority of experience I'd never questioned. Neary was a grown man. But then, so was Brendan. He'd finished school before I'd started. Brendan knowing Neary went with him knowing the Criely boy, Colin, who'd died before I was born, and with him knowing why Mr Criely cut the gate, but not being able to explain it because there were things I didn't understand.

'You just don't do it, right?' he said. 'You think it's the same as messing with Criely's birds. It's not.'

I'd never messed with Mr Criely's birds, and Lonan showed no interest in them. They seemed off-limits in their sad walk-in aviary, which was really just a glorified cage. It was like Lonan knew the birds had some other significance for his dad beyond their frantic bursts of interrupted flight each time he lifted the latch.

Brendan worked nights at the club and drove during the day. The back door was always open and he came and went as though he owned the place. When he spoke about Colin Criely and about his sister, Susan, who was married now and moved away, it was like he was talking about another place altogether that shared a common boundary with the place I knew.

'That bedroom you're in,' he said. 'That's my room.'

The top shelf of the wardrobe was stacked with schoolbooks and trophies he'd won for sport and a wireless set he'd built himself but never got to work. In the bathroom there were creams and razors, and a badger-hair brush in a ceramic pot with his name printed on the side. It was like my world was something borrowed, and each time I opened a cupboard door I caught a glimpse of something more real and substantial that occupied the space behind it. Some nights I felt, if I opened the bedroom door and stepped out to the lounge room, they'd be there: Mum and Dad and Brendan, only Brendan would be my age in his pyjamas sitting between them, and they'd look right through me.

'So what was the other room?' I asked.

'The other room,' he said. 'That's what it was: the other room.'

'Then it was yours?'

'Not really. It wasn't like that.'

'What was it like?' I asked.

'Like nothing. You just don't mess with Neary's horse, hear?' he said. 'You leave it or you'll end up the same,' and he pulled his fist up between his legs like a stab.

*

I thought maybe Lonan would be there when I arrived. But there was no sign, and the horse stood with its back to the wind, staring out across the paddock to what remained of Neary's land. I'd brought a stone with me in case. It banged against my thigh all the way through the estate and out past the cutting to where the last of the fences stopped short against open sky, then further out to where the horse stood at an indeterminate point that seemed as far removed from home as it was from the flat horizon in the distance. The only feature of the place was the horse itself.

I laid my bike on the grass and stepped towards the horse. All the way out, from the moment I'd turned onto Boundary Road, thinking about Lonan and where he might have gone, the horse had been a fixed mark in the middle distance that I'd steadily made my way towards. It seemed it had always been there. It was like a hill or the set foundations of a house that had long since vanished but still staked its claim without asking anything of anyone. It simply was.

As I pedalled, the low fences and skeleton-frames of half-finished houses slipped away on either side and the smells of cut wood and turned clay gradually opened to the expansive smell of grassland. The wind carried me through it. When I passed the cutting and the open mouth of the drain, I might not have been pedalling at all had it not been for the weight of the stone against my leg. The grass billowed in the wind like a living pelt beside me and I seemed to float above it, moving yet strangely still with the horse always the same distance ahead.

And now, with the horse beside me, I looked out across the same flat expanse of featureless paddock that the horse saw with no fixed point to give it depth or focus. The sky was immense above it. There was no horizon now. No distance. I don't know how long I stood there with the horse breathing beside me, and the relentless sound of the wind. The grass and open sky might have extended behind me as far as it did in front.

There was no sign of Lonan. Other times he'd disappeared, it was with his father, birding. It was the saddest thing, he'd said. They'd drive out to the country, just the two of them, and barely speak. Then they'd watch great flocks of birds, starlings or sparrows, wheeling above them in the sky. And when they were done, they would drive to a friend of his father's who bred birds and his father would buy one or two brown quail for his aviary and place them on the back seat in a cage the size of a shoebox. When they got home, his father would introduce them into the aviary and stand there watching to see what they would do. It was like he was looking for something, Lonan said. Like he wanted something he couldn't have.

When the horse shifted its weight I gripped the stone in my pocket. I was surprised at how hard and cold it still was. I had no real idea how big a stone would have to be to choke a horse but I'd taken a piece of basalt from my box, half the size of my fist. It should do, I thought.

The horse had done nothing to acknowledge my arrival. It didn't care whether I was there or not. I could see its sheath between its haunches and the puckered scar where Neary had cut its balls.

Lonan would do it. I knew he would. Without thinking. He'd feed it to him just for being there.

*

Lonan was a year ahead of me at school. We'd pass each other in the yard and not acknowledge that we knew each other. Each afternoon, though, he was there, through the fence as quick as a wink. He ate with us. He dropped his clothes in the TV room. He was more a brother than Brendan was. My mother picked up after him and set his place at the table, with his own serviette from the kitchen drawer. Christmas and Easter, he came with us to Mass, and took communion and stood and knelt and crossed himself.

Brendan said it only made sense. Mr Criely wasn't Catholic. Mrs Criely only went when she felt the need.

'Colin never went at all,' he said. 'First of church Colin ever saw, he was already dead.'

Colin Criely had been the same age as Brendan. He belonged to that otherworld that Lonan and I had never been a part of, and each time Brendan spoke of him, it was like a window opened.

'I was with him the day he died,' Brendan said.

He'd come into my room late one night and I could smell the cigarettes and beer from the club.

'Who?' I said.

'Colin. Who else?'

He was pulling things from the wardrobe and laying them out on the floor.

'We were both working for Neary, planting carnations for the markets.'

There was a leather case filled with books and bits of folded paper.

'Not Neary, Neary. Old Mr Neary. All of it was his then. Everywhere you looked it was market gardens.'

He flicked through each of the books and unfolded the papers, then put them back the way they were.

'What are you looking for?' I asked.

'Nothing. Just nothing. You wouldn't understand. Anyway, I left him to it 'cause Colin Criely never knew when to stop. He'd work into the night if you let him. One more row. One more row. He was a good worker; I'll give him that. So I left him.'

He opened each of the drawers as he spoke and jammed it shut, then went back to the wardrobe.

'His dad knew something was wrong when he hadn't fed his birds. The covers were still up and the birds were restless for their food. And he went out to the paddocks on dark and found him underneath the tractor.'

I didn't know what to say to him. What could I say?

'He never said it was my fault. For leaving him, I mean. He never said.'

*

I didn't know what time the girl was coming, but I was expected to be there.

It would only take a minute to choke the horse. So far, it had taken what was offered. I thought about where to stand to do it. Would it keel over, or go down on its knees? Would it kick? It seemed so resolute and indifferent to my presence, I found it hard to imagine it doing anything but standing there and accepting its lot. Would it even know?

That same night, when Brendan had come into my room, he spoke about Lonan and how trouble seemed to follow him.

'He's not like us,' he said. 'He's not like you, I mean. He thinks he is, but he's not.'

I wondered what he meant about not like me. What was I like, then? What did Lonan want? At school, he ran with the boys who played rough and made their own rules. If anything, I thought it was them he wanted to be like.

They had a boy down once, in the dirt at the back of the oval.

I don't know what he'd done. He was on his knees and they were standing over him. Lonan was there too, on the edge at first, but then not. Each time the boy tried to get up, they pushed him down. That's all it was. He'd get up and they'd push him down. Over and over. It went on longer than it should have, and the boy never made a sound. Then Lonan was in there. I thought he was going to stop it. But he bent down and picked up a handful of dirt from the ground and when the boy was on his knees again he pushed it into his mouth and leant his knee against his back till the boy gave up and howled. It was over then. Just the howling and the boy lying in the dirt.

I thought we'd talk about it, but we never did. I guess there's things best left unsaid.

There was a wilfulness about him that put his own needs first, as though there was something owed, and if it wasn't given, he would take it. If I were more like him, I might have stayed longer with the horse and fed the stone to it. Its breathing was slow and regular, a constant beside me, like the wind. I wondered what would happen if it stopped. And what would the damage deliver?

I stooped and tugged a fistful of grass from the ground and approached the horse. It swung its head and took it from my fingers with barely a brush of its lips. All I felt was its hot breath soft against my skin.

*

The girl was sitting at the kitchen table with my mother and Mrs Criely when I got back. She was older than I'd thought, barely a girl at all. Mrs Criely must have walked the long way round.

'Michael,' my mother said, 'this is Liddy. She's come to visit.'

The girl started from her chair toward me then stopped, and there was a moment of awkwardness that has stayed with me where I didn't know what to say or whether to reach out or smile or nod. I had no idea why she was there. She braced herself against the table as though she might fall into the space between us.

'Hello,' I said.

She was Brendan's age or older, a woman really. She had pale, washed-out eyes and thin lips smudged with lipstick.

'I'm Liddy,' she said. 'I'm ...'

Her fingernails were bitten to the quick.

'Liddy. I'm Liddy.'

She was like some creature in a spotlight. She looked from me to Mum to Mrs Criely, then sat down again and folded her hands in her lap. There was a crucifix around her neck, the kind you bought on card from the piety stall at the back of the church.

She must have been there a while. There were cups of tea and a half-finished plate of biscuits. Mrs Criely pushed the plate towards me.

'Where's Dad?' I asked.

'Out,' Mum said. 'He's gone out.'

Liddy didn't take her eyes off me.

'Michael collects stones,' Mum said, as though to change the subject. 'Don't you, Michael?'

Liddy leaned further towards me and smiled. She wanted something from me that I couldn't hope to understand.

'Sort of,' I said. 'They're not very good.'

'Why don't you show them to Liddy?' Mum said. 'She'd like that.'

She was out of her chair before I could answer.

'Go on,' Mum said, and I could tell she and Mrs Criely wanted to talk.

*

I kept the stones in a box by the side of the shed. Most of them were unremarkable: sandstone, bluestone, limestone. Some shards of quartz. But there were some with lichen stains that might have been fossils, and a piece of polished chalcedony I'd bought from a shop. I'd made a start on grouping them. I had labels stuck to the inside of the box and a coloured chart on cardboard.

Liddy wanted to know about every one: where I'd found it, how long I'd had it, how I knew what it was called. She stood closer to me than she needed. There was the faint smell of mothballs about her, beneath some cheap perfume.

'They're lovely, Michael,' she said. 'They're really lovely. They are.' Though even I could tell they weren't. 'Is it what you want to do?' she asked.

'What?'

'When you grow up. Is it what you want to do? The stones?'

She was only asking, but she didn't take her eyes off me and it made the whole thing – the box, the handwritten labels, the earnest attempts at scientific classification – seem like something I should have outgrown.

'Not really,' I said. 'It's just something.'

'It's more than something,' she said. 'You should do the things you like.'

I could feel the piece of basalt, still heavy against my leg. There were more like it in the box, dull black specimens of ordinary rock. I should have thrown it on my way back home, or left it near the horse. But I hadn't. I'd carried it back, and as I pulled it from my pocket to put back in the box, she saw it.

'That's a nice stone,' she said. 'Did you collect it today?'

She moved even closer to me. I could smell her hair and see the small cracks in her lips where she'd chewed the lipstick off.

'It's nothing,' I said, and I pointed to the other pieces in the box. 'It's just basalt.'

She reached out to me then and touched my hand, and when I didn't move, she closed her thin fingers over mine to hold the stone. She was trembling. The longer we stood there, the tighter she clasped my hand. But still, her arm kept shaking and her eyes kept their hold on mine.

'Michael,' she said.

Nothing else. Just 'Michael,' in a broken sort of voice as though she was about to cry.

Eventually, I prised my fingers free and handed her the stone. She held it to her chest like something precious.

*

'They never wanted him, really,' Brendan said. 'Neither of them, but they couldn't say it.'

It was the same night when he'd come searching. He'd given up looking for whatever it was he wanted, and was stretched out on the floor.

'You couldn't blame them. I mean, Mr Criely never wanted a replacement. He wanted his own boy back. How's he meant to feel? Colin was hardly gone when they handed him over the fence like a parcel of meat.'

'Who?' I said, but he kept talking, lying flat on the floor like I wasn't there. It took me longer than it should have to realise he was talking about Lonan.

'Right there where they cut the gate. Dad was happy to see him go. I mean, they never asked. They never even asked. For all those years, there'd only been me. You weren't coming in a hurry and they just assumed that was it. There's the three of us, and the other room with no one in it, so they just thought. Only they didn't think. Did they? I mean, how's Dad supposed to feel? Like there's only the one, then nothing. Then the nuns come knocking at the door like they do and Mum can't say no because they're nuns and we're Catholic, and it's only for a while.'

'For a while?' I say. Everything changed then. How could I not have known? 'How long did he live here?' I asked.

'Eight months,' Brendan said. 'He was as good as ours. As good as Mum's, anyway. Then Colin Criely goes and dies, and there's a gap next door in need of filling.'

I don't know how long he lay there on the floor, but in the morning, he was gone, and not long after that, he left for Queensland and the mines. The only times we saw him were when he flew back for a visit.

*

Liddy was gone by the time Lonan returned. Mum and Mrs Criely kept refreshing the pot and stayed talking in the kitchen for an hour or more, their voices rising and falling in degrees of confidentiality when I came near.

Eventually, there was a knock at the door, and it was the nuns. Lonan was standing between them. They didn't come in, just delivered him to the door and left. Lonan told me he'd been with them all day. He was going to make his confirmation so he'd been to church first, then he'd worked all afternoon in the nuns' garden, pulling weeds and shovelling dirt into the beds. We didn't talk about the horse. Mrs Criely finished her tea and the two of them walked home together. Later, I heard Mr Criely sweeping out the birds and muttering to them the way he did.

They're long gone now of course, the Crielys and the birds. The fence was replaced some years after they left and the aviary went with it. I remember thinking how long Mr Criely used to spend there and how little time it took for it to go. There was nothing to it really, just a rectangle of open space enclosed by wire.

I eventually found what Brendan had been looking for in my room that night. It was years later. The Crielys had gone. Brendan had married and moved back to Melbourne and his stuff was still jammed in the wardrobe, all but forgotten when he'd cleared out the other room. It was at the back of the chest of drawers where it had fallen into a closed space.

I didn't realise what it was at first. I assumed the handwriting was Brendan's. It was small and neat with twenty-five entries to a page. Half the pages were filled: more than five hundred sightings recorded in his small, tight script. *Greenfinch. Song Thrush. Indian Mynah. Spotted Pardalote. Magpie Lark.* Each was dated and annotated. *On the wing. Perched. Nesting.* And on the centre page, in an even smaller script, Colin Criely had recorded his tally of sightings and birds he'd yet to claim.

I thought of him and Brendan out there, working for Neary with one eye on the plantings and one on the open sky, looking to fill the gaps. *Black Kite. Satin Bowerbird. Golden Whistler.* And after that, empty page after empty page.

Aftermath

Kevin Brophy

They were good people and perhaps this was the real cause of their troubles. The hallway in their house had two bicycles leaning on the wall, an old wedding photo hanging precariously by a nail that had chipped the plaster when Matt had hammered it in. There were scarves on the back of the front door, some helmets rolling under the wheels of the bikes and their son's razor scooter down the far end near the kitchen. It was tricky walking to the front door, and they had learnt, more or less, to angle themselves away from the scooter, sway past the bikes, step over the helmets, avoid scraping an ear on the wedding photo and brush aside the scarves to get to the doorknob that opened the front door to a rare visitor. Mostly they used the back door from the side lane. Their friends had learnt to do this too. It took a surprisingly long time to get to the front door from the kitchen where they spent most of their lives, so whatever stranger was knocking would usually knock again, louder, or sometimes walk away before the door was opened. Matt would call out, 'Coming, coming,' but not so loud that the sound of his voice penetrated to the outside. It was more like an instruction to himself to gather his person into a social presence in preparation for the stranger at the door.

On this day he managed to open the door before the third round of knocking to find in front of him in the sunshine of the late afternoon two young men in crumpled suits. They had

American accents. One of them looked vaguely Japanese. They smiled as though they had just begun their day and it was going to be a good one. Of course he understood what they were and what they wanted. They were concerned about the world, and he was too. They wanted a better world, and he did too. It was almost enough to break your heart to see two young men so sure that they had all the important answers and the important questions as well in a pamphlet in their hands, the whole text learnt by heart. He asked them in. Sarah was not happy about it but she put on the kettle and got out some fruit scones. The fruit scones were fresh but a bit crumbly. She had put a little too much butter in the mix because she'd been watching one of those American crime shows while she made up the batch. No end of evil in the world to entertain and distract us, Matt was fond of saying. In this particular series the evil ones were not truly evil, for they were usually dim characters who acted impulsively then tried to cover their tracks, which they could not do against the formidable brains of the team on the side of the law. She told Matt that these stories were modern allegories, small miracle stories that Jesus would have made up if he had arrived two thousand years too late for his crucifixion. He would have written screenplays instead of sermons, because that's what screenplays really are, they're sermons.

'Here you are, boys,' she said, as she arranged the scones and butter and jam in front of them with their steaming cups. She could see that they considered they were receiving an authentic welcome from authentic locals. This was something they would write about on a postcard, an experience brief enough with the main ingredients clear and unmistakable.

They spoke of Jesus and of the end of the world and of the church just opened down the road with a new preacher and a new message, one that would bring people's hearts closer to the divine presence. Matt asked them if they had experienced the divine presence themselves. He was curious in that way. They nodded gravely. He asked them to describe what it had felt like for them, but he asked so quietly that they did not feel they were being set up for ridicule. They spoke openly of the way their hearts had burst in their chests, their heads had been spinning and their vision had blurred so that light was spreading everywhere until they were inside the very dawn itself. Their hands had been shaking, they said, and their tongues were loosened in their mouths, their teeth felt like they were being smashed on stones and their ears were ringing. Sarah exclaimed, 'That's enough, that's enough for anyone. Don't tell us any more.'

The missionaries sipped their tea. A boy of about eleven or twelve came in from the backyard where he had been sitting with the cat, teasing it as usual with a furry toy on the end of a string. Either the cat would never learn it was being tricked or it enjoyed the game as much as he did. The boy, Tristan, their son, was introduced to Malchiel ('Mal') and Joshua, who stood up and shook hands solemnly with him, one then the other. They also greeted Tristan by using his name back to him, 'So good to meet with you, brother Tristan, on this fine afternoon.'

Tristan got himself a scone too and sat down at the table for he wanted to listen to these formal men who seemed to be so awkward in the world and so new to it. They are like kittens, he thought, but they're so big. Matt did not ask more questions for he knew that the answers would be long-winded, over-confident and infuriatingly short on logic. Tristan, though, wanted to know if the devil was as real to them as God. 'Anyone,' Mal said, 'who slanders the Lord speaks the words of Satan. You know the devil when you feel the walls of his prison building up inside you, trapping you away from the light, and you can smell the flames that would eat you for eternity.'

Matt steered the talk to somewhere else, asking where they came from. They said they were both from Kansas, from a town that hosted the largest military prison in the United States. Malchiel said his father was a lawyer who dealt in properties. Joshua's father worked in a hospital as a guard. They were both from wholesome Christian families, they said, and they complimented Matt and Sarah on the homeliness of their cottage. They said that this was the first cottage they had been invited into. They found it delightful. They had no idea that tea could taste so refreshing. Almost like a drug, Joshua laughed. He was slightly less pious than his partner. Tristan wanted them to leave now so that the family could go back to saying whatever came into their heads, which was usually much the same things in much the same phrases every day, but it felt right and it felt comfortable, as comfortable as the soft sound of rain on their roof that went on for months and months, eventually greening everything around them. The boys made no sign of being about to leave. They wanted to know if Matt and Sarah and Tristan too would come to just one service in the hall down the other end of the village next Sunday. It will be just simple Christian folks, they said. The word 'folks,' it sounded special in their mouths. They lengthened the 'o' in the middle and almost made a thing of the silent 'l' in their cheeks as they pushed out the last two consonants. Tristan wondered if the word really did have a plural form but he let it go. He would look out for it in books, he might even look up the dictionary at school if he got there early enough in the morning and Mrs Scillion the librarian would let him into her *domain*, as she called it.

Matt finally said yes, they might go, and the boys were pleased with themselves, and with the luck the Lord had brought them. They could have sung a hymn right there in their suits and no one would have been surprised if they had then revealed wings kept under their coats. There were handshakes all round. Matt's handshake was limp. He did not know properly how to shake hands because it had happened rarely in his life that anyone shook his hand. Either people knew him too well to need to touch him or the situation was so formal and Matt so insignificant that he did not put himself forward for a shake with anyone's hand. He felt special, however, when these boys held out their big hands. He smiled without having meant to smile. After they had left, Tristan leaned over to the plate of scones to help himself to another one. 'They're good, Mum,' he said, 'but they could have been more cakey.'

The service in the old guild hall at the end of High Street was an occasion that rattled the couple. There was so much singing, and more shaking of hands, and then there was the moaning that came from the congregation as the sermon on the topic of the wounds of Christ was delivered. None of the people they knew from their many years of drinking and eating at the White Horse or the Cock on the Corner were there. The couple supposed that the people who had materialised for the service must have mostly been staying at one of the string of caravan parks between this town and the next along the coast. Afterwards the two boys crowded round and begged them to come again, saying that they could feel the two of them were such good people that their goodness had spread among the others in the room, making a golden atmosphere. They said yes, they would come again.

So they fell into it, and further into it, so far into it that Sarah was taking scones up there on Sundays and Matt was scraping up whatever coins and notes he had around the house at the end of the week to give to the new church. That's what they called it. The New Church. Those who went there began to think of themselves as the New People. Matt rather liked thinking of himself as one of these New People, even though he was contradicted by the mirror in the bathroom and by the way his bones were becoming exquisite carriers of many fine distinctions in arthritic pain. Tristan noticed changes in the way his parents spoke and thought. None of it he liked. As far as he was concerned his parents had been bewitched. There are no new people, nobody has ever been new, not for two or three hundred thousand years, he thought to himself as he scooted around the streets after his friends or just went to and from the café where that girl with bright cheeks, brown eyes and sarcastic lips served him his soft drink. Maybe not for five hundred thousand years, he decided contradictiously. Those American boys knew nothing. He had been reading a bit in the library at school where Mrs Scillion, librarian to the bottom of her soul, had taken a liking to him and had begun to say, 'My domain is your kingdom, young man. I've never seen such a reader in this school.' Mrs Scillion showed him books that explained how ancient was the species we call human according to Darwin and those who follow him. Tristan was pleased to read these books. The pictures and the colourful timelines in diagrams made a lot of sense to him. He preferred these books to television for a while. He thought that one day he might be a librarian himself. Or an archaeologist. He would try to talk to Sandra at the café about which she thought would suit him better in the end.

'You c'n dig around in books or you c'n dig around in swampy peat, it's all the same to me,' she said, sarcastically. He liked her for it, but he seemed to be getting nowhere with her. He noticed that his razor scooter was looking dusty and spotty over in the corner of the café. It was looking neglected, like the two bicycles in the hallway at home, like everything in that house. Like everything in my life, he thought.

*

Twenty years later Tristan sat in his own cottage with a woman who had not been a waitress in the corner café in Cromer, but one who nevertheless had bright cheeks and a certain way with her mouth that made you think she thought something she was not saying, something that amused her. He liked that, he liked being puzzled by her, having to guess about her. Their baby was rolling on the floor at their feet, almost under the television.

'Cakey? What do you mean, it could have been more cakey?' the woman asked him.

'Light and sweet, you know, lightness and sweetness, it's in the temperature of the butter when you make the first crumbling, though you mustn't handle it too much. Sweetness and lightness, you know what I'm talking about, it's not easy to come by.'

'Next time,' she answered, bending down now to the baby so that the sunlight coming through the window caught itself in her deep ropes and rivers of hair, sparking almost.

'What?' she demanded in answer to the way he looked at her.

'Your hair, it should be in one of those fifteenth-century paintings in the national gallery, you know, a national treasure, something audio guides would tell people about as they stand there wondering what to look at when they look at a masterpiece.'

'Stop. Stop or I'll have it all cut off.'

Before he had started on the scone thing, when she had taken the tray out of the oven, he had suddenly mentioned two missionaries who had come to his parents' home twenty years ago and changed their lives. Almost ruined their lives, he had told her, until the devil had rescued them. She asked him now how the devil could have saved his parents.

He told her that not long after his father had sold their car to give yet more money to the church they'd joined, to help pay for a new organ or maybe a new house for the preacher who had come across from Belgium, for something or other that God needed done, because God seemed to need endless small injections of money, at the time when he was thirteen and so lonely he wanted to die, and so ugly he was afraid to become a corpse because he thought he would be laughed at, he had woken one night with his arm on fire. He could smell the flesh of his arm burning and the retching stink of blackened smoke from it was in his nostrils. His fear made him rigid at first, then he leapt from his bed into the corner of the room and screamed until his mother came in to cradle him. This happened for three nights in a row. His mother reported on the third night that she could smell the burning flesh too just before his screams woke her. They took him up to the local doctor who examined the arm carefully. It was true that it was a little numb and lacked muscle tone. It was true that his heart was racing faster than it should, that his temperature was slightly raised and in general he was listless. But there was nothing wrong, the doctor said, that a good game of football wouldn't fix.

That week, when his parents prepared to go to the church on the Sunday, he told them he could smell smoke leaking into the house through cracks in the walls, coming under the doors and in between the window panes. He said that if they left the house he would be trapped there with the smoke, and flames would leap up his arm again. He was sweating and shaking with fear. They stood and looked at each other for a long time. Matt and Sarah stood near the doorway to the hall. Matt looked weary. The bicycles were perfectly still, the scarves too. The photo on the wall seemed about to fall. Everything was suspended, the world itself was so perfectly balanced between possibilities that in a moment it might split in two.

'And that was it,' he said. 'They never went back to that church. I think they were relieved. Secretly I think they felt saved. Though they were worried those missionary boys would return one day.'

He did not tell her that they could never speak about it again, that it became something they could never look into or point at. It was as if there was no word for this thing so close by. But they had left something there, something alive and compact, something that waited and never slept.

'And the devil did that for you? Gave your parents back to you?'

'Yes, but in exchange for our souls.'

'Ah, your souls,' she repeated in that half-poetical way she had of savouring a word. She was scanning the room. 'Now where did I put my book?'

Market Porter

Greg Bogaerts

Pierre leans on his shiny black cane. It is hot in the middle of Paris near the markets. It is only early, barely seven in the morning, and already he is perspiring, the dirty runnels of thick salt water running down his face. He surreptitiously wipes his puffy cheeks, trying at the same time not to smear the thick pink powder he stole from his wife's bureau back in the tiny apartment in Montmartre. Pierre plastered it carefully over the lines and pits in his face, hoping to hide his age so that he might continue to get work as a porter in the markets.

Besides, he thinks, as he looks at his powder-blotched hand, I've been working here for years, decades. They won't forget me; they'll remember what a good porter, a good worker I was. Still am, he tells himself, but he feels the cane slip on the cobblestones made slippery by the congealed lard of slaughtered animals hauled across the narrow square to be strung up for sale.

He almost stumbles, just rights himself in time as some of the younger market porters stroll past. They greet him with familiar hellos, chide him good naturedly, calling him granddad. Pierre despises them, and refuses to acknowledge their existence.

He pulls down his big round straw hat, almost covering his eyes, blocking out the sight of their muscular arms and big hands, their easy animal gait. The men cannot see the anger in his eyes. They cannot see the hurt as well. In his heart Pierre knows they are not being unkind to him; it is just that he is jealous of their youth and strength, their ability to cart and carry heavy boxes of fruit and vegetables and dead animals about the marketplace without the slightest sign of fatigue.

Once upon a time, before that mad Baron von Haussmann tore down the old heart of Paris so dear to Pierre, the porter could work all day, and at the end of his shift he was always ready to take on more work, and ready, always, to make love to his Eugenie when he finally got home and slipped in under the beetling brow of the Montmartre butt and into his small apartment, perched halfway up the Rue Lepic.

Now he is weary and he hasn't done any work today; he is waiting for some of the produce owners or one of the market overseers to come along and offer him paid toil. Pierre flatters himself that his loss of strength is more than compensated for by his dapper appearance. His cane once belonged to a duke, the antique-shop dealer assured Pierre; his long smock once belonged to a prince, the back-street peddler in clothes promised. The smock is draped about Pierre, hiding, he hopes, his corpulent body. His exotic hat is an object of envy among the other porters, he tells himself, and the hand-tooled leather boots Eugenie polishes early every morning should be enough, he convinces himself, for an overseer or owner to hire him.

And even if he can't manage the work anymore, he is entitled, because of his years of long and loyal service, to help from one of the younger porters, someone who might serve as an apprentice to him, thinks Pierre, puffing his chest out with importance and pride.

Pierre remembers Monsieur le Grand, one of the big owners of produce in the markets, years ago. Le Grand brought eggs, vegetables and fruit by the crate load to the market every day, and he always sought out Pierre, telling all in the marketplace that Pierre was the best market porter he'd seen, that his blood should be bottled and the other porters, far lesser men, should be made to drink small sips of the thick, vital, bright-red substance to make them into the tireless worker Pierre was. But not too much of that blood for each man, le Grand always warned; he said that too much richness of strength and determination might harm some of the pale shadows of men who slouched about the market, barely able to stand upright let alone cart a box full of sheep heads across the cobblestones.

Ahh, those were the days, thinks Pierre, and he pulls himself upright, balancing his weight between the cane planted in the cleft formed by two cobblestones and his other hand, which holds the ornate cast-iron lamppost. He stands slightly forward, hoping to disguise his hand gripping the post. He holds on to the ornate metal head of a snake, cast by some mad artist in a garret or a cellar somewhere, he thinks.

That's the trouble, says Pierre out loud, since Haussmann ruined the city and the Bohemians came to stay, things have gone to rack and ruin. One of the lady shoppers, passing him, gives him a strange look. Pierre realises it is because he was talking out loud to himself. He pulls himself together, grits his teeth, but bites the tip of his tongue so the blood spatters down his fleshy double chins. I must stop talking to myself; people will think I'm mad, he chides.

Only the other day his Eugenie stopped in the middle of dusting, came over to where he was sitting with his legs raised (so that his puffy ankles would go down) and said: 'Good God, Pierre, you've been talking to yourself for the past half hour, and I don't think it's that glass of wine you're drinking. For goodness sake, man, be quiet. I can't think to do my housework. If you're going to talk to yourself, go into the bedroom and sit in front of the big mirror. At least that way you'll have someone to talk to.'

Her mocking words were close to the vinegar sting of sarcasm, and they hurt Pierre. He loves his Eugenie with a passion, even if not much of that passion translates anymore into love making. He got out of the chair with difficulty and left, but not before a parting shot of hot acid words caught him.

'And if you're going to use my face powder all of the time then you should go out on the streets with the working girls. At least if you sold your fabulous body we might be able to pay the rent on time.'

Pierre blushes at the thought of her words; the heat is thick like the molasses that arrives in the market in big stone bottles from Africa, and he feels faint. For a moment he thinks the iron snake he is holding has come alive; for a second he is convinced it will bite him and sting him to death. It is a delusion, he tells himself, and forces himself to stand still, not to cry out in fear.

It's not the first time he's imagined such things. Last week, on the Sunday, when he was climbing the Rue Lepic to buy bread from the bakery near the summit, he imagined the loaves had turned into sharks and that they were swimming out of the bakery door down the incline towards him. He screamed, afraid they would tear him limb from limb, devour his flabby body with their rapacious jaws.

The baker, drawn by Pierre's screams, came from his shop and looked with only mild interest at the terrified man. Passers-by regarded him with amused curiosity until Pierre got himself under control, went into the bakery and, gritting his teeth, ignoring the jibes of the baker, purchased some of the man-eating sharks. He took them from the shop, holding the bag at arm's length, convinced, still, that if he held the warm loaves close, the escaped beasts of the sea would bite him.

Now he forces himself upright once more. His head swims, the cobblestones of the market rise and fall like a big tide, rushing down the Seine during the spring thaw; shoppers float by him, vendors seem to expand and contract as if they are made from some strange plasma, alien forms of life. And they are to Pierre; they no longer know him, no longer care about him.

Suddenly he is brought back; everything stills. The smell, the stink is rank, so strong it brings back images to Pierre's mind, pictures of the live wild animals that used occasionally to be sold in the market. He turns and sees the big black and yellow striped Bengali tiger in a wooden cage being man-handled across the market square by four burly porters. The animal opens its mouth; the stench hits Pierre like death. The men sweat and curse with the heat and the heaviness of the animal; their fear makes them weak, Pierre can tell, and who could blame them. The long tarnished teeth of the animal are only inches from their bodies.

Then the tiger screams and roars, the noise echoing against the building walls of the marketplace, stopping every man, woman and child in their tracks. Pierre sees the fear etched on every face, and this gives him some solace, some satisfaction he cannot fathom.

The tiger is placed on a stone stand in the middle of the square where it will be sold to the highest bidder, probably a circus owner or a rich man wanting something exotic to roam the parklands of his estate to amuse his lovers and wife. The wooden crate and the animal disappear from Pierre's view. He is dizzy again and reaches for his moustache, which he regards as his one vanity. The magnificent edifice of hair, plastered with wax under his nose, is his good-luck charm, the talisman he has stroked and worried for years.

He touches it, but there is almost nothing there other than a bare line of greying bristles, and then he remembers, almost sobbing with the grief the memory brings to him. Last week, after work, he'd sat in the cool of evening on the front step of his landlord's apartment, waxing his moustache the way he did almost every night. But he'd put too much wax on the hair, saturated it so it hardened into a long line of hair and wax.

He'd fallen asleep, and one of the gang of urchins that marauded up and down the Rue Lepic came along, took hold of the mustache, and, with one strong yank, tore the adornment from under Pierre's nose. The pain was excruciating, but not as painful as seeing the ragged boy, running down the hill, holding Pierre's moustache above his head, yelling to his grimy comrades that one of the working girls had just donated her muff to his collection of bric-a-brac.

The prostitutes who ply their trade up and down the Rue Lepic and along the Boulevard de Clichy, have a reputation for whipping up egg whites and plastering them through their pubic hair. Sexual tastes come in all shapes and forms in Paris.

Soon, the whole street knew of Pierre's loss and, for days, he had to suffer the jibes and jokes of his neighbours about escaped hairy caterpillars and the dangers of loss one might have to bear when munching the vagina of one of the working girls. The girls were inspected by government authorities once a week for syphilis. The butcher on the Rue Lepic suggested that a deputation from the street should accompany the inspectors to see if Pierre's moustache could be discovered and reclaimed.

Pierre has had enough; he can't keep up his pose of strength and sartorial magnificence any longer. He slumps over his cane, eventually stands up straight, and decides to go to the small café at the edge of the marketplace. Here, he thinks, I will revive myself with coffee and a plain roll. No butter is needed to make it slide more easily down his pelican gullet of a throat.

He sits at a small table and fishes into the pocket of his smock for the franc he is sure is there, but it isn't. But that won't matter, he thinks. The café owner has known him for years, they are almost comrades, almost friends. The big, bald, bullet-headed man comes to Pierre, and the porter is taken aback for a second by the look of distrust that creeps like river mud across the man's face.

'A cup of black coffee and a roll without butter if you please, monsieur,' says Pierre in his best merry and bluff voice.

The café owner leans on the edge of Pierre's table; the man's hands are enormous and, for a moment, Pierre forgets to be afraid because he is jealous; he would like to have those hands because he would always have work if he had them. But then the fear takes hold of the old porter, and he struggles to meet the cold, hard, iron-grey eyes of the owner.

'Show me the colour of your money first, monsieur,' he demands in a voice sharper than the blade of the guillotine.

Pierre reaches to rub his throat, but he can't find it among the multiple layers of fat chins that spill down to his grimy white collar.

'Wh … what do you m … mean, m … monsieur?' he stammers.

He grins at the man. Pierre looks like one of the African monkeys that used to be sold in the market, creatures that always wore a perpetual grimace as if they were pleading for mercy and compassion from their captors and future owners.

'I mean that your credit has run out. You owe me at least ten francs for rolls and coffee and you cannot have any more until you pay me,' says the owner, who turns on his heel, pauses a moment to present the disdain of his back to Pierre, then marches off.

Pierre, blushing bright red, rises, totters away; the markets are a roiling ocean of confusion to him. He searches out his iron pole and takes hold. Hanging his head, he closes his eyes. He does not care anymore about keeping up appearances and hoping for work. He takes no notice when the screams of horror and terror rise in the marketplace. His head still hangs in defeat like the head of one of the bullocks, its throat cut from ear to ear, its body hauled up by a chain for the market butcher to carve steaks from to sell to shoppers.

The commotion grows louder so that Pierre cannot ignore it. He raises his head and there, standing next to him, is the Bengali tiger, crouched back on its steel haunches, ready to spring. Its jaws are open, its teeth glow dully; Pierre, for a mad moment, thinks it is smiling at him.

'Go on, piss off, you bastard! Go and have a good laugh at my expense with the others,' he tells the beast.

The tiger, maybe having grown used to the human reaction of fear to its presence, seems puzzled by this short fat man speaking angrily to it. Its muscles relax a little; it turns its head to one side and regards the porter with glistening eyes in which the jungles of the subcontinent still live dimly.

'Go on, piss off, I said! Go away!' says Pierre.

The tiger does not move. Pierre opens his eyes and sees what he thinks is a throng of shoppers crouched low, hiding behind boxes and doors, whatever is at hand, looking at him with fear and relief. They look at him that way because once the porter is eaten they think the tiger will not eat them.

Pierre, seeing the attention of the throng focused on him, loses his temper, stands up straight and strikes the tiger with his cane. The animal is infuriated and the roar is terrifying, sobering Pierre, wrenching him back to reality. He looks at the big cat and finally realises it is the tiger he saw carried past before, and he understands that it has somehow escaped.

The tiger screams again, bunches its hard neck muscles, and the porter sees that it is about to spring, and he will be killed. Desperately he thinks, and an image of his wife and her cat rises in his brain. He sees Eugenie and the way she scratches her cat, Leon, under the chin and between its eyes, and the porter hears the purr of contentment. Pierre knows he has no choice; his life is miserable, but continuing to live a miserable life seems preferable to being eaten alive by a tiger in front of so many people. Such a mess, thinks Pierre. All that blood, and my poor white body would be revealed to all and sundry and they would laugh about it later.

Carefully he reaches forward, leaning on his cane, and carefully he reaches out. The tiger growls a warning, but Pierre manages to scratch between those cold and merciless eyes. He continues scratching a bit harder when the tiger doesn't bite off his hand. Gradually the tiger's eyes close, its body relaxes, its head lowers. Pierre has to bend forward more to reach between its eyes. The pain of stretching down is excruciating, but the porter thinks it could not be worse than being eaten raw.

Fleas from the tiger's fur hop onto Pierre's hand; they bite hard, drawing the man's sugary blood into their bodies. Pierre grits his teeth, stopping the sound of irritation from escaping. He does not want to bring the tiger out of its torpor.

From the corner of his eye, Pierre sees the shoppers, some of them standing, some of them moving a bit closer to the porter and his tiger. Clearly they are impressed, Pierre understands. He bends even lower, slips his hand under the thick muff of the tiger's chin, and begins to stroke and scratch. The beast begins to purr, and that purr sounds like a growl of anger, but the old porter keeps on. Besides, he is beginning to bask in the growing admiration of the shoppers and market vendors. With satisfaction, Pierre notices the look of awe and respect on the café owner's face.

There is movement behind the crowd; someone, it seems, has been found to do something about the escaped animal, hopes Pierre. And he is right.

'Keep on stroking him there, monsieur,' says the man dressed all in white, holding a long black whip and wearing long black leather boots.

By luck a travelling circus has set up close to the market, and their lion tamer has been called upon by one of the market overseers to come and save all of his customers.

'Now, when I tell you, monsieur, step away from the tiger. Keep on moving away so I can confront the cat. All will be well once you do that. He will not harm you once I am between him and you,' the tamer says.

Pierre continues to scratch; the tiger's eyes are almost closed. Its head almost rests on the cobblestones.

'Now, monsieur, my brave lad, move away as quick as you can.'

Pierre doesn't need to be told twice. He steps away; the tiger does not move. Pierre takes more steps. He is dizzy and he begins to fall backward, but the arms of the admiring crowd catch him, pull him to his feet, then raise him high above their heads. The last thing Pierre sees, before he looks up at the blue oblivion of the sky, is the tamer brandishing his whip, holding the mad animal in check, and the young porters advancing on the tiger with the wooden crate.

Pierre is pleased with the attention, flattered by the praise of the shoppers as they carry him on high towards the café. But the old man is reminded of his father's death. His father was a coal miner in the Loire Valley and died in a mine collapse. Pierre remembers, as he is sat at a table and the café owner plies him with coffee and dozens of buttered rolls, his father brought home, his body held high by fellow miners, the corpse left on the kitchen table for Pierre's mother to wash before burial.

But that sobering memory vanishes as he answers the breathless questions of the shoppers. He replies that he was not scared for a moment. He tells them he has been a porter in the markets for years, and there was no way he was going to let a mere tiger upset the daily routine of selling produce. His newfound admirers stuff many francs into the pocket of his smock, and Pierre pretends to be embarrassed, pretends not to want the money, but he makes sure he stuffs the coins and notes further down into the pocket to make way for more.

A market overseer hires a horse and carriage so Pierre goes home in style. The horse steps high and fast, but news of the porter's heroic deed travels faster. When he gets to the Rue Lepic, the crowd is dense out the front of his apartment. Pierre alights, and immediately he is besieged by well-wishers and the curious, wanting him to tell them how he tamed the tiger. Pierre obliges his many devotees many times, and they ply him with drinks and food. They run up and down the steep street in straight lines, fetching delicacies for him to consume.

Pierre looks up into the black sky; the stars circle in bright wreaths of fire. He drinks the Green Fairy, many glasses, but he feels unaffected, as though the spirit of the old man is now more than a match for the deadly green spirit.

Finally they let him go, and Eugenie helps him to the couch in the small sitting room. He lies down; his heart is beating hard like the hammering of the steel foundry on the banks of the Seine just south of the city. The walls of the apartment seem to melt, and Pierre sees the man and woman when he turns his head to one side. His mother and father stand on the cusp of a room Pierre did not know was there. They smile at their son; their radiance falls upon his bloated body and sweaty brow. He smiles back.

But suddenly, Eugenie stands in front of him, blocking Pierre's parents from his view. The light of their radiance dims, almost eclipsed by the naked and plentiful body of the woman. She wears black stockings and high-laced black leather boots, the same as the washerwomen and seamstresses of Montmartre wear.

'Now, my darling Pierre, you have tamed a tiger, you have tamed the marketplace and you have tamed our creditors. I think it is time for you to tame me as you used to do,' she says.

The woman thrusts forward her plump pubis. Pierre looks at her with horror. He wonders if he reaches out and scratches her under the chin and between her eyes whether she might go away.

Southerly

I Can Hear the Ice Singing

Sean Rabin

Unnar Eyjólfsdóttir, Paris, France, 1982
Jónas? Of course I knew him. We grew up in the same village. You've heard the story? Well, I was the person who first discovered him in the ice. My goodness that was a long time ago. Wherever did you come across his name? I haven't thought of him in years. I was only a girl then, thirteen or fourteen. But already serious about skating. The harbour in front of my village froze solid every winter and I would go out there before school to practise. Even then the only thing I wanted was to become a famous skater and travel the world. And now look at me! I can still remember that morning. As usual I'd walked down to the pebble beach in the dark then started to lace up my skates. I didn't notice Jónas at first. But as the sun rose I saw something about two hundred yards from the shore. It was large and brown, so I thought it must be a seal. They sometimes crawled onto the ice if they were injured, and in the morning one of the fishermen would have to put the poor creature out of its misery. I skated out to investigate and quickly realised it was a man, not a seal. It happened every few years. Someone would drink too much, then go for a walk on the ice and freeze to death. I was scared it was going to be a relation, and considered going back to the village for help, when suddenly the body sat up. I must have screamed with fright, because Jónas turned around and waved for me to skate closer. I couldn't understand what he was

doing out there and thought perhaps he was too injured to walk. But when I skated in front of him I couldn't see any blood or broken ankle. In fact, I couldn't see any ankles at all because both his legs were below the ice. Not all of the leg, just his feet and shins, so he could still bend his knees and lie backwards. It was so confusing I kept skating around Jónas to make sure that what I was seeing was real. I'd always thought he was handsome. All the girls did. Jónas was never too loud or boastful, and never drank more than the rest of the men. Any girl would have been happy to marry him. Including myself. Probably that's why I flirted and asked what he'd give me if I went for help. And you know what he replied? That a girl as pretty as me shouldn't have to ask for anything. Well, after that I couldn't even look him in the eye. I just kept skating around and around as Jónas offered to take me to the pictures. I'll be wanting a Coke as well, I said. And chocolates. I thought I was so sassy. But when Jónas asked if I'd also like a kiss, it sent me to the shore as fast as my skates would carry me. Oh, I know it probably didn't happen exactly that way, but it's how I like to remember it. There is one thing I am certain of, though. Just before I left to get my brother I noticed there wasn't a mark on the ice. Usually my skates made lines everywhere, but that morning, even though I had been tracing the same spot over and over, there was nothing. Not the slightest scratch.

Ulrik Andrésson, Kópavogur, Iceland, 1979
He threatened to kill me when I arrived on the ice. Shouted in front of everyone that if he lost his legs there'd be nowhere I could hide; he'd hunt me down and kill me. Hans as well. I was still hung over so it came as quite a shock. Jónas and I had been friends since kindergarten. We drank together, worked the same fishing boats; I couldn't understand why he was so angry with me. Then finally I realised he thought Hans and I were responsible for him being stuck in the ice. Jónas couldn't remember how he got there – never could – so he assumed we had plied him with drink and played a prank. But it wasn't true. Sure, we'd been out the night before – it was Jónas' twenty-third birthday – but he'd left early. Said he'd had enough. There were people on the ice that morning who even confirmed it. Baldur owned the tavern,

and told Jónas that Tumi and I had stayed until closing time. All right, Hans left soon after Jónas, but it wasn't to play a prank. I don't know if I should tell you this. Hans is married now with kids. His wife might not like it. You see, Hans went home with Freyja that night. It was why he wasn't on the ice that morning. They were still in bed. Maybe you shouldn't write that part down, I don't want Hans to get in trouble. Jónas could tell I was telling the truth. We'd been friends so long that he knew when I was lying. Jónas was always a steady man. Never lost his temper unless there was a good reason. So he calmed down. But the loss of certainty about who was responsible for him being stuck in the ice left him confused – I could see it on his face. I said we'd have him out in no time, but I was late to the ice. There was a whole circle of spectators standing around him by the time I arrived. And I didn't realise they'd already tried most things. Hammers, chisels, but nothing made so much as a dent. Nobody had ever seen ice so hard. Even the hand drills we used for ice fishing couldn't make a mark, and it takes two men to turn them. Everyone had an opinion about how best to get Jónas out. Gunnar fetched his hoe, and the crowd laughed themselves silly when its wooden handle snapped in two. The same when Kettil tried his pick and it ricocheted back over his head so fast that it pulled him down onto his bottom. Young boys wielded crowbars and screwdrivers, but nothing worked. You should have heard the old men muttering about how young people didn't work hard enough, and that's why they had no strength. It seemed ridiculous to them that ice could not be broken. Pétur arrived with his axe, and badly gashed open his own leg when its blade slid sideways. After that we all stood around scratching our heads. Ice that would not even chip made no sense. But we refused to give up. So the children were sent for firewood and any coal their mothers could spare. We thought a fire might weaken the surface of the ice and allow our tools to get a hold underneath. The coal was put down first, covered with straw and twigs before a layer of wood. Everyone stood behind Jónas to avoid the smoke. We tied a rope around his waist in case the ice suddenly cracked, but the blaze only burned the twigs and wood. The coal refused to catch. Someone suggested pouring vodka on the fire, and you should have heard the cheer go up. People were acting like it was a party.

Teitur Dagfinnsson, Elmey Island, Iceland, 1978
Jónas Arnmundsson ruined this village. That's all I've got to say about him.

Magnús Arnmundsson, Reykjavík, Iceland, 1980
Our mother took great care of us when we were kids; loved her husband, and adored her grandchildren, but she was a habitual crier. No matter if she was reading a book, dancing at a wedding, or burning something on the stove; down would flow the tears. She wasn't an especially sad person. Her emotions just lived near the surface where it was difficult for her to control them. All her friends were used to it, and so were her children, but it can't have been easy for Jónas when she stood in front of him and sobbed like that. I thought her tears had been bad as we hurried across the ice, but when she saw how his legs were stuck, the floodgates just burst open. Our father sighed and said: Didn't I warn you about drinking too much last night? Elín was sixteen at the time and thought everything was funny. She gave Jónas a kiss and told him how we'd all assumed he was still in bed sleeping it off. Jónas called me over and quietly asked if I could find a bottle for him to pee in. When I got back they were about to pour vodka on the fire. Father had taken charge. He didn't want anyone accidentally setting his son alight. I handed Jónas the jar, then moved back with the rest of the crowd to avoid the smoke. Father joined us when the vodka was finished, and Jónas took advantage of the moment of privacy to relieve himself. When the fire burned out we saw that nothing had happened to the ice. Not even a black scar. People started to return to the village. Jónas might be stuck, but there was still work to do. Our mother fetched food, while Father tried all the tools that had been used before he arrived. Elín stood with her friends and started to feel embarrassed at how ridiculous her brother looked. I began my shift at the cannery, but came back in the afternoon with blankets for Jónas to sit on. Because it was the middle of winter there were fewer hours of daylight, so only Father remained on the ice. I was eighteen at the time and happy to take over keeping Jónas company. Elín brought us supper, and as we ate Jónas told me how when he woke that morning he thought he was still dreaming. But no matter how hard he slapped his own face, he

remained stuck in the ice. So he started to hack at it with his pocketknife, and when that failed he unbuckled his belt to try and slide out of his trousers. It might have worked if the space around his ankles hadn't been too narrow for his feet to pass through. He assumed they were swollen with cold, and poor Jónas, he kept asking over and over if I thought he was going to lose his legs. How could he be a fisherman without legs? He was exhausted ... and so was I. My head kept nodding forward. I remember Jónas telling me to go home. He had wrapped himself in blankets and pulled a hunting hat over his ears. By the time I reached the shore he was lying down. It was too far away to see if his eyes were open, but I hoped they were because the winter lights had appeared and I thought they could keep him company.

Dr Ragnarsson, Hafnarfjörður, Iceland, 1981
According to my records there was nothing wrong with Jónas. When I examined him his blood pressure was normal, his pulse was steady, and his temperature was only point two of a degree higher than it should have been, which I attributed to stress. It was quite remarkable considering the situation he was in. Hypothermia was just one of the problems I expected to face when I walked onto the ice that day. It was the middle of winter for heaven's sake. I had never performed an amputation before, but I anticipated the need to do both legs if they couldn't get him free. I tried not to let such a grim prospect show on my face. And certainly everyone else was doing their best to keep up Jónas' morale. People were standing around talking and eating, and sipping vodka to stave off the chill. I could see Jónas trying to remain calm, but when Unnar skated back onto the ice it signalled that school was over and still no progress had been made. Jónas' face filled with fear, and I told everyone to stand back to give the man some privacy. I asked him to drop his trousers so I could examine the skin of his legs. I even managed to squeeze a finger down behind his calves, but everything appeared normal; they didn't even feel cold. He said he could wiggle his toes inside his shoes, though I didn't give it too much credence. His feet could have been frozen solid and he was just imagining them moving, like an itch on an arm that has long

ago been amputated. After he dressed I asked about appetite, and passing water, and if he felt any pain. I won't deny the results puzzled me. To a man of science it made no sense. By that stage Jónas had been stuck in the ice for more than twelve hours, and though his clothes were cut for cold weather, their protective qualities could explain his good health only to a point. The rest was beyond me. I kept visiting Jónas every day, but there was no change to his condition. And eventually our appointments stretched to once a week. Frostbite had become more of a distant possibility than a looming certainty, and Jónas no longer feared losing his legs. In fact, I believe he'd stopped even feeling the cold, though I haven't any scientific evidence to prove it.

Magnús Arnmundsson, Reykjavík, Iceland, 1980
When the first blizzard hit there was nothing we could do. It was the middle of the night, and such a big storm that to go outside was suicide. We all thought Jónas was going to die. Elín panicked. Mother cried. And Father yelled at them both to calm down. I wanted to try to make it to Jónas, but no one would let me leave the house. We sat up all night listening to the howl of the wind, until the sun finally rose and revealed just how severe the storm was. It continued for another two or three hours then passed out to sea. By that stage we held no hope of finding Jónas alive. Father put on his snowshoes and carried a shovel out onto the ice. It was covered with four feet of snow, so he walked towards where he could only assume the body was. He knew Jónas sat about two hundred yards from the pebble beach, but before he had counted one hundred and eighty steps a well appeared in the snow with his son sitting in the middle of it, apparently unharmed. Jónas turned at the sound of his father and waved. The way the snow had refused to settle on him, or near him, was as much of a surprise to Jónas as it was to our father. The well was ten yards in diameter and perfectly round, and Father thought Jónas had somehow built it as a form of protection. But there were no tools. Only a bucket, a bottle of water – still unfrozen – umbrella, and the small wooden box where Jónas stored his toothbrush, flashlight and newspaper. They were all tied to tails that had been cut in a canvas sheet

we'd laid under the blankets Jónas sat on. It was a system I'd devised to stop his possessions being blown across the ice, and when I looked down into the well I felt proud at how successfully it had worked. Jónas told me the worst part of the blizzard was boredom. The wind made it impossible to read, and with no one able to visit he quickly grew weary of his own thoughts and lonesome for his view. Jónas said that despite the noise he just went to sleep, and all night felt perfectly warm. Father couldn't stop smiling, and Mother wouldn't stop crying, and Elín ran back home to cook her brother's favourite fish cakes. People from the village with less invested in Jónas' welfare were shocked by his survival and unable to conceal their disappointment that he was not as dead as they had predicted he would be. It was unnatural. An aberration. No one could survive a blizzard like that. Some mothers told their children not to go near, and men who had even worked with Jónas sat in the tavern that night mumbling how it would bring the village bad luck. Grandmothers recited prayers whenever they saw the tiny figure in the distance, and refused to relinquish their fears of the Devil's handiwork even after Jónas had eaten the sacrament. The local priest had walked onto the ice expecting to recite prayers for the dead, but instead found Dr Ragnarsson with his stethoscope out, listening to Jónas' heart.

Ulrik Andrésson, Kópavogur, Iceland, 1979

By the time Hans and I reached Jónas, Hallmar had hold of his shirt and was shouting at him to melt the ice. Spring was already two weeks old, and while the rest of the island had ceased to be locked in, our harbour remained frozen. All through winter we assumed the sea would melt like it always did. It was why we had stopped trying to set Jónas free. No one thought he was going to die of frostbite anymore, so it was easier to just wait for spring than blunt another drill or saw. Everyone was tired of failing, and the men in the village said it wasn't their fault Jónas had got himself stuck in the ice. He pushed Hallmar away and yelled at the other drunken fishermen that he had watched people hammer all through winter without making a scratch, so what was he supposed to do, break it with his fists? Teitur swayed on his feet and suggested that maybe it wasn't the ice that needed breaking.

That's when Hans and I stepped in. We wanted the fishing boats back in the water as much as anyone, but would not stand by and watch Jónas be harmed. Teitur and Hallmar sized us up, yet lacked the courage to take on opponents who were not at a disadvantage. The other men grumbled and complained, then slowly began to make their way back across the ice to the village. When they were gone, Hans pulled a bottle out of his coat and declared we all deserved a drink. The next thing I remember I felt a sharp pain in my neck, and Jónas was pestering Hans about whether he still owned his rowboat. The sun had started to rise, and Hans refused to open his eyes or listen to anything about Otom's Point. Everyone in the village knew there was nothing out there to catch. Something to do with the currents, or the water's temperature. But Jónas kept insisting he'd give us anything we wanted if only we'd row out there and try. I had always admired his boning knife, and there was nothing else to do that day, so I stood up and kicked Hans awake. It was his boat, and I needed help to drag it across the ice. I reckon it took us three trips to get all the fish back to the village. Hans' dinghy was so full that if there'd been the slightest swell I'm sure we would have been swamped and drowned. Jónas said it felt like one of the flying dreams he'd had as a boy, but this time he was free of the ice and in a boat, yanking in fish as fast as he could drop a line. You should have seen the tavern that night. The whole village was happy for us. But no one would believe Jónas had anything to do with it. They all thought it was a fluke and we were making up stories to protect our friend from another mob. Only when we came in the next day from Black Bottom with another big haul, and the day after that from the edge of the reef, did the idea of Jónas giving fishing tips start to gain traction.

Bryndís Einarsdóttir, Elmey Island, Iceland, 1978

Jónas believed the ice was as alive as the sea it had come from. He understood that to everyone else it appeared as just a slab of frozen water, because that's how he used to see it as well. But after his legs became stuck he realised the ice was always changing, always evolving. Jónas used to say that even if he lived two lifetimes he would never be able to discover all its secrets. I'm sure you and I can imagine it shimmering like a jewel when the sun came up, but to Jónas it was also like a fountain, and a tortoise, and a tin can. I know, it sounds silly, doesn't it? But remember when you were a kid and you tied a piece of string between two cans to pretend it was a telephone? Well, that's what Jónas said the ice was like for him. The frozen harbour was one can, and the ocean was the string that connected him to everywhere else in the world. He would tell me about what he sensed through the ice whenever we lay next to each other. It was a little ritual that had started the first night we were together. Jónas must have been in the ice for three years by then, as it was the night of his twenty-sixth birthday. I was so late I think I woke him up. My grandmother had been unable to get to sleep, and I couldn't let her hear me leave the house. She was in no position to judge people, but it was hard for her not to be a little superstitious about Jónas … it was just her generation. I had only recently come back to Elmey to take care of her. There was no one else, and she had raised me from when I was six. Anyway, it was better I visited Jónas after everyone had left. Five years on the mainland meant I was still a worthy topic of gossip. He was shy when I sat next to him. We knew each other from school, but Jónas had been stuck in the ice while his friends were out gaining experience with girls, so he couldn't help but feel nervous. He offered me a drink. And pickled herring, of all things. Then said if I closed my eyes he would show me a trick. I told him I didn't really like surprises, but Jónas insisted so sweetly, and looked so unthreatening, that in the end I agreed to play along. When I opened my eyes I found myself sitting in the middle of a circle of light glowing up from beneath the ice. I couldn't remember the last time I had seen something so beautiful, and when the light finally faded I gave a small shiver of loss. Jónas offered me his coat. He said he didn't feel the cold anymore. That he'd almost forgotten what it was like. He only wore heavy clothes to stop people accusing him of being possessed by the Devil. I pretended to doubt such a claim and dared him to take off his shirt. I might have been the first woman Jónas slept with but he was not naïve enough to think my visit was an accident. He realised Hans and Ulrik had something to do with it, and as he got dressed he said he was too happy to care. It's what I liked about Jónas. He was calmer than most men. Maybe because he knew he couldn't go anywhere or do anything else, and had accepted his life. Don't get me wrong, he was still ambitious. Jónas had set up a business with the fishermen, and he was determined to see me again. It wasn't the first time a virgin had fallen in love with me, but I was newly retired and told Jónas on the night of his birthday that it was just a favour I had done for Ulrik and Hans. So instead he sent me food. My grandmother lived on a tiny pension, and the cannery would only give me shifts when someone was off sick, so Jónas arranged for boxes of groceries to be delivered to our door. Each time a different friend would do the buying, but I knew where they were coming from and ran down to the ice to tell him I wasn't for sale, not to him or anyone else. So, Jónas being Jónas, he apologised and asked if I would come work for him. He wanted someone to tell him all they knew about the world beyond Elmey Island. Explain how loud aeroplanes were; what a city smelled like; if the theatre was really as wonderful as it sounded in the books he had read. I agreed to do it thinking I was calling his bluff, but for the next two years I visited the ice every day and answered his questions about the mainland. I suppose it's no surprise we eventually fell in love and married, but that wasn't until my grandmother was dead and the war was over.

Hallmar Bergsson, Mosfellsbær, Iceland, 1980

In the beginning, before everyone got greedy, it was a terrific system. Someone was always struggling to make repayments on their boat, or had too much credit owing at Tumi's, but when Jónas started giving tips on where to fish we all began to earn enough to pay off our debts. There were only six boats then, so every morning one of the captains would go down to Jónas and be told where to drop his nets. I don't know how he did it. Some people said he felt the fish through the ice, but I couldn't say for certain. He just always led us to a good catch. Better than good. A fantastic catch, every time. The captain with the day's tip was always given an hour's lead. That way no one could follow him to the fishing spot. Jónas came up with the system himself. Said he wanted it to be fair to everyone, which was pretty generous considering how we'd treated him when the ice didn't melt that first spring. I don't know if I could have done the same. I'd probably have just kept giving tips to my friends. But when we all walked onto the ice Jónas pretended like he had never been threatened, and said that if we wanted to fish like Ulrik and Hans we had to work together. First to get the boats across the ice, because Jónas doubted if it was going to melt any time soon, and then to build a temporary pier. At that stage not even Jónas believed the ice was going to last through the summer. But it did. It lasted for years and years, and eventually we had to make the pier at the mouth of the harbour permanent. Jónas helped pay for it. He was always fair with money. All he ever asked for was two per cent of the profit each captain made on the day he received a tip. And a further three per cent to be deposited into a pension and accident fund. No one liked it at first. You've got to understand that we were used to taking what we wanted from the sea and not paying anyone for it. Even after Jónas explained the savings we'd make on fuel if we didn't have to search from one fishing spot to the next, it still wasn't popular. Of course, no one was forcing us to join. But Jónas made a good point that the men in the village who worked as crew would probably favour boats that were guaranteed at least one big catch a week. I knew there were captains already thinking of ways to cheat Jónas' system, but he warned us that anyone caught following the first boat of the morning, or lying about the size of their catch, was stealing from the entire village, not just him, and if it happened he would give them no more advice. We all agreed, and asked Jónas about the last day of the week. There were seven days and only six captains. But Jónas said Sunday was a day of rest, for us as well as the fish. There were no rules about where we dropped our nets on the days we didn't receive a tip, but I can tell you I looked forward to the mornings it was my turn to visit Jónas on the ice. I'd never had hauls like it before, and certainly never have since. I paid off my boat in five years, and so did pretty much everyone else. Even the cannery started to make a profit. And all the while Jónas just kept taking his two per cent. I don't know what he spent it on. He didn't have a house. And didn't buy any more clothes than what he could wear because he had nowhere to put them. I guess he supported his wife, but they weren't married straight away. And even his food was free. As part of the deal about telling us where to fish, Jónas said it was the responsibility of the captain he spoke with each morning to provide his meals for that day. Breakfast, lunch and dinner. My wife didn't mind taking him a plate of whatever we were eating, and I know the other captains, when they realised how much Jónas' advice was worth, didn't think twice about it. Some would get the village restaurant to deliver to him, while others asked their mother or sister to help.

Teitur Dagfinnsson, Elmey Island, Iceland, 1979
And another thing. His wife was a whore. Everyone knew it. I don't care what people say now. Once a whore, always a whore.

Unnar Eyjólfsdóttir, Paris, France, 1982
I usually went back to Elmey during the summer months. People aren't interested in ice-skating when it's warm, I can understand that. And after so much touring I enjoyed the chance to spend time with my parents and friends. When the taxi brought me over the hill and the harbour came into view, I would see Jónas' tiny figure among that great expanse of white and know at last I was home. It was always a relief to see he had survived another year. Because I was the one who had found him in the ice I felt we had a special bond. Nothing romantic, just good friends. And I made sure I always brought him back a gift. He didn't have anywhere to store trinkets or postcards, so it would either be a delicacy he could eat or some unusual liqueur. Jonas insisted I tell him about the places I had played that year. Most people in the village didn't ask about my travels in case I'd seen somewhere better than their island, but Jónas wanted to learn how things were different in Russia and America and Canada. He couldn't believe what I told him about China, and made me repeat the same stories over and over until they were clear in his imagination. That's not to say the people in the village didn't treat me well. They did. Of course they did. I was famous, and they'd insist I give them a show. It would have been impossible without Jónas' ice, so I always thought of us as a team, and that together we helped start the tradition of a summer festival. Every year the village would set up food stalls and a beer tent on the ice, and organise games for the children. One time there

was even a merry-go-round. Jónas never admitted that he paid for it to be brought over, but everyone knew he had. He loved the festival because it was the only day of the year he was surrounded by the entire village. He even devised a game of strength where everyone had a turn at swinging a large wooden mallet against the ice to try and break him free. Sometimes Jónas said he felt something, especially if a child was trying their hardest, but I can assure you there was never a scratch on that ice. Dirt didn't even seem to stain it. If you're having a festival there's going to be drinks spilled and food dropped, and somebody always has too much beer. I would sometimes look at the ice after everything was packed away and think, oh my goodness, look how dirty it is. But the next morning it would be back to its brilliant self. I don't know if the wind blew away the litter and birds ate the scraps, or Jónas' family came down to clean it for him, but it was always so perfectly white that it was hard to believe it was made from the same stuff that turned grey and slushy in every other town I visited. I was so proud of that. But not everything stayed the same. Things did gradually change in the village. Some summers I'd spend performing in Australia and New Zealand, after which I'd go straight into my winter tour, so I would be away from home for almost two years, and when I came back I'd notice girls wearing finely made clothes or restaurants charging mainland prices. I was never around long enough to get to the bottom of it, but there were rumours Jónas was helping the men find more fish. I thought somebody was just making it up to play a trick on me; to see if they could get the worldly traveller to believe a silly story. People in small communities sometimes do things like that, and I've learnt not to take it personally. It reveals more about their own insecurities than anything about me.

Elín Arnmundsdóttir, Elmey Island, Iceland, 1978
Jónas got bored just like everyone else. Who wouldn't looking at the same view day after day? But the only time I remember him being sad was when our father died. It might seem strange, but Mother and Father grew to like having Jónas stuck in the ice. Every parent worries about where their children are, no matter how old they grow, so the fact they always knew where Jónas was

gave them a sort of comfort. I don't think a day went by when Father and Jónas didn't talk. Even during the coldest weeks of winter he would walk down for a visit. And every time he would give Jónas a kiss. We all did. It was a family tradition that had started the day he had been found in the ice, and we kept it up so Jónas knew that even though he wasn't with us in the house, we were always thinking of him. Jónas and Father could talk about anything. The newspaper; how the fish were running; whether there was a chance of snow; or what they were going to eat for lunch. Father never said what he thought about Jónas' fate. I don't think he cared just so long as his son was alive and happy. That type of unconditional love doesn't appear often in anyone's life, and I could see that Jónas was devastated when Father's coffin was carried down to the ice. He leaned in to whisper a private farewell, touched Father's cheek, then nodded for the pallbearers to carry the coffin away. I think our mother drove Jónas a little crazy with all the time she started to spend on the ice. He never complained, but in the end it was probably why he proposed to Bryndís. I don't mean he didn't love her, but there was no reason for them to get married. They couldn't live together, and everyone already knew they were lovers. We didn't care what the rest of the village thought of Bryndís. We had long ago stopped paying attention to what people said about our family. But in the end the whole village turned out for the wedding. I remember it was the clearest day of the year. No wind. And Bryndís looked beautiful as she walked onto the ice. Everyone said so. We spread out rugs and cushions, and because it was summer it stayed light for most of the night. I don't think I ever saw Jónas more happy, except maybe when Kjartan was born. And he was right, it did help Mother realise there was still plenty for her to enjoy in life. She already had two grandchildren by then. Tumi and I were married a few years before, and we'd had twins. Eydís and Vagn. We lived a little outside of the village so Jónas could see us without needing to turn his head too far. It was only fair considering he had bought us the house as a wedding present. When Eydís and Vagn were older they rode their sleds across the ice to say hello, or to show Jónas their school reports. Whenever they did well he'd send them to the village to buy a reward. All the businesses gave Jónas credit. They knew he had money to pay his bills. But none of us had any idea how rich he was. If it hadn't been for what Jónas left us in his will, I don't think we would have been able to stay on the island. I'm glad he did, because it meant Eydís and Vagn could grow up away from the city. And I wouldn't have liked to leave. Just being near the harbour makes me feel closer to Jónas.

Ulrik Andrésson, Kópavogur, Iceland, 1979

Jónas saved a lot of lives during the war. If it wasn't for him, Elmey might have lost its entire fishing fleet. Other islands did. Iceland was supposed to be neutral, but the rest of the world didn't seem to want to accept it. When the Germans took Denmark the British panicked and sent in twenty-five thousand troops. It wasn't called an invasion, but I'm not exactly sure how else you'd describe it. Nobody paid much attention to our island. We offered no logistical advantage, and a harbour still frozen in summer implied a brutal climate. We built a small shed around Jónas. He hated it, but understood what would happen if the military learnt the ice was strong enough to land aircraft on. Eventually even Reykjavík got too cold for the British, and the Americans took over. Forty thousand of them, and at that stage they were supposed to be neutral as well! The British still hunted U-boats, and their explosions scattered the fish so deep it was hard for Jónas to tell us where to drop our nets. Then one morning he called all the captains to the ice and said we had to stay ashore for at least a week. He'd given similar warnings when the weather was set to turn, and as a result we hadn't lost a vessel in eight years. But everyone could see the skies were clear, and it was the wrong time of year for storms. Jónas then explained how he could feel mines drifting in the ocean. The British had given us depth charges for such an occasion, but what was the use of them when all they did was scare away the fish? And fish was all we wanted. Without them we didn't eat. Not much grows on Elmey, and the mainland kept buying our sheep for the Americans. This had to happen only five or six times before we all needed to mortgage our boats again. One day Finnbjörn announced he didn't care what Jónas said, he was going to fish. But his nets must have hit a mine as soon as they dropped, and after that no one went fishing unless Jónas gave the all clear. We managed to catch enough to feed the village, but there was little left over for the cannery. It had to cut shifts. And even though I didn't know it at the time, Jónas bought fifty per cent of the business when it started to run out of cash. He also set about improving the village. If there wasn't money to be made in the sea, then he paid men to paint the town hall and build a new boardwalk for the beachfront. Despite a world war going on, our village never looked better.

Teitur Dagfinnsson, Elmey Island, Iceland, 1979
A hero? You've got to be kidding. How many people slipped on that ice of his? No one ever thinks about that, do they? If it wasn't for Jónas Arnmundsson I'd still be a fisherman. Shattered my elbow and hip and never worked again. No, I don't think anyone ever died, but lives were ruined, which is the same as dying, isn't it? I wasn't drunk. I can hold my liquor better than anyone in this village.

Bryndís Einarsdóttir, Elmey Island, Iceland, 1978
As a honeymoon present Jónas sent me travelling. Down to Italy, Greece, across to Spain, then into England. He knew I wasn't afraid to leave the village, and insisted that just because he had to stay in one place didn't mean I had to as well. And he wanted me to tell him what I saw. How it felt to have the sun burn your skin, and to swim in warm water. I wrote him letters about the people I met and the food I ate, and the way the world was rebuilding itself after the war. I also sent him gifts, like a pouch of sand, with instructions to pour it through his fingers, and a jar of water from the Mediterranean Sea that he could sip and taste the difference. I bought him a silk shirt in Italy, an umbrella in London, and always books from Paris. Jónas was a great reader. He would finish two or three books every week. Ásta, our village librarian, would bring them down to the ice and hold long conversations with him about writers and the latest journals from Europe. Jónas had taught himself to read French and Italian, and would sometimes ask me to hunt down specific books while I was away. Whatever I sent back he donated to the library. It was only a tiny room at the back of the school when I was a girl, but after the war Jónas bought an old house and had it converted into a proper library with deep armchairs and even

index cards. It was no wonder Ásta fell in love with him. On the day I returned from my travels I would always visit the library as a way of letting her know that any dreams of me not coming back would have to be put on hold for another nine months, then run down to the ice and smother Jónas with kisses. Most of the time I travelled during the winter because it was difficult to visit Jónas with the wind blowing and snow falling. I always felt warm enough by his side, but I could never stay out there for long. Jónas would also worry about me walking back home, and insist I wave a lantern in the window to signal I was safely back inside. When I came home in the spring the hillside behind the village would be covered with wild flowers, and I could pick Jónas a fresh bunch every morning. He couldn't smell them otherwise. The scent of the sea was too strong. He said the flowers cleansed his senses and made everything around him seem fresh and new again. I would cut his hair and trim his beard. Both had turned white years ago, even before his father died. Jónas assumed it was an effect of forming a connection with the ice so deep that he could feel when it was changing, and hear when it was singing. Jónas said it was a low, rumbling music – muscular and textual – that would sometimes be accompanied by the calls of passing whales. I thought my travels would finish when I fell pregnant, but Jónas didn't want his baby brought down to the ice in the middle of a blizzard. And why shouldn't his son see the world? Parents usually want their children to have the things they couldn't … it's only natural. I also think it helped Kjartan grow up knowing that though the world is a wonderful place, his home was just as beautiful and worthy as anywhere else.

Hallmar Bergsson, Mosfellsbær, Iceland, 1980
Because we'd been kept out of the water so much during the war, fish stocks had increased. Even on days when Jónas didn't tell me where to drop my nets, I could still bring in a quality catch. The debts everyone made during the war were quickly repaid, and soon we all started to make some real money. And the more we made, the more there was to buy. You're probably too young to remember what it was like back then, but every week there seemed to be a new invention. Electric washing machines. Electric refrigerators, though I never understood why

you'd need one in a place this cold. And when TVs arrived everybody wanted one. As soon as the fishermen started making money, the rest of the village did as well. The whole community relied upon us. Tumi's supply shop. Baldur's tavern. The cannery stayed open twenty-four hours just so it could fill its orders. The council began planning new roads and fancy street signs, and at one stage even considered building a hospital, but there weren't enough people on Elmey to support something like that. Even the farmers started to ask if they could work the boats. Bird eggs and sheep would never earn them as much as fish, and they could put up with seasickness if it meant paying off the banks. Some of the men who worked as crew eventually saved enough to make a down payment on a boat of their own, and the ones they bought were bigger, more efficient, with better equipment. Jónas gave them advice as well. It was only fair, he said. They were from the village like the rest of us. So instead of visiting him once a week, I'd go down to the ice every eighth day, and then every ninth. Soon our fleet had grown from six to eleven, but then there weren't enough men to work all the boats. Some boys left their studies early. They wanted to be fishermen anyway, and if they were working on their father's boat it just meant more money for their family. People stopped caring whether it was Sunday or not. They said the fish didn't know what day of the week it was. This continued for about ten or twelve years, and it never occurred to anyone we might be taking too much from the sea. We just wanted to keep fishing and making money. But eventually, no matter if Jónas gave us advice or not, our hauls started to grow smaller. And some days we didn't bring in enough even to pay for fuel. Then Jónas stopped dreaming about fish altogether. He couldn't explain it. Said they just weren't there anymore. Those who didn't already own their boats struggled to repay their debts, and when they lost everything to the banks they blamed Jónas. We even had to stand guard over him for a few nights when a rumour started that he'd purposely sent the fish away. His son got bullied about it at school, and someone slipped a few cruel letters beneath Bryndís' front door. But it wasn't Jónas who decided how many fish were in the sea. He suggested we all stop for a year or two to let the stocks replenish themselves, but what were we supposed to live on in the meantime? And there was no guarantee the fish would come back, or that boats from other islands wouldn't come to take our catch. People started to move to the mainland so they could fish further south. But Jónas had to stay. He couldn't go anywhere. I don't think the village was the same after that. I hear the cannery is still open, but not many people eat canned fish anymore, do they?

Unnar Eyjólfsdóttir, Paris, France, 1982
My mother passed away at the end of spring, and Paris is insufferable when it's hot, so I was happy to spend summer on the island. I took my skates and did a little performance for the festival, but I was out of practice, and the villagers didn't seem to want to celebrate like they used to. I had read about the problems with the fishing industry and wasn't surprised to see some businesses had closed down. Jónas was still there, of course, and his son Kjartan as well. He was ten or eleven by that stage and had a laugh just like his father's. Jónas apologised for not being able to attend my mother's service. He told me stories of her walking down to the ice with my latest letter, or to show him a cutting from a foreign newspaper. I spent the summer sorting through boxes of such correspondence, and every day saw Jónas eating with his family. Sometimes Bryndís would take Kjartan fishing, or on a hike to the other side of the island, and other days Jónas would read to him, or tell stories about how the ice had changed. In the end there was nothing left for me to do but sell my parents' house, and at that stage I knew there would be no buyers. I asked Bryndís to take care of the keys and said I expected to see her and Kjartan in Paris very soon. Her son had excellent French, which he told me his father had taught him, though I can't imagine whom Jónas learnt it from. They never did come to visit. I suppose Bryndís and I were not that close. I was more Jónas' friend. I remember the last time I saw him because it was raining. Autumn usually started that way on the island, and it made the ice treacherous to walk upon, but I knew it might be the last time I made it back to the village so I was determined to say goodbye to Jónas. My life has always been that way – bidding adieu to friends before I move on to the next town or city. Jónas sat under a broad umbrella, which made it difficult

for me to claim the kiss he had offered that day I found him in the ice. Instead we shook hands and smiled in the knowledge that we would probably never see each other again. I think Jónas had grown used to goodbyes as well. A lot of people had moved away by then. Ulrik and Hans, and even his brother Magnús had left for the mainland. There were still some fishermen in the village, but I don't think they made much of a living. I looked back at the frozen harbour as the taxi drove over the hill, but all I could see was Jónas' umbrella. I'm sorry to hear he died, but I must admit I haven't thought of him in years. Not until you mentioned his name. It's so nice to speak Icelandic. You must visit again. It's wonderful practice for me. But that's enough about Jónas. Your article is about me, isn't it?

Teitur Dagfinnsson, Elmey Island, Iceland, 1979
I do a few odd jobs here and there, but yeah, I live on one of the pensions Jónas set up. Why shouldn't I? I worked the fishing boats like everyone else. We all made him rich, and what did he do? Nothing. Just sat there with his legs stuck in the ice.

Elín Arnmundsdóttir, Elmey Island, Iceland, 1978
I don't care who you are, being outside all those years takes its toll on a body. Humans aren't made for it. And you could tell Jónas wasn't well. Even under a beard you could see his cheeks were sunken. Dr Ragnarsson said Jónas' blood pressure was low, and his pulse slower than it should have been. But it had been a hard winter, with more blizzards than usual, so we assumed the warmer weather would restore his strength. Except it never happened. The white of the ice started to fade. Patches of dirt appeared on the surface. Jónas stopped reading. Took less food. He was always happy to see Bryndís and Kjartan, but sometimes when I visited he would ask if he had made a mistake telling people about the fish. Had he betrayed the ice? One day he would weep for all he had lost – not just friends, but the chance to fulfill his potential. Then the next he would say how lucky he had been to stay in the same place, because if he had seen a palm tree or sand dune he might never have realised how special they were. When a small crack appeared at the edge of the ice, Bryndís panicked and refused to leave Jónas' side. The summer

light usually made it hard for him to sleep, but more and more he felt compelled to lie back and close his eyes. Kjartan stayed with us and kept watch over his parents through our kitchen window. My two children gathered flowers and spread them around their uncle. Ásta read aloud to Jónas from his favourite books. Magnús came back from the mainland. Then one day a large crack appeared and Jónas sent everybody to the shore. Yelled that the ice was no longer safe and he would have no more lives ruined because of him. I remember people standing along the pebble beach discussing what to do, then without warning Tumi walked out onto the ice. I don't think I have ever been more proud of my husband than when I saw him crouch beside Jónas and shake his hand. He gave him a kiss on the cheek like we always did, then returned to the shore. For the rest of the day I watched everybody in our village do the same, one at a time, until Bryndís and Kjartan were the last. The three of them stayed together until it grew dark, then Kjartan walked back with his father's wooden box under one arm, and his mother's shaking shoulders under the other. All through the night we listened to the cracks in the ice grow longer, wider, until morning arrived and Jónas was gone. The ice in the harbour had broken apart and drifted out to sea. Men with boats went searching, and didn't stop until all trace of the ice had melted away. It was hard to give Jónas a funeral because we felt like there was a chance he was still alive, floating in the sea, looking for fish. In the past few years they have started to come back, and Kjartan seems to share his father's gift of knowing where to find them. The harbour no longer freezes, even in winter, so he and the other fishermen go out all through the year. Bryndís doesn't worry when the weather is bad. She knows Jónas would never let anything happen to their son. She bought out the other partners in the cannery, and now runs it herself. Everyone has work if they want it, just like it was when I was young. In fact the whole village is pretty much how it used to be. As if Jónas had never existed. But there are other people who still remember him. You should go in to the village and talk to them. They'll tell you all about Jónas.

Permafrost

Scott

Kate Simonian

Scott managed to get a part-time job at McDonald's, not as a cashier, but in the kitchen. I was driving him home from a shift when he asked, 'You know how you're always saying I should have friends, Brendan?'

'Yeah. You do have friends. Like me and Mum. And Billy.' How I hated Billy. He thought because he used sign language no one could understand what he meant when he pointed at a girl and imitated squeezing melons. Whenever I picked Scott up from school and saw Billy I wanted to punch his head. Do some more damage to his soft-boiled brain.

'Billy is a boy. I want a girlfriend.'

'Right. Have you talked to Mum about this?'

'No. I was just thinking.' He stared out the window.

Scott started buying clothes. They were his wages, so there was nothing Mum could do about it. He bought his own ticket, caught the train to the shopping centre, and returned with bags held triumphantly aloft. Everything he bought was deeply uncool: a sleeveless shirt with 'hero' emblazoned across the front, a black matching tracksuit set, and white sneakers he wouldn't wear outside. One afternoon the bathroom sink was dirtied with black coils of hair that looked pubic. Scott showed me his nipples and their proudly trimmed halos of hair.

'Looking good, Scotty,' I said. 'Who's the lucky lady?' Poor Scott. He didn't have a chance. He'd asked me to buy him dirty magazines when he was fourteen, and I'd taught him to hide his porn in a special file named 'm.exe.Scott.doc/'. That file was pretty full, if I recalled.

He dropped his shirt. 'Not telling.'

We were driving back from his shift at Macca's when he brought it up again. 'One day, I'm going to get married,' he said.

'Course you will, buddy. And then you'll have lots of kids.' I pulled the car around a bend in a smooth arc and hit the accelerator.

'Mum would love that.' He stuck a sheaf of chips into his mouth and chewed.

'Close your mouth, buddy.'

He ignored me. 'I'm going to marry Lara.'

'Nice one. Close your mouth.'

'Yeah. I need your help, but.'

'Right, bro. I don't see what I can do.'

'You can tell Mum we're going to the movies and then you can take us home to watch *The West Wing*.'

I couldn't stop the car right there, but I kept my eyes ahead and said very slowly, like I was measuring the length of each word, 'Oh no. Remember what we said? It's okay to have girl friends at school, but you can't have them around, because it looks funny.'

'Brendan. I want the funny business.'

'I'm not sure you do. It isn't as fun as it looks in those videos.'

'Please, Brendan.' He gave me the same limp, imploring look he gave Mum whenever he wanted something. The 'help me, I'm retarded' look.

'No way, buddy. And anyway, you have to be in love to do what you're talking about.'

'She's my girlfriend.'

'Hold on. D'you mean – do you kiss her?'

He rolled his eyes. 'Of course. When no one's watching.'

I'd have to have a word with Mrs McGrath about the centre's supposedly close supervision of students. We drove in silence. It was that nice time of day, around seven o'clock, when the suburb was in shadow and shreds of light caught in the treetops. I pulled into our street and parked. Scott sat in the passenger seat and rubbed one hand over his nipple. There was no way of telling whether he wanted this like he wanted a new PlayStation controller, or if he felt it like a burning need. Maybe there wasn't a difference.

'Scott.' He looked at me. 'Even when you want things, there are some things you can't have. It would mean lying. You don't want to lie to Mum, do you?'

'I guess not,' he said.

The next morning was Saturday, and I mooched around the house avoiding my Criminal Law assignment. I ate a packet of salt-and-vinegar crackers and strained to remember what we'd learnt about diminished responsibility. I had to touch on the accused's mental incapacity. But it wouldn't be that simple. As our lecturer said, 'There's never a bright-line concept.' She'd obviously had fun setting the assignment, because the schizophrenic plaintiff who'd drowned her children was called Medea. Ha.

I got myself a glass of milk and thought about the situation. Brendan, *compos mentis*, helps his seventeen-year-old retarded brother Scott inflict a sexual assault on a sixteen-year-old retarded girl. Brendan shows foresight and actively conspires to lure the girl away from her parents. He is fully aware of the consequences of his actions.

I went back to the study and started to search on Google. Retard. Retard. He was a fucking retard. It gave me an angry thrill to think the word, type it and see it glowing in the search bar, obscene. When I typed into the search bar, 'Do retarded people,' it pre-empted my questions with 'Do retarded people have super strength?' and 'Do retarded people have retarded souls?' I deleted my words and typed in, 'Can I help my retard brother have retard sex?' I posted the question on a bulletin board and I got a quick reply from Sputnik_65:

> I am really offended that you would use the word 'retard.' My sister is mentally challenged and that is not the proper or nicest word to say about someone with challenges. Would you like to be called a retard if you had daily challenges? You make me sick.

Fuck you, Sputnik_65. Scott had it easy. He had one mode of being. I had to juggle talking to him like an adult and trying to stretch him with not letting him know there was a gaping chasm between him and other people. Mum glossed over everything with greasy platitudes, but I couldn't. There was more to it. Like, did I owe Scott a duty of care? Where were his rights? Mum didn't think beyond protecting Scott's right not to have his body fiddled with. What about his right to share his body? I leaned back in my chair and pictured myself standing in shadows behind a naked Scott. Brendan, the vicarious deflowerer. The one who was to blame, who knew what he was doing. Just the action of picturing myself guilty was enough to make up my mind.

When I told Scott I'd help him he made a thrusting move with his hips, like he was fucking the air. We didn't get a chance to put our plan into action for a good month, until Mum said she was going on a health retreat.

The weekend before she went away I asked Scott for his class list. There she was, right at the top: Lara Applebaum. Scott sat uncomfortably close to me while I dialled. When her dad picked up, I slipped into a reserved, parental tone. I was Scott's older brother. Much older brother. Scott had mentioned that he and Lara were friends at school. Would Lara like to accompany Scott and me to a movie next weekend? I'd be chaperoning, of course.

There was concern in his voice. 'I'll have to talk to my wife.' A muted background conversation followed. 'Can I get back to you?'

When he called back he was hedging, but I knew how to play it. 'They're friends at school,' I said. Then I dropped the bomb. 'It'd be good for their social skills. You know, that's what teenagers do. They hang out, boys and girls, as friends?' That was it, refer to the program objectives.

'Why don't you two come around for dinner on, say, Tuesday night? Lara will be here, and we'd like to meet Scott first. If that's okay with you.'

That Tuesday night, Scott insisted on wearing his new jacket, the one with the Superman 'S' in diamantés on the back. It was a girl's jacket. 'Looking good, bro,' I said. 'Mind if I borrow your hair gel?' He opened the tub and scraped some onto my hand.

Oh God, her parents were nice, so nice. Mr Applebaum shook my hand. 'This is my wife, Judy,' he said. She took my hand, pressed once.

'This is Scott,' I said. He stepped forward and gave a bow. They laughed at that. I'd told Scott to keep his distance from Lara – you touch, you die – and when she came out, he looked at me. 'Go on, then,' I said. He gave her hand a shake, and let go. Lara curtsied.

Mrs Applebaum laughed. They were doing it! Socially interacting! 'What polite children we have.'

Scott kept it coming. At dinner not only did he tuck in his napkin, but he also remembered to compliment Mrs Applebaum on her steak. 'I really like it cooked like this,' he said. 'It's much better than my mum's.' When Scott excused himself from the table to use the bathroom, Mr Applebaum grasped the inside of my arm. 'Your brother is a *real* gentleman.'

He wants to fuck your daughter. He wants to fuck your retard daughter. 'Thanks. He tries very hard,' I said. We kept the conversation on the surface so that Scott and Lara could chip in. Lara told us that she was going to start playing hockey.

'Lara is very good at sport,' said Scott.

'Not,' said Lara.

We all laughed. Poor Lara. She was all right looking, but she had these technicolour blue braces and there was a strand of chicken caught in them.

'And what do you do, Brendan?' asked Mrs Applebaum.

'I'm studying law.'

'That must take up a lot of your time.'

'Yes, well, the readings do. But study load depends on how much you work. It's like I tell Scott, you only get out what you put in.'

'Absolutely. We take the same attitude with Lara.'

I looked at Mrs Applebaum. Maybe if I explained the whole situation, they'd agree that Lara should have sex. Why not, with a boy like Scott? Scott would make sweet love to their daughter. I'd grilled him on sexual etiquette for the past week. He even knew, theoretically, how to go down on a girl. He knew you spent half the time on her, half on you. Didn't they want someone to go down on their daughter, sweetly, lovingly?

But I couldn't shift the blanket of decorum that rested just above our cautious, moving forks. It was with a sick feeling that I cast the bait at the end of the night. They took it. Yes, Mr Applebaum said. Lara could see *Hookwinked!*

'I promise to have her home by three,' I said. 'And don't worry about the classification. It's PG.'

Laugh, laugh. We shared a big laugh.

On the morning of, Scott got up at seven and made me breakfast. The sink was a waste of burnt egg and crumbs. 'Great stuff, buddy,' I said, hoeing into the stiff toast. 'They're teaching you some great stuff at that school.'

In the car we went over it all again. He kept saying I know. I know I have to go fifty-fifty. I know I won't be selfish. I know I have to lick her vagina. Brendan, I'm wearing the watch, see? Yes, I promise I'll look at it to make sure the timing is fifty-fifty.

We pulled up at the house, and there were the three Applebaums, clustered in the same spot on the corner of the veranda. Why did they have to look so vulnerable, so nice? Lara was wearing a red dress with flowers on it. Daisies. She had her hair out. Were her parents suspicious that she was making such an effort? They didn't seem to be. They shook my hand, then Scott's.

'We'll see you at three, Lara,' said Mrs Applebaum. 'Have fun! Oh and Brendan, I've given Lara money for her ticket and sweets, but she can only have one ice-cream and a small popcorn. No chippies or fast food. They make her mad.'

'Of course,' I said, and looked at Lara's hand. Her wallet was attached to her wrist with a rainbow shoestring. 'She won't be losing that.'

We drove home in silence. Scott was on his best behaviour and kept his head forward. When we got in the house, I pointed to the couch, and the two of them shambled over and sat down. I picked up a PlayStation controller and tried not to tell Scott off for leaving it on the ground. I sank into the couch facing them.

'All right, Lara. How are you?'

'Good.' She had her hands in her lap and kept rolling her shoulders. I had to scope her out. Maybe she wasn't even his girlfriend and Scott had dreamed the whole thing up. Or maybe she thought sex was kissing, and in five minutes she'd run out of the room, screaming and bleeding.

'I just need to run through some things. Now, Lara, you're going to be left with Scott in his room for about two hours. Is that all right?'

She shrugged.

'That's how she says yes,' said Scott.

I shushed him. 'Now, is Scott your boyfriend?'

'Yes.'

'And do you know what boyfriends and girlfriends do?'

'Yes. They have babies,' she said.

'No. No they do not. They get close together and they have sex but they do not, under any circumstances, have babies. If you have babies your parents will be very upset. I've told Scott about using a condom. If you don't use a condom I'll be taking you straight home, and I will tell your parents everything, do you understand?'

'Yes I understand.' That didn't mean anything. What if she thought she wanted it and then told her parents? I couldn't believe anything she said, not because she was deceitful, but because she might not understand the question. Scott shifted his hand across the leather surface of the couch and gripped her hand.

'Right. Now, how old are you?'

'Sixteen and a half.'

'Excellent. Wonderful. You have to use the condoms, and I'm going to inspect the condom at the end of it, so don't try to be sneaky. And what is the safe word?'

'Broccoli,' they said.

'Right, and the safe word is what you say when you don't like what is happening. Say it loud and clear so I can hear it. You have to leave the door a bit open, and if you say broccoli I will come straight in. Do you both understand that?' Neither of them moved. They knew if they played it right, I'd go away. 'I've put a jug of water in there, and if you have sex – and you don't have to, Lara, only if you want—'

'I want.'

'Well then afterwards you have to put this towel on and go and wee in the bathroom, otherwise you might get an infection in your wee. Do you understand? Say it back to me.'

'When I have sex I have to come out in the towel and go wee.'

'And the safe word is?'

'Broccoli.'

I gave them a last look. They could be a couple. A slightly mad couple: Scott with his boy-woman face, Lara damaged but still pretty, maybe normal. I smiled at them. I hoped it wasn't a terrible, sad smile.

They went into Scott's room. I soon heard through the open door the sound of the R'n'B album Scott had played on loop for the past week. First up, 'Ignition Remix.'

Thirty minutes in, Lara came out in the towel. She looked at me, spooked, and walked awkwardly to the bathroom. As she walked back past me I saw the rainbow wallet string.

'Oh no, have you had this on?' I got up and she surrendered her wrist, holding the towel tight to her breasts. I held my breath and tried not to smell her. My fingernails tore at the evil knot. 'Your mum did a good job of this.'

'It has my bus pass in it.'

I let the wallet go. 'Just leave it, then.'

She went back to the bedroom.

There was nothing I could do, only sit and wait. It was a relief, that feeling of surrender. I could stare at the wall opposite me, at the still life of giant pomegranates Mum had bought years ago. They were obscene, really: two bulbous, fleshy globes, one cut to the core and weeping red seeds. At an hour to go I stopped waiting for 'broccoli.' I picked up my book and tried to read the first chapter, but it was hopeless. I couldn't relax. Instead I ran over the schedule. It was one, and they'd be done by two. That left us half an hour to get ready to go, and twenty minutes to drive back. We'd be ten minutes early back to her place. Everything would be okay. Promise fulfilled: here's your daughter. She's fine.

After another half hour, they appeared, fully dressed. Scott's face was red and his upper lip dotted with sweat.

'That's it? All done?'

'Yup,' said Scott.

'Lara, you have to go to the toilet. No, wait.' I looked at her hair, and the perspiration at her temples. They'd smell the sex on her. 'You have to take a shower.'

What choice did I have? I had to get in the bathroom with her to make sure she didn't just stand there and, I dunno, just run the water over her feet. I kept my face turned away while she undressed, and made sure the bathroom door was a bit open.

'Okay, Lara. Get in the shower,' I said to the wall. 'Wash everywhere.'

'Brendan.'

'Yes?'

I looked at her. She was holding her wallet out of the shower. I took the wallet and held it for her out the shower door, while she washed herself with one hand. Oh fuck. I had seen it, her entire body. I had perved on a retarded girl. Her nipples were like little cones that pointed outward, and her arse was flat. How could I not have noticed her huge bush? It spread from her pelvis onto her legs. It was luxuriant, extravagant.

'Wash it,' I said.

'What?'

'Your vagina.'

I kept my eyes on the half-open door. Slowly, very slowly, it opened itself, and Scott's face peeped through. He was on his hands and knees, smiling.

'Fuck off, Scott!'

Lara had seen him, and started laughing. She gripped one of her boobs and shook it. Then they were both laughing: a dumb idiot laugh. I stood there, the bottom of my pants wet, holding a velcro wallet out of the shower door. I felt pissed off, then sick. What a bastard I was. They weren't children. They had every right, and there I was, feeling mad.

'Look at my girlfriend!' said Scott.

'Yep, what a girl! Good one, guys. Lara, just turn off the water – don't get your hair wet! – yep, turn the hot off first, now quickly, the cold.'

I wanted them out of the house, and oh God, I'd almost got a whiff of freedom by the time we got in the car. That was until I saw the wallet, its waterproof surface flecked with droplets.

'Oh fuck. Your change. Your mum's change. Oh fuck oh fuck oh fuck.'

I looked at my watch: thirty-five minutes. 'We're going to Macca's drive-through,' I said, and swung the car around.

They cheered.

At the drive-through we ordered two large quarter-pounder meals and a chocolate sundae. That came to twenty-one fifty: an acceptable price for a movie ticket and snacks. By the time we got the food we had twenty minutes to spare. I pulled into the car park so I could make sure they ate it all.

Lara ripped into her hamburger. Jesus, that girl could eat. When she finished she had a sliver of sauce on her chin. I watched

Scott in the rearview mirror, watching her. Every so often he would take a bite, then put his arm over her shoulder, then move his hand back to secure his burger.

'Hey,' he said when he was finished. 'You have some sauce on your face.' He gripped her head and gave her chin a kiss. 'I ate it away.' She continued demolishing her fries.

We made it back to her house at three. Of course her parents were in the same spot: they needed a bench or something. Lara played it to a tee. She'd really liked *Hoodwinked!* The wolf was scary. Grandma had a funny voice. Mrs Applebaum looked at her daughter chasing the dog around the lawn. 'Lara seems to have really enjoyed herself! Maybe we can make this a monthly event. Our turn next time, though, Brendan. It was Brendan, wasn't it?'

When we got home, I went straight to my room. I was exhausted, and I didn't want to be anywhere near Scott. As I was about to drift off, I heard a knock at my door.

'What?'

It was Scott. He was holding a package, bound clumsily in Christmas wrapping. He stood awkwardly at the end of my bed and stuck out his hand.

'Is it for me?'

He nodded. I ripped it open. It was a red bandanna with paisley eyelets over it: the kind Tupak Shakur wore, that only looks good on gangsters. 'Wow.' I unfolded and refolded it into a fat band, and tied it around my head. Surely I looked like an idiot. 'Thanks, buddy. Hold up, did you put the condoms in a bag in the bin?'

'Yep.'

It was over, then. I pulled off my shoes and threw one at Scott's feet. 'Hey bro, how do I look?'

Two thumbs up.

Hide Your Fires

Guns 'N Coffee

A.S. Patric

I work in the middle of the damned city. I start when every other son of a bitch is about to clock in as well. It doesn't matter where I go, I can't get a coffee without waiting for fifteen minutes in a queue. No one likes lines, right? I'm not saying I'm different, but lately, these coffee lines seem to be slowly moving us along like a hissing snake, swallowing all our minds in a milky swirl of white poison.

These days there's less space in front and behind. The breath of those who haven't eaten or brushed since the day before, spiced up with a cigarette or two before coming into the crowded café and snuggling up right behind my shoulder, is the kind of stuff that is going to challenge the most equanimous. Me? I only know what 'equanimous' means because it was word of the day on my screensaver yesterday.

If it's not that, then it's those women with that angry industrial-strength perfume that burns like a corrosive through my nasal passages and leaves a chemical taste on my tongue. I used to think they had lost their sense of smell. Now I know it's an attempt to get some space in these coffee queues.

None of this is going to explain why I brought a handgun along with me today. I'm just saying, there's too many people in this damned city, and they're all starting work around the time I need a coffee.

*

It's a modest gun. I'm not a closet Dirty Harry wanting someone to make my day. I only want someone to make my coffee.

When I pull it out for the first time the woman in front of me blinks sleepily and goes back to daydreaming about her strong latte with two sugars.

'Hey,' I say to her. She's ignoring me so I give her a wave of black steel near her right ear. 'Hey,' I say again. 'I'm not kidding.'

I fire the gun through the wide doors of the café and out into the street. The shot travels above the heads of the masses of people pushing along the footpaths. The bullet shatters a pane of thick glass in the fashion store across the road. People get a bit cut up from the crashing glass and a man begins screaming like someone has cut off his toes. The pedestrians keep passing, barely pausing, crushing the glass beneath their shoes as they make their way to work.

My wrist is limp from the kickback. I transfer the gun to my left hand as if it's all the better to display the weapon. The double-sugar-latte woman steps aside. The rest of the folks in the line follow her example.

Bradley the Barista knows how I like my coffee. His arms move with speed and precision – a perfection of machine engineering in human form. It's as though I press his fast-forward button and then the stop button when he finishes my ristretto-strength long black with three grips and three sugars.

I pay him and tell him he can keep the change on a ten-dollar bill. It's only polite to show an appreciation for good service.

'How's your day been, Brad?' I ask after my first satisfying sip.

'It's been pretty busy, Mr Bushnell. This is the first time I've had a moment of stillness for two hours.'

'Are you enjoying it, Brad?' I ask.

'I am indeed, Mr Bushnell,' he replies, and adds, 'There's something about a loaded gun that makes one appreciate a moment like this. Thanks for that, Mr Bushnell.'

'Glad I could do that for you, Brad. I'll now have the pleasure of strolling to work rather than the unwelcome power slalom through those frustrated crowds outside. I'm going to have a lovely amble to work today.'

As soon as I move away from the counter the line resumes its shape, longer and angrier than ever. A rattler of a line extending outside the front doors, the furious tail shaking with the anger of twenty smartphones going off simultaneously. It's a soothing sound when you have discovered the ways of the snake charmer as I have.

*

I come in the next morning with a smile in my stride and a spring in my face. I'm eager to display my Kimber 1911 Compact again. I want to get that snake dancing out of my way.

I don't have a problem until I arrive at the head of the line and a high-powered exec smiles like his teeth are made out of diamonds and he eats crystal croissants with his coffee. He's been held in the purgatory of the line for the last fifteen minutes and can't swallow me moving past everyone with a royal wave of black steel. Maybe he didn't see my warning yesterday but I can tell he is a natural-born hero.

'You are not going to shoot me for a coffee. That's ridiculous! It's only a few dollars and a few moments. You can't kill a human being with such little motivation.'

'What's your game, Mr Suit?' I ask him.

'I don't want to play. I'm just going to get a coffee and go to work.'

'Well, Mr Suit, I'm not going to go into a lengthy analysis of the situation here. But I will say this – it's not about a few minutes or a few dollars. It's about an accretion of time that mummifies my brain and turns my thoughts into sand. More than anything, it's about the brief, black, bitter taste of liberty in those cups. You're standing in the way of my freedom, Mr Suit. I advise you to step aside and give me a moment with Bradley the Barista.'

'I don't think so,' Mr Suit tells me with his diamond grin.

'Mr Suit,' I say and step forward. I raise the gun to the height of his heart. 'Reconsider, please,' I say and wiggle the Kimber 1911 Compact. I polished it last night and I know it has a lethal gleam.

He looks at it like it's a water pistol and turns around and asks Bradley for an affogato. It's more of a dessert than it is a coffee. An affogato! It also happens to be the most time-consuming thing he could have asked Bradley to make him. I take it as a personal affront. Mr Suit says he also wants two scoops of ice-cream and not just one. I give him two bullets instead and I'm not sorry.

Mr Suit dies in a very elegant creaseless crumple of the best Italian fabric and design. A macchiato stain of blood spreads across the immaculate collar of his white shirt and drips onto the black marble of the café's floor. Everyone lines up behind me. Bradley's hands fly to the handles and dials of his Gaggia Deco D espresso machine.

*

The next morning I walk into the café and feel sure there will be no more need for gun-waving and I won't have to kill anyone to get a coffee. I had a difficult night getting to sleep. For hours I tried to rest my mind and body. Even when I managed to drift away I found myself waking in a fevered state, my sheets wet right through and my pillow soaked. In short, too much coffee. There have to be limits even to these dark pleasures, I suppose.

The line is long and I can barely get through the doors of the café. I announce myself but no one moves.

The double-sugar-latte woman stands before me again and I tell her, 'Surely, my mettle has been tested. My resolve can't still be in question.'

She turns around and a wash of her perfume breaks over me in a dizzying ocean of petals and pollen, bouquets of sweet-smelling chemicals rushing down my throat. I take a step back but I stumble and grab a chair to steady myself.

'You don't look good,' she tells me.

'I didn't sleep very well,' I explain. 'Frankly, my experiences in the toilet haven't been too pleasant either. I'm sweating a lot and my stomach feels uneasy. Queasy, I feel very queasy.'

'Coffee's not for everyone. Perhaps you should drink tea instead. Take a few moments every morning, perhaps – treat yourself to a pot of Orange Pekoe leaf. You'll find it's better suited to your nervous system. Our culture has so many problems and diseases that stem from stress and anxiety, and there's nothing that generates and promotes these things like the addiction to the coffee bean.'

I'm starting to feel disorientated. People are pushing past me to get into the store and others are coming out with steaming takeaway cups filled with the delicious beverage that will give me the boost I need to get through the next few hours of my life. 'Shut up, you scandalous hypocrite. You're here for the same reason I am. You need the coffee bean as well.'

'I drink decaf.'

'Decaf?' I say. 'Decaf!'

'Yes, decaf. Decaf indeed.'

'Don't talk to me about decaffeinated coffee. It's like taking a shower in a raincoat.'

'I don't think so,' she says.

'It's like eating one of those burgers made out of lentils and cabbage.'

'No, it's not,' she says, looking at me like I'm someone to be pitied.

'Should I remind you I'm carrying a weapon?' I reach below my arm and remove my Kimber 1911 Compact from a holster I bought for it yesterday afternoon. 'You don't require further demonstrations, do you?' I pull it out and hold it before her.

'It's not a good idea. There's a room full of coffee drinkers here, after all. Every single one of them desperate for that first hit, just like you. There's no way you can keep a trump card like that in a room full of losing gamblers.'

'What?' I blink at her. 'Just move!' I wave the gun with two sharp movements to the right.

She steps aside with a sorrowful expression. I see the line has changed. Everyone in it has removed a firearm from a pocket or handbag and they all have these guns pointed at me. Thirty barrels are trained on my head, chest and stomach. I blink. I can't really take in the image of all these respectable city workers armed with such deadly weapons.

I look over to Bradley the Barista and ask him, 'What's going on here, Brad? Didn't I invent the game? It's my ball, isn't it? I get to say how we play. Bradley – tell these people!'

The Barista wipes his hands with a tea towel and a regretful look passes across his face. He says, 'I'm sorry, Mr Bushnell. No more coffee for you.'

'What?' I ask the question meekly but I feel my heart kick in my chest at the thought of never having another morning jolt from Bradley's beans. 'What?' It comes out as a roar this time.

'You can't be serious. I've been coming here for years. I've been working in this damned city …'

*

My anger had begun to foam like milk in the bottom of a metal jug and I was spitting with my eyes closed when I said 'damned city.' My weapon might have been raised. It was more a gesticulation than an intent to harm anyone. Coffee drinkers are jumpy though and their fingers get twitchy.

fourW

Yia Yia on Papou

Zoe Norton Lodge

If my name is Koula and your name is Mick and we shall be met and we shall be married under the auspices of the father in the Greek Orthodox Parish & Community of Saints Raphael, Nicholas & Irene, then you shall remember this, you shall remember this forever, and if you shall remember this, then you may begin to understand my eternal contempt.

If my name is Koula and your name is Mick and we shall be met and we shall be married and we shall cohabitate in a house-familius in Suburbingford with our two children and our patio and our various Shih Tzus named Dadie and Sadie and similar and our Carltonware, our plastic-covered couches, our china horses, cups of tea, brass statuette of the harbour bridge, our security blinds and tobacco, our flannelettes and mouthwash. If one day in this situation unto which we have found ourselves you shall ask unto me:

Koula, pou ine tou alago thacktilithi mou favourite? I will say: How the fuck should I know, Mick. If it's not on your butso-glifti finger, then pous thialo would I know where your stupid favourite ring with the horseshoe is? If you shall suggest that blame for this ring misplacement lies outside the gelatinous boundaries of yourself, perhaps with me or our children or our Shih Tzus and you shall make us search the house. If one day, two weeks after you have lost the ring, and we have searched the house, you shall cry out unto me from your seat on the toilet, whilst peering southward, with a repulsive strain over your gut, down to your knee-ward underpants: Koula! Do echo vriso. Ine sta y front vrakya mou!

If you shall find, sitting there in your underpants, your favourite horseshoe ring, understand that I shall know you have not changed your underpants for two weeks. Understand that the fact that you did not notice a ring with a jagged horseshoe setting burring into your buttocks for two weeks suggests a disturbing deficit in observation and a medically significant lack of somatic response in your fat arse. You should see several kinds of doctors.

Furthermore, understand, Mick, understand that I have never lost anything. Understand that I have no sympathy for you. Understand this and you shall begin to understand the emergence of my eternal contempt.

If my name is Koula and your name is Mick and we have been met and we have been married and you have no feeling in your arse and one day you tell me you are taking our seven-year-old son to the Maritime Museum. If, instead of taking him to the museum, you leave him in the car for four hours while you drink at the RSL with other arseholes like you, who you are friends with because you all share ninety per cent of your genes with elephant seals. If you do this Mick, our son will remember forever, and I will never forget. And when you are old and vague and I am old, I shall carry my blackened memories of you forever in my mouth ulcers.

If my name is Koula and your name is Mick and we have been married and you have no feeling in your arse and you have previously left our son in a car for four hours and you are sixty-eight and you are not dead and I have not forgotten and we are flatting together for apathy and convenience. If one day in this situation unto which we have delivered ourselves, you shall suppose to comment on my cooking. If one day you shall squint and wheeze as the pencil shavings and hairy sodden bath plugs comprising your brain attempt to inhale, interpret and re-release information back into the ether. If your brain shall miraculously evade electrocution through unprecedented usage, and you manage to sneeze out of your teeth bucket the premature stillborn of a would-be verbalised thought. Should this premi-thought call into the arena of question an aspect of my cooking. Understand this.

Understand that every day for fifty years, I have, in spite of the emergence and subsequent exponential growth of my eternal contempt cooked you three perfect meals every day. Understand that perfection is my only weakness. Understand that my kitchen has a fucking chef's hat. And understand that in order to ensure that nothing of this sort recurs I shall beat you repeatedly over the head with a Christmas placemat.

If my name is Koula and your name is Mick and we have been met and we have been married and you have no feeling in your arse and you once left our seven-year-old son in the car and I have beaten almost every last drop of your ambition to engage with the world out of your head with a Christmas placemat and you are seventy-five and you are not dead and I have not forgotten. If one morning before dawn, in this situation unto which we have found ourselves, I encounter you in our driveway, with a garbage bag full of tissues and ornaments, wearing nothing but a pair of white stubbies, waiting for your eight-year-old grandson to drive you to your lacrosse game. Understand that you seem to have gone completely mad. Understand that the only upsetting part of this situation for me is that I briefly had to look at you without a shirt on.

If my name is Koula and your name is Mick and we have been met and we have been married and you have no feeling in your arse and one day you left our son in the car and I have beaten your churlishness with a Christmas placemat and you have gone mad and you have disappointingly recovered quickly and we have moved to stou thiavolou ti manna retirement villa and one day you shall sit at your windowsill, staring at the happenstance in your visual field, and you shall say: Koula, you have to come and see this. There is a little white dog, just sitting there on the grass. It's so still. I wonder if it's lonely. It's so beautiful. Parakalo Koula.

And I will refuse.

Parakalo.

No.

Parakalo, just one little look.

No.

Koula …

Fine …

Mick, I will say as I disgust myself by eventually humouring you, Mick that is a FUCKING MAILBOX.

Understand that if you mention how low your cholesterol is in spite of eighty years of treating your body like a hospital-grade bag of infected rubbish, understand that if Lady Life renews her lease on you, and you develop a penchant for 'walks,' understand that in bitterness, in unbridled bitterness, I shall have a segment of my lower bowel removed.

If my name is Koula and your name is Mick and one day having served you lunch I shall ask for a sip of your beer. If I shall ask for but one sip of your beer and you shall look me in the eyes, you shall look me in the eyes with sixty-five years of hatred, you shall look me in the eyes and I shall meet your eyes, and without taking your eyes off me you shall pick up the beer in your pig hand and take it to your pink and crusty discarded-by-the-butcher-and-left-in-the-sun poisoned ham lips. And you shall swig from it. If you shall swig from it and then exhale beer, particles of lunch, and air all at once. If then, after this brothel performance you shall offer unto me your beer, I will put a curse on you.

If after I put a curse on you, you shall summon, from within your gingivitis cavernous death-pot mouth, a phlegmatic viscous. If you shall spit this phlegmatic viscous and chart it on a course toward my face. If you shall do this Mick, then understand you shall have regrets.

If my name is Koula and your name is Mick and one day you spit in my face. Understand that with all my will I will reach behind me for a knife. Understand that if all I can place my hands upon without looking, without unlocking our hating eyes, understand that if I cannot reach a knife, if all I can reach is a colander, understand that I shall use the colander like a sort of knife-hat. And I shall drive it onto your head.

And there you shall be, drunk and vague with nothing but your colander-hat and what remains of your beer and the dishrag of your soul.

Mick, if you understand these things, if you understand them, then you shall begin to understand me and my eternal contempt.

Going Down Swinging

Cold Patch

Jon Bauer

She lay there listening to the rain and thinking about her washing. It'd been on the line since that sunny Thursday. Now it was Friday night and she was in bed, the downpour dirtying her sheets and her husband blowing his nose in the sink.

She pulled the doona more tightly around her, sausage-rolling herself in some warmth. His footfalls stopped halfway along the corridor.

'Did you turn the heating up again?' he said. She was facing the wall, a grimy area on it where he rubbed against it during sleep – coming to bed filthy. She looked at that smudge, the shape of it.

'Did you?' he said, arriving in the bedroom.

'You're obsessed.'

'Can't you put some warm clothes on rather than heating the whole house?'

He was undressing with his back to her, knick-knacks wobbling on the chest of drawers as he balanced on one leg to get a sock off. Then again for the other.

'I put the machine on,' he said, his voice still showing the strain of balancing.

'Mm.'

He crawled up from the foot of the bed to slide in between her and the wall. She sat straight up and swung her legs round, put her feet in her slippers and went off down the corridor.

'Forgot to floss.'

The wind gusted rain hard against the window, as if it were suddenly falling more heavily. The downpour drumming on the roof.

She was coming back, her footsteps pausing.

'Love?'

'Coming,' she said.

She sat on the bed, deposited her slippers, then lay down and flung the covers over herself, banging her heels up and down on the mattress and blowing out her cheeks.

'Cold one tonight,' he said.

'Mm.'

'When I said we needed rain, I didn't mean this much.'

'This bed's *freezing*!'

'It'll get there.'

They listened to the rain.

'Lights out?' he said.

She leaned over and turned out the lamp but the security light blinked on outside – light coming in through the curtains. Over and over she had begged him to adjust the sensor. 'It's your sensor that needs adjusting,' he had replied. Which she took to mean he didn't know how to fix it.

The security light blinked off, the rain beat down. They lay in the dark, looking up at the sound.

'There's a cold patch,' she said, her hand on the space between them. He turned over to face his grimy wall. 'It'll warm,' he said, his voice already softening in sleep's shadow.

She plonked her body over the cold like a broody hen. She hated it when he fell asleep before her; the sense of abandonment you could feel lying right beside someone. People were never further away than when they were sleeping right beside you. Like her father laid out in state. The smell of rosewater.

'It's still there,' she said in a loud whisper, as if not to wake him.

'What?' he said, his voice coming long distance.

'The cold patch. I've been on it and it's still there.' She had to speak over the rain intensifying on the roof. It sounded like cattle feed landing in a metal trough, her father holding the weight of the sack but her steering it – feeling like she was pouring. The feed powder coming up. She had adored that smell.

'Love!'

He snorted. 'What?' He sat up, turned the wrong way to face her in the dark. 'It's *really* raining,' he said, his voice a little sing-song with sleep. The security light blinked on again, etching the room with light and shadow.

'Feel it.'

He reached out and she found his hand, directing it.

'See?' she said. 'I've been lying on it and it's still like that.'

'P'raps it's wet. Is it wet? Maybe the roof's leaking again.'

She turned the lamp on and they squinted, staring down at the spot on the bed where their hands had been, then up at the dry ceiling.

He shuffled down the bed and got out.

'Where you going?'

'Water bottle'll fix that,' he said. 'Cuppa?'

'No thanks,' she said, looking from him – naked from the waist down – to the spot on the bed. 'Don't be long.'

When he'd gone she positioned herself on the cold again, looking up at the architrave to help her sense the temperature better.

'You *did* turn it up, godammit!'

He huffed on down the corridor to the kitchen. Eventually she heard the faint growl of the kettle.

They were both in bed now, the hot-water bottle in place, the lamp too bright. She reached over and snatched up his dressing gown from the floor. The lamp giving off a tainted green light after she'd flung his prized garment over it as an extra shade.

'Careful with that,' he said.

'This is ridiculous. It's you and that bloody thermostat.'

'Wear more round the house.'

'Some husbands would appreciate their wife uncovered.'

'Maybe husbands that like to look at a dish they can't eat.' He turned over in bed.

'You're going to *sleep*?'

'It's night time. People traditionally sleep then.'

She got up and peeked between the bedroom curtains, the water pooling on the flowerbeds, his dressing gown starting to smell warm on the light bulb. She had begged him to throw it away for years, the polyester polished grotesquely smooth. She glanced across to see if he could smell it but he'd put a pillow over his face.

'Lights out, please,' he said through the old feathers and drool clouds.

'Your roses are getting a drowning.'

'*Lights*, love.'

'What about the cold patch?'

He growled a sigh. 'You're imagining it. Besides, the hotty's on it. It's a hot patch.' The faintest smoke rising from the dressing gown.

She lifted the hot-water bottle and felt the bed. She thought about how her dad had touched her with two spoons at once, one from his tea, one from his ice-cream, and she'd not been able to tell the difference. She thought about how not knowing the difference had been exciting back then. She thought about all this rain pooling on his grave. They said she wouldn't be allowed to put in the stone for weeks, until the ground had settled. Her reflection looked at her from the wet window glass, a drear picture of the passing of life – time's teeth marks all over her face, and her father in an unmarked grave in the rain.

She stared down at the dressing gown, the room smelling of sweat and singed fabric, a slight burn forming. She lifted the gown, all the time checking for the pillow still over his face, his breathing evening out. The gown was stuck. She lifted harder, panicking a little, trying to tease it from the hot bulb without tearing it. When he fidgeted she dropped it – turned the light off, opening the door a little to let the smell out.

She got into bed, her face turned to the lamp, worrying about fire. The rain had almost stopped, his breathing starting towards the first gurgle of snores. The light from the bulb now a remnant splodge in her eyes, floating between her and the darkness, her brain trying to make meaning out of it.

'What if we can't tell anymore?' she whispered to him in the darkness. 'What if we can't tell how cold it's got?'

She reached for his hand and he gave her a little squeeze, even in his sleep – a sign of cold habit, or of warmth beautifully engrained. She worried which.

While he drifted off she lay there looking at the darkness, his dressing gown still stuck, smelling, to the cooling bulb. Her hand too nervous to check the cold patch now. The hair-trigger security light coming on again.

Rosewater, she thought, picturing her washing sagging in the Friday night weather, and thinking about that sunny day when she'd hung it all out there, clean and fresh and bright.

She sighed and got up, unplugged the lamp, crept with it out into the corridor and closed the bedroom door to, the security light shining in through the window over the front door – the corridor freezing.

The light went out, her body rigid in the cold and the black, the house especially sombre with the downpour gone, the eaves dripping water, his snoring percolating through their bedroom door. She wrapped her arms round herself, wondering why it was that women had to feel more than their fair share of the cold. And yet she remained in the corridor, stuck between not wanting to stay up alone, and not wanting to slide in next to somebody who wasn't there.

She waved at the sensor, hoping it would take pity on her through the window, but it was the thermostat that clicked.

Kill Your Darlings

Your Voice Is Lead

David Sornig

The lieutenant, to give her the credit she's due, did not ever say *don't tell the truth.* What she did say, and what I signed up to in the schedule of field operations about which I was forbidden to report, was item number twenty-five: *The embedded journalist is precluded from communicating the contents of this schedule to any individual or organisation not duly authorised to have knowledge of its contents.* So the terms of the agreement don't require me to tell the truth. It can't reach that deep. Not even now. What it says is that the truth isn't what you say, it's who you say it to.

*

It was on the seventh morning of my captivity that I was again blindfolded and seated in the back of the small car. We drove for some hours and when the car finally stopped and the driver had killed the engine I was taken out and held by the arm before my blindfold was removed. The three men, with their faces, as always, covered in my presence, stood around me in a circle. Two of them held pistols and the third an automatic rifle. They bore their weapons as if they were items of jewellery or toys that they had somehow forgotten to put down. I searched for any sign of a building or some other mark of human life. But there was only the car, the road, and away down towards a river, which ran wide and slow around the curve of a hill, a poppy field. With a nudge, the man carrying the automatic rifle, the one with the blue sneakers, directed me to walk with him down into the poppies. We traced a line roughly perpendicular to the road some way towards the river, and once we were well out of earshot of the other men, perhaps five or six hundred meters away, he tied the blindfold on me again. He gripped me by the back of the neck and pushed me a little further along. Then, with his hand pressing down on my shoulder, he sat me down on what felt like a large flat stone that was still cold from the night. When he lifted his hand off my shoulder I listened for any sound, a snap or a click, that might have been the loading action of his rifle as he prepared to fire it.

*

The roadhouse I had been taken from was the last stop for those truckers who had decided to chance it and cut through the valley rather than negotiate the safer but much longer and more expensive route to the south. Between getting themselves greasy and black under the axles of their half-broken machines, the drivers who hung around the place ate watermelon, drank tea and seemed to take final measure of how the lead of their fear weighed in the emptiness of their purses.

One of these drivers, whose face and name I have now forgotten, sat with me on a mat on the floor and in English told me that his childhood friend, who was also a driver and the son of his father's cousin, had been held up and shot to small pieces (this is how he put it) by a gang just the day before. The driver was scared now to drive but had little choice. He had a large family and no other income. I gave him my card and said that if he ever needed to tell his story, I would be the one to tell it to. I don't know why I thought at the time that this would be a good idea, but it seemed compassionate and the driver took the card gratefully. 'Yes. I will telephone you,' he said. The way he used the word 'telephone' sounded as if he had learnt his English in a time when placing a call was still an activity that required some commitment of time and energy. So when he said it I did not doubt that he would call me.

The only detail of him I remember now with any clarity is the smile he gave me as he stood to leave. He showed his full set of shining teeth and I imagined he was using them to bite into the future that was now bearing down on him.

I noticed as the driver's shadow passed out into the light that I was being openly watched by the three men who remained. They were staring at me with expressions that I could not identify as either curious or hostile and that seemed to me at the time the only attitude available for them to take towards me. While their stares did not in themselves unnerve me, I began to wonder why it was that none of them, not even the driver who had been so friendly to me, had thought to ask what I was doing there. I did not know what answer I would have given in any case, and so that it did not seem to them that I was anything but purposeful I left some money on the table, a US ten-dollar note on which someone had written the word 'shit' in fat black letters, and walked out to the veranda. Outside there was a group of barefooted boys kicking a ball around a dusty paddock on the far side of a potholed track, and I passed some time in the pleasant abandon of watching their perpetual motion. It was only when the ball had been inadvertently kicked across the road and it somehow hopped up from a stone or a step and fell to a stop at my feet that I came to myself. The boy who had kicked it came running towards me as the others stood with their hands on their hips and behind their heads. I took up the ball and made to hand it over the wooden rail that drew the boundary between the road and the roadhouse. The boy had pulled up short, just out of reach, so that I could not simply hand over the ball, and when he looked up at me I saw he was not a boy at all but a girl, with her hair cropped close to her scalp. She said something that I took to mean that I should throw the ball to her and I did. I let the ball drop to the ground and the girl picked it up and ran back to her friends, who, I now realised, were all girls.

It seemed by then that no one would ever come to claim me and I began to worry a little about how I would get back to the base before dark. It was only when the pressure in my bladder had begun to grow uncomfortable, owing to the volume of tea and watermelon I had consumed, that I once again entered the roadhouse. Inside nothing seemed to have shifted, the men had not moved, nor did they seem to have drunk any more from their glasses of tea. I called out into a small niche behind a curtain, and in moments the owner of the place emerged. He was a tidy man in all aspects of his appearance, apart from the small pieces of food stuck to his beard. I asked in English for the way to the lavatory and when he did not understand, I tried out the few words I could remember in the local language. When he still did not understand I made a gesture that I hoped he would not take as lewd. He laughed to show that he had understood and he pointed me to the back of the building. The other men, I saw, were now laughing as well. Out back there was a lime tree that had had a narrow moat dug about it. I went to it and I pissed into the moat and it was when I had finished that they took me.

*

My captors, in the week that they held me, made many threats to my life. They held guns to my head and brandished knives at me, and in that way I suppose they more or less abused my mind and my emotions. Otherwise they treated me well enough. The only physical injury I suffered was inflicted by the force they used to drag me to the car from the lime tree; the hessian sack that was roped over my head had burned a wedge of skin from just under my earlobe across to the peak of my Adam's apple and by the time I was in the poppy field sitting on the cold stone the wound had grown septic and was suppurating. Now, all these months later, the scar looks as though it spells out a word in an alphabet no one has yet invented. A curse probably.

It was as much punishment as I deserved I guess for looking too closely at the life of Rasheed Omar.

*

Time passed as I sat on that stone but it seemed to stretch, to grow sticky. I wondered whether my captors were not simply playing a cruel trick on me, whether they were standing by silently, watching my every move, anticipating the moment when I would risk removing the blindfold, to finally kill me. When, after some time, I did remove it and my eyes adjusted to the light I saw that the man with the rifle had left a flat trail through the poppies that led back to the road. The car was gone and so, too, were the men. I followed the track back to the road, but once I was there I realised that I did not know which way was forward and which was back. I did not know where I had come from and I did not know in which direction I should head. So I simply chose one direction even though, as I tell it now, I don't remember which it was, because through the hours that followed, as I walked in steps that grew steadily less certain, the landscape did not seem to change. There was always the river and always the mountain. By the time the day had grown hot, and I did not know whether it was the sun or the fever that was to blame, I heard the crackle of an approaching vehicle. It was an APC that I recognised as the type that had been sold to the local force by the Polish government, but this one seemed to have been commandeered by an American contractor.

'Muthafucker,' said the driver when I told him where I had been taken from. 'That's at least a thousand muthafucking miles from here.'

Inside the APC I sat beside a man named John Oates whose skin glistened in the slitted light. It gave him the sheen of a young man even though he was probably in his mid-forties or even fifty. When I asked him why he was doing such a shitty job so late in his life, I saw his comrades laugh a little.

'You sick, buddy,' he said. 'You got fever. Best you shut the fuck up a little.'

He was right. I did shut the fuck up and let the fever quiet me into a kind of sleep so that I did not have to endure the small shame I felt at having embarrassed him.

When I woke it took me some minutes to work out that I was now in another vehicle. The light had faded and I'd been strapped by my wrists to a gurney and had an intravenous drip in my arm held fast by a strip of grubby tape. John Oates and his company were gone, or rather I seemed to have left them, but this did not strike me as the order of things at the time. I came to again in a bed. A man's voice was singing a lullaby in a quiet language. I knew the melody but not the words and I hummed it to myself. It was, I suppose, like a cat's purr. Something healing.

Once I had regained clarity I established that I had been evacuated to a hospital in the large Flemish base in the north of the country. The ward itself was populated by journalists and private paramilitary contractors who called it the Mercenary Wing. It had taken three days from the time I had been found by the side of the road to get there. The voice that I had heard singing belonged to a Brazilian photojournalist who was in the bed across the aisle from me. He had been blinded in a helicopter gunship attack on a maternity clinic. We spoke about our work and our families. His wife was a singer and an intellectual and he didn't feel worthy of her.

'My eyes are my intelligence,' he said. 'And now they are gone.'

I told him I had left my son with his grandmother to come here.

'He thinks I am a hero. He is ten. I am his hero. War is heroic to a ten-year-old.' The Brazilian made a face that I could not properly read because of the bandages over his eyes.

The following day the lieutenant arrived with a thin man whose tag said *Howard Sherlock*. Sherlock's face was neat and eager. He struck me as probably new to his job and wanting to please someone. The purpose of the visit was, as he put it, for them to ask me questions and for me to answer them. I remembered the terms of the schedule and I imagined that this was more or less an obligation. Whenever I spoke Sherlock keyed notes into his device. I guessed it was also recording the sound of our words.

I told them about the roadhouse, about the call from the man who spoke English with such a ringing Geordie accent that I wondered it wasn't a joke someone was playing on me.

'Do you know who the source was?' the lieutenant asked.

Her tone was generous and her round head tilted towards her shoulder, the crease of a smile on her lips. It was an act, of course. But it didn't matter. I liked the lieutenant and I liked her pretending to like me. I think for a time she actually did.

'No,' I said. 'There was no way of knowing who the source was. The tip was anonymous.'

Sherlock came to life then.

'What kind of information did this source have?' he said.

I resisted rolling my eyes.

'Obviously there *was* no information,' I said. 'It was a trap.'

'Of course it was a trap. But what kind of information were you expecting?'

When I said Rasheed Omar's name the lieutenant shifted in her chair. I noticed it. Sherlock noticed it. I wondered if he knew how to read it.

'You think there's more to know about him?' he said.

Sherlock seemed earnest and even more naïve perhaps than I was but I wasn't sure if it had been trained into him the way it had been trained into the lieutenant. The lieutenant had been there three years already. She knew what went down but pretended she didn't. It had crossed my mind more than once that the kidnap was a warning for me to play nice, to say nice things about Omar. I still didn't really know anything more about Rasheed Omar than the rumours. So I didn't know what to say. The only things I ever say are things I know for certain.

'I can't say,' I said.

Sherlock made a face at this semantic gap. I guessed it gave him the impression that I was playing a game with him, trying to be evasive.

'I mean I can't say. I don't know.'

Again I looked to the lieutenant. She seemed to relax, to rest back in her chair a little, happy, now that I had refused to be drawn on Omar, to let Sherlock take over.

'Where did they take you?' he said.

'I don't know. I was in the boot of a car for ages.'

'Ages? For an hour?'

'Maybe. Maybe more. It was hard to tell. I was scared. I wasn't worrying about how long I'd been travelling. I was worrying about how much time I still had left to live. You measure it differently.'

'Did the car stop along the way?'

'No. There were no stops.'

'No checkpoints?'

'Not that I could tell. The car never stopped.'

'Did you hear traffic?'

'No.'

'Animals? Were you on a farm?'

'No, there were no animals. No planes. No children. Just …'

'Yes?'

'Wind.'

'Wind?'

'Yes. Wind. It whistled.'

I made a whistling sound to demonstrate and Sherlock made an earnest note of it in his device. I asked him how it might be significant.

'I'm the one asking the questions here,' he said. 'Now, tell me about the people who held you. How many of them were there?'

'There were three.'

'You seem very sure. Are you sure? What did they look like?'

'I don't know. Whenever they were in the room they had their faces covered.'

'But you're sure there were three. How?'

'I saw their shoes. There were only ever three different pairs of shoes. The brown loafers, the black shiny shoes, and the blue sneakers.'

Again Sherlock made a note.

'And how did you communicate? Did they speak English?'

'Nope. At least they didn't speak it to me. They asked me no questions and I gave them no answers. I was not tortured. I was fed. I was taken to a toilet blindfolded. If it weren't for my neck, I think I would even have slept comfortably.'

'Is this the truth?'

'Yes, it is the truth.'

Sherlock looked from me to his screen and back again as if he were making a portrait. The lieutenant leaned across to him and pointed to something on the screen and he nodded, typing another note. When he was done he closed the screen and stood.

'Thank you for your cooperation,' he said.

He did not offer a hand for me to shake or wish me a speedy recovery or anything friendly of that nature.

*

Two days later the lieutenant came to visit me again and we took a walk through the hospital grounds, past the broken walls of buildings that had been abandoned perhaps back in the days of another foreign occupation, or more recently even. I did not know the country so well.

'We sent out men to look for you,' said the lieutenant. 'They put their lives on the line for you.'

'I didn't ask for that.'

I thought she might spit but knew that it was a projection. A cliché. This wasn't a movie.

'He doesn't even believe you were taken hostage, you know. No one ever made any demands.'

I could not say anything to that.

When we returned to the ward, the Brazilian looked as if he had been waiting the whole time just to greet us. We had become friends, of a sort, in the way that hospital roommates are forced into a basic bodily camaraderie.

'I know who that is with you,' he said as we passed. 'That's the lovely soldier. She smells so nice.'

The lieutenant did not smile or frown. If anything I thought the compliment seemed to tire her. I sat on the side of the bed and bounced on it lightly. The lieutenant stood back against a wall.

'Do you want to go home?' she said.

'Do I have a choice?'

'Yes. Technically you've still got a few months left on your embed. We have an agreement after all. A contract. It's your choice.'

I guessed that Sherlock wanted the lieutenant to keep me close. Better to have me where I could be seen than allowed to make mischief elsewhere.

'I'll let you know.'

When she turned to leave and had walked halfway to the door, I called after her.

'Petra,' I said. I waited until she had returned to my bedside to show her a face that said I had something to confide in her.

I looked over to the Brazilian. He was pretending not to listen, so I lowered my voice to a whisper. She leaned into it.

'When they left me at the side of the road back there, the one with the blue sneakers put his hand on my shoulder and said "Sorry." That's it. That's the only thing he said to me, the only thing any of them said to me directly the whole time. He tied the blindfold on me and I thought he was about to shoot me and was apologising for it. Maybe he really was going to shoot me but changed his mind when I felt for his shoulder. "It's okay," I said to him. "It's okay."'

*

It had just gone night when I arrived back at the base. There were two soldiers on security detail at the gate. One of them trained a gun and a bright light on my face while the other frisked me. I'd been there for five weeks before I was captured and I had supposed these men would have known me, but they did not show a single sign of recognition. The soldier who frisked me took a good hard look through my credentials and my kit. He found the camera I'd paid the Brazilian photojournalist a thousand US dollars for on my last day in the hospital. Without him knowing I had copied his pictures onto my memory card and now the soldier was scrolling through them. They were the last pictures the Brazilian had taken before he was blinded; among them were delicate portraits of an expectant mother in the maternity clinic who, moments later, would be dead.

'I'll want that back,' I said.

'Sure,' he said. 'You'll get it back.'

Inside the gates a group of soldiers had formed a ring of chairs around a campfire. When I approached, one or two nodded their acknowledgment and one lifted a can of Coke in salute. None of the others followed.

The only spare camp chair left in the circle was beside a muscular Queenslander whom I had only ever heard addressed as Jezza. He had been the first to turn his head away when the other soldier had tried to lead the toast. I folded my arms into my university pullover and made a show of not looking in his direction but a moment later he nudged me with a fist in my ribs. When I turned to him, he looked long and hard into my face. He was pale, freckled, and blinked his long white lashes often as if sand had been blown into his eyes.

'You know,' he said, and he paused in a way that gave the appearance of having chosen his words with great consideration. 'Back in Bundy mine was a cock to be reckoned with.'

I grinned in the way I had learnt to as a man in Australia with other men who were drinking, even if now they were only pretending at it with Coke and Red Bull. And in so doing I met the provocation. I was trying to show him I was sound.

'I bet it was,' I said.

He put his arm about my shoulder and gripped my chin with his free hand.

'I did my fucking money on you, you weasely cunt. I thought they'd got your fucking head for sure.'

I tried to hold my grin as he said this, but felt it turning sour beyond my control.

'Hey Smalls,' he yelled. A wide-lipped boy at the opposite end of the circle lifted his head and nodded in our direction. Jezza had also found the attention of the entire group. 'Here's your hundred bucks, cunt.'

He crumpled a note and tossed it Smalls' way. It unfurled and fluttered to the ground, almost into the fire.

'Pick the fucking thing up and give it to him before it melts.'

It took me a moment to realise that Jezza was talking to me. I stood and picked up the note and handed it towards Smalls. He snatched it from me and a ripple of laughter tracked around the circle.

I sat back down and pulled the hood over my head, self-conscious now about the dressing on my throat, no longer convinced that it looked as heroic as I had first thought it to be when I was being treated in hospital.

*

In the morning I reported to the lieutenant, who handed the camera back to me.

'I've taken those images and passed them on to Mil Intel. They'll have to be vetted before we can release them back to you. You haven't made copies for anyone else have you?'

'No,' I said. I didn't know how she thought she could trust only my word. But it was the truth. I had made copies for no one but myself.

'Well you can sign to say so just the same.'

I signed on the form she offered.

*

The election was coming and even though he didn't need them Rasheed Omar wanted votes. He had decided to pull a PR stunt in the nearby town, a walk through, pressing the flesh. The lieutenant had signed up to it and was sending along a couple of soldiers and a compliant media body to give it the spin she wanted. Local cooperation. Democracy. Delivering autonomy. The two soldiers were a South African named John and the Queenslander, Jezza. I was the media.

I met with the soldiers at the camp gates just before ten in the morning. Jezza barely acknowledged me. When I made an extra signal of greeting to him he had to ask for my name.

'Oh, yeah. The journo, right?'

'Yeah. The journo.'

The South African pointed us in the direction of a white car parked a short distance away on the open road.

The man in the driver's seat drew a finger across his wispy moustache as we neared. The man beside him swigged from a clear plastic bottle of water. This was Omar.

At the car I stepped ahead of the soldiers and the young man pushed the door out so that I had to move back. He stepped out as if he were the one to be greeted.

'What do you want?' he said.

It was the man with the gentle Geordie accent I had spoken with on the phone and who had given me the tip about the roadhouse. I looked at his shoes. They were the blue sneakers.

'Media,' I said. 'Australian media.' I held out my pass.

He smiled, nodding, and made a long introduction through the open door of the car. I guessed it told the story about the kidnap. At the end of it Omar's face spread into a broad smile. I thought then that it was the smile that drew the permanent squint across his face and that made him look as if he were always staring into the sun. I found out only later that he was almost blind in both eyes. This is how the truth of a person arrives: in pieces and usually late.

We shook hands and he said something that the translator listened to and repeated back to me. While his accent was coal-mining Geordie, I couldn't fit him together because he spoke in sentences that were overly formal; the rhythm of his words didn't have a clear pattern of belonging.

'Rasheed Omar is very pleased to make your company. He has heard of your recent troubles and hopes that you have recovered.'

Omar pinched his hand about his throat, smiled and spoke again.

'He says that while the criminals who kidnapped you must be brought to justice he wonders if you are a changed man after your experience.'

I looked the translator in the eye, then down at his shoes again. He followed me. He seemed embarrassed, as if he had not until then realised that he had given himself away.

'I still aim to tell the truth,' I said.

The translator made a grim face and turned to pass on my message. Omar nodded sagely. I guessed there was a kind of respect in it but I knew that I'd been shut out.

Our group walked the short distance along the approach road from the camp into the town. The South African soldier moved into a forward position. He kept perhaps ten or twenty paces ahead of us. The translator kept by Omar's side. I tried to nudge my way between them but when I tried to ask a question the translator ignored me. Instead he touched at Omar's elbow, guiding him away. Jezza gave me a look.

'Leave him alone,' he said. 'Just watch and see what happens, okay? That's your job.'

Under the terms of the schedule I was obliged to follow Jezza's directions and to stick beside him.

In the town proper we were joined by a few local men who carried on conversations with Omar. Each time someone approached, the translator spoke into Omar's ear, and the blind man nodded once, as if keeping score in this way of who had shown proper deference and who had not.

A little further along a group of women passed by and Jezza leaned over to me.

'You ever think about what it'd be like to fuck one of them?' he said. 'Tell me the truth.'

I made to answer him, but hesitated. I stopped. He wasn't really waiting for an answer. He had moved on already. In any case it was a private truth, immaterial, inconsequential. I thought about the schedule. What did it matter if I really had thought about fucking one of the local women when it was a thought I would never act on? I didn't have to tell him.

Our group and its growing entourage of children and men came to a stop near another group of women who were standing outside a house. Its open front window doubled as the storefront for a bakery. I watched as Omar spoke to the women. He moved his hands freely and they all laughed together. There was, I noticed then, an unguarded softness in his face and it swallowed my doubts about him the way the ocean swallows an oar. I was certain in that moment that I had misread him.

It was just then that I saw a boy who was maybe seven or eight years old come forward to us from the bakery door. He swept into the robes of the women and disappeared from view. Seconds later he appeared again. Now he was holding a loaf of bread out to us. In English he said, 'Take, take.'

Jezza was the one who stepped forward and gave out his hand to take the loaf.

In the same moment the boy raised his free hand. In it was a shiny black pistol, which he gripped now into his two fists. He fired once, solidly, into the soldier's face. The man fell. The boy turned then and pointed the gun at me. We faced off for a bare second and I saw white. I heard a scream and there was something in that scream that allowed me to see again. The boy let off another shot and then another. I let myself fall to the ground and I wriggled like a child, feeling for blood. But there was none. And no pain came. It was only when I looked up towards the second soldier, who was running in my direction, screaming something, trying to take control over the uncontrollable, that I saw Rasheed Omar's dark, dusty robe bunched on the ground beside Jezza and beside him the blue sneakers of the translator, his leg still twitching.

Where the women had been standing I now saw maybe four or five men standing in their places, all of them dumb with shock. One of the younger children had stood his ground with his finger in his mouth.

The boy with the gun was gone.

The South African soldier knelt beside Jezza and spoke into his radio. His voice was panicked, urgent. He spoke in codes that I could not understand.

The dead soldier's face was a ruin. I knew it only from its clean white lashes. His fingers were blunted and heavy and I unfolded them from the bread.

*

In the evening I was sitting alone at a long table in the mess hall when the soldier named Smalls came to hand back to me the memory card the lieutenant had given to Mil Intel. Smalls sat beside me and I offered him a piece of the bread that I had been cutting into morsels and chewing on all afternoon. He took it and swallowed it down. I plugged the card into the camera and scrolled through the four or five images that remained on it. I took some comfort in knowing that the original pictures were still with the Brazilian and that when he finally uploaded them he would use them to tell the story he had lived through. It would give the dignity back to his eyes. Smalls did not know that and neither did he probably care. He was just the delivery boy. But clearly I was expected to accept that the fate of the photographs had been determined for all time by someone like Howard Sherlock.

'Lieutenant says you have to give a statement,' Smalls said. 'No one else is talking. No one saw nothing.'

'Sure,' I said. 'I've been waiting.'

One of the images still on the card was of a boy who looked to me to be remarkably similar to the one who had shot the three men in the town. Of course it couldn't have been him; the Brazilian had been far to the north of the country when he had taken these pictures. But it looked so like the boy that I couldn't turn my eyes away.

'So, did *you* see who did it?' said Smalls.

The image of the boy was a colour portrait taken indoors. It showed his clear laughing smile and upper body as it relaxed against a wall. He was lifting a cigarette to his mouth and was flanked by two sources of light. Over his left shoulder was the even orange glow of a kitchen stove and behind the other was a television that showed what looked like a cartoon. Marvin the Martian, I thought.

'Yep,' I said. 'I saw it. I saw it all.'

What would happen was this. It would take maybe an hour for a contingent from the Australian force to track the boy down. I imagined a wide-footed soldier kicking in the front door of his mother's house, which stood more or less in the middle of a dirt track a kilometre or so out of the town. The Australians would take the boy into custody and after a week they would hand him over to the police in the regional capital. And that would be the end of him; the cartoons would leave his smile. And for what? What admission could he make except to repeat the local saying, that in the footsteps of every hero a thousand assassins follow?

'So?' said Smalls. 'Who was it?'

*

In the interview room Sherlock had given up trying to keep his poker face together. He was fidgety and impatient and would not look at me. This had fallen out of his control. Either he no longer knew where the truth was, or he suspected there was another world of it that had eluded him the entire time, that all he'd been able to put together from his strings of data and information was a false approximation of what was really going on. The lieutenant stared right through me. I no longer existed for her. And I felt myself dissolving.

There was a third person in the room. He was a local police recruit whose uniform hung loose from his shoulders, as if it had once belonged to someone else, a much larger man, or would one day be inherited by another body. He was smiling. He got it. He had made it this far. He waved his hand and invited me to sit down. I sat, and for a moment they left me in silence. I waited for a sign, for a gesture that said that they wanted me to begin. To tell them the truth. And when the sign came – what was it? A nod? A smile? – I looked down at the local man's shiny black shoes and felt for the words at my throat.

Harvard Review

Human Beans

Eric Yoshiaki Dando

We have a problem – Laurel from the Community Centre is not sure if I have actually written a proper curriculum for my Certificate 1 Horticulture course. She wants to look at my syllabus, she wants to have a coffee with me so that we can look over it together and get it up to scratch. 'Look,' says Laurel, 'I know you are a good teacher. I don't want to tell your grandmother how to suck eggs.'

'What does that mean?' I suppose I am a bit wounded. 'My grandmother is dead,' I say. 'Why does she need to suck eggs?'

Laurel is shocked. She takes a step back to regroup. All she wants to do is talk about how we can work together, she says. All she wants to do is move forward, she says.

'Well, I think I am doing a bang-up job,' I say.

'What does that mean,' she asks, 'a bang-up job?'

'A good job,' I say. 'It means I am doing a good job.'

I'm not even sure I know what a syllabus is; I thought a syllabus was a curriculum. Either way I haven't written one.

Pedagogy

We are going to plant some small citrus trees in the vegetable garden of the Lutheran Church after morning tea. I offer the students oranges and mandarins and lemons from my trees at home. I dissect a mandarin and an orange on a plate and offer the segments around but they are all smoking cigarettes. Nobody will even taste one. I have to eat most of the plate myself just to save face.

I try to get everybody to Learn by Doing with a hidden curriculum of sensory experiences – you know, a synthesis. To promote dissonance. To ignite interest and provoke life-long learning.

'I can't eat fruit during the day,' says H, clutching his stomach. 'It gives me gas.'

'Well do you want to just take some for tonight then?'

'Nah, thanks. I don't eat fruit during the night either.'

'Come on, H,' I say. 'Well, why don't you take a few home for your kids?'

'My kids won't eat fruit either. If we buy it, it just goes brown.'

'You have to eat fruit,' I say. 'Your children have to eat fruit – it's part of the course. You have to enjoy fruit. I am going to check on this and grade you before I can give you any sort of certificate.'

'Well,' says H, stuffing a lemon and a couple of mandarins into his overalls, 'if it's part of the course I s'pose we'll have to.'

Hot Showers

H tells us not to have hot showers because it makes you hairy. Unless you are going bald, then hot showers are good if you can handle them. He tells us about this woman he had a shower with once. The water was very hot and her nipples had all this hair growing out of them. She told him she always had hot showers like this and H put two and two together.

'See,' says H, ruffling up his hair so that we can see the roots, 'I got a good head of hair, that's 'cos I don't have my showers too hot. I don't have cold showers, though,' he is quick to add, 'just in-between.'

A Type of Horse

All the women who run the Community Centre are losing their hair – Jasmine says that the condition is called *alopecia*. They try to cover it up with comb-overs and pomade and hats, but it is no good. It just makes it worse. I can't stop looking. I try not to look, I really do – but it just makes me want to look even more.

Every three months my supervisor becomes overstressed from overwork and is replaced, but each replacement has been a woman with this condition – this alopecia. I don't hate bald women; I don't usually even think about bald women. I didn't even know what alopecia meant before I started working here. I thought it was a type of horse.

A Baby Horse

Jasmine always teases me about the day we met and I pretended I knew everything. I told her that a pony was a baby horse.

'Um, that's a foal,' she said.

'No, it's not,' I said.

'Yeah it is,' she said.

'It could have been a deal breaker,' she says now. 'I thought you were a fucking idiot,' she says. I do feel like an idiot now – back then, I just did not understand or appreciate Jasmine's experience and expertise with animals.

Yellow Mitsubishi L300

Jasmine is worried about how conspicuous I am. My students seem to know a lot about me. I drive a bright yellow Mitsubishi L300 Express, and they know my full name, and suburb. They know that I live in a sharehouse in Richmond and that I have a girlfriend and that her name is Jasmine.

'They don't know your last name, though,' I say.

'Yeah, well, they know your middle name. One of them sent you an email. They know your mobile phone number, for fuck's sake,' says Jasmine. 'What sort of people are you working for down there? They should have just *given* you a phone and a car. To make it harder for the criminals to find you. Why don't you just *tell* them where we live? Why don't you just tell them we've got a spare room?'

'Don't worry,' I say. 'It will be okay,' I say. 'That's why they are paying me so much money.'

I try to show her all the new blisters I have on my hands but she will not be distracted.

'It's danger money,' I say.

The Code

Laurel says that my privacy problems can be solved with *misinformation.*

'Jesus,' I say to myself, 'she's balding like a man.'

Laurel is very proud of her new car because it has a keypad lock on the door and the ignition. The key is in her head.

'Go on,' she says to Jay and Dee and H in the car park. 'Have a go. I bet you can't figure out the PIN. It's a five-digit number, I'll tell you that much.'

Later in the kitchen, Laurel confides to me that this was a lie, that the PIN is actually a seven-digit number. Though I do not know if this is more misinformation to confuse and confound me further.

It's probably a six-digit number.

Self Assessment

I write an email to Laurel at the Community Centre with an outline of the assessment criteria for my Certificate 1 Horticulture course. These students have extremely low self-esteem and extremely low literacy, I write. All students will make their own garden with plants that they will make at work. If the students have no garden at home then a space in the Community Centre garden will be allocated to them. They will take 'before' and 'after' photos of their garden, and talk to the group about them. There will be many opportunities to improve our reading and writing.

Let's celebrate what the students *can* do, I write. Let's celebrate what they already know. A picture tells a thousand words – two pictures equals two thousand words. Let us read them and weep, I write.

I talk about the photos that will be taken and the words they represent. I wax lyrical like Jerry Maguire, or some hippy do-gooder who is crying out to be manipulated. What a complete wanker I am, I tell myself as I drive over the Westgate, what a complete fucking lunatic I am. They are going to eat me alive.

A Breath of Fresh Air

Laurel is here to take more photos. She says that everyone seems to be enjoying the Certificate 1 Horticulture Program, everybody seems to be really getting into it.

She takes more photos of us hammering in stakes for the snow peas. 'What are those other plants?' she asks, not wanting to walk any further because it is muddy.

'Well, don't ask me,' I say, 'ask them.' I want my students to demonstrate what we have learned, to increase their self-esteem, to reinforce what we already know.

'H can tell you about it,' I say. 'What are those, H?'

'Broad beans,' says H. 'They put fertiliser back into the soil.' And I am pretty impressed that H is playing his part and has learnt his lines and is saying what I had hoped he would say.

Laurel says they are entering our program into the National Innovation Awards. 'Oh,' I say, 'an award. Do we get some kind of trophy?'

'No,' she says, 'it's a certificate.'

'Fantastic,' I say to the students, 'we will have to get it *laminated*.'

'I can do that for you,' says H. 'I've got a laminating machine at home.'

'I bet you do, H,' says Laurel, raising her eyeballs. H is actually very sweet to her, but perhaps that's so he can cultivate some sort of advantage for himself sometime in the future. I am very nice to Laurel, too, so I must be just like H in that respect, although it is unlikely that I will take out my cock to impress her, as H has suggested doing.

'You don't think that thing I wrote was too hippy?' I say.

'No, no, no. Positive is good,' says Laurel. 'It was a breath of fresh air, actually.'

Broken

Laurel calls my mobile and says Corrective Services is keen for us to take a lot more photos of all the fantastic things we are doing. Someone from the local paper will also be along to take pictures. 'A picture tells a thousand words,' she says, and I am pleased because she seems to be quoting from the crazy manifesto I emailed her.

She says they are going to use us as the new face of Corrective Services, although our faces are not allowed to be in the actual photos. They are certain we will win the National Innovation Award. 'It's a shoo-in,' she says.

'A shoe-in?' I say. 'What does that mean?'

'It means we are doing fine,' says Laurel.

Laurel says that what I have written for the assessment criteria sounds fine, but she has changed the official submission for the award a bit.

'*Fixed* it,' I think she said.

Assessment

Jay is very worried and anxious about the homework assignment for the Horticulture assessment. I did not anticipate it being so tricky for everybody when I wrote the curriculum or the syllabus or the rationale. I thought my students would appreciate not having to write anything.

'Me mother-in-law's not gonna like me messing with her garden,' says Jay. 'She wasn't too happy the last time.'

'Tell her you can't finish the course unless you grow a little garden at home,' I say. 'If she still says no, tell her I will ring her. Or she can come and see me when she picks you up.'

'Okay, I'll tell her. She doesn't like me in the garden because I ripped out all her plants and grew dope plants and the police came and ripped them all out.'

I call Laurel and explain that we need to organise a space at the back of the Community Centre for the students who can't make a garden at home.

Enough Coloured Pencils for Everyone

It's raining pretty hard so I get my clients to sit around the heater in the lunch-room and draw cognitive 'mind maps' of a garden or barbecue area they would like to have at home. I thought the barbecue area would appeal to H because, although I am sure he does not like gardening, he does like sausages.

'Just draw the garden or barbecue area that you would like to own. Maybe you would like a spa or a big fountain. Or a gazebo. Or lots of concrete and cactus and gnomes. If you want a monkey house, you can draw a monkey house. I don't care. But on account of the rain, this is all that I need today for my assessment of your Certificate 1 Horticulture. Everybody who hands in a design will get an instant H1 credit for garden planning/ cognitive mapping for Certificate 1 Horticulture. There are no rules to this project. But you've got to have a go and think about it and be honest. It takes a different sort of guts to do this, I know, but you will get credit for it, I promise.'

I have lots of coloured pencils. I sit with them and draw a garden I would like to have one day – a small fish farm that recycles itself into a small vegetable garden. And a hermitage for my hermit, who I will point out to visitors but never, ever speak to face to face. And a large, bronze sculpture of an upturned foot,

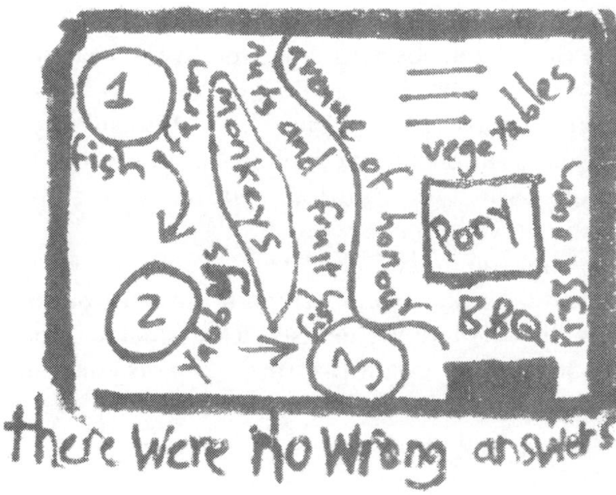

like a giant's foot sticking out of the ground, that you can sit on, like a park bench. With a perfect view of the fish farm and the hermit being wretched and unkempt. Because that is what my visitors have come to see.

The Children

H comes to talk to me at lunchtime. He is having trouble getting to work on time because he has to take his kids to school. I call Laurel and write a passionate email to Corrective Services. I write, 'The kids should be the priority here,' and 'who are we really punishing here?' and stuff like that.

I got a call from Laurel and it's all official now – H can arrive late to work but he must work through lunchtime to make up for it. I stick my neck out for H.

I find it truly amazing that I still like H even though I know all the truly horrible things he has done to animals, plants and people.

'I'm such a good boss,' I tell myself as I drive home over the Westgate.

That's All Well and Good

Dee says he has been clean for three years. I overhear him telling H how good it is to be able to save money and go into shops and buy little luxuries and clothes and electronics whenever he wants. To not funnel all his time and money and energy into a black hole that just keeps getting bigger. Just so that he can stay well.

H flails his hands up like a giant bird. 'But isn't there something missing? I'm on the methadone program too, but there are some times when there's just something missing. Know what I mean?'

'I know what you mean,' says Dee.

I walk past later and H has written down a list of dodgy doctors and a list of dodgy chemists, as a special favour to be redeemed later. They go on like this, like ants communicating in their secret language.

I am really pissed off at H, and next time we are alone I will let him have it, but for now the damage is done.

I Thought She Was Just Pleased to See Me

I keep bringing in fruit from my garden and putting it in a big communal fruit bowl in the kitchen. Strange fruit – pepinos, babacos and tamarillos – but it remains uneaten for a long time. But then, this week, some of it is missing. I get excited at first, but then I realise that my students wouldn't have eaten it. They would have told me they had eaten it or eaten it in front of me to get more marks on their *assessment* for Certificate 1 Horticulture.

I think the Buddhists have been stealing our fruit. I saw the Nasty Old Buddhist Administrator as she was leaving and she had a pepino-shaped bulge in her trousers.

It Was Like Some Sort of Secret Competition

I have noticed that H is jealous of Dee, or is angry at him for giving up heroin. H is always suggesting dodgy doctors and chemists to Dee in case he needs to start using again. He always makes a point of talking about heroin when Dee is around. H is on the methadone program but he still uses. 'Sometimes I just like to take a little holiday,' says H. 'Does that make me a bad person?'

When I drive H to Bunnings to buy him overalls, I tell him to stop talking about heroin to Dee. 'You hate him for giving up, don't you?' I say. I say it politely.

'He hasn't given up,' snorts H. 'You're a nice guy, but you just believe every little thing ya hear.'

'Well, I think from now on we have to agree that we can't talk about heroin or dodgy chemists around Dee, okay?' I narrow my eyes at him, to see if he sees that I am serious.

'Ahhh,' he says, covering his face with his hands.

H understands my eyes, but not the situation. 'Okay,' he says, 'I never would do anything to fuck things up. Sorry.'

My Own Personal Golem

H is late for work again. He has been down at the Sheriff's Office, he says, brokering employment deals for my future. H says that he has been putting in a good word for me.

H is continuing to leave work very early and arrive very late. He always has the paperwork to support his stories. He always gives me some sort of conspiratorial slap on the back as he is leaving each day. I have created a monster.

I keep wondering if the criticisms of my program are becoming true – that somehow my students are taking advantage of my goodwill and trust-building exercises.

A Monster

I don't know about H. He is doing my head in. I have created a monster. A golem. He comes in at 10.30 or 11 a.m. or 12 p.m. sometimes, but still expects me to sign him in for 9 a.m. All he does is make cup after cup of sweet, sweet tea. H gets stoned on sugar and flicks through the paper, just looking at the pictures – because he is illiterate, they told me at the Community Centre.

I ask him, could he re-pot the lavender, sow all the vegetable seeds for the vegetable garden, clean the coffee cups and sweep the floor. 'And if there's any time, could you pick up papers in the car park?' He keeps wanting to push the boundaries. We agree that he works through lunch to make up for being late, but then he somehow makes me drive him to McDonald's. I sit with him near the playground while he eats.

He gives me the seventy cents he borrowed a week ago. 'You thought I had forgotten,' he says, 'but I always repay my debts. Some cunts don't, but I do.'

Brass in Pocket

Laurel thinks that my clients are taking advantage of me; she says she is telling me as a friend. This makes me uncomfortable because I know we are not friends. I point out that I was employed as a horticulture teacher and the formerly disengaged students are learning about horticulture as per my curriculum or rationale or syllabus. Everyone is working hard and respecting each other so what's the problem? I certainly don't feel like my students are taking advantage of me. I feel like we are a team, that I have the support of my students. I feel like we are fighting *for* each other rather than *against* each other. I really do believe all this claptrap and bunkum and hogwash.

I tell Jasmine about it but she is not amused. She agrees with Laurel. 'They probably *are* taking advantage of you,' she says, 'but you just don't know how yet. But you will and then it will be too late.'

Maybe I *am* a soft touch; maybe they are taking advantage of me. I must come off sounding like a terrible hippy when I open my arms out wide, saying things like, 'We can build trust' in the kitchen of the Lutheran Church, as the rain comes down on a Monday morning in Werribee.

Pirate Among the Pigeons

H is preparing to take advantage of me, but of course I don't realise this until much later.

First, he says, 'Do you know what my favourite show is? *The Simpsons*. Who likes *The Simpsons*? Know my favourite character? Bart. Because he gets away with everything. Who's your favourite character on *The Simpsons*?'

I give this serious thought. 'I don't know,' I say. 'Maybe Moe or Mr Burns. I like a lot of the supporting and cameo characters like Lenny and Disco Stu. Lenny. I think my favourite character is Lenny,' I say. 'Nuts,' I say, in a little Lenny voice.

Everyone talks about their favourite character on *The Simpsons*. Everyone has a go at their favourite catchphrases from their favourite characters.

'I think I've seen every episode three times,' says H, 'because it's the type of show you can watch again and again and again, even if you've seen it before.'

Now everything is set up nicely for H, he is going to sell us pirate DVDs, and we are all ready to buy them. 'Well listen,' says H, 'I've got heaps of *Simpsons* boxsets here, three for ten dollars. Take 'em home and if they don't work just bring 'em back to me. I'll give you some that do.'

Everyone starts ordering pirate *Simpsons* boxsets and I take a little walk to the toilet until they have finished. I didn't see anything. I don't know anything. Later on, I have a little talk to H. I tell him I don't really care about whatever it is he is doing, just not to do it in front of me. Just don't do it here. They haven't said anything about it but I'm sure we are not allowed to sell pirate DVDs during work time. And I don't even know who *they* are, but *they* will not be pleased.

'So, just save it for down the pub,' I say.

'Sorry,' says H, rubbing his hands against each other like he is trying to start a fire with them, rolling up little cigars of dirt in his palms. 'I'd never do anything to get you into trouble,' he says.

H goes to the pub after work and moves the whole bag of *Simpsons* boxsets and gets orders for more. I overhear him telling Jay about it – he deliberately says it within earshot so that I can hear. H is a fantastic salesman – it is just something that he wants me to know. It's like he wants me to give him extra marks on his Certificate 1 Horticulture or something.

Vegemite Soldiers

I go out in the morning in my pyjamas to warm up my yellow Mitsubishi L300 and I find Dee asleep in the back in my sleeping bag. I check all the doors and windows for forced entry but there is no damage. I can't figure out how he got in but he is a professional, I suppose. He wakes up when I start the engine but only for a few seconds. It must all seem like a horrible dream.

I go back inside and make some coffee and get dressed for work. It's okay, I'm not going to get in trouble because Jasmine has already left for the day. I make Dee some Vegemite on toast. I cut the toast into thin Vegemite soldiers the way my grandmother did for me.

I cut Dee's toast in this way because I believe Dee missed out on lots of experiences like this when he was growing up. I believe the Vegemite soldiers will cause some sort of chemical reaction in his brain. I believe it will be a catalyst for good things to happen in his future. It's only toast so I probably won't tell Jasmine about it. It is probably something she doesn't need to know.

Dee is leaning against my car, having his first cigarette for the day.

'I had a fight with me wife,' says Dee. He smokes the rest of his cigarette and eats the toast at the same time. I must confess that I have never seen this done before. He tastes the coffee and is shocked that it is not instant coffee. He is not sure if he should drink it now or save it for later.

He must think I am rich, I think.

'This coffee works better than instant coffee,' I say. I am relieved and proud that I know more about coffee than Dee does.

'How did you know where I lived?' I say.

'Everyone knows where you live,' says Dee.

Later that day, I overhear Dee talking to ATM about the

Vegemite soldiers and the real coffee that I made for him. 'You should have seen the breakfast this cunt made for me,' says Dee.

Dee keeps referring to me as a cunt but I know that he means I am a good cunt and not a rat cunt or a dog cunt or a cunt rat fucking dog cunt or anything like that.

Crack

We are having our morning cup of tea in the ugly, ugly winter drizzle, sitting under the veranda so that they can smoke. Everyone is complaining about the rain but the truth is that everybody is much happier when it is raining because we don't have to work.

'Good weather for ducks,' says H.

'It's good for the peas,' I say. It is the second cup of tea for our second morning tea break. On days like these our morning tea is sometimes interrupted by lunch.

H takes a cigarette out of his shirt and I notice that it has a little twist on the end like a joint. He has this funny look on his face like a naughty boy about to do something naughty.

'H,' I say, with a little menace in my voice, 'is that a joint?'

'Nah, don't worry. It's not dope. Don't worry,' he says with confidence, lighting it up, puffing away, 'it doesn't have any smell.'

He takes short, deep little drags as it sizzles and burns down one side, all sticky and black and moist, burning blue smoke with a fizzle.

Oh my fucking god, I think.

I glare at H.

'Nobody will know,' he says, 'for shizzle my nizzle.'

'What does that mean?' I say, frowning and rubbing my brain firmly with one hand.

H shrugs; he does not know what it means. Then he actually offers me the butt-end of whatever it is he is smoking.

'Jesus, H, I can't believe you're doing this,' I say, walking away in disgust. I can't believe any of this. Jasmine and the women at the Community Centre were right – H is taking advantage of me.

I don't feel as though I can really rat him out to the Community Centre but I tell him that he has to go home for the day. I sign him out, saying that he is sick. He doesn't go home right away, he makes a big production out of weeding all the peas and beans and making sure they are all supported. It is the most work he has done in weeks. It's like having a baby elephant loose in the garden. He tries to engage me in a conversation about the peas but I stonewall him and then he leaves, slamming the side gate behind him.

Fooled Again

Later, when we are alone, Dee tells me the real reason H is late every day – he is out finding his morning taste. 'You didn't hear this from me,' says Dee.

Even though he is on the methadone program, H has to shoot up before he is well enough to come to work. Dee says that H's wife takes the kids to school anyway. 'Everybody knows that, even those bald bitches at the Community Centre,' says Dee. 'Why would they let you get sucked in like that? There's going to be trouble now,' says Dee.

Dee says that H's problem is that he is just too disorganised. Dee says that when *he* was using, he always planned his heroin use a few days in advance, unlike H, who never knows where his next taste is coming from. 'He's always got his hand out and his leg up,' says Dee.

'H is making a fool of you,' says Dee, 'you have to do something. Or *they* will come down here and do something. He's going to fuck it up for everybody.'

I feel really confused about Dee. I really thought he was interested in gardening, but now I realise it is just an easy work dodge.

Like I said, at least we are all learning something new and getting some exercise and not hurting anybody.

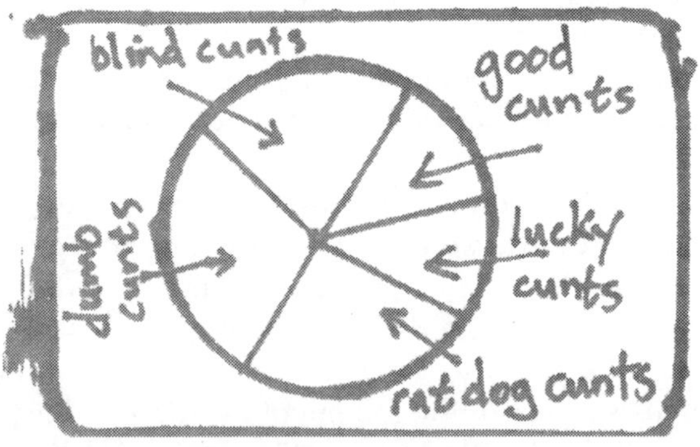

Debriefing H

The next day I talk to H about using drugs at work and letting me down. H doesn't really understand what the problem is. I try to see it from his side but I just can't.

'You can't do it here,' I say. I have to take a deep breath. I think I am getting asthma or something. 'You have to wait until you get home,' I say.

'You think that got me stoned?' he says. 'That didn't have any effect whatsoever.'

'I know what you mean,' I say. 'You are an elephant, so you need more.' H looks at me funny – he probably thinks that I am calling him fat, but I mean that he needs a big dose because he has built up such a resistance. Maybe he thought I meant he had a good memory; you would have to have a good memory to be such a good liar.

'The thing is,' I say, 'I don't want you doing that here. I don't want you talking about it and tempting people with it. I don't want you coming here loaded again. Otherwise you will have to find a different course to do and we would really miss you here.'

'You know what?' says H, taking a step closer to me. 'You do this funny thing with your eyes when you're angry, that's when I know I am really in trouble.'

Positively Punitive

I am really angry with H but it's not like extra punishment is going to help him take fewer drugs. *They* are already watching him. I think about H's children. I have to make things clear. The thing I am really pissed off about is that he did it in front of Dee and then offered him some. Dee just looked at me and shook his head.

Later, I see Dee speaking very quietly and intensely to H about something and H waving his arms around and slapping himself in the head and the chest and the back of the legs. Then he tries to offer Dee his hand, but Dee spits on the ground and walks away without shaking it.

Peas

Laurel has sent me a crop of new students today. I talk firmly about working in a drug-free environment and I give a short talk to them about what is expected in case they have heard anything different from H or somebody who knows H. He keeps working really hard and breaking a sweat and looking over at me like a little puppy.

H loves helping with the peas, or says he does. He loves helping the peas grab onto the string, although sometimes his act is a little wooden. 'Look at their little hands,' he says, jabbing his enormous sausage fingers into the tangled loom of peas. 'I tied this string up here for them to grab onto,' he reminds us. 'I can't wait to eat some of these,' he claims, 'straight off the fucken bush.'

I think H has just worked out the things I like to hear. I think he is just faking his transformation and his reconnection with the natural world. I don't know if he really feels this way about the little pea sprouts or if he is just pissing in my pocket again.

The Sleepers Almanac

David Davis at Coldpigeon Dot Com

Meredi Ortega

There were a lot of people in the world named David Davis but David Davis had got in early, he had snaffled DavidDavis at Coldpigeon dot com before anyone else. Consequently, all the David-come-latelies had to choose names that were not their own but close approximations or name-scrap stews such as davidavis and dddaviddavis and david.daviddavis.davis42 at Coldpigeon dot com. There were countless varieties of David Davis but there was only one David Davis. He was the precursor and when he logged into his mail, he took some comfort in knowing he had not compromised himself, at least in regard to his name. It was something.

As the Coldpigeon webmail service grew, David began receiving emails intended for other Davids. The people who sent them thought they were sending them to their own particular Davids but, in reading the scrawl on the back of a docket or in half remembering the email address they had been given, they omitted the full stops or the extra ds or the numbers which differentiated their Davids from the first one.

To begin with, David Davis blocked these senders and relegated their misdirected mail to his Deleted Items and Junk folders but as time passed he began to read them and even to hold on to them. He didn't receive many personal emails and when he watched the pigeon icon flapping its wings during Send and Receive and did not perceive the cooing sound which accompanied new messages in his Inbox, he felt a sad emptiness in his stomach. So when a message did appear, though not meant for him, it was easy to pretend it was his, especially as its salutation so often began with 'Hi David.'

'Hi David.' As time passed he not only read and held on to these emails but he began to reply to them. He didn't reply in a helpful manner in the way that, for instance, a person might inform someone they had dialled the wrong number. When he received an email reminding him about a Christmas party at the home of Pastor John and Debra in Dallas, Texas, from a woman named Carol, he replied, 'Thanks, but no thanks.'

From: Carol

Sent: Wednesday, 8 December 2010 9:39 AM

To: DavidDavis@Coldpigeon.com

Subject: Re: Christmas Party Reminder

What does that mean?

Blessings

Carol

From: DavidDavis@Coldpigeon.com

Sent: Monday, 13 December 2010 2:29 PM

To: Carol

Subject: Re: Christmas Party Reminder

It means stop sending me this junk.

David

From: Carol

Sent: Wednesday, 15 December 2010 12:15 AM

To: DavidDavis@Coldpigeon.com

Subject: Re: Christmas Party Reminder

OK, Mr Davis, are you saying that information regarding the ministry that you work in and the church that you attend is junk?
I hope you are having a truly blessed day!
Carol

From: DavidDavis@Coldpigeon.com
Sent: Thursday, 16 December 2010 2:43 PM
To: Carol
Subject: Re: Christmas Party Reminder

That's right. Christmas parties, churches, Jesus. They are all forms of spam.
David

David didn't hear back from Carol but the exchange left him wanting more. It gave him a warm, treacly feeling which he hadn't felt since he was seven, a golden age when he believed he could will lightning storms and electrical blackouts. And again he wanted to see what havoc he could unleash from his fingertips, along the cable, shooting up then down from a satellite in the sky. It was conceivable that he could ruin the life of another David Davis, an inferior copy, on the other side of the world. And why not, if it created a little diversion in the day-to-day minutiae of specifications, calculations, data sheets, vendors and clients, meetings, cup after cup of milky tea? It wasn't like steaming open envelopes and reading other people's mail.

For one thing, it was easier. Electric kettles were problematic because they turned themselves off when they had a good jet of steam going and then there were the inevitable little scalds that occurred if you held the envelope at the wrong angle. Also, you didn't want the ink to run. A tricky business and when you tried to put the flap back as it was, it never really looked as unopened as it had, prior to being opened. Especially not to the person who had opened it, their perspective probably altered by the knowledge that it had in fact been opened. Although his ex-wife had never seemed to notice. And that was the other problem. Christ, it was bor-ing. There was never any illicit love letter containing erotic photos or a statement from a secret bank account in Luxembourg. It was always a reminder for her annual check-up at the dentist or a special discount on tents at a camping shop where she'd bought one white enamel mug last century.

Certainly, he opened his fair share of uninteresting emails intended for other Davids: a tennis academy urging him to come along and burn calories at cardio drills to *The Sound of Music* and a request for him to bring along his secateurs and trim lilly-pillies at a primary school working bee. Didn't schools have gardeners anymore and how could anyone work up a sweat to *Edelweiss*? Sometimes, an email was only humdrum to begin with, until he breathed some life into it. He received a picture of a large vase sitting on a faux column.

From: Julie Brown

Sent: Thursday, 13 January 2011 4:22 AM

To: DavidDavis@Coldpigeon.com

Subject: Mum

I got this one.

Julie

Sent from my iPhone

From: DavidDavis@Coldpigeon.com

Sent: Thursday, 13 January 2011 6:47 PM

To: Julie Brown

Subject: Re: Mum

Don't tell me you actually paid money for

that. It looks like a spittoon. She will hate it.

David

From: Julie Brown

Sent: Friday, 14 January 2011 4:02 AM

To: DavidDavis@Coldpigeon.com

Subject: Re: Mum

I paid 4 it but the money is cmng out of the estate. Since U couldn't B bothered cmng here 4 the funeral I don't think U have the right 2B choosy about the urn. What would U know about what Mum liked since U always sent her gerberas and she Fking hated gerberas.

Julie

Sent from my iPhone

He looked at the picture again and noticed the vase had a lid. All the same, it sounded as though that David Davis deserved a good kick up the pants for not going to his mum's funeral, what a piece of low life. Still, he couldn't resist sending one more mail.

From: DavidDavis@Coldpigeon.com

Sent: Friday, 14 January 2011 7:25 PM

To: Julie Brown

Subject: Re: Mum

Just so you know. Mum said I was always her favourite.

David

From: Julie Brown

Sent: Saturday, 15 January 2011 4:47 AM

To: DavidDavis@Coldpigeon.com

Subject: Re: Mum

Just so U know. Mum always said U were a mistake and yr real dad was Uncle Bob.

Julie

Sent from my iPhone

Yes, he still had lightning in his fingers as he ended friendships, had people sacked, meeting places changed, reputations ruined, the whole while remaining outside it all like a faceless god. Sometimes people would confer in real life and realise they had been deceived and they would send him angry and threatening emails about their imaginary lawyers who they claimed were going to sue his sorry ass off. Americans mainly, but what could they in fact do? They had emailed *him*, after all and he had only replied. They didn't know who he was, only that he was David Davis and there were a lot of them in the world. Too many, it sometimes seemed.

From: Stefanie

Sent: Sunday, 20 February 2011 2:39 PM

To: DavidDavis@Coldpigeon.com

Subject: picnic

Hi Dave

OK I will bring blankets to sit on. What food are you bringing?

Cheers

Stef

From: DavidDavis@Coldpigeon.com

Sent: Monday, 21 February 2011 10:22 AM

To: Stefanie

Subject: Re: picnic

Stef

I will bring a sheep's head.

Dave

From: Mathew

Sent: Thursday, 17 March 2011 9:09 PM

To: DavidDavis@Coldpigeon.com

Subject: Davis Mountain Cottages

Hi David

We have booked a cottage with you in Nov. Is it possible to upgrade it to a deluxe cottage?

thanks

Mathew

From: DavidDavis@Coldpigeon.com

Sent: Friday, 18 March 2011 11:18 AM

To: Mathew

Subject: Re: Davis Mountain Cottages

Hi Mathew

That is no problem. I will make sure you have the one with the toilet seat.

David

He smiled when he opened a mail which greeted him with 'Hey Tiger.' It was Jessica telling him she thought they could make this whole long distance thing work. She told him that if two people were meant to be together then a two-hour flight was not such a big deal and she was counting down the weeks. She then startled the under-utilised X button by firing off a barrage of kisses. He typed 'Hey Gorgeous' and told her how he likewise thought it could work with the proviso that they could still see other people because maybe they were meant to be together but then maybe he was meant to be with Kelly or Angela or Rachel. Oh, he nearly forgot Melissa. He didn't want to rule anyone out at this stage and he signed off with 'I love you heaps, too' and clicked Send. He wondered if he'd changed the future. Perhaps they were going to marry and have children and perhaps, with one click of a button, he'd deleted their prospective children and their children's lives and all that would have branched from them. If two people were meant to be together, that's what she'd said. He wasn't just designing gas platforms and refineries and filling out tag numbers for valves like his colleagues. He was engineering destiny. His fingers tingled at the thought. Another mail deposited in his Inbox.

From: Erasmus Erastus

Sent: Wednesday, 4 May 2011 12:47 PM

To: DavidDavis@Coldpigeon.com

Subject: Poetry Symposium

Hi David

I don't know if you will remember me but we spoke recently at the Poetry Symposium. You said you would be happy to give me some feedback on my work. Thank you for your generosity. Please find a poem attached. Please feel free to be critical.

Kind regards

Erasmus

Poetry, snorted David. He opened the attachment. It was titled *a poem for emergencies* and it began, 'away from the road / cast anchor in a hard place / slide your music box / your well sweep / under the unloved / jester of gilbert.' Plainly it was poetry because it was complete gibberish. He didn't finish reading it.

From: DavidDavis@Coldpigeon.com

Sent: Wednesday, 4 May 2011 1:25 PM

To: Erasmus Erastus

Subject: Re: Poetry Symposium

Erasmus

This poem seems like it was written by a Vogan. Are you from the planet Vogsphere by any chance?

David

From: Erasmus Erastus

Sent: Wednesday, 4 May 2011 2:05 PM

To: DavidDavis@Coldpigeon.com

Subject: Re: Poetry Symposium

David

I confess I am a little bit surprised by the harshness of your response. Would you care to elaborate? Something constructive would be greatly appreciated. Many thanks.

Regards

Erasmus

David looked at the poem again, 'unmask the hub, brace / each honeycomb / left and loose / raise it higher / - release - / that which gyves / the orb to its gyre.' Seriously, what claptrap. He was annoyed at himself for even reading the second stanza, for wasting his time on this wally with the stupid name. Erasmus Erastus. He'd made that name up. Two similar names like David Davis except anyone could tell David Davis was a real name whereas Erasmus Erastus sounded like a stage name for a second-rate magician. Except the only things he made disappear, apparently, were upper case letters and full stops. What a sad act. David clasped his fingers together, stretched his arms and cracked his knuckles. A blue electrostatic discharge sparked from his fingertips.

From: DavidDavis@Coldpigeon.com

Sent: Wednesday, 4 May 2011 2:15 PM

To: Erasmus Erastus

Subject: Re: Poetry Symposium

Erasmus

The only way this poem could be useful in an emergency is if you were lost in the wilderness and you had a flint and steel but no tinder. In this scenario, your poem could start a cracking good fire.

David

From: Erasmus Erastus

Sent: Wednesday, 4 May 2011 3:03 PM

To: DavidDavis@Coldpigeon.com

Subject: Re: Poetry Symposium

David

I had no idea my poem was that bad. I think it must be the medication I'm on. It takes away the lows but it also

takes away the highs. Maybe it makes my poetry middling, too. I think I was better without it. Thank you for your time.
Erasmus

So Erasmus Erastus the poet was depressed. How clichéd. But still, David was drawn to look at the poem again. The third and fourth stanzas were nonsense as well, 'find a notch / on the forbidden fruit / slit a drink-straw hole / sting like a biro bee.' What was he on about? Why couldn't Erasmus just say what he wanted to say in plain English like a normal person? David tried to put the strange poem out of his mind but it kept teasing him like a puzzle. Random lines intruded into his thoughts, 'bring the fifth / to the four.' What did it mean? The fifth what and why four? He tossed and turned in bed that night with the lines 'a pen that does not breathe / will need a rekindled heart.'

Perhaps poems came from the same place as dreams because when he awoke, he realised with sudden clarity that the poem contained instructions on how to change a flat tyre and perform an emergency tracheotomy. Of course, if you were changing a flat tyre, the poem was only going to confuse matters if you had left-threaded wheel nuts, more than four or decagon-shaped wheel nuts. No matter, now he wished he'd written something along the lines of, 'The only way this poem could be useful during a tracheotomy would be if it was rolled into a tube.' How he wished he'd written that instead of the one about tinder!

*

A week later, it was the name that leapt out at him from an online news site. There it was again, that implausible name, Erasmus Erastus. David winced at the part where he'd jumped off a bridge. A promising undergraduate in creative writing. Really, you could get a degree in that? People got degrees in anything these days, surfing and wine tasting. Nice for some. Except not this time. No, well, you had to have thick skin to be a writer. You couldn't throw yourself off a bridge every time someone looked at you the wrong way. Hardly his fault. Erasmus had said, hadn't he, 'Please feel free to be critical.' David tried to think about how a poem might be useful in that sort of emergency, the sort where you were jumping from a bridge. He could have written something else to Erasmus, something helpful, 'The only way this poem could be useful in an emergency is if you held it above your head like an umbrella and held on to it for dear life.' He'd just needed enough drag to slow his fall like that barmaid who was saved by her crinoline. But then again he probably hadn't printed it out, hadn't made it real. Also, A4 encompassed a fairly small surface area and in any event, Erasmus had jumped from an overpass. It was useless really, the poem. He'd been right all along. He was going to dwell on it some more when he was distracted by the soothing sound of a cooing pigeon. He had mail. Oh look, it was Carol from Dallas again, inviting him to a prayer meeting. All was forgiven.

The Raid on Australian Poetry

Alan Gould

'Here, Australian poets, I will like you to sleep off your night with the gravestones.' Branca showed us through their apartment. 'Then please, I will like it if you come to our big conference and ask the exploding questions. Your name-tags I will arrange, it is easy.'

Honoured, we said, and marvelled at our luck.

Their rooms were peculiarly sumptuous given the austerity common to both poetry and communist regimes. Lofty ceilings were decorated with plaster moldings of swains and maidens. A kitchenette and a narrow balcony above the Rio Santa Moisé both came off the wide parlour, while two bedrooms, each furnished with a double bed of modern wrought metal and spread high with snowy doonas and several scarlet-covered pillows, were placed discreetly on a corridor.

'I see what you think of us.' Branca was apologetic. 'Here are two communist women who enjoy the pretty good fortune with International Poetry.'

'Good luck to you, I reckon.'

'Poetry is like the socialism,' she continued quickly. 'It has no national borders.'

'Blood oath,' I said.

'Poets meet each other at the level of mystery, not politics.'

'Absolutely,' Henry said.

It was intriguing how she glanced uncertainly at us, endowed us with presence on the simple basis we had declared ourselves to be poets. She was old enough to be our mother.

'My government likes this idea. So for poetry it is always the big handshake for poets, and if you translate the poetry then you also enjoy.' She gestured around the room, her spiel having been at once deprecating and playful. This gave the ironic liveliness to her eyes.

'Why not, ma'am?'

'Perhaps your country is the same.'

Australia was also fond of the big handshake, Henry assured her.

'Just so.' She nodded her head, glad that we knew how to be complicit. 'And you see,' she rested her eye on Henry, 'Jelenska and I, we must be good scouts for our country in the literatoor. Poets are a good foreign exchange for a communist country.'

'Poetry is a kind of money,' Henry stated.

Branca regarded him appreciatively. 'You are authentic Australian poet.'

Now Jelena reappeared from the bathroom to hurry her mother to the conference. The amenities of the apartment were explained to us: coffee, bread rolls, honey. We would see our hosts later. Then they were gone to their work and we were left alone.

'We've hit gold.'

'They are very trusting,' Henry qualified.

We helped ourselves to their coffee, then Henry read in one of the armchairs and soon was fast asleep. Wandering from the apartment, I took this street and that, came out at the Grand Canal again and, in the casual manner of Venice, found myself gazing across the water at the Chiesa Di Santa Maria Della Salute. Built (as I read in Frommer) to rejoice Venice's deliverance from the plague, the dome of this baroque church appeared spectral and magnificent against the milky overcast. So was this city truly all about death and beauty? It seemed so, and once more Henry seemed to have summed up a thing in advance of being exposed to it, like Byron, whom he had mocked for doing so.

When I returned to the apartment he had woken and was reading again.

He glanced up. 'Where have you been?'

'Checking out death and beauty in this city.' I described the extraordinary church I had seen across the water. I should say that, whenever I fell into line with any of Henry's airy pronouncements, he did not preen himself. Egotist that he was, a personal supremacy was never the point. It was my acquiescence in his view of the conditions of existence that he sought, an assurance my mind had been cleared of non-poetic clutter.

So I framed my question to him carefully. 'Hal, when you tell me this city is about death and beauty, do you actually see in your mind's eye those people writhing and vomiting from plague, and the measure of relief when the contagion departs such that they can raise some magnificent church in thanksgiving?'

I wanted him to assure me that the particulars of what was suffered by living folk down the eras were embraced by the poetic shorthand of his 'Venice is about Death and Beauty.'

But he evaded my attempt to probe the quick of how he imagined things. 'Let's check out this poetry conference.' He jumped to his feet.

We found our way to the Casa Foscari, and entered its foyer to be confronted by its opulence.

Henry was buoyant. 'What's an image for that stairwell?'

'Uh—'

'Too late, too late. It is a conch shell.'

And naturally the image was vivid and judicious for the lucent, upwardly spiralling balustrade that disappeared into darkness.

He went off to collect the name-tags Branca had promised while I sat on the lustrous stair and cast my eye over the crowded foyer. The encampments of poets seemed arranged more by attitude than nation. Above one group a calico sign read, 'We are poets and we are millions,' while similar banners advertising similar solidarity hung here and there in various languages. I saw islands of argument and faces of studied hauteur. Many notepads rested on many knees and wordspray was being set down on their lined pages. I recognised a Ken, a Laurie and a couple of Kates from the Australian scene. Aware that, as Arden poets, Henry and I were sometimes called the School of Ardour, I nodded curtly to these fellow nationals and, when Henry reappeared, I ascended the conch shell with him to the theatre where the session that included Peter was being held. We took our seats near the back.

Money was being spent on poetry here. Each seat in the auditorium was equipped with headphones and wired to a cockpit at the back where sat several translators ready to give simultaneous translations in a diversity of languages to each speaker as they presented themselves. I could see Jelena among them, but not her mother. The title of this session – in its English translation – was *New Lions from Old Lines: The Poetics of Post-Colonial Societies.*

'Bring it on!' Henry settled into his seat and fitted his headset.

The lights dimmed with the exception of spotlights that illumined our panel. There was a poet from Mauritius, groomed like a film star, pulling nervously at his graying temples. Next to him sat a woman poet from Surinam, like a tropical fish in the turquoise and orange of her national costume. And there was Peter, wearing a braided waistcoat, tight black trousers: the matador among them, perhaps.

The Mauritian gentleman spoke first, and for a time I tried to follow the translation from his French, but it was a disconcerting metallic English coming through the headphone. The word 'historicising' seemed to recur and one glorious phrase I recall was how it was 'the nymphomaniacal desire of a post-colonial poetics to engage the interest of the ex-colonial power.' This prompted a squeal of laughter from Henry, for all that it seemed to be taken soberly by the rest of the packed audience. In the end I preferred to listen to the musicality of the fellow's French, for French sounds so articulate in French. The Mauritian finished with a poem where we were encouraged to join in a refrain line – 'Man-deh-lah' repeated thrice on each occasion, and a chant of support for Robben Island's indomitable prisoner.

Peter was next. He had listened to the 'Mand-deh-lahs' with a small smile on his face. Now he leaned to his microphone and paused, regarding us for an interval.

'Like, poetry is always poetry,' he said, and stroked his jowls ruminatively. I expected the English channel on my headphones to be silent for an English-speaking poet and was surprised to hear Jelena's voice rendering the English from the English.

'The Australian poet conveys the greetings from his country,' came her voice through the headphones.

'Like man, you can forget the historicising bullshit,' was Peter's next advice.

'In Australia are many kinds of poetry,' Jelena translated. I indicated to Henry he should switch to the English channel.

'Like …' Peter contemplated us all, 'maybe the most important thing I can say to you might be …' and he went to the nearby wall and abruptly stood on his head, attaining his balance immediately.

'It is poetry written from the point of view of being upside down on the other side of the world,' Jelena translated calmly. There were eruptions of laughter from parts of the audience, puzzlement elsewhere.

From his upside-down perspective, Peter needed to speak up to be heard, but he had commenced to tell us how the mind needed to be open to find poetry anywhere.

'Australia is mostly an urban country,' came Jelena's gloss.

The poet came down from his headstand, leapt onto the panel's bench in front of the Surinam lady, went down on his haunches and then, placing his hands on the surface and pressing his knees against his elbows, he commenced to crabwalk from right to left under the noses of his two panel colleagues.

'Like, Olson, man, like Rimbaud. Like, how do you tell what is inside the poem and what is on the outside?'

'In Australia it is possible to watch how poetry can disappear entirely from poetry,' Jelena supplied.

Peter reached the end of the bench and manoeuvred himself to face the audience. 'Like …' I feared he was beginning to feel the strain on his arms, sinewy as they appeared to be. 'Like, doing this is a poem.'

'The Australian poet says Australia is a hot desert land where mirages are quite common.'

Peter dissolved the crab posture and leapt down from the table. 'I've even got a book with some of my poems in it.' He went to his chair and rummaged in a shoulder bag.

'The Australian poet will now present some of his mirages.' There was laughter from larger sections of the audience now as more people had discovered the English-into-English.

Peter's was a breathy voice and the poems he gave us seemed more purred than recited. Sleeping pills were mentioned, a dedication or two to an American poet, and some mention about the poem being about itself. He came to an end, walked to the side of the auditorium, quickly assessed the space available to him, then performed three cartwheels across the breadth of the stage and sat down. Sustained applause followed. Indeed, I clapped too, feeling that Peter deserved the hurrahs for something, whether his gymnastics or the light he had shed on our topic.

'Ho hum,' said Henry.

'It was agile, Hal.'

'If he wants to stand on his head, why not become a PE teacher?'

After the two male performances, the Surinam lady did not have a chance and this was unfair because her preamble was intelligent, and her several poems coming through the headphones, in their translation from the Dutch, seemed to be lucid and amusing. The session broke up. Henry spied Bernard Hickey and went over for a chat. I met Jelena coming from the cockpit.

'You're a translator of creative brilliance,' I told her warmly. 'Do you have any idea of the service you have just done for Australian poetry?'

'Australian poetry, what do I care about your Australian poetry?' she said. 'You may buy me some coffee.'

We sat at a small table, and I asked her, 'Will you be in trouble for your creativity?'

'Of course not,' she said. 'It is poetry. Who cares? Tell me something interesting about yourself.'

The Loveliest Night of the Year

Anthony Lynch

One lunchtime, on a day off from the well-paid tedium of my middle-management position, I visited my mama and papa, letting myself in the front door and following voices down the carpeted hallway until I came to my old bedroom, in which stood a woman in her early thirties. A woman my age, in *my* old room.

I'd moved to a place of my own a decade before, but when I stayed over it was in this room I still slept. It had the same discoloured Degas print on the wall, and the wardrobe housed a few favourite old dresses and dolls, including a jungle Barbie, from when I was a girl. Now, in some primitive, urban jungle way, I felt my space invaded.

The woman adjusted a colour chart; Papa adjusted his hearing aid. She turned a page, pointed to a square of colour she described as 'the brighter side of olive.'

Papa caught the word *olive.* He had a mature tree he netted every year.

Turning my way, the woman introduced herself as Lisbeth. Mama, catching up on the game, introduced us again, but she struggled with the lack of an *e* at the start of Lisbeth's name. Lisbeth sans *e,* a *home and office interior design consultant* (her business card was attached to every brochure), had showered that morning under a waterfall of Issey Miyake. It seemed to fill the house. This was not the only impression she gave of a big presence. Aided by the fact of Papa's malfunctioning hearing aid, she shouted a thesaurus of absurd colour names in his ear. Autumn plum. Harvest moon. Languedoc. LANG-UE-DOC.

That was the first I knew of it. The renovation. *The move.*

She left three hours later, the house awash with colour charts, sample tiles and swatches of carpet. Brochures for whitegoods, tapwear and blinds littered the dining table. Small asterisks decorated the charts and brochures, with 'Kitchen,' 'Bdm 1' or 'Lounge feature' jotted neatly in the margins.

'Why?' I asked.

'Adding value,' said Papa, as if at a marketing meeting.

'It's tired,' said Mama. 'The house.'

Lisbeth had also used *tired*, as if the family home of thirty-five years should be pensioned off.

'I like it as is. What's this about *value*?'

'Market value,' said Papa. 'We're making it attractive to a prospect buyer.'

'Prospective.'

'I don't need a smartypants.'

'You don't need a buyer.'

*

One morning, a month later, two housepainters arrived. They scraped away the wallpaper that depicted trellised grapes growing skyward after Papa had laid the pattern upside down when we were kids. They sanded and puttied. Cut in and rolled.

The hallway, lounge and dining room were repainted in what Lisbeth had advised were colours *akin* – another word she liked, you could see she'd once opened a dictionary – to those of the deco period when the house was built. Off white, cream, two different greens. I think one of them was Languedoc. Rose for a feature wall, contrast white for period detail. A bit of a lolly shop. I'd paid no attention to the period features of the home I grew up in, they were always just there, but ceiling roses, curved mantelpieces, the half columns in the hallway, all now came to life.

Carpets and linoleum that Bruno, aka Papa, had laid down decades ago were lifted, exposing blackwood boards. These were now polished to a mirror finish. Ribbed sisal was laid in bedrooms that suddenly smelt like upmarket rope factories. Cross-over curtains, fake teak daddo and faux marble benchtops made a short journey from the house to a skip on the nature strip. The oven, cooktop and dishwasher were replaced with new models in matching stainless steel. Miele, for God's sake. Skylights opened up patches of blue in the kitchen, laundry and bathroom, which featured cool, *inner urban* textiles. The outdoor decking was sanded and received a new membrane of varnish.

The only room to escape censure, save a coat of ceiling paint, was the small sixties sunroom with geometric wallpaper deemed sufficiently retro by Lisbeth to warrant salvage.

Having spared themselves the labour of DIY, my parents busied themselves with dozens of coffees, teas, biscuits, cakes, sandwiches and even hot lunches for the tradesmen in the upended house.

The accumulated belongings of suburban life were shipped back and forth. I had dinner at Mama and Papa's every Tuesday night, and on each visit would find the furniture in a new configuration. The sideboard that hadn't budged since I was a teen was shunted from the dining room to the hall, to the lounge, to my old bedroom, and back to the dining room. Papa, who in his maintenance of the house had until now shown little regard for aesthetics, reinvented the family home. After first declining to replace the beige bathroom tiles, which were good enough for anyone's feet, he relented, and broke his attachment to all things old. He despatched to the skip anything taking temporary residence in the front yard. Even Lisbeth sans *e* had to remind him to retain some original fittings.

When the last tradie gathered up his ladders and throw sheets and backed his van from the drive, the skip bloated with our past was docked on the back of a truck. I rescued jungle Barbie for old time's sake, but much of our family furniture remained in the garage, where it stayed until it sold or failed to sell at a garage sale, and was picked up by St Vinnies or taken to the tip.

*

The house looked bigger and brighter, as if it had gone to a fitness farm and come back reduced in some areas and expanded in others. But also more spare, with so many old belongings gone, some character lost. Too much anti-wrinkle cream in some areas, too much make-up in others. It made me sad, like when I found my nonna painted up like a clown in her nursing home not long before she died.

But a buyer would be impressed, you'd reckon, and that was what Mama and Papa wanted. *A buyer.* Because suddenly, they had it in their heads that they wanted a unit in a new block being developed in the next suburb, where houses just like theirs had been bulldozed to make way. They'd picked one out already, a unit at the rear with its own courtyard, ensuite bathroom and with cupboard doors that would open and shut in just the way you'd like them to. The ones in their current, newly gym-fit house now did that too, of course, but they'd be needing a packet for it to get back all they'd suddenly spent.

*

Mama and Papa had bought the house decades ago through an agent called John Bigelow. They had kept the paperwork, and the original advert with a black and white photo. Bigelow and Son still operated from a small office, dwarfed by their opposition's brightly lit expanses of glass and signage. I guess they had a local following. John Bigelow had since moved to a small plot of land in the Eastern Cemetery, so when I rang – despite spending all his adult life in Melbourne, Bruno still didn't trust his English – I got the son, Graeme. He sounded quite advanced in years himself, and he recounted how so many clients had come back to the firm over the years, how they'd bought and sold properties for three generations of some families, how helping people find new homes was one of the pleasures of the business. I conveyed a precied version of this to Papa, who snatched the phone and excitedly told Bigelow Jnr all over again how he, Bruno Valenti and his wife Rita, had bought the house through his father. Not-so-young Graeme repeated how rewarding it was to help people find a good home and, years later, help those same people again when their circumstances changed. As if he were some do-gooder social worker.

Bigelow the social worker didn't come to inspect the house. He sent two underlings – one a bit green, very dapper and polite; the other, Gillespie, in early middle age, pudgy and with an aftershave that hung around long after he'd gone. But sharp. You could see his mind ticking over. You knew he had a figure in his head before he offered his hand in greeting.

Gillespie said we should go to auction. 'Harness the competition.' Bruno thought auctions were about game playing. He preferred the surety of sale price. *Private sale*, as agents say, as if it's not them but the owner plonking a hand-painted For Sale sign out front. They put $995,000 on it because it was such a great property, but also because the million-dollar figure would scare some folks off. The young agent, whose name was Peter Duncan-Green and whom I dubbed Green Peter, did most of the selling. He was a nice guy, I liked him better than Gillespie, who always looked on the make, but he was over-anxious, too eager to please.

It took Papa a while to get used to the idea that $995,000 was a starting point, not the figure someone was likely to cough up. Then a couple came who were going to fork out something near it, but the woman got cold feet and the deal fell through. Mama and Papa could hardly believe it.

'Should have had the experienced one,' Rita kept saying. 'That boy, he got no sales smarts!'

In fairness to Green Peter, he worked hard and got other offers, but Bruno would accept nothing less than what was on the table when the first deal collapsed. Rita convinced him, eventually, to surrender attachment to the office-bound Bigelow and go elsewhere.

HBT were a bigger outfit, with a glitzy glass cube of an office down the road from the last mob. After Bruno and Rita signed, they sent around a minibus – I'm not kidding – with all their agents, who slid out in their black suits like a murder of crows, conducted a three-minute inspection with handshakes sprayed in all directions, collected themselves and drove off again. Apparently they did this with every new property on the books, so that all their agents, even those who had nothing to do with a sale, could provide a recommendation.

The agent responsible for Papa and Mama's property was Wayde Tinkel. He was about the same age as Gillespie, late forties, when agents, the men at least, hit their spinmaster, lying bastard prime. But he was fitter, with cropped hair going silver above a tanned face, and a body that looked as if it might have been a rower's or at least seen the inside of a gym. He wore, unusually, an open-neck shirt, an expensive grey suit that matched his hair, and an air of being a statesman of the realty world. He was assisted by a young woman named Kirsten, who carried a clipboard that probably held nothing but blank forms, and who wore tight grey skirts that approximated the grey of Wayde's hair, so it looked as if they always read from the same *über* urban corporate page. A youngster, John, who was on a different page, sometimes hovered in the background in an ill-fitting black suit, checking his mobile and failing to wipe the remains of his lunch from the side of his mouth.

Like the previous agents, the buffed Wayde Tinkel recommended auction. My parents this time agreed, hoping to spare themselves the grief of another collapsed sale.

'Once someone puts their hand up at auction, there's no pulling it down,' assured Wayde. He said anything less than a million would be giving the house away.

Being a middle manager has occasional advantages, so I took a long lunch to sit in with Bruno and Rita when they signed with HBT. Whenever mention was made of the previous agents, Wayde Tinkel would give a small shake of his head, say he was loath to criticise competitors, but some agents didn't know how to garner interest in challenging market conditions.

'For quality properties such as yours, there's always a market.'

'Exactly!' said Rita, shaking her hands so that the gold bracelet she wore for important occasions bounced noisily on her wrist. 'That boy with the last mob not sharp enough.'

'Some agents,' said Wayde, and he shook his head again. John-with-lunch-on-his-cheek grunted agreement.

HBT already had, we were told, a number of clients on their books seeking a property just like Bruno and Rita's. For the first week of the marketing campaign, apparently the most important, Wayde convinced my parents to take out a full-page advertisement in the local rag. At the first open inspection, after complimenting them on their immaculate presentation – there was not a speck of lint on the carpets, not a dust mote on the polished blackwood boards – Wayde, aided by the full-page advertisement and his easy charm, ushered through scores of would-be buyers while Bruno and Rita took coffee in the backyard.

My parents had heard on radio that, according to an article once written by Bryce Courtenay, who could attest to the fact thanks to the happy experience of selling his own small mansion on Darling Harbour or wherever, the aroma of coffee and freshly baked bread created happy associations for potential buyers. Before each inspection, Bruno and Rita would make a large pot of coffee. Bruno would buy a loaf of something white and crusty, rip it open, shove it in an oven and turn to medium for twelve minutes. By the time Wayde Tinkel or Kirsten or crumb-faced John knocked on the door, the coffee and bread would be swept away, but the kitchen and dining area would have the comforting aromas of a bakery.

My parents had rarely tolerated mess, but they now set new benchmarks in tidiness. When I visited, Mama immediately gathered my keys, jacket, bag and the newspaper or magazine I'd thrown on the kitchen table, and make of them a neat pile folded onto a chair. The house once cheerfully cluttered with gold-leaf cups, florid cushions, decorative plates featuring royal couplings, family photos and bad art, took on an air of austerity if not heightened alert. Even the hallway crucifix was temporarily laid to rest in a drawer, and Jesus and his fellow diners now took their last supper in the garage.

Mama often repeated the line Wayde Tinkel had gifted her: 'Anything less than a million would be giving the house away.' When Wayde or the tight-skirted Kirsten ushered casually well-shod buyers in and out, it felt as if that million dollars was fluttering through our family home, waiting for the right moment to deposit itself on a leather armchair.

But as the auction date approached, I noticed Wayde, Kirsten and even young John Boy, catching up on his craft, tweak their words. 'If we can get up towards that magic seven figures, that'll be a great result for you,' they said. Or, 'We're still confident we can achieve a fantastic outcome.' A week before the auction, only a handful came to the open inspection, and few requests were made for the contract of sale. Kirsten said this was normal. Those interested ('and we *have* had interest') had done their homework already. Papa frowned. Kirsten patted his arm. 'In any case the auction itself is only one stage of the campaign.'

By the final days pre-auction, Bruno and Rita's campaign of neatness had a military air. A chair once sat on would be inched back into place with slide-rule precision, windows were cleaned to the point of invisibility. The new bedroom carpets, which moulted wisps of sisal every time someone stepped on them, were vacuumed daily, as were the timber floors. Every bench and ledge – nearly every horizontal surface – was dusted almost on the hour, and a vase or lamp would be repositioned millimetre perfect. Outside, the lawn wore a permanent buzz cut. Any leaf with the temerity to rest on a concrete paver would quickly be met with Bruno's fanatical broom.

*

The night before auction, I had dinner at Papa and Mama's. Bruno said grace, adding to the usual spiel a prayer that the house would sell, that the new owners would take as much joy and happiness in our family home as we had. Amen to that. He and Rita were on high alert. I was scrubbing dishes – no way would anyone find a dirty pot in our dishwasher – when the doorbell rang. Bruno was gone two minutes. Male voices, his and another, floated down the hallway. A mix of exclamations and pauses, footsteps on the dust-free floorboards. Heavy steps, and a familiar voice that rang loudly in the de-cluttered house. A voice I hadn't heard in five years.

My little brother looked both wiry and large when he walked in. He wrenched a swollen rucksack off his shoulder and swung it in an arc to the clean-swept tiles of the kitchen floor, accompanied by an equally expansive 'Well!' This was directed partly at Mama and me, partly at the renovated space before him.

Mama didn't move. She held a knife with which she'd been scraping scraps from a plate. She stood still, plate in one hand, knife held mid air in the other. She stood like that nearly half a minute, staring at my brother. Then she scraped the plate.

My brother remained stationary, hand and mouth both slightly open. He held on tightly to a smile.

'You've lost weight, Mickey,' I said. He turned, took a step forward and put his arms around me. I smelt train station lockers, fast food. I kissed him quickly on each cheek, then gave the burp-the-baby pat that says let go. He held me at arm's length, like in a Hollywood soap.

'Big sis, it's good to see you.'

He went to Mama, stuck out his arms. She half turned away but accepted a peck on her cheek. He hugged her briefly. Released, she dropped the plate and knife into the sink.

'Why you here?'

'Nostalgia, Mama.'

She looked for more dirty plates, but they were in the sink or washed already. She grabbed a tea towel.

'Just kidding,' he said. He maintained a big smile. 'I wanted to see my family again. And the old family home. What's that lit-up billboard about?' He gestured towards the front of the house.

'You forgotten how to read?' said Mama.

Papa stepped forward. 'Mickey thought he might stay a couple of nights.' He patted Mickey in a fatherly way on the arm. A nervous action, I thought, desperate to summon cheer.

'Only if that's okay, of course,' said Mickey. He lowered his head, turned his hands out in stagey supplication. 'I know the last time I was here was not a happy time. My behaviour was appalling. For that, I'm truly sorry.'

*

We'd last seen Mickey after he walked out of another failed rehab. By his second night back home, he'd relieved the house of the flat-screen TV – a replacement for the previous model that had vanished six months earlier – the stereo, a rack of CDs and my old PC. How it was worth his while lugging a Pentium III out the back door was beyond me, but the loss of the stereo pushed Mama over the edge. When Papa had retired, he'd bought a Bose with separate CD, tuner, amp and speakers with subwoofer. MP3 compatible. A curiously top-dollar affair, given Bruno barely knew what to do with a CD. He listened mostly to talkback radio or watched TV news services that repeated each other. But the Bose was a mature-age rite of passage. He proudly showed visitors its discreet black lines, the digital welcome when it came to life, how effortlessly the earnest voices on talkback or SBS Italian news bellowed through its three-way speakers. It was a signature piece marking Bruno's decades of managing storerooms. And it was gone.

Rita shouted at Mickey and declared this the last of many straws. Screechingly asked how he could pawn his own sister's computer. Gestured at the space from where the flat-screen had disappeared as if at the loss of a minor da Vinci. She moved to where the Bose had sat and screamed at him as to how, *how* he could possibly have sunk so low as to steal his own father's loved music box, and for a quick quirt in the arm sell it to some, some ... For one of the few times in my mother's life, words failed her.

'Your own papa!' she yelled. 'Fifty years shifting boxes for this!' In his later years he'd had others shift the boxes for him, but never mind.

Mickey roused himself from momentary silence. He turned to her and swore. Viciously. Papa stepped forward with hands raised in a vain attempt to foster calm.

'You don't talk to your mama like that.'

Mickey punched him in the stomach, twice. Short jabs that took his breath away. When Papa's breath returned it came in little sobs, and he stood crying while Mickey stormed from the house and into the night in a cyclone of screaming and slammed doors. Later, Mickey phoned to check if it was safe to come pick up his stuff. He could pick up his stuff from the rubbish tip, I told him.

Bruno, most sinned against, was the most forgiving. Rita maintained her rage. When Mickey's name came up she would let loose on his appalling abuse of our family. She muddled sentences in her anger. 'The first order of an arsehole,' he was. He was that and more, of course, but her outbursts were mostly enough for both of us, and I had little to add, saving my anger for private rages. After two years, Rita moderated hers to releasing a short breath, shaking her head a dozen times and slamming whatever was to hand on a table or benchtop. Once she broke a cheese platter. Bruno made vague noises to the effect that this was what God had offered, and we must bear with it.

*

I helped Mama prepare the bed in his old room, now with a feature wall in some designer shade of olive. Methodically, silently, we unfolded blankets and pulled the sheets tight as Mama's face. I patted down the bed, patted her shoulder. She straightened the pillow with a slap, as if Mickey's head were on it already.

I stayed until eleven. Mickey, after making a conspicuous point of washing our cups and wiping down the already clean bench top, sat at the kitchen table with a tumbler of Frangelico poured from a bottle he'd extracted from his grubby rucksack as a gift for Papa.

'Cin cin,' he said as I was leaving, and emptied the glass.

*

Next morning, auction day, I was met with the black smell of burning toast, the front door having been thrown open before I reached it. Papa had put the oven on full, only to forget the torn loaf he'd placed inside to counterfeit a bakery. An acrid fog filled the kitchen; smoke decanted from the oven. They were in near panic, yelling in Italian, Papa waving his hands to clear the air and placate Mama in a series of frenzied movements.

Mickey hadn't emerged. It was Mickey's fault their routine was up in smoke.

Rita confined to the bin the charcoal carcase of what had once been a loaf of bread.

I knocked on Mickey's door and entered. The room was a cartoon dog kennel. Clothes had spilled from the belly of the rucksack all over the floor; the tumbler and half-empty bottle of Frangelico sat beside the bed. The blanket was largely detached from the bed itself, and an odour of sweat and a muffled groan rose from the hump of bedclothes, from which protruded a scruffy head of hair. I gave the hump a violent shove, five years in the making.

'Get up. Pronto!'

Over their protests I steered Bruno and Rita, still fussing with windows and fans, to chairs. Into their hands I put cups of coffee, remade after the previous pot had burnt as badly as the bread. When the greasy-haired rag that was Mickey staggered into the room, I slapped a cup in front of him too.

'Service,' he said.

'You know what day it is?'

'Friday. Saturday. That'd be it.'

I looked at him.

'Oh yeah. The sign out the front.'

'One hour,' said Rita, near hysterical. 'One hour and everyone will be here!'

'Milk?'

I gestured towards a carton.

'It was good to be back in my old bed. Have you seen my leather coat, by the way? Knee-length? Whatever. I was thinking if I could stay a while, I could sort my next move. You know, stability. Family. Roots. That's all I need. If I could hunker down, like Kafka's little beetle, I'd be sweet.'

Mama walked from the room. Mickey yawned.

'Is it just me or has something burnt?'

'Shower. Get dressed. Now.' I shoved him towards the bathroom. Perhaps it was my meaner, inner jungle Barbie, but I could get to like the shove.

He made a big thing of tidying his room. He wrestled his clothes back into the rucksack, which he threw to into a wardrobe. He straightened the bedclothes, centred his pillow.

'Mama, Pops, this house is a credit to you.' He put his arm around Papa's shoulders and squeezed, as if he were the greatest son any father could want. 'Sure you want to sell?'

*

Wayde Tinkel agreed the house at 31 George Parade was a credit to my parents. He would tell his audience so this morning. He arrived with Kirsten, John Boy and a tall suit I recalled from the minibus visit a month earlier. Another flurry of handshakes. The sun shone on what all agreed was a perfect auction day. John had removed breakfast from his cheek for the occasion.

Ten minutes before the auction, the family home was a public thoroughfare, a department store where the only item for sale was the store itself. Parents towing kids shuffled from room to room, the kids opening and poking everything and no doubt wiping their snot on the bedspreads and lounge. The adults walked with their arms strapped across their chests, except when they too opened a cupboard door to check the storage or our belongings, and they nodded or frowned and shook their heads or just locked their thoughts down. Kafka's little beetle sat on his bed, staring as if stoned at everyone who walked into his room. I manoeuvred him out the front door, along the garden path, and lodged him up against a picket fence on the opposite side of the street.

'Don't fuck this up for Mama and Papa,' I spat at him. He looked at me, shame-faced.

'Sis, I hear you.'

'Stay here,' I said, motioning with my hand as if instructing a dog, looking back as I walked away to check he hadn't moved.

At 11 a.m. Kirsten rang a bell, the sort once used in schoolyards, which everyone seemed to think was very amusing. The parents, their snot-nosed kids and a smattering of tradie and investor types assembled. I joined Mama and Papa in the lounge room at the front of the house, where they stood by the window, too tense to sit.

After motoring through the requisite legalese, Wayde extolled the virtues of this premium property in a *tightly held pocket* of a sought-after suburb with so much *local amenity* – a term that probably owed its existence to estate agents. The cafés, the public transport, the schools, the parks, the twenty minutes to the CBD. The charm of the house, the meticulous renovation that retained and enhanced magnificent period features and melded them with contemporary design. A property the vendors could rightly take pride in. And one in which, over many years, they had made an immense emotional investment. Here Wayde hit his spinmeister straps. This was a very emotional day for the vendors, the whole family, he said. A family he'd come to know and respect, one that had put so much time and love into this residence. Stepping into this much cared-for and loved family home, all would feel the warmth of thirty-five years of family life. It was a very special property, and it was with great emotion that this close-knit family now offered it, *entrusted* it, to the market. With that, Wayde cast his arms out wide, Christ-like, and declared himself in the hands of his audience.

Mama gripped Papa's arm; I got ludicrously misty-eyed. Wayde had obviously spent insufficient time in our textbook family home, but, sentimentally, as he spoke I recalled marathon backyard totem tennis rallies, my first make-up kit, long lunches for ridiculously extended family. And when Mickey was plain Michael, a ten-year-old hypnotised by PlayStation, whose greatest grief to his parents had been his childish, lewd versions of TV jingles.

A great silence wafted through the lounge-room window, Wayde's audience evidently overcome with the emotional charge of our familial bonds.

'I see we've gone shy,' said Wayde, and smiled.

It was a tough gig, I have to admit.

Wayde said he knew there were buyers among the many gathered, and he extolled again the virtues of location and the stunning renovation. After another silence he offered a vendor bid of 850, and said he'd take ten.

Following talk of a million plus, this seemed inordinately low. But Wayde had met with Mama and Papa the day before, and after much subtle arm-twisting convinced them that the reserve they had wanted all along was 950 – a shrewd decision on their part, he said, one that would ignite bidding once the property was *on the market.*

'Hands tend to come out of pockets and start being raised. Like little ducks lifting their heads from a golden pond.' Wayde was a closet poet.

HBT had, I sensed, told my parents one figure, would-be buyers another. In a tough market you had to get that first nibble, Wayde advised. The million mark remained a 'possibility.'

Wayde Tinkel's voice continued floating through the open window, but except for when we lowered our heads briefly into the frame, we saw neither him nor his gaggle of ducklings gathered in strange, mute observance at the front of the house. Rita shook her head and cursed the silence. I motioned her to keep her own. The neighbour's Pomeranian barked.

'Did I hear 860?' asked Wayde, and won a laugh.

When he threatened to pass the property in, a man with a broad Australian accent, whom I imagined to be a tradie but was probably an office manager or local politician, gave him 860. Another bidder took it to 870, and it rose in tens to 890, in fives to 905, in ones to 910. Then it stopped. I peeked through the window. The underbidder, a woman in her late fifties, was shaking her head.

'What's happening?' said Papa. 'I can't hear.'

'It's against you, madam,' said Wayde. If people had been holding fire, now was the time to join the bidding for this exceptional property, otherwise the gentleman to his right, this astute bidder who could see *tremendous value* in this wonderfully presented home, would have first and exclusive negotiating rights with the vendors. But with no other takers, Wayde called a halt to 'consult the vendors.'

Offstage, Wayde's voice was hushed. People were keeping their hands in their pockets, he said, their cards close to their chests. How they could do both these things at the same time was beyond me. But according to Wayde, if we could declare the property *on the market* we might get new bidders involved.

I saw Papa hesitate.

'And if no one gets involved?' I asked. 'It sells for forty grand under an already low reserve?'

'It's a difficult market,' nodded Wayde.

'No. No way Papa and Mama are selling for that.'

'No pressure. It's entirely up to you.'

Wayde Tinkel returned to the lonely stage that the front of our house had become. I looked out and saw Mickey. *Dancing.* Dancing with the woman who lived opposite with her stitched-up husband, two kids and labradoodle. Holding her closely, spinning her in a kind of energetic waltz. He seemed to be singing while guiding her, and she was smiling, broadly but nervously, as if this were the kind of fun she'd like to end soon.

'Fuck,' I said.

'Dancing in the streets!' Wayde said. 'If only all my auctions had that effect.'

The reluctant dancer tapped Mickey, who continued to rock her energetically about the footpath, on the arm, and gestured towards Wayde. Mickey stopped, raised his hands in a comic gesture of apology. He gave an extravagant bow to his dancing partner, and resumed his position by the picket fence. A few people clapped. I let out a deep breath.

Wayde spoke again of the exceptional advantages of our property. He was met with another great silence, almost as excruciating as Mickey's dance. With no further bids, Wayde passed the property in. He thanked all for their participation, and made a beeline for the highest bidder, a corporate type in shades and camel cargo pants with too many pockets.

After a brief exchange, he ushered the man and his linen-clad wife through the front door for *further discussion.* They went to the living room out the back, white linen ghosting Mr Cargo Pants down the hallway.

Mickey stepped through the door. Mouse-like, looked in at us. 'No cigar? Think I might take a kip.'

In another part of the house, hushed negotiations commenced. Something like Camp David for Planet Real Estate. Wayde walked up the hallway to give us a figure. Suffice to say it was not within a bovine roar of a million. We sent him back down the hallway. Five minutes later he returned with a figure slightly above the last. Then he went back.

After twenty minutes, Wayde travelled the hallway for the last time.

'I've got them up to 935. Sixty-day settlement. I don't think they'll come further. It's entirely your call, but under the circumstances it's not a bad offer.'

Papa was silent, Mama dismayed.

'Bruno, this is not what we agreed to!'

Papa put his hand to his head.

'This is less than what that useless boy could have got for us,' Mama continued.

'No pressure, of course,' said Wayde. 'But it's a tough market, so have a good think before you let them walk away. Sometimes it's best to take an offer while it's on the table. They walk and we might not see them again.'

He spoke softly but deliberately, his head lowered confidentially to Mama and Papa's height, his hands framing small, invisible pictures of demand and supply.

Papa opened his mouth, but nothing came out.

'Bruno!' said Mama. The gold bracelet on her wrist was going crazy.

'I'm in your hands,' said Wayde.

I took Papa's hand, soft and sweaty. 'Take your time, Papa.'

He looked out to the hallway, to the polished floorboards and freshly painted walls. As if the house itself might have the answer.

From along the hallway, a few muffled strains of song drifted to us. A voice, unaccompanied, from Mickey's bedroom. Humming, sometimes singing, a tune eerily familiar from an ancient past. A waltz. And then I knew. It was 'The Loveliest Night of the Year.' A version of which, recorded long ago by Maria Lanza, Mama and Papa had played on cassette and later CD on the ill-fated Bose. As he'd danced briefly with the mother of two across the street, 'The Loveliest Night of the Year' must have been the half-remembered song Mickey heard in his head.

I stood with Papa and Mama, holding Papa's hand. Mickey's voice dropped in and out of earshot. Lilting and strangely soulful. A little bit beautiful.

The Swan

David Brooks

There is at least one man who has seen it, covering the figure of the tall, pale woman who lives on the attic floor of the grey house on Cathedral Street near the wooden footbridge, on the eastern side of the river. A large, white bird, moving slowly, with a kind of concentrated violence. Intense. Erotic. Frightening. A glimpse of it, nothing more, as if through a light mist, although there can't have been mist in the room. Nor can he, this man, ever have been there to see. Not mist then but the veil of dream. It is not, after all, as if he knows her, or could in any way have been prepared to find himself stumbling upon them in this way, with shock – awe – in some dark corridor of one of the almost-nightmares that have been assailing him, like the sounds of people beating on a wall. A woman he has only seen four or five times, in the market or on Poets Square, near the entrance to the alley of the booksellers. And noticed, of course, every time: he could not deny that. A single man alone in the city, too intent on his project to contemplate a relationship, yet longing for one. And now he was both desperate to glimpse her again and almost afraid of doing so. To him, after so vivid a dream, it would be as if he knew her intimately. To her it would mean nothing at all.

But there seems to be a law to such things. The more you want a glimpse of this kind, the less likely it is that a glimpse will occur. As if the very intensity of a desire serves to distance its object.

His book proceeds slowly. The chapter he has been working on he has been months in compiling. Each day a few paragraphs, if he is lucky, and twice already, with the process considerably advanced, a tearing up of the draft, a beginning again, the tone, the point of view off-target, bringing him to an impasse. Writing each morning from eight until noon, then showering, dressing, going to one of the restaurants on the other side of the river, coming back through the market, shopping for his evening meal. A piece of fish sometimes at first – supposedly it was good for thought – but increasingly just cheese, bread, vegetables, the idea of dead flesh locked up and rotting inside him more and more repulsive. And now as he shops – buying vegetables, purchasing stationery, searching out a rare volume – he is looking for her, every moment, through the market, in the squares, in the alley of the booksellers, along River Street, along the St Michael passage, along Cathedral Street. But nothing. She is nowhere. Nothing.

She becomes an obsession; *swans* become an obsession. As if they betoken her, might be a means of summoning. One day he is coming back by a different route, along the old stone galleries cut into the riverbank, where the fishmongers have traditionally set up their stalls to keep their wares fresh in the warm summer months, and they are there, as he turns to mount the street-level stair. Four of them, gleaming white on the black water, gliding majestically with the slow current, crimson-beaked, astonishing in their brightness. So that now he looks for them too, each day, and extends his riverside walks to improve his chances.

On his way to interview an elderly woman in his grandfather's native village, he drives to the river marshes on the edge of the city in the vain hope that he might find them nesting there. Another day he travels by bus across the city to the Royal Gardens and feeds the swans on the lake with pieces from a large pretzel he has bought at the cart by the entrance. They have a strange, spongy knob between and below their eyes, and some of them have raw-looking, puce-coloured bills, as opposed to the predominant orange. A gardener who comes over to talk to him, a short, muscular woman with bright-blue, spiky hair, tells him that they are called *mute* swans. They shouldn't be eating pretzel, she says: their diet is water weed. They live on the small island in the middle of the lake. None of them are breeding pairs, she tells him. There are breeding pairs on more isolated lakes elsewhere in the country, but these are largely un-mated swans. They wander. When he tells her that he has seen them on the river near the markets, she nods and says that those are probably from this group. She asks him if he has heard the rumour – that is all it is, she says, an urban myth – of the swan that wanders the streets around the market at night. It isn't true, she says, though people keep thinking they have seen it.

One night, after a long day's work, he watches a program about Trumpeter swans, huge birds on a vast lake in Alaska, then dreams of them taking off, lumbering into the air where they form a great V as they fly southward across the pink Arctic sunset. There is something about them that seems deeply familiar, as if he might be one of them. Or perhaps it is just his loneliness, without the woman.

He is writing a biography of his grandfather, who came to live with him and his mother after the death of his father, and who therefore, from when he, this writer, was seven, was almost a father to him, teaching him about the forest, teaching him to fish, teaching him to garden, and so much more. His grandfather the war hero, the leader of partisans. Some of his earliest memories are of following him about their small plot on the edge of the city, helping him with his various chores. His grandfather's shadow, his mother used to call him, though this has come to mean something else after recent discoveries. Twenty-seven years dead now, his grandfather can no longer be asked anything, and nor can his mother, who died ten years after him. If he is to find out anything it must be from the village itself, but no one there is talking.

He has a photograph on his desk of his grandfather, wearing a beret, rifle slung over his shoulder. A man in his early forties, virile, strong, only a few years older than the writer is now. Beside it is a photograph of his mother, taken at what must have been nearly the same time, a beautiful girl with long blonde hair, dressed in white for a church festival, her arms around her younger sisters. One of them, he knows, died before the war ended. The other one her mother and her grandfather lost trace of soon afterward, and presumed dead also. A shadow, all through his childhood, like a dark lake in the background. And beside these photographs are now photographs of swans. He wishes implausibly that he could have a photograph of the woman from the house on Cathedral Street, but knows that this is absurd. For all he knows, she has moved away; indeed she may never have existed.

And then suddenly she is there. He has just arrived at his usual restaurant, the Ifel, on the other side of the river, near the university. It is a warm late-summer day – no hint yet of autumn, though in most years the season would have already shown signs of its coming – and he has taken a seat outside. Having carried a thought with him for the last hundred metres or so, he has taken out his notebook and started to write, and, looking up, the note finished, has seen her, being seated at the table opposite. She is wearing a soft-yellow blouse and light summer skirt, of an intricate Indian pattern. Her long, pale legs are bare, and she is wearing light, elegant sandals. He tries to keep his eyes off her, perhaps unnecessarily since she seems quite unaware of him, but while she reads the menu he surreptitiously studies her face. She has a long, slim nose, high cheekbones, eyes set so deeply that they would probably convey the impression of a tired sadness no matter what her mood. Wan, he thinks: a *wan*ness.

When his meal arrives – he has taken the daily special so consistently that the waitress has felt no need to ask him – he eats slowly, turned slightly so that she is just at the edge of his vision. At one point he hears a shifting of her metal table and glances up at her more directly. She is adjusting it – one of the legs must need bracing – and for a moment, oblivious to his watching, she parts her legs slightly as she tries to steady the table with her knee. For a few seconds – it is no more than that – he sees her inner thigh, white, secret, forbidden, and has to wrench his eyes away, in fear that she might glance up at him.

Kept at bay for months, his dream now flushes through him, like a drug suddenly released into a vein. It is all that he can do to continue his meal, for the burning consciousness of her proximity. Her own meal, meanwhile, arrives, is eaten, paid for. When she leaves he watches her walk westward along the riverbank and then rises, pays for his own meal, and walks off quickly in the opposite direction. Forsaking his daily market visit – he can do that later – he goes directly to his apartment and into its tiny bathroom. Closing the door, not turning on the light, he braces himself against the wall, in total darkness, and masturbates, more rapidly and violently than he has done in years.

*

It is weeks later. He has not seen her. Again she seems to have disappeared. The weather is closing in. People are now wearing overcoats, scarves, heavy sweaters. Although a few of the cafés and restaurants still have outdoor tables, they are for the braver clients who want either to be seen or to take advantage of the occasional outbreaks of sun. Evening comes earlier. He is in the local delicatessen for bread and wine and olives when he hears two elderly ladies by the cheese counter talking quietly about a swan. He pretends to be looking for cheese himself, in order to listen more closely. They are speaking of a third, a friend, Vladka, who has seen something in the Bishop's Lane, hard by the cathedral. 'The one with the mushroom sellers?' asks one. 'No,' says the other, 'that little lane that runs off it, near the bible shop, then runs down to the river.' Nor is it clear whether what Vladka saw was the swan at all – the word 'swan' that initially caught his attention was merely the first reaction of the smaller of these two women, when the other mentioned it – but it was large, and feathered, or appeared to be, in a very dark part of the alley, an alcove, near some rubbish bins. She only glimpsed it, Vladka, when someone opened a door to let out a cat; it might just have been a bundle of rags, but she could have sworn. 'Did she try to touch it, poke it with her stick?' the smaller woman asks. 'No! Of course not,' says the other. 'Imagine if it had moved! hissed at her! She would probably have fallen and broken something.' 'And it might have been a person after all, a man, trying to sleep.' 'Yes, a man, and he wouldn't have taken kindly to being poked by a stick!'

Back in the apartment, hours later, his dinner over and his wine half finished, he washes the dishes and, turning out the kitchen light, about to go back to his desk, looks out the window at the moon rising above the hill behind the house. It is a clear night. He can even see a few stars. And, hearing one of his neighbours coming slowly up the ancient stairs from the street below, resolves something. Rummaging in the cupboard beneath the kitchen bench, he locates his torch, checks it, changes its batteries, and sets out for the Bishop's Lane. He is there within minutes, at first walking its length, trying to accustom himself to the pitch dark, then retracing his steps, using the torch carefully, keeping its beam on the ground close by him, aware that whoever lives in these houses – priests, most of them – may not take kindly to someone searching their alleyway. But, although he finds three or four likely alcoves, a couple of them containing bins, there is nothing untoward. No pile of rags, no homeless person trying to sleep, no swan.

The idea, however, stays with him. The next day he must go back to his grandfather's village. A lead has opened; there is someone who might be willing to talk. As he drives – it is almost two hours away – he finds himself counting up how many such alleys there are in the old part of the city. He can think of at least eleven, on either side of the river, and certainly there are more; alleys, and some ancient cobbled arcades, with darker and more likely spaces even than the alcoves he had found in the Bishop's Lane. He decides to search them all, if only to convince himself that there is nothing.

He drives back, frustrated but also more hopeful about his project than usual, since although this person claimed they knew nothing, they told him of a man in another village who had been a young partisan in his grandfather's brigade. Rain begins to fall, light at first but eventually torrential. It sets in for days. There is no possibility, until it thoroughly clears, that anything would think to forage, let alone sleep in the alleys. Yet the idea of them nags at him, seems to want to draw him in.

It is a week before he can explore the first of them, and a month before he has visited them all, and by that time he has long realised that the process is much more complicated than he envisioned. Why should the swan, if the swan exists, stay in one place? What is to say that at one time it is not in an alley not yet visited, and at another in an alley he has searched already?

When the winter nights allow, he begins to go through them again – the alleys, the lanes, the impasses – and to visit them randomly. Not every night, and sometimes not for a week or more. He comes to think of it more as an evening walk than as a hunt. He is *drawn to* it, he would probably say, if there were ever anyone to ask him; it is not even something that he has consciously chosen. Some nights he does not bother to take a torch.

On one such night he is walking slowly through a lane that has become quite familiar to him. Though cobbled and as ancient as any, it is a little wider than most, with an arcade along one of its sides, and towards the centre a section built in overhead so that it becomes, for six or seven metres, a kind of tunnel. He has just come through this section when he senses – it is senses, rather than sees – something in a dark passageway, a space barely a shoulder's width wide, off to his right. He has just decided that it can have been no more than a cat, or a large rat, and turned to resume his progress, when a door opens a few metres ahead to the left, and someone comes out, caught briefly in silhouette in the sudden light from a stairway. He steps back into the narrow passage, not wanting to be seen, knowing how disturbing some might find it to encounter a stranger in their alley at this time. A small, curtained window opposite him is throwing a little light into the alley, barely sufficient to see his own hand by. As the figure passes, however, he can make out enough, and the racing in his chest, a kind of giddiness, confirms it. It is her.

The next day, on the way to his lunch, he goes back to find the door. There is a plaque beside it, and a picture of a broad white beach. A travel agency. Perhaps she is employed there. Perhaps, the evening before, she had been working late. He goes up the stairs to a small landing. A door to the left, a door to the right, and before him the door to the agency. He knocks and, when there is no response, opens the door. A small, cluttered office. A thin, bald man with round, wire-rimmed glasses and a drooping moustache, and a gum-chewing secretary with lank blonde hair and an acned face, each of them looking so bemused they might have forgotten what a customer looks like. He asks them – it is the first thing that comes to his mind – about airfares to Thailand. They cannot help him. They deal only with eastern Europe. The beach, he calculates, as he walks back down the stairs, must be somewhere on the Black Sea. Clearly she does not work there. Perhaps she lives or works behind one of the other doors. Or has a friend there. Or lover. Unless he watches the place – and that for the moment seems impossible – he will never know.

He changes his lunch-hour walk and for a time passes through the lane almost daily, but never sees her. His book is drawing towards an end; at least, his most difficult chapters are. Hopefully the rest will recompose itself around them. The person in the other village – it was in fact a hospice, and the man, although eighty-five and clearly dying, had a lucid memory and was anxious to unburden himself – told him more than enough. He had been just twenty when the war ended, a partisan for almost three years. And his – the writer's – grandfather was the leader of the local brigade. When the war finished they had all thought their work over but it was clear that it wasn't. For weeks after the Germans had withdrawn there had been a steady flow of collaborators following them, in fear of their lives, and now, with the fighting over and the neighbouring countries refusing to harbour them, there began a steady flow back. Contingents, in forced marches. The collaborators who found themselves delivered back to the villages in their area had a nasty time of it. There were beatings, murders, executions, rapes. From leading the local fight against the occupiers, the writer's grandfather and those of the men under him who were prepared to help now found themselves more like peace-keepers, trying to hold back a flood of fury and revenge. And it wasn't just locals forced to return. There were others, passing through, on their way to the next border. A miserable lot, going back as some of them were – for some had worked in extermination camps – to almost certain death.

The brigade was part of a system of safe passage. They would meet another brigade, from villages to the west, and a party of deportees would be handed over. They would take them through the woods, avoiding the villages, where things could get out of hand, and would hand them over to the next brigade, a few kilometres to the east. They had done this four times already, but there was something different about the fifth group. Maybe it was because there was some particular person in it, or maybe there was some change of policy: he, the man in the nursing home, was not told. They took them to an old mine entrance, high up along the ridges, that they had used to rest the earlier groups, under guard. And as they had before, they fed them, issued them blankets and straw and lamps, and locked them in behind the huge wooden doors that had been put in place when the mine closed. Only this time – it was a group of almost twenty, men mainly but a few women, a couple of the men and women quite elderly – his grandfather ordered them to brick the entrance closed. Not straight away. At first they went to a nearby village for a meeting, and for some food of their own; but then they went back and did the brickwork by torchlight. He, the man in the nursing home, only did what he was told; others – there were seven of them altogether – seemed to follow the orders without question, and so he did likewise.

It was eerily silent behind the wooden doors as they worked. As if everyone within were too deeply asleep to hear. When they finished they went back down to the village and behaved as normal. As far as anyone knew they had passed this group on to the next brigade just as they had the others. And no one spoke. There was an unvoiced understanding that no one would ever talk about it, and apparently very few had. But now that the bones had been found, now that the other partisans were all dead, and he himself as good as dead, he could tell it all at last. Whether the writer's grandfather had done it on his own initiative or whether he was following orders from elsewhere, however, the man in the nursing home simply couldn't say. He had always assumed it was the latter. One of the other partisans, after a long night of drinking, twenty years later, when at last they had spoken about that eerie silence, had said something about strychnine in the food: that they had been taken away for their 'meeting' so that they couldn't hear the screaming, the hammering on the wood. But who knows. Perhaps, after all, that would have been the kindest way. He has had dreams, he tells the writer, all his life since, terrible dreams.

It is a grey day. The bells have woken him again. The Angelus. Normally he can sleep through it, or at least go back to sleep, but there are mornings, and it seems this is one of them, when he knows that this will be impossible. He must, in any case, write. He is just a sentence away from the end of this last, difficult chapter, and he might as well type it while it is clear in his mind. He gets up and, beginning to dress, looks back at the bedsheets and the strange, bird-like shape that has formed itself among them – almost expected by now, almost familiar – and wonders if he will ever know how it gets there, ever know what it means.

Parts Unknown

David Francis

Will looked out to sea through the blurry circles of his small tin binoculars. The flap of his yellow sunhat kept blowing up and he could feel his lips burning. They'd blister, he knew that. The pins of sea spray stung his cheeks, bit him like invisible insects. He was too pale for a place like this. It was 1963 and he was six, or he would be in a month. They were somewhere off the coast of New Guinea.

He listened to the clunk of the boat against the waves underneath him. No sign of land or anything but the greeny-blue water and the smoke from the engine that smelt like burning tyres. His mother lay in her folding chair, one pale leg stretched out and braced against the engine room to keep the chair from sliding. He'd rarely seen her in a sundress, the blue ridges of her *very-close* veins. That's what he called the bulging rivers that ran down her calves, but he knew it wasn't quite the name.

She was only here *under sufferance*, to get to the *bottom of things.* That's what she said.

As he let the binoculars fall, he glanced around at the native men. *Islanders*, his father called them. He'd barely seen an Italian back on the farm in Victoria, let alone anyone like these New Guineans. He didn't like the way they watched him back, especially the one on the box who peeled a strange orange fruit and had a piece of metal hanging from his nose. No shirt or sandals, just a cloth about his middle. A lap lap, his father called it. And the way the man chewed red stuff made him look as if his teeth were bleeding. Then he spat crimson juice on the deck and stared with bloodshot eyes. This place wasn't like his father had promised. It wasn't anything like *Paradise.*

His father stood over by the far rail with his pipe and cream safari jacket, trying out his pidgin English on a short native in baggy yellow shorts who chewed the red stuff too. *Beetlenut*, his father called it, but his father was unreliable. His mother was *the brains of the outfit* but she seemed out of her element here. She'd gone more silent as the day wore on. It was his father who seemed to be at home, but he'd been to *The Islands* before. Three times. He had his *interests in the Tropics*, or so his mother had recently learnt. Will still didn't know exactly what those interests included; something to do with his father's best friend Carson, a room-mate from boarding school, Malvern Grammar. Will had always heard about Carson and how his family owned Nuguria, a tiny island way north of New Guinea, *on the way to the Marianas*, as his father put it. But there was no sign of Marianas. Not yet. Will had seen photos – rows of coconut palms and thatched-roof huts, canoes on beaches. He'd touched the giant axe his father had brought home with the black and brown grass-woven handle and the big black blade.

His father had pointed to the mountains on a map and said, 'That's where the head-hunters live,' as if that was a lucky thing. Will knew his father was only trying to scare him into being interested. He talked about copra, some crop from coconuts that had to do with fuel. He knew this was the reason his parents barely spoke. His mother hadn't known his father had sent Carson money from the joint account, eight hundred pounds a year since 1957. She hadn't known about it until the month before. She'd called his father a *sloven and a slut.* Will had never heard her use those words.

Now he held the map up to his face in the wind and stared at where his father had marked it with a Texta, charting their course from Rabaul in small red dots to a speck in the middle of the blue that wasn't named. His father had written *Nuguria* in big loopy letters. Will whispered it to himself and the sound of the word reminded him of the stuff in a bag that his mother used to fertilise the garden back home at Broadford, the powder that smelled like pee and looked like ground-up bone.

The boat pitched and the purple-faced captain spun the wheel, shouted at a knotty-haired man who disappeared down the steps. Will wondered if there was a fire to be stoked below, but then he wasn't sure if there'd be a furnace separate from the engine. He'd never been on a boat before.

From beside the steps that went down underneath, the man on the fruit box stared. It made Will feel uneasy, kind of seasick, so he edged closer to his mother, reached out and touched her leg but she moved it away; she was sweaty. He didn't talk to her, didn't dare – it was too late in the day for that. They'd been on board for too many hours. Under the shade of her big straw hat, behind her sunglasses, she buried herself in her Hammond Innes. Earlier, she'd read him bits – the haunted ship that ran loose in the English Channel, *The Wreck of the Mary Deare.* But that boat was different from this. It had English people who were *scary in a different way*, according to his mother.

The short brown man listened to his father as if he had no choice, then suddenly showed his crimson teeth, said *cah cah*, and retreated to the end of the deck. The sound of the words *cah cah* made Will want to laugh but his father wasn't smiling, just chewing on his unlit pipe and surveying the sea as if he contemplated a long-distance swim or dreamed of an island of his own. Maybe he was looking for Carson. His father had said that *back in the good old days* Nuguria had been too far for Carson to get home from boarding school for the holidays, so Carson spent them on the farm at Broadford. After they matriculated, Will's father inherited the farm and Carson inherited the *Plantation.* That was what Will's mother said: *we have a piece of* now and she needed to *get to the truth of the matter.* That's why they were here. *Pissing more money away to get to the truth.* He imagined peeing coins out into the sea, how you'd have to swallow them first. The thought of it made his doodle hurt.

To get to New Guinea they'd driven the brown Vauxhall sedan for three days from Melbourne to Brisbane, sleeping out at night near Forbes, then Moree. They left the car at the Brisbane airport and waited for their flight to New Guinea. Will fell deep asleep on the linoleum corridor, where the passengers had to step right over him. His parents thought it was funny, both of them together. It was unusual to hear them laugh at the same thing. Then he got up and slept on the carousel because it was rubber and softer, but it started to move and he jumped up in fright. They thought that was even funnier.

But they weren't laughing now, the sea in every direction, no other white people but the captain who drank straight from a brown glass bottle, his cigarette somehow glued to his lip and his face sweating. A pig lay dead with its legs twined to a stick across the back of the boat. A gull sat on its head, pecking at its eyes. Someone should stop that, he thought.

The staring native with the nose ring spat betel nut on the back of his father's safari jacket and Will shrank back into himself, moved against his mother's pale leg as the New Guinean glared at him as though daring him to tell. *No place to bring a child*, that's what his mother had said, but she stayed in her book on that other boat in England.

Will couldn't stop watching the bright red slag that sat on the cream of his father's jacket, so he raised his binoculars to the sea and focused on what his father seemed to be gazing at, but all he could feel were the eyes of the spitter on him like the sun burning through his shirt, on the back of his neck and the bowls of his shoulders.

At first he thought he only imagined the trees on the lip of the water, then a line of white that could have been sand. He dropped his binoculars. A rickety pier and a white man surrounded by natives.

'Carson's there,' Will shouted. He'd never met the man but Will could feel his strength from here, and his own excitement. 'King Carson,' he said triumphantly.

His mother stood and folded her chair, made her complaining noises. 'Let the games begin,' she said. His mother knew Carson from before, back on the mainland a *lifetime ago*. She'd fancied Carson then, so his father said, but she'd said, 'Please don't be ridiculous.'

Near the entrance to a lagoon the anchor splashed into the glassy blue water, so clear and shallow he saw a fish, a velvety thing that could have been a manta ray. It was bluer even than the sea. He wanted to show it to his mother but the spitter dived from the rail and the ray was gone, just the swimmer underwater like an eel, a plastic bag trailing in his hand.

The boat had settled about a hundred yards out, as far as the sprint at school, his distance, but it seemed like a long way to swim. A woman he hadn't seen appeared from below the deck, her whole body wrapped in orange like the sun. She had a dead thing bleeding from a sack. As he climbed down a rusty iron ladder looking up at it, he prayed it wasn't one of those shrunken heads he'd seen in a photo of his father's, or a small severed animal, or a baby.

His father waved at Will to go ahead, so he stepped down from a ledge into an enormous dug-out canoe already half-full with natives emerging from under the deck, some hanging onto the sides in the crystally water. Others clambered in beside him and made the whole thing rock. He was feeling claustrophobic and his foot was sore so he sat between men on a ledge. A hand from above him played with his hair; he was surrounded by dark legs as his mother and father got in and the lip of the canoe began to take water. His mother moved through with her chair and stood over him. None of the men got up. 'Stay put,' she said, then added, 'Lucky your father's a swimmer,' though they both knew he couldn't swim. He was a farmer, although when he filled in the travel forms he called himself a *pastoralist*. He had *delusions of grandmother.* His mother said he was a *grazier, at best.*

Through all the legs Will noticed a man who was rowing, sweat on his face, lathering white under his arms, yelling at the others. People jumped to it when he spoke and hands were cupped to dredge the canoe because there were no buckets. The oarsman had a small wooden sculpture hanging from his ear and he stared at Will too, but unlike the spitter he seemed to be laughing without moving his mouth. His lap lap hung open as a smile and Will couldn't help glancing into its shadows. He couldn't be sure what was moving in there as the oarsman reached back and forth, rowing.

'He's airing his differences,' his mother said and gave Will a fright; he'd gone off into his *own world* but he could feel his face go redder than his arms, even than the burns on the arches of his feet. He made himself look away but he kept being drawn to the oarsman's eyes and down to his lap lap. He rows for me, Will thought, but he didn't know why.

As the jetty approached, he turned to the shore. Carson stood still at the centre of things. His legs looked solid as a wrestler's, but tanned and hairy – they made his father's seem skinny as rakes.

The oarsman threw the rope up, lassoed it tight around a post and knotted it, and Will slid past, trying not to look as he climbed onto the rickety slats of the pier. 'Is everything *flimsy* here?' he asked his mother, but she was already moving to the front, navigating through the natives unloading and talking in their language with red in their teeth. She *loathed* crowds, and his father was further on greeting Carson while Will stood on the jetty, mesmerised wherever he looked. Palm trees leaned away from the sea and dark women stopped to watch him, bright-coloured bundles on their heads. One had bosoms that drooped so low they reminded him of the pair of sleepy Dachshund puppies he'd seen at the Kilmore gymkhana. The nipples nothing like his mother's, small and pellet-sized, hidden from sight.

When he looked back towards the sea, the captain stood alone on the drifting boat getting smaller and Will realised they'd been left. The late afternoon sun jutted through the trees like swords in his eyes and he felt as though his parents had forgotten him. His mother swept ahead to a house on stilts that resembled a giant thatched insect. Carson had his arm around his father, doing their *catching up* as they walked along a path to a weatherboard house among the trees. A garden of bright yellow flowers and a pair of palms towered like giant green-topped matchsticks on either side. Coconut palms, that's what the money had been pissed into. Not like the straggly date palm in the garden at home that dropped its clumps on the lawn, then died.

Will hung back, waited for their bags – he was afraid of them being left – his transistor clock and travel Scrabble in the small green suitcase, his woollen pony he was not supposed to bring. Their suitcases were pulled on a cart by an old man who wore a long shirt just barely covering him, as if it was a uniform. He clunked the old wheelbarrow with its wooden spokes and squared-off wheel along the jetty. Will followed the bags along a path to the tall hut with legs where his mother stood waiting.

Someone else touched his hair. It was the oarsman, guiding him forward, and he tried not to look at the man's waist, afraid of a glimpse of the oarsman's *possible* at such close range. His grandmother always said *wash down as far as possible, and up as far as possible, but for heaven's sake don't touch possible.* His grandmother who looked after him, but she'd been left back at Broadford to *keep an eye on things.* Will would keep an eye on things here.

Carson turned and shouted to his mother, 'Annie, let Nonti put your bags up.'

He'd never heard anyone call her Annie. She was supposed to be Anne. And he'd never thought of his father as small, but compared to Carson he seemed short and narrow, Carson squinting, handsome and broad under his faded canvas hat, like the father in *Swiss Family Robinson.* 'Come up and have a cuppa.' He motioned Will's mother towards the painted house but didn't seem to notice Will.

'Go, my manki,' said the oarsman, who touched Will's ear and walked off down the path through the trees along the beach.

Will watched him for a moment then walked over a square of thick lawn towards where his parents and Carson already sat in wicker chairs on an open patio in the shade of a faded grey blind. Everything seemed so green; it was as if the plants were growing before his eyes. The yellow flowers with thin red tongues from their middles, the petals like ears pushing in from the sides like they were listening. He looked back but the oarsman was gone, just the hut and the jetty and a row of canoes on the lagoon, and one small boat painted blue. Everywhere else was jungle.

He knelt at a low table made from a big slab of wood. A teenage boy served iced coffee from a glass jug, pouring it into cups just like his grandmother's Royal Doulton. Will looked at the boy's long dark feet. A fine layer of skin seemed to stretch between his toes. At first Will thought it was some sort of shadow and reached to touch them to be sure they were real. 'He's a mermaid,' whispered his mother as she lit a Virginia Slim.

'Orpheus grew up in the water,' said Carson, 'comes from generations of fishermen. Don't you, son?'

The boy nodded and smiled, walked into the house in his narrow cut-off shorts, his feet barely hitting the ground. Then they all looked out at the small fishing boats on the lagoon. 'You can't pretend it isn't beautiful,' said Carson.

'Indeed,' Will's father said, removing his Akubra hat and running his fingers through his hair to stop it flopping over his face. His *beak* and bright blue eyes with their pink rims, the zinc cream white on his nose and the lumps in his jaw from grinding his teeth and always chewing on his pipe. 'What do you think, Annie?'

Now he was calling her that.

'I only came to see what we're getting for our money,' she said.

'What's that?' asked Carson as if he'd misheard, and for a moment there was silence. Carson's jaw was all bone and broader than Will's father's, his skin even more out in the weather. His hands were like leather plates.

Will's father took a drink from his cup, his little finger looking broken the way it bent. 'I told her we'd been helping out up here.'

'Who's *we*, white man?' said his mother, then let her cigarette arm swing wide as though she already owned the place. She was beaky too.

'I mean us,' his father said, 'as a family.' They looked like brother and sister, not parents; maybe that's why they didn't get on. Both of them sharp like birds. His mother looked red in the face. Strange sounds emanated from the forests and talking came from inside the house. Words that repeated like music.

When Carson asked about their trip his father said, 'The crossing was calm as a Hindu cow,' and Carson laughed but it wasn't funny, just one of his father's stupid sayings.

'It was endless,' his mother said, drawing deeply on her cigarette. She blew a smoke ring in Will's direction because she knew he didn't like her smoking, and he didn't like coffee cold or hot. He was so tired he lay down on the straw rug beside the table and wished there was a dog. No sign of children his age, he'd only seen a baby being nursed by a girl as she walked along, a girl who looked much too young for a mother. He looked over at Carson's legs, so muscly and hairy, his feet brown and wide, just inches away, sandals strapped across the veins. Skin leathery like his hands but the hair on his shins looked soft and bleached by the sun.

Gently, Will reached out, touched Carson's calf and stroked it, so softly Carson didn't seem to notice. Soft as the purr of a cat against his palm. He wanted to rest his head on Carson's foot and sleep.

'What's happening down there?' Carson shifted his leg and Will sat up and pretended to drink some iced coffee but it tasted like manure. His mother brushed the corner of her mouth with her little finger as if there was something to flick from there, then gave his father the *hairy-eye* like he was supposed to say something.

'Would you like a biscuit?' Carson asked her, then yelled for the boy, who came out with a tray of thin brown wafers shaped like fingers. Will examined the boy's strange toes again as the tray was passed around.

'We came to talk about a repayment plan,' his mother said.

'Must we talk about this in front of ...?' Carson tipped his cup towards the boy, who walked away. 'They understand more than you think.'

'*Do* they?' said his mother.

'Annie, Carson's our host,' his father said. 'He'll pay us back if he can.'

'*When* he can,' his mother said. She pushed her cigarette into an ashtray even though it was only half done and Will wished she wouldn't waste cigarettes and he wished the wafer he'd taken wasn't so stale. But he liked the red flowers in the vase; hibiscus like the yellow ones, the same as his grandmother had in a tub beside her front door. The ones he used to call *hibiscuits.* They belonged here, he could tell, not in his grandmother's garden. As he wondered if flowers got homesick, he noticed a hairy grey creature like a big-eared bat nestled in a corner of the overhang, right against the awning.

'We're almost breaking even,' said Carson. 'If the next few years are kinder than the last ...' He trailed off.

A chorus of croaking began and Will looked out through the glare at greenish-brown shapes that now sat on the lawn like barking cowpats. His mother breathed out smoke from a new cigarette. 'I just happened upon the bank statements,' she said. 'You can imagine my surprise.' She was *on a mission.*

'Look,' said Carson, 'you've both been very generous.'

Will looked up at the black eyes of the silent bat, its ears like a dog's, and listened to the croaking lawn.

'I wasn't given the chance to be generous,' said his mother.

Will was sick of this conversation and the looks on everyone's face, as if the mean tide was coming in. 'What's making the noise?' he asked.

'Cane toads,' said his father.

'I have an old cricket bat,' said Carson. 'Would you like to go and practise on them?'

'No thanks,' said Will and then he hesitated, looked down at Carson's legs. 'What's manki mean?'

'It means *my little man*,' said Carson, a wafer almost in his mouth. 'How do you know that?'

Will just shrugged and pretended to sip from his cup.

*

The sound of the toads faded to an echo as they walked in procession through the rows of coconut palms, the late afternoon a bright purple line above the clouds that lay on the water. A man with a machete up a tree cut coconuts that thudded to the ground like severed heads. Another man shinned up a nearby trunk, quick as a lizard. They were headed to the sing sing his father had promised.

'The place looks well,' his father said.

'What part's ours?' his mother asked. She was a dog with a bone and Will could tell that Carson wasn't pleased, the way he glanced at his father so seriously.

'Anne, darling, for Christ's sake, must you?' His father poked his pipe towards his mother.

She touched at the top button of her dress as if offended. 'I'm just looking for some satisfaction,' she said.

A whooping sound rose like a bird that was laughing and Will's foot was hurting, from the sunburn and the place where the blister had almost healed, but it was blistering afresh, he could feel it. The foot hurt from the day he'd gone to the steeplechase, when he took the thermos to the car and promised his mother he wouldn't open it. But before he placed it in the picnic basket he broke the promise, turned the lid to see inside and accidentally tipped it. Boiling water poured into his gumboot.

That whole morning he walked around the point-to-point course in agony, watching the horses jump the brush fences in straggly groups, too afraid to admit what he'd done.

'Tough is good, but stupid is stupid,' his mother told him in the hospital waiting room. He didn't let her see him cry.

As they walked through the palms his foot rubbed against the strap of his sandal. He stopped and leaned down to examine it. 'Most likely sunstroke,' his father said but his father had already forgotten about the trip to the hospital where he'd admired the nurses.

'It's my foot,' Will looked up and said to him, 'you *priceless idiot*.'

His father looked at Carson, shrugged.

'You let him talk to you like that?' asked Carson.

'Someone has to,' said his mother.

An angular dog with a gash on its flank sniffed along behind her and when Carson shooed it away, Will wondered if the man was nice or not. Then a native was walking through the trees. He wore a headdress of red feathers and white paint on his face. It was the oarsman dressed up as a chief. He had on an elaborate red-patterned lap lap that was longer than the one he wore in the canoe, and a necklace of what looked like teeth all strung together. More like miniature elephant tusks.

'Annie, this is Loodstar,' said Carson. 'He's our local leader.'

His mother raised her new cigarette. 'We saw him on the canoe,' she said. 'Very festive.'

But Will wasn't sure if she meant festive now or festive then, and what sort of name was Loodstar? He noticed how his father didn't greet the man, though he typically said hello to everyone, even waved at buses in Alice Springs in case there might be someone on board he knew. Instead, his father turned to the boy from the house. 'Could you carry Will on your shoulders?'

'I take him,' said the oarsman-chief and Will was hoisted up, hands tight around his calves. It took the breath right out of him. But up on the tribesman's shoulders, his thighs against the man's neck, watching out between red feathers that sprouted from the oarsman's head, was like being stroked by the sun. He could see everything – a woman with a papoose walking at an angle through the rows of tall trees, a stooped man in the distance with a bow and arrow who hid behind a narrow trunk. Will played the lookout among the knots and feathers in the tribesman's hair and he realised his foot barely hurt at all. He could feel his doodle against the oarsman's neck and wasn't sure he wanted to get down.

They approached a clearing, a group of huts that weren't on stilts. A crowd of women emerged in grass skirts with shells at their waists. Some of their breasts looked out like parking lights, others fell low to their bellies. A pig with its legs tied lay upside down above a fire. The pig from the boat. Tied up and burning.

The chief lowered Will, careful not to mess with the feathers, and as the women danced their beads and bosoms bounced. Black stripes streaked their cheeks; their mouths smiled but their eyes didn't. A few of them reached to play with Will's hair but he stayed close to the chief, who sent them away. A man crouched up a tree with a mask like a bird of paradise; others appeared from the forest. A woman whirled a cloth that turned like a kaleidoscope. This was a sing sing. Drums beat and dancers painted in white clay did a follow-the-leader around the shaking women.

'*Mudmen*,' his father said proudly as if he knew them all, and he did seem to know some, the way they smiled and nodded. His mother unfolded her chair and sat, and the chief was given a tall chair of his own.

Will tried to get the right angle so he might see inside the new lap lap but his mother threw a stick at him. 'Watch the limbo,' she said. She was *onto him*, so he watched his father hold the limbo broom. A woman bent back so low her shoulders almost brushed the earth, and still her breasts got caught on the broomstick. His father's face gleamed as he flipped the stick so each bosom flopped down by her side. His father was an expert at this – the nipples met the dirt and the native men laughed, the betel nut bloody in their teeth. All except the chief, who watched his mother and Carson whisper. A boy about Will's age swung a bunch of nuts tied on the end of a stick that made a clacking sound and Will wondered if the boy would play but all he did was look at Will strangely and make a face.

Carson crouched beside his mother and she whispered hard.

'It was eight hundred pounds,' she said through her gritted teeth, 'for six years. Every year of Will's life.'

'Don't you get on your high horse,'said Carson, but that made no sense – she hadn't ridden a horse since Will was five, after she hurt her back.

'We need that money,' she said. 'He needs to go to boarding school.'

Will almost said he didn't want to go to boarding school but he didn't interrupt. They talked as if no one noticed, watching the natives line up behind a strip of leaves on the ground.

'It's time for the dash,' said his father. He handed Will the broom and went to join in. His father looked like a child in his shorts and jacket, enthusiastic, lined up with all the others, the spitter from the boat and the man who said *cah cah*.

'Annie, I would have lost the place,' Carson said, almost pleading. He put his hand on *Annie's* shoulder but she shrugged it off; still, her whole body shuddered in a way he'd never seen.

'We'd settle for the deed to the island,' she whispered but still she didn't look at Carson, her eyes glassy in the fading light. Carson rose, his whispering finished, took off his hat and pushed a knuckle against his mouth. His head was shaking slowly as if he didn't know what to do.

'Car, you could have come back to the mainland and lived like a normal person,' his mother said, looking up. He had a play name too.

'I couldn't do it, Annie,' he said. 'You know that.' His hands clasped themselves into a prayer. 'Live that life. All bottled trout and polo.'

Will's mother turned away at a sudden clap of two coconuts banged together. His father started out fast and took the lead across the clearing. Will almost cheered him on but he felt the oarsman's eyes on him and his mother staring up at Carson, whose eyes were on the sprint. His father's little white legs covered ground so quickly they couldn't contain him. Then he was airborne, falling face first in the dirt as the *mudmen* ran right over him. It even made the oarsman laugh out loud.

His father stood and dusted himself off, but still seemed quite pleased.

'Look at him,' said Will's mother. 'Albert Bloody Schweitzer.'

'He's happy here,' said Carson, not seeming to notice the betel-nut stains all over Will's father's jacket, or the way the chief man listened.

*

Will had trouble sleeping, on the floor of a small alcove next door to his parents. The faces of the *mudmen* and the spitter, the shadows of the chief, then the sound of his parents quietly arguing through the wall, through the buzz of the mosquitoes swarming outside the net. When he woke up with the thatched roof above him, it was morning. He went out into the sun and stood on the deck. A group of half-naked men scooped out the insides of a log with small axes, making a canoe, and then his father appeared from among the trees with a tray of fruit. Will turned to wake his mother.

'Leave her,' his father said. 'She got into the Halcyon.' That meant she'd sleep late. *Halcyon* was a bird that floated in its nest on the sea. She'd pretend the hut was a nest and go *on a voyage of her own*. That's what she called it.

His father put a tray down on a wooden bench, orange slices of pawpaw cut up on the plate. White water in a plastic jug. 'I think the sing sing went well.' He said it in his *rah-rah* voice. Will decided not to say anything, took a slice of the fruit and looked out towards the men at the canoe, others with their nets in the water.

'Three thousand miles to the farm,' his father said.

It looked further than that. 'What's going to happen?' asked Will. 'About the money?'

His father poured from the jug into cups. 'Oh, they'll sort it out.'

Will wondered if his father really was *an imbecile*. He tried the drink, thought it was water, but it tasted sickly sweet and made him wince. 'Coconut milk,' his father said.

If we're relying on coconuts *it doesn't bode well*, he thought, as a dark-blue Jeep bumped along the track. It wasn't as dusty as the farm at home, but damp and more humid; everything sweated. Carson pulled up in front with the boy from the house and another dark man in a safari suit like his father's. It was Brazen, the plantation manager. Will had seen him in photos, standing with his father in their matching outfits. One face brown and one pink. He wore a cap that said *Nuguria Plantation*. Carson stood and waved like a prime minister and Brazen frowned.

'Can I have a hat like Brazen?' asked Will but his father was already down the steps. 'Can I come?' he shouted after him.

His father turned as he got into the back of the Jeep, put his hands on Brazen's shoulders. 'Sorry, son, we have our business to attend to.' His father was all smiles. 'Orpheus will look after you.'

Orpheus backed away and the Jeep drove off into the undusty jungle. Will spat pawpaw pips and looked down at Orpheus's webbed toes, his bare feet in the sand. The toenails were chalky and the soles like shoes, but the skin between the toes was so fine Will could almost see through it. Orpheus lifted Will's foot to examine his blister. 'No shoes. We go swim. Salty water good healing.'

From the bench, Will climbed up Orpheus's back and they went down to the water like that. He gripped with his arms and legs as Orpheus kneeled in the soft waves and he let out a whine as the salt hit his blister. 'Only a pain,' said Orpheus and then it went away and he was on Orpheus's back being swum along like that – he felt like he was his own bird at sea. The water was warm and Orpheus paddled along the shallows. Will felt as if he were riding a long brown fish. This would be a thing of his own.

They swam along the shore of the lagoon, Orpheus's head up in the air and Will's legs gripping tight around his ribs and he didn't know how they stayed afloat with only Orpheus kicking, his arms around Will's legs to keep him from sliding off into the thick warm water. There was a kind of market ahead in the trees on the beach. Orpheus rose up and splashed in towards it, keeping Will piggy-backed, and they walked right up the sand. 'Why is your mother so belly hot with us?' Orpheus asked.

Will didn't know what to say because it wasn't Orpheus she was angry at. 'She doesn't like my father,' he said.

Orpheus nodded. 'Your *father*,' he repeated.

Native men and women sold goods from tables made of slats, piles of sugar cane and cut coconuts with bright insides. Will looked out over Orpheus's shoulders; he liked the feel of the arms around his calves. Orpheus spoke to a woman with big round earrings who handed Will a slice of coconut. He sucked on the flesh and it was sweet but crunchy, better than the milk as it dripped from his mouth onto Orpheus's shoulder. It tasted like frosting, like Cherry Ripe without the cherry. Maybe there was hope for coconuts after all.

Orpheus lowered him to the ground and the woman offered him a drink from a mug carved out like the canoe. She removed his hat and the sun made it hard to see, the glare in his eyes as Orpheus led him into the shade where a dog lay on an angle that made it look like part of the tree root. Orpheus took him by the hand into a small hut behind the market stalls. Dark inside with coloured sheets that hung from the ceiling and the market noisy through the wall. A row of heads in the corner gave him a fright until he realised they were masks carved in coconuts. A machete leaned against a ledge and the oarsman was there in his head-dress, sitting on a kind of throne among the sheets, his face painted red as his teeth.

'Manki,' he said and it sounded like *monkey*. Orpheus was gone.

The oarsman-chief stood up and gently lifted Will's shirt. A *skin a bunny* up over his head even though it had buttons – did they want his clothes? His mouth was dry and the oarsman's skin shone like oil and his *possible* was right there, let out of a crack in the lap lap, watching like an eye. A stale sweat smell as the chief took Will's hand and placed it on the dark soft skin.

'Do you own the island?' asked the chief and Will nodded even though he wasn't sure. He thought of his mother alone in the hut and how she might be waking but the chief played with his hair now, guided him down to the beginning of a secret, lips resting soft against the black wrinkled skin, the smell of it scary and strange, stale against the coconut flakes on his tongue. The *possible* kissing his lips, back and forth around them and it had him imagine the eyes of the spitter, the betel nut red as a lady-bird's coat, and the taste on his lips as if nothing else ever existed.

'All because your father,' said the chief and Will had a feeling he was supposed to do more but his breath sounded loud in his head and a struggle came up from inside him, made him reel away. He saw a dog lying under a table watching and wondered if the dog was for him but it was a carving from wood like the one that hung from the chief's own ear, which was being presented to him now like a gift.

'Special for you,' said the chief. Something to show his parents or hide in the garden as a secret for home, the strong smell smeared on his lips.

He ran through the sheets and into the light and it was even brighter than before. Orpheus crouched against a tree with the woman who wore Will's hat with her earrings hanging down from under it. He ran past, the burn in his feet like a fire, running straight back through the trees, smearing the smell from the chief that mixed up with his tears as his hands wiped his hair and branches slapped at his arms, ferns slapped against his legs, stung by things he couldn't see, lush and green and hot and running. He didn't call out because there was no one to answer, no one who'd understand, all the way back on his own with the carving in his fingers and the water in sight to the place on stilts where the sun sat high. But he would tell. He would tell her. They'd have to leave. They had to go home. It was all wrong here.

He came out of the trees, the sky a deep translucent blue above him, a toad noise like the cry he kept inside his throat. The Jeep was parked outside the hut and finally he shouted 'Mum!' But it was Carson who came out of the hut. Had she not woken from her nest?

Will stood there breathless at the foot of the steps, holding his tears. He could smell her cigarette and there she was beside Carson in her dressing gown; her hair was a mess. She blunted out her cigarette and walked down to him. She had bare feet. He'd never seen her outside with no shoes. She knelt and patted him lightly on the head, not seeming to notice that he'd lost his shirt. She didn't notice anything at all, just smiled into his eyes from far away.

'Carson and I were talking,' she said. Will looked up at Carson's legs on the deck, then back into his mother's face. She'd been crying.

'You only need to hug me,' he said to himself, words that stayed inside his head.

'How would you like to live here?' she asked.

He felt the carving tight in his fist. He could not show her; he could not tell her anything.

Meanjin

The Inconvenient Dead

James Bradley

A week after he killed himself, Dane Johnson came to visit Toby at the service station. It was a Friday, which wasn't usually one of Toby's nights, but Toby was working anyway because one of the other guys had quit unexpectedly and the manager hadn't had time to put a replacement through the two-day unpaid customer service accreditation scheme new employees were required to complete before beginning their trial period.

Dane appeared at the edge of the light in the service area at about ten. Toby was watching the television screen that repeated advertisements above the fridges, and though he wasn't looking in Dane's direction something about him caught Toby's eye and made him turn.

He knew straight away that whoever it was was Dead: the slow shambling motion of their walk was unmistakable. But it took a moment or two longer for him to recognise the hair and clothes, and to rise to his feet in surprise.

For a few seconds he didn't know what to do. He supposed he should have been frightened, but what he felt wasn't fear, more like a sense of slippage, a queasiness, as if the world was shifting beneath him. On the screen above the fridges, the advertising montage began again, the images of people smiling photogenically at each other flickering silently across it, but Toby barely noticed. Instead he flicked the safety on the register, set down his drink and stepped out through the sliding doors.

Dane didn't move as Toby crossed the service area towards him, and for a moment Toby was reminded of his sister, who sleepwalked, of the way she looked when he or his parents found her in the hall or the kitchen in the small hours of the morning, the way she could appear to be awake yet somehow absent at the same time. Once people believed sleepwalkers would die if you woke them. That was a lie, Toby knew, but still he was unsure what to do when Dane did not seem to notice him, even when Toby was standing right in front of him. So he just said his name, first once and then again, until something seemed to register and Dane turned towards him, his eyes fixing on Toby briefly before moving on and away. Yet it was only when he spoke for a third time, to ask him if he was okay, that Dane finally focused on him. On the other side of the service area a car had drawn up and a man was standing by the petrol pump, watching them. Toby glanced round at him, then back at Dane.

'Do you want to come in?' he asked.

*

It had been happening for a while, of course, the Dead-coming-back thing. Not often, but often enough. Nobody seemed to know why it had started, nor did there seem to be any particular rhyme or reason to who came back. In the beginning people tended to assume their return must mean something, that those who came back had left things unsaid or undone that they needed to set right. But after a while it became clear this was not the case. Although a few of the Dead did want to return to the life they had known when they were alive, most did not, preferring instead to move on, leave behind wives and husbands, children and parents.

For all the pain it caused there was no malice in this, no desire to harm or distress. Indeed for the most part the Dead seemed almost entirely uninterested in the repercussions of their presence. Instead they were just *there*: heavily, inconveniently there.

*

Once they were back inside, Toby offered Dane a seat in the corner behind the counter. He wasn't crazy about having Dane there but it was better than leaving him out in the service area or standing near the food. His manager, Ahmed, would be pissed whatever happened but at least this way he could argue he'd put him somewhere the customers were less likely to see him.

Not, of course, that they wouldn't know what he was if they did. Like all the Dead, Dane's body seemed unable to shed the rigor of the grave, meaning his every action had a jerking quality, a quality that in Dane's case was underlined by the angry line of the ligature beneath his jaw and the unnatural angle of his head upon his neck.

Nor was it just about his pallor or his neck. Last summer, riding home after a party, Toby had seen one of the Dead in a park, standing quietly just out of the reach of the streetlights. He hadn't seen her face, but he knew at once from the way she stood, the passive waitingness of it, that she was Dead.

He hadn't been frightened that night. In fact, as he coasted past he had looked back, struck by a feeling he couldn't name, something more like yearning, or sadness.

He wasn't sure Dane made him feel like that, exactly. Yet it was difficult to avoid the sense that Dane had come loose from whatever held him to his former life, that however much he tried he was no longer part of it, of this. And, as the customers came and went, he could see they felt it as well. One by one, they started, or did double takes, some going so far as to place a hand over their hearts or mouths in surprise. The living Dane probably would have relished the response; now he seemed barely to notice it.

Yet as the night wore on Toby began to wonder if there wasn't something more to it. Dane himself might not want anything, but his presence, the unwanting thereness of it, weighed upon him, made him uncomfortable. It was as if just by being there Dane demanded something of him, something Toby had no idea how to give. Once or twice he glanced across at him, expecting to find Dane looking his way, but he never was. Instead he sat staring off into space, his eyes fixed on some invisible point in the middle distance.

Nor was making conversation any easier. Dane never spoke unless spoken to, and even when he did his replies were halting, distracted, meaning any exchange sputtered out almost as soon as it began.

Of course Dane hadn't been much of a talker when he was alive, either. But this was different. Now his silence made Toby so uncomfortable and frustrated that it was almost a relief when, just before dawn, Dane stood and, after hesitating for a moment, shuffled out from behind the counter towards the door.

Rising, Toby hurried after him.

'Dane?' he said, first once and then again, louder this time.

In front of him Dane stopped.

'Where are you going?'

Dane didn't answer. For a moment Toby thought about reaching out, taking hold of his arm, but he didn't.

'Will you be back?'

This time Dane hesitated, then shrugged.

'Sure,' he said, 'maybe.' Then, turning away again, he headed out across the service area and away into the soft grey of the pre-dawn light.

*

Toby had been at home the week before when Dane's father rang. He heard his mother answer, then she was at his door, the phone clasped to her chest.

Afterwards he opened his computer, pulled up Facebook. People were already leaving messages on Dane's profile, little notes of shock or grief saying things like 'I'm crying for you, Dane' and 'Sometimes the world is just too sad,' or just lines of hearts and little pictograms. He knew he should have written something, if only because he had known Dane the longest, but as he watched the messages appear, one after another, the things he wanted to say all seemed somehow to miss the point, to be too weak, too obvious.

They hadn't been friends, of course, not really, not for a while. Indeed as he sat there in his room with the computer he found he couldn't remember the last time they'd spoken properly. Now he thought about it, he wasn't sure when he'd last seen Dane having a proper conversation with anybody. It wasn't just that Dane was mopey or weird or angry, though he was all those things. It was that he was so obviously in pain, and that was too difficult to deal with.

*

When he woke up that afternoon he called Mav. When Toby told him about the night before, Mav whistled.

'No way,' he said. 'For real?'

Hearing Mav speak, Toby felt suddenly uneasy, the events of last summer reasserting themselves.

'For real.'

'Are you on again tonight? I have to see this.'

Afterwards he wondered why he had called Mav instead of somebody who had known Dane a little better. Had he thought Mav would be impressed? Or was it just that he thought Mav understood the strangeness that sometimes came with night shifts at the service station, the way the gap between the fluorescent light and plastic surfaces within and the sodium-tinted dark without could combine to make the world seem both too real and oddly distant, as if one had fallen unexpectedly out of sleep into sudden wakefulness.

Either way, the result was that at ten, when Dane appeared on the edge of the light again, Mav was seated inside with Toby. Seeing Dane shuffle into view he stood and gave a low whistle.

'Where do you reckon he's been all day?' he asked. 'Do they go back underground or something?'

Toby remembered the Dead woman in the park, her quiet presence in the shade of the trees when he went back the next day, the way she had seemed part of that green. 'I don't know,' he said. 'Perhaps.'

As Dane approached, Toby wrinkled his nose. The night before Dane had smelt of earth and hospital, the close reek of the dirt mingling with the medicinal tang of disinfectant and surgical soap, but there was a new note to it now, something sweet and slightly foul.

As Dane drew near Mav grinned and nodded his head as he did when appraising a car or a girl he admired.

'Hey, Dane,' he said.

Dane stopped and jerked his head around. 'Mav,' he said, his voice coming loose and rasping from his ruined windpipe.

*

When Toby started work at the servo the summer before, neither he nor Dane had ever really spoken to Mav. A year ahead of them at school, the captain of the rugby team, Mav would usually have looked straight through both of them, which meant Toby was surprised when he turned up for his first shift and found Mav working behind the counter in the Mountain Bean Café ('Real Coffee! Real Baristas!') that occupied the other half of the building.

That first night Toby was more absorbed with trying not to mess up the intricacies of the register and the toilet checks and the cash drops than the question of what he would say to Mav when or if he had to speak to him, which is why he was surprised when, at around eleven, Mav appeared at the counter.

'You're Toby, right?' he'd asked, and when Toby told him he was he shook his head, grinned, and said, 'Welcome to the crappiest job in town.'

Toby never deluded himself into thinking Mav would seek out his company if they weren't stuck working together. But as the weeks passed it became a sort of habit, and on those nights the two of them were both rostered on Mav would usually drop past and waste an hour or two with Toby before heading home or out to meet his mates. It wasn't friendship exactly, but as time passed Toby found himself coming to enjoy the shared bullshit of his company. There was something cheerfully uncaring about Mav, a casual arrogance that made him surprisingly easy to be with.

Then, a month or so after he started working at the station, Toby heard the sound of skateboard wheels bumping in across the service area. Beside him, Mav made a face.

'Jesus. Look at this loser.'

Seeing it was Dane, Toby got to his feet in surprise.

'What?' Mav asked. 'You know him?'

Toby hesitated for a moment.

Mav snorted in disbelief. 'No skateboards!' he said.

Dane glanced around, then, placing one foot on his board, flicked it up and caught it. For a long moment he'd stood staring at Mav, then turning, had looked at Toby and said, 'Hey.'

Toby didn't know why he'd come: the two of them hadn't really spoken for the last year or so. Exactly why wasn't clear to Toby. When he was with Dane it was impossible to escape the feeling Dane felt Toby was missing some bar Dane had set, not giving enough or pushing hard enough; yet however hard Toby tried, Dane would just lift the bar higher, until one day it just seemed too hard, and Toby stopped trying.

Yet when Dane walked in that night it was as if none of that had ever happened, and so, even with Mav there, it didn't take them long to fall back into the rhythm they had always had when they were alone together.

After that night it became a routine: every Friday and Saturday night at around ten Dane would coast his skateboard to the doors and step off it with a practised flick. If Toby was serving Dane would pause by the magazines or flip through the CDs on the counter, lingering over the ones called things like *Death Metal Madness Vol 6*, until eventually the customers left and Toby was able to talk.

Looking back, Toby realised he didn't really remember what they talked about, or even whether they talked much at all. Dane was often distracted, and the constant flow of customers meant it was difficult to have a proper conversation, but in a weird way that seemed to make the whole thing easier, almost as if the interruptions kept Dane from focusing for too long on any one thing, or from trying to push Toby about this or that.

All the same, Toby couldn't have said he wanted Dane there. Although he was pretty certain Ahmed didn't check the CCTV footage all that often, he'd made a big deal about friends not being welcome when Toby did his training, and the one time Ahmed had caught Dane there he'd asked Toby the sort of pointed questions about who Dane was and what he was doing hanging around that made it clear he suspected Dane was more than just a blow-in on a skateboard.

But the real problem was Mav. After that first night he seemed to make a point of coming through to hang out when Dane was there. Exactly why wasn't clear to Toby. He and Mav weren't friends precisely, and in the scheme of things Dane was nobody, especially to Mav. Yet something about Dane, or perhaps Dane's relationship with Toby, seemed to bother Mav, and not in a good way. On nights when Dane didn't turn up Mav used to ask Toby about him, about what Dane had been like when they were kids, about why they'd been friends, about what it was Toby saw in him now. Not that they actually were questions, not really: as Toby quickly came to understand, they were better seen as a sort of riff, an extended speculation on why anybody, and in particular Toby, would be friends with somebody like Dane.

Nor was it much different when Dane was there. Although after a time it settled into an uneasy banter, Toby saw how Dane tensed up when Mav appeared, the way his jaw set and his hand closed tighter over whatever he was holding, the way he grew still as if he might disappear.

But Mav wouldn't let him. Leaning on the counter he made a point of asking Dane's opinions, of including him in the discussion. 'Hey cockhead,' he'd call, grinning as he paused so Dane would have time to recognise his failure to respond to the insult. 'You listen to this metal shit, right? What's the point of it?' Or, 'Is it guys' cocks or their arses that turn you on?'

There was something oddly coercive about Mav's manner, a sense in which the openness and ease of his belligerence made it almost impossible to protest without seeming unreasonable. Part of it was that he was often genuinely funny, but it was more than that. For Toby understood that to complain would be to show he was like Dane as well, and that to do so would be a mistake.

What made it worse was that Toby understood how much Dane hated it. Although he only rarely responded it was impossible to watch the two of them together and not see the way Dane tensed up in Mav's presence, the way Mav's taunts unmanned him.

All of which made it stranger to see the two of them here again, to see Mav staring at Dane in his demanding way and Dane, his face obscured behind his hair and his mouth loose where the piercing in his lip protruded, staring, refusing to meet their eyes, his gaze sliding down, or away over their shoulders, as it always had.

At first Mav seemed unsure how to engage with Dane, preferring to stare at him while he asked Toby questions about when he had turned up, how long he had stayed, whether he had looked this fucking bad last night. But then he paused, his manner growing more deliberate as he asked Dane how he had got out.

For a brief moment Toby had an image of Dane swimming up through the earth like something quick and slippery, the flash throwing him off balance for a moment.

'I dunno,' Dane said. 'Dug.'

Mav shook his head. 'Jesus,' he said. 'With your hands?'

Dane nodded.

'And they're not all torn and shit?'

As if the question had not occurred to him before, Dane looked down at his hands. Still covered here and there with black nail polish, his small, bitten fingernails were chipped and broken, his fingertips black with grime. But it wasn't his fingers or fingernails Toby found himself staring at but Dane's skin, which was waxen pale and mottled purple and green, as if with fading bruises.

'Huh,' said Mav. For a moment nobody said anything, so when Toby's voice came again it sounded loud, uncertain.

'What was it like?'

'What?'

'Dying.'

There was a pause. Dane tilted his head and looked past Toby. 'I dunno.'

'What do you mean, you dunno?' Mav asked incredulously.

Toby glanced at Mav, willing him to be quiet. 'Was there a light or a tunnel or something?'

Dane shook his head. 'Not really. I remember being on the rope, being afraid, and fighting, then next thing I knew I woke up in the coffin.'

'So you weren't, you know, aware?'

Dane shook his head.

'And it didn't hurt?' Mav asked.

'No,' Dane said. 'I don't think so.' He paused. 'I remember being cold, I think. And alone.'

'And now? Does it hurt now?' Toby asked then, one hand rising, as if to touch the mark on Dane's neck. Opposite him Dane lifted his head, his eyes meeting Toby's.

'No,' he said. 'At least, not compared to being alive.'

*

It was after three before Dane left, and although Mav wanted to follow him, Toby held him back, telling him it was better to leave Dane be. But as they watched him lurch off into the dark, Toby could see Mav already had some new object in mind.

'We should get some of the others around,' he said, once Dane was out of sight. 'Get some kind of party going.'

Toby hesitated. 'I'm not sure that's such a good idea,' he said.

'Don't be a dickhead,' Mav said, flicking his phone on. 'It'll be cool.'

Which is how there came to be twenty people waiting in Mountain Bean when Dane turned up the next night. A couple were friends of Mav's, the rest kids from school, a group of girls, a couple of guys Dane had been friendly with years before.

Released from his shift, Toby lingered on the edge of the group, listening and watching. There was something skittish and stagey about the gathering. Several of the girls kept bursting into tears, while the guys talked too loudly, their movements forced and oafish.

Some time around ten it occurred to Toby that Dane might not come, that his first two visits might have severed whatever vestige of his past life remained. But then one of the girls gasped and, glancing around, he saw Dane approaching.

Despite the nervous energy of that past half-hour the room fell silent as Dane entered. Part of it was the fact of his presence, the way he looked, but Toby could see from the way several of them stepped back, hands raised to their mouths, or the protective way one or two of the guys closed their arms around their girlfriends, that it was more than that as well. For a long moment nobody moved, then Mav stepped forward, and with an oddly solicitous gesture placed a hand on Dane's shoulder and drew him into the group.

*

As Toby watched Mav's guests take Dane's hand and clap him on the shoulder he found himself wondering at Dane's manner with them. The Dane he knew would have hated this, would have sneered at the fake emotion, said they weren't here for him but for themselves. Toby had hated his anger, hated the way Dane could never leave it be, never stop riding the people around him until he provoked exactly the reaction that would confirm what he believed. Until he made them hate him.

Yet the Dane he could see tonight wasn't that Dane. It was as if the anger had drained away and in its place there was only a sort of emptiness, as if Dane was already gone.

At first that didn't seem to matter. Just as at the funeral the girls cried and hugged each other, though now they also made a show of sitting with Dane and talking to him. Some held his hand. The guys embraced him or shook his hand. Mav called him brother. People said you should have told us, and you know you can talk to me, we're always here. And for a while that was enough.

But as the night progressed, Toby felt something begin to shift in the mood of the group. Whether the others felt it or not he wasn't sure, but to him it felt like a sort of dissatisfaction was setting in. It wasn't enough, it seemed, for Dane to be there; he needed to give them something as well, to be grateful for their grief.

At first he wasn't sure whether he was imagining it or not. But as midnight approached it was obvious something was wrong. Even Caitlin, who had been crying on and off all night, burying her face in Amber's shoulder and sobbing about how much she missed him, seemed almost angry when she came to say good night.

'I'm so sorry,' she said, but Dane just looked at her without speaking. Then he nodded. Yet that moment, that space of seconds, was enough for something to turn cold in Caitlin, for her to pull away, cheated.

Afterwards, when it was just Mav, Toby asked how it had gone. Mav glanced over at Dane.

'You'd think he'd be pleased, wouldn't you?'

'About what?'

'All these people turning up. That they're so upset.'

Toby shrugged. 'I suppose.'

Mav shook his head. 'You don't think there's something really passive-aggressive about it?'

Toby turned to look at Dane, remembering all those Friday and Saturday nights the year before, the way Mav had tormented Dane.

'What?' Mav asked, but Toby only shook his head.

'Fuck you, Mav,' he said.

*

Outside, Dane was sitting in the air and water bay, his arms wrapped around his legs. Toby walked over, sat down beside him. Dane was doing the staring thing again, his eyes fixed on some invisible spot up on the service station roof, his expression blank. But when Toby spoke he knew Dane was listening.

'Are you okay?' he asked. Seated beside him, he could see the line of stitches running up the side of Dane's head, the white of the skull beneath. Suddenly he remembered something he'd heard about the pathologists removing people's brains to do toxicology and wondered whether Dane's was in there or not.

'They could have done that whole evening without me, couldn't they? I was only there to give them a chance to feel good about themselves.' When Toby didn't answer Dane looked at him. 'Is that what my funeral was like?'

Toby hesitated. 'A bit.'

Dane looked away again. When he spoke again his voice was quieter. 'I spoilt it, didn't I?'

'Spoilt what?'

'This. Before. All of it.'

Toby didn't reply at once. 'Why did you do it?'

Dane shrugged. 'I don't know. I just wanted it to stop, I think, just wanted it to be over.'

'You could have tried to talk to me.'

'Would you have listened?'

Toby didn't answer, the blood rising to his face. 'I'm sorry,' he said at last.

For a long time neither of them spoke. Then Dane rose.

'I have to go,' he said.

'Go where?' Toby asked, looking up at him.

Dane did not answer, just turned, began to walk away.

'Wait,' Toby said, standing up. 'Isn't there something I can do?'

As he spoke Dane hesitated and looked around. 'No,' he said. 'Not anymore.'

For a moment Toby thought to run after him, tell him to stay, but he knew there was no point, that however much the thing in front of him looked like Dane it was not, or not in any way that mattered, that everything that mattered about Dane, all his anger, all his need, had died with him, and all that remained was a memory of that need. And as he did, he understood something else, something about the Dead. People wondered why they were here, what they wanted, what they needed. But that was the wrong question. The Dead didn't want anything: it was the Living who wanted, who needed. And this was their tragedy, to be caught in a story that would not end, to be inconvenient, to be extraneous. To be alive.

Overland

The First Day of the Season

Brooke Dunnell

The Districts' cricket clubhouse was a dark brick bungalow at the edge of a large suburban oval. Although the approaching summer would soon dry the grass to a stubbly hay and force spectators onto the marginally cooler cement veranda, on this spring morning the ground was still damp and green under Brian Gerrity's shoes. Sliding his key into the door of the clubhouse, he smiled as the heavy weights of the lock shifted at his touch.

Months earlier the trusty deadbolt had been replaced by a PIN-pad system after Bev Hammond, the club's match-day kiosk manager, complained about boxes of jelly snakes and packets of Twisties being lifted from behind the counter. The new electronic system had been the brainchild of their fellow board member Paul Selby, who used words like 'synergy' and 'brand management' and basically wanted to turn the clubhouse into a licensed bar. The rest of the board, blinded by his capped teeth and shiny new Prius, had voted in favour of the new security, while Gerrity made sure his objection was noted in the board's minutes.

Vindication came not two weeks after the technology was fitted, when someone gained unauthorised access to the building. Flouting the new system, the perpetrator stole a twenty-four pack of Coke and took a rich dump in one of the boardroom chairs. With the entry code compromised the board hastily met in the change-rooms, where the stink wasn't so bad, and voted to have a new lock fitted.

Gerrity felt a wash of familiarity as he stepped inside. He'd played for Districts for twenty-five years, and the clubhouse was his home away from home: the peeling lino kiosk his kitchen, the windowless boardroom his lounge, the display cases his memories. Unbeknown to the rest of the board, at his lowest the place had actually become home: during the cold May nights after Joanne kicked him out he'd slept on one of the battered couches with an open yearbook held over his face, turning the link-armed photo of his first Seniors team into a crinkled grey smear. In the boardroom the soiled seat had been replaced. Gerrity took the new chair, the only one that didn't expel air from cracks in its vinyl the moment weight was lowered onto it. Though no one else was around, he had consciously appropriated the ceremonial air he associated with the new cricket season – the smell of bore sprinklers on mown grass, the breezy sensation of untrousered knees – and he didn't want to spoil it by sinking into a chair that farted. He settled into the new seat and exhaled with relief.

Gerrity didn't know what he would do without the cricket club. He'd been a lover of the game from a young age, hitting a tennis ball against the shed with a plastic bat while in the house his dad captained the Aussies from his armchair. Gerrity liked to sit back with a coldie in front of the TV as much as anyone, but his preference was to be involved, to feel the solidness of the ball in his hands and the cut of the willow through the air. It was the classiness of the game that he loved: the perfection of its geometry; the devoted strain for the ball; the respect each team afforded the other, which harked back to a more genteel time. He'd never made it to any sort of professional or representative side, but he now felt this was a good thing. Instead he did his nine-to-five at the Department and in the evenings traded shirt and tie for the formal whites of the most beautiful sporting uniform in the world.

Their league had fixtures from mid October to mid April, and during the off-seasons Gerrity was untethered. This year had been particularly bad – all the time he was looking for a new place and begging Joanne's sisters for her new phone number. Later, finally meeting with a lawyer, he had ached for a return to the simple life of meeting and coaching and keeping. A calendar tacked to the wall of his one-bedroom rental had the days to 16 October crossed out with a thick black marker, and now the morning had actually arrived he felt sick with excitement. Just two hours until the season opened with the traditional intra-club match. Sitting in his new chair, Gerrity could almost feel himself crouching deep into the warm grass behind the wicket, the faint rushing in his ears becoming the roar of an out. Turning to the sidelines to see Joanne under the eucalypts, clapping primly and smiling at him. It could happen.

There were voices in the main room. Max Hammond, chair of the board, appeared in the doorway first, his belly the exact size of a full-term pregnancy. The big man coached the under-18s, the most successful Districts team in the league, earning him the right to be chair. In reality the team's success was due, Gerrity had calmly calculated, 49 per cent to the star bowler, Brent Ryland; 49 per cent to their best batsman, Robbie Miller (whose one-day average was a very Bradman-like 99.9); and only 2 per cent to Hammond's coaching, which consisted largely of whooping like a demented crane every time Miller hit a six or Ryland sent the bails flying. Max Hammond smiled with one side of his mouth. 'Morning, Brian.'

'Max.' Gerrity nodded as Max stepped aside for his wife. 'Bev.'

'Hello, Brian,' Bev Hammond said brightly, sliding an apron over her head. 'No problems getting in?'

Bev had been thrilled by the glowing numbers and merry welcoming beeps of the short-lived PIN system. She and Paul Selby had been the two to vote against the new deadlock, and she now claimed its heaviness made her wrist hurt.

Gerrity fixed a smile. 'Easy as pie.'

Max settled into a chair, which raspberried as he lowered his right buttock. He pouted. 'Nightmare, Brian. Absolute nightmare.'

Bev immediately looked concerned and Gerrity's guts wrung in preparation for the sentiment that was sure to follow. For the past five months people had been dispensing sympathy and advice to him in grave tones, their expressions twisted as if they too felt his pain – It was like a cricket bat to the chest. (They weren't far wrong.) They told him 'These things happen' and that 'Some things weren't meant to be.' He objected to the flimsy noun. His marriage had not been a 'thing'; it had been meaningful, unlike their vague homilies. As if they knew this, the well-wishers tried to supplement their blather with touch. Men clamped his shoulder reassuringly and women had, unsolicited, hugged him, something that hadn't happened since he was married. The foreign breasts pressed against him made him feel awkward and empty. He didn't think he could bear the same performance from Max Hammond.

But as usual, Hammond was talking about himself. In September Brent Ryland had turned eighteen, which meant he could no longer ditch lethal spinners at the faces of knock-kneed teenage boys but would instead be joining the Seniors. Hammond's lower lip drooped, showing aubergine gums. 'It's going to be a tough season,' he moaned. 'A tough season.'

Gerrity couldn't help but agree as he heard clipped footsteps outside.

'Hello, all.'

Paul Selby, self-appointed club marketing guru, environmental avenger and Seniors' coach, stood surveying the room, thumbs hooked casually through his belt loops. This drew attention to the zippered area of his jeans, which were just a stitch too tight: when he stepped forward there was the tiniest hint of lumpiness, of weights rearranging behind his fly. Selby was built like a jockey and was as cocky as a game hen, visiting the houses of recently separated women in his easily identifiable low-emissions car.

'Paul,' Gerrity acknowledged stonily.

Selby strode over to the table and pounded his fists smartly against it. The sudden slam made Bev shriek a little in the back of her throat. 'Big season! Best season!' Selby announced, looking right at him.

'I heartily agree, Paul,' Gerrity said, trying to keep his tone even.

'I'm glad you do, Brian.' Selby glanced at the Hammonds. 'Because there's something we wanted to talk to you about.'

'Of course,' Gerrity said automatically, feeling sweat forming on his forehead. So they were going to be out with it. In front of the rest of the board, no less. Well, fine, he thought dizzily, massaging his collarbone. Not like it wasn't a club issue. This was where he and Joanne had met in the first place; how the short-arse had got to know them. In fact, if Paul Selby was now fucking Brian Gerrity's wife, and Gerrity strongly believed he must be, it really should go down in the minutes. 'Bev,' he began.

But Paul Selby deflated as the last Districts board member joined them: Tim Tynam, an excellent bowler but a complete idiot. With his wrists starting to deteriorate Tynam had been looking for a coaching position, but this was not a good idea. He was both a sore loser and a bad winner, and his cherub-like yellow curls and glossy Red Delicious cheeks made it difficult to take him seriously. The man was a giant baby. He'd be useless with the under-12s, who required the tight herding of a sheep-dog, and the smart-arsed under-14s would rip him to shreds. All the other coaching spots were taken.

Not that Gerrity ever said any of this to Tynam. They all tried to avoid the sucking black hole of a conversation with Tynam.

Tynam nodded at them as he made his way over to the last empty seat. Two months previously, the seat in that same spot had cradled a turd. 'How youse all going, all right?'

Max Hammond nodded but didn't make eye contact. 'I call this meeting to order. Bev, love, would you take the minutes.'

Despite the unresolved look in Paul Selby's eye, Gerrity felt excited as the five of them righted their posture and assumed their board faces. This was the moment he'd been waiting for all those cold, lonely months of winter. For the first time since May, the withdrawal of his wife's love and his eviction to the portside suburbs were no longer the most important thing: cricket was the most important thing. With his arse in the new chair and the faint tang of disinfectant sharpening the air he felt refreshed, renewed. Gerrity almost didn't mind if the bastard Selby was sleeping with Joanne, just so long as he could still play cricket.

'As we all know,' Max began, 'it's customary to begin the meeting with a nomination of the board members for the current season.' Bev's pen scratched against her paper. 'Five are required, with each nomination to be seconded. I nominate Paul Selby.'

'Second!' Bev trilled, copying the name down.

'Carried.'

'Thank you, Max,' Selby said. He rested his hands high on his spread upper thighs, framing his crotch. 'I nominate Bev Hammond.'

'Second,' Max said immediately.

Bev blushed and printed her own name in the minutes, then nominated her husband. Selby seconded vigorously.

Gerrity looked over at Tim, who was unusually quiet. In past years he'd stumbled all over the procedure like an excited foal, seconding names before they'd been nominated, calling 'Carried!' when it wasn't his place. Tynam crossed his arms and stared down at the table. Pouting about not coaching, probably. After a moment Gerrity said, 'Well, nominate Tim.' Bev looked at her husband as if for confirmation. Hammond nodded shortly. 'Second.'

Silence fell again, drawing out longer this time. Gerrity looked around the table expectantly but couldn't meet anyone's eye. The scent of disinfectant bit his nasal passages and made his eyes water. He was beginning to get a bad feeling: the feeling of waking up alone in his bare flat; of meeting with the expressionless lawyer; of driving past the house on a Saturday night to see Joanne's car missing from the garage. 'Well, I know I can't nominate myself.'

Paul Selby drummed his fingers against the table for a second and looked elsewhere.

'Brian,' Max Hammond began, leaning into the balloon of his stomach, which threatened to pop. 'We wondered if you might want to take a break this season.'

Gerrity coughed. 'I beg your pardon?'

Bev was no longer taking minutes. Her eyes were moist.

'You've had a tough time of late. What with Joanne – leaving ...' Hammond faltered. 'Maybe you need some time to yourself.'

'I've had the whole bloody winter to myself,' Gerrity responded, trying to keep his voice even. 'What I'd like is to get back into it.'

'Oh, we'd still like you to play,' Hammond interrupted, as if Gerrity himself had suggested otherwise. 'And coach.'

'The under-16s are doing fantastically under your stewardship,'

Bev told him, reaching across the table and gripping his wrist. This too was an action women had been performing on him of late, and like their hugs it made him feel trapped. He pulled gently against her grasp and she released him, frowning a little.

'Well, if someone would nominate me …'

Selby opened his mouth, paused, then spoke. 'We just think you'd be more comfortable steering away from the board for a while.'

'Why?' Gerrity asked, anxiety eroding his tone into a yelp. 'Why is that, exactly?'

Selby glanced at Tim Tynam for assistance but Tynam was still hunched over, hands buried in his armpits.

Gerrity could feel his chest pumping with shallow breaths. He knew what he would do if Selby forced the issue: he would confront him. Have you had sex with my wife? Have you had sex with my wife, you little shit-licker arsehole?

Selby let out a deep sigh and dropped his hands back into his lap. 'All right, fine.' He frowned. 'Nominating Brian Gerrity.'

Gerrity waited.

A grunt came from Tim Tynam. 'I second.'

Selby sighed again.

Gerrity's windpipe loosened with relief. 'Thank you,' he told Tynam weakly.

Tim looked up. 'Next bit of business.' His eyes were flat and still as dead grass on an airless day. 'I want to coach a team this year.'

*

Opening the season with a barbecue and an all-age intra-club match had been Gerrity's idea and, unlike Paul Selby's whiz-bang security plans, this one was a success. That afternoon Bev's troupe turned sausages while the two team captains, Selby and Max Hammond, stood at the side of the oval and picked names from an upturned cap. Gerrity tried to remain calm as player after player was selected, and finally Max waved the last slip and shouted his name.

Sagging with relief, Gerrity slid in next to Hammond as the team gathered. 'Thank goodness for that, Max. I don't know if I could handle being sidled out of another thing today.'

Hammond's look was so full of concern that Gerrity had to force laughter. 'Only joking. Only joking.'

Over at Paul Selby's bench Tim Tynam stood with his arms crossed, a faint smile tightening his round cheeks. He should have been pleased. That morning the board had named him the new coach of the under-16s, four votes to one. It wasn't clear why a peevish Paul Selby had voted against; probably because Tynam had thwarted his plan to have Gerrity kicked off the board. It had needled Gerrity to vote for the change, but if these bastards with their faux-sympathy were going to wrest one of his club positions from him under the guise of 'concern,' let it be the one with the least glory. The under-16s were crap.

Selby's men won the toss and fanned out across the oval. Hammond offered Gerrity the fourth batsman's slot and gripped his shoulder as he sat on the bench. 'You were a brave man today, Brian.' Gerrity didn't want to turn around for fear there would be tears in the chairman's eyes. 'A very brave man.'

'Well, you know, the board's very important to me.'

Hammond squeezed him harder. 'To give up the coaching, though.'

'No one's in charge of the under-12s yet.'

As if sharing the vision of toothy preteens swinging bats into one another's faces, Hammond sucked in a breath and gave Gerrity a final reassuring slap. 'You'll be fine.'

But he wasn't. As soon as Hammond moved off Gerrity took the opportunity to turn his head against the cramp in his shoulder and saw what Hammond's wide frame had blocked: his wife, Joanne, standing in the shade, floral dress lapping against her thighs. Just as he had imagined. She was watching the action on the field. Forgetting the painful twist in his neck, Gerrity stared. Stared as Jo took a step forward. Stared as she reacted and clapped. Stared as she set off around the perimeter of the oval for where Paul Selby stood, frowning into the midafternoon sun. Gerrity stood up.

A seventeen-year-old leaving the field scowled as he dodged around him. 'Jeremy isn't out,' he muttered.

Gerrity looked at him blankly.

'You're not batting yet,' the kid squeaked. He put a hand to his face before anyone saw, but Gerrity recognised the proud kid bowled for a golden duck in the very first game of the season, and he sympathised. Right now he felt about the same way.

He was distracted by cheers from the fielders as Jeremy also left the pitch, his bat held shield-like in front of him. He shoved it at Gerrity. 'Tynam's a dickhead,' the teenager seethed, and stomped off towards the change-rooms.

Gerrity took the bat and looked over at Tim Tynam, who was gazing at the other side of the field. As Gerrity watched, the bowler pressed his hand to his mouth, then held the palm in the air. Gerrity looked across the oval, confused. For a second he thought the gesture was aimed at Selby, who had his hands in the pockets of his jeans and his crotch thrust outwards. When Selby didn't react, Gerrity shifted his gaze two metres over to where Joanne stood, so pretty in her summery outfit it made his heart hurt.

Jo had a hand to her own chest. The fist was closed tightly, as if gripping something precious. She was staring back across the oval at Tim Tynam as if he was holding the Ashes high above his head.

For a moment the ground seemed to move under Brian Gerrity's feet. He swayed a little and put his foot out to steady himself. This step taken, he kept going, moving automatically over to the spot where two young men had just been bowled out, cuckolded in front of the entire club. Taking up his position, Gerrity felt oddly calm. The spring air was soft at his cheeks and the sun warm on his forehead as he hunched into the bat. It was a beautiful day for cricket.

Tim Tynam was still looking over at Joanne, and when he finally resumed his concentration he seemed surprised by the appearance of the new batsman. Gerrity gave him a lizard smile and ground his bat into the dirt.

Tynam's first ball was wide and Gerrity didn't flinch. The wicket-keeper belted off to retrieve it and Gerrity saw Tynam's Adam's apple bob uncertainly in his throat. Good.

The next delivery was perfect and as it loomed in his vision Gerrity was overtaken by grace. His dance down the pitch was elegant; the arc of the bat perfect. A ringing crack sent the ball back along its trajectory, and there was an echo as it connected with Tim Tynam's nose, turning it into a glorious crimson spout. Gerrity's gliding follow-through felt like freefall.

He hadn't felt so good in ages. It was even better than taking a shit in Paul Selby's chair.

Meanjin

Publication Details

Romy Ash's 'Underwater' was first published in *Griffith Review 34: The Annual Fiction Edition*, October 2011.

David Astle's 'Oxtales' was first published in *Griffith Review 36: What Is Australia For?*, April 2012.

Jon Bauer's 'Cold Patch' was first published in *Kill Your Darlings*, number 10, July 2012.

Greg Bogaerts's 'Market Porter' was first published in *Southerly*, volume 71, number 3, Winter 2012.

James Bradley's 'The Inconvenient Dead' was first published in *Overland 206*, Autumn 2012.

Michel Dignand's 'She Knows How to Look After Herself' was first published in *fourW twenty-two*, November 2011.

Brooke Dunnell's 'The First Day of the Season' was first published in *Meanjin*, volume 70, number 4, Summer 2011.

David Francis's 'Parts Unknown' was first published in *Meanjin*, volume 71, number 3, Spring 2012.

Matt Gabriel's 'Other People' was first published in *Meanjin*, volume 71, number 2, Winter 2012.

Erin Gough's 'Benny Wins Powerball' was first published in *Going Down Swinging*, number 32, September 2011.

Martin Lindsay's 'Someone Called Rob' was first published in *[untitled]*, issue 5, Busybird Publishing, June 2012.

Eva Lomski's 'And Senseless Acts' was first published in *The Sleepers Almanac No. 7*, Sleepers Publishing, Melbourne, 2011.

Zoe Norton Lodge's 'Yia Yia on Papou' was first published in *Going Down Swinging*, number 32, September 2011.

A.S. Patric's 'Guns 'N Coffee' was first published in *fourW twenty-two*, November 2011. It has since been published in *Las Vegas for Vegans*, Wakefield Press, Melbourne, 2012.

Bram Presser's 'Crumbs' won the 2011 *Age* Short-Story Award and was first published in the *Age*, 7 January 2012. It has since been published in *Award Winning Australian Writing 2012*, Melbourne Books, Melbourne, 2012.

Sean Rabin's 'I Can Hear the Ice Singing' was first published in *Permafrost*, volume 43, issue 1, University of Alaska, Fairbanks, Winter 2012.

Emma Schwarcz's 'Sidney' was first published in the *Big Issue*, number 388, 30 August–12 September 2011.

Kate Simonian's 'Scott' was first published in the *UTS Writers' Anthology: Hide Your Fires*, number 26, May 2012.

David Sornig's 'Your Voice Is Lead' was first published in *Harvard Review 41*, Fall/Winter 2011.

Chris Womersley's 'A Lovely and Terrible Thing' was first published online in *Granta*, 21 October 2012. It has since been shortlisted for the 2012 BBC International Short Story Award.

Eric Yoshiaki Dando's 'Human Beans' was first published in *The Sleepers Almanac No. 7*, Sleepers Publishing, Melbourne, 2011.

Notes on Contributors

The Editor

Sonya Hartnett is the internationally acclaimed author of many novels. In 2003, her adult novel *Of a Boy* won the *Age* Book of the Year and was shortlisted for the Miles Franklin Award. In 2000 and again in 2003, she was named one of the *Sydney Morning Herald* Young Novelists of the Year. Her work has been published internationally with editions available in the United Kingdom, the United States, Canada, Germany, Italy, Norway and Denmark. In 2008, she was the first Australian recipient of the Astrid Lindgren Memorial Award. She lives in Melbourne with her dog, Shilo, and cats, Marcus and Morgan.

The Authors

Romy Ash's debut novel, *Floundering*, is published by Text Publishing. She has written for *Griffith Review*, the *Big Issue* and *frankie* magazine. She writes a cooking column for *Yen* magazine and the blog *Trotski & Ash*. She was co-winner of the 2011 *Griffith Review* Emerging Writers Prize for fiction.

David Astle is a puzzle-maker with a lifelong bent for storytelling. He has written two novels, a true-crime thriller, a trivia/travel guide to Australia and a memoir, *Puzzled*, just relaunched in the UK. His latest book is *Puzzles and Words* (Allen & Unwin, 2012).

Jon Bauer is the author of short stories and plays and a novel, *Rocks in the Belly*, which won Best Debut in the Indie Awards, was longlisted for the Miles Franklin and was shortlisted for the International IMPAC Dublin Literary Award. It has been published in eight countries.

Greg Bogaerts lives in Cooranbong, New South Wales. He has had many short stories published in journals, anthologies and newspapers. His novel, *Black Diamonds and Dust*, was published by Vulgar Press.

James Bradley is a novelist and critic. His books include three novels, *Wrack*, *The Deep Field* and *The Resurrectionist*, all of which have won or been shortlisted for major literary awards and been widely translated; a book of poetry, *Paper Nautilus*; and *The Penguin Book of the Ocean*. He writes and reviews for a wide range of newspapers and magazines in Australia and internationally, and blogs at cityoftongues.com. In 2012 he won the Pascall Prize for Criticism.

David Brooks has published numerous novels, works of poetry and short fiction. He teaches Australian literature at the University of Sydney and is co-editor of *Southerly*. His latest book is a novel, *The Conversation* (UQP, 2012).

Kevin Brophy teaches creative writing at the University of Melbourne. He has had twelve books of poetry, fiction and essays published. The latest is *Radar* (Walleah Press, 2012), a collection of prose poems co-authored with Nathan Curnow. From 1980 to 1994 he was founding editor of *Going Down Swinging* with Myron Lysenko. He was awarded the Martha Richardson Medal for poetry in 2005 and in 2009 he was co-winner of the Calibre Prize for an outstanding essay.

Liam Davison has published four novels and two collections of short fiction. He has received numerous awards for his work, including the National Book Council Award for Fiction for his novel *Soundings*. His short fiction has been widely anthologised and has previously appeared in *The Best Australian Stories 1999*,

2001, 2002, 2003 and *2011*, and *The Best Australian Stories: A Ten-Year Collection*. He is a regular contributor to the books pages of the *Australian* and lives in Melbourne.

Michel Dignand was a freelance writer, mostly for the *Sydney Morning Herald* but for other newspapers and magazines as well, from roughly 1985 to 1990. He was a copywriter for an award-winning advertising agency, senior copywriter for the radio station 2WG, and then joined a department of the New South Wales government as an editor and publisher for eighteen years. He now writes fiction full time.

Brooke Dunnell's short stories have been published in *Meanjin, Westerly, New Australian Stories 2, The Best Australian Stories 2009, Allnighter* and *Voiceworks*. Born in Perth, she has a PhD in Creative Writing and is currently working on her first novel.

David Francis's first novel, *Agapanthus Tango*, was published internationally in seven languages and in the United States as *The Great Inland Sea*. His second novel, *Stray Dog Winter*, was named Book of the Year in the *Advocate* and Novel of the Year in the *Australian Literature Review*. It was a 2009 Lambda Literary Award finalist and won the 2010 American Library Association Stonewall Book Award – Barbara Gittings Literature Award. His short fiction has appeared in the *Harvard Review, The Best Australian Stories 2010, Griffith Review* and *Meanjin*. Film rights to *The Great Inland Sea* and *Stray Dog Winter* have been optioned in France and Australia respectively. For more information go to www.straydogwinter.com.

Matthew Gabriel has lived and worked for most of his life in Melbourne. He is now doing that in Adelaide. He is a writer of short stories and is currently working on a novel as part of his Masters in Creative Writing at the University of Adelaide.

Erin Gough's award-winning short stories have been published in a number of journals and collections, including *Southerly, Overland, Small Wonder, Going Down Swinging* and *The Best Australian Stories 2004*. She is currently writing a novel for young adults.

Alan Gould has published eight novels, twelve volumes of poetry and a collection of essays. Among his awards are the New South Wales Premier's Literary Award (1981), the NBC Banjo Award (1992), the Grace Leven Prize for Poetry (2006) and shortlistings for both the Miles Franklin and the Prime Minister's Literary Awards. His latest novel, autobiographical in substance, is *The Seaglass Spiral* (Finlay Lloyd, 2012) and he has a second collection of essays, *Bolero and the Sea*, due to be published in 2013.

Marion Halligan was born in Newcastle, New South Wales. She grew up by the sea and has lived most of her adult life in Canberra, with periods in Paris. She writes novels, short stories and essays. *Valley of Grace* (Allen & Unwin, 2009) won the ACT Book of the Year and was longlisted for the 2011 International IMPAC Dublin Literary Award. Her latest is a collection of short stories, *Shooting the Fox* (Allen & Unwin, 2011).

Rebecca Harrison has degrees in English and philosophy and this year completed a Masters of Creative Writing at the University of Sydney. The story 'Scissors' comes from a suite of related stories that she is presently turning into her first novel.

Ashley Hay has published four books of narrative non-fiction and a novel, *The Body in the Clouds*, which was shortlisted for various Australian prizes and longlisted for the 2011 International IMPAC Dublin Literary Award. A former literary editor of the *Bulletin*, her work has appeared in publications including *Australian Geographic*, the *Australian*, the *Monthly*, *Good Weekend*, *Griffith Review* and the *Guardian*. This year, her story 'The Aussie Mozzie Posse' has been shortlisted for a Eureka Prize and selected for the *Best Australian Science Writing* (NewSouth Publishing, 2012). Her new novel, *The Railwayman's Wife*, will be published next April by Allen & Unwin.

Sarah Holland-Batt's first book, *Aria*, won the Arts ACT Judith Wright Prize, the Anne Elder Award and the Thomas Shapcott Poetry Prize, and was shortlisted in both the New South Wales and Queensland Premiers' Literary Awards. She was recently a

Fulbright Scholar at New York University, where she completed her MFA.

Martin Lindsay, based in Perth, is the author of three plays. He is wantonly procrastinating over a novel. He breaks things for a living as a software tester.

Eva Lomski lives and writes in Melbourne. Her stories have been published in *The Sleepers Almanac, Kill Your Darlings, Griffith Review* and *Island*. In 2012 she was awarded a Grace Marion Wilson Mentorship and is currently working on her first novel.

Anthony Lynch lives on the Bellarine Peninsula in Victoria. His work has appeared in the *Age*, *Island*, *Southerly* and *The Best Australian Poems 2010* and *2011*, and been read on ABC Radio National. His short-story collection *Redfin* (Arcadia, 2007) was shortlisted for the Queensland Premier's Literary Awards. His poetry collection *Night Train*, published in 2011 by Clouds of Magellan, was runner-up in the 2012 Wesley Michel Wright Poetry Prize.

Alex Miller is the author of ten novels. His books are published internationally and have been translated into many languages. He has twice won the Miles Franklin Literary Award, in 1993 for *The Ancestor Game* and in 2003 for *Journey to the Stone Country*. He has been an overall winner of the Commonwealth Writers' Prize and has twice won the Christina Stead Prize for Fiction in the New South Wales Premier's Literary Awards. He received the *Age* Book of the Year Award in 2010 for his bestselling novel *Lovesong*. In the same year he was awarded the Manning Clark Medal for an Outstanding Contribution to Australian Cultural Life. He was elected a Fellow of the Australian Academy of the Humanities in 2011. His most recent novel is *Autumn Laing*, published by Allen & Unwin in 2011.

Zoe Norton Lodge is a storyteller and theatre maker. Over the last few years she has worked as associate artist at Tamarama Rock Surfers Theatre Company and as manager of the National Young Writers' Festival. In 2012 she worked with The Chaser on

The Hamster Wheel. Her short stories have been published in literary journals and she is now working on a book. She is co-creator of the Sydney storytelling night *Story Club* and presents the 'Bluffer's Guides' on Radio National.

Meredi Ortega was born in Albany and grew up in the mining town of Tom Price, Western Australia. Her short stories have appeared in *The Kid on the Karaoke Stage & Other Stories* (Fremantle Press, 2011) and *indigo*, and her poems in *Westerly*, *indigo*, *Cordite* and the Science Made Marvellous chapbooks.

A.S. Patric is the author of *Las Vegas for Vegans*, published in 2012 by Transit Lounge. His debut book, *The Rattler & Other Stories*, was published in 2011. He has been published in *The Best Australian Stories 2010*, the *Sydney Morning Herald*, *Meanjin*, *Overland*, *Southerly*, *Quadrant* and many other literary journals.

Bram Presser schlepped around the world for ten years in the acclaimed punk band Yidcore. His story 'The Prisoner of Babel' was published in *The Sleepers Almanac* in 2011. 'Crumbs,' a story based on his grandfather's 1930 escape from a small shtetl, won the 2011 *Age* Short Story Award. When not writing fiction, Bram pens the literary blog *Bait for Bookworms* and occasionally works as a criminal lawyer.

Sean Rabin was born in Hobart but now lives in Sydney. He is a freelance writer and recently completed his first novel.

Emma Schwarcz is a Melbourne-based writer and editor. Her stories have been published in *New Australian Stories 2*, the *Big Issue*, the *Age* and *harvest* magazine.

Kate Simonian recently graduated with a Masters of Creative Writing from the University of Technology, Sydney. Her work has been published in *Blue Crow*, *Visible Ink* and *The UTS Writers' Anthology 2012: Hide Your Fires.* She currently lives in Brooklyn, New York, where she is studying fiction at the City University of New York.

David Sornig's published writing includes short fiction, memoir, essays, reviews and literary criticism. His novel *Spiel* was published by UWAP in 2009. He is a fiction editor for *Wet Ink* and literary reviewer for the *Melbourne Review*, and he has taught creative writing at Deakin, Victoria and Flinders universities. In 2008–09 he was the Charles Pick Fellow in Creative Writing at the University of East Anglia and in 2011 was awarded grants by the Australia Council and Arts SA to continue work on a new novel. He lives in Melbourne and can be found at www.davidsornig.com.

Chris Womersley's fiction and reviews have appeared in *Granta*, *The Best Australian Stories 2006*, *2010* and *2011*, *Griffith Review*, *Meanjin* and the *Age*. His first novel, *The Low Road*, won the Ned Kelly Award. His second, *Bereft*, won the Indie Award for Best Fiction and was shortlisted for the Miles Franklin, the UK Crime Writers' Association Gold Dagger Award and the Australian Society of Literature Gold Medal. You can visit him at www.chriswomersley.com.

Eric Yoshiaki Dando was born in Japan but now lives in Daylesford. He has had stories, cartoons and poems published here and there. He is best known for his cult classic novel *Snail*. 'Human Beans' is taken from his new graphic novel, *Beautiful Useful Things*. He blogs at www.ericdando.com.

Lightning Source UK Ltd.
Milton Keynes UK
UKOW041947230113

205293UK00017B/807/P

9 781863 955805